The Scars Inside Us

The Scars Inside Us

L. GRATA

Contents

One

LuLu groaned as her alarm buzzed relentlessly at 9:00 a.m. She rolled over, her muscles aching from the late night. The faint aroma of stale beer and disinfectant wafted up from below, a constant reminder of her commitment. She didn't think being twenty-four would be this hard. She swung her legs out of bed and gave Doodle, her faithful Mini-Goldendoodle, a quick scratch behind the ears. He thumped his tail and looked at her with expectant eyes. Despite not being much of a guard dog, she loved him. LuLu went to the bathroom, downed her anti-anxiety medication, and took a deep breath to start the day. She grabbed a breakfast bar and her iced coffee from the frig and was on her way. She was lucky. It was the last she had.

The Pour Decision was just a flight of stairs away, filled with memories of her parents. Each detail, from the polished mahogany bar to the vintage neon sign, was imprinted in her mind. She could almost hear her mother laughing as her father told one of his many stories. The weight of this legacy was palpable as she headed downstairs, focusing on her commitment to preserving it.

The bar was quiet, a stark contrast to the lively chaos of the night before. She walked past the tables, her fingers trailing over the worn wood, each groove and scratch telling a story. LuLu grabbed a broom and started sweeping, Doodle trotting alongside her. The framed photos on the walls—snapshots of happier times, including her college graduation degree—reminded her of the promises made and the sacrifices endured. Her decision to stay and run the bar, despite everything, its challenges, her challenges, was more than a responsibility; it was a tribute to her parents and a path to healing.

Stepping outside, she paused for a moment, feeling the weight of the day's first chore tug at her. The mailbox wasn't far, just a short walk to the end of the sidewalk, but it still felt like a burden she'd rather avoid. The morning air wrapped around her, cool and crisp against her warm skin, offering a brief reprieve. She inhaled deeply, savoring the freshness before slowly making her way to the mailbox. With a reluctant sigh, she opened it to find the usual mix of bills and responsibilities staring back at her—each envelope a small reminder of the constant pressures she faced. Among them was another offer from the condo developer, the bold figures promising over a million dollars, making her heart twist. Selling the bar would be like severing a piece of herself, yet the idea of starting over whispered seductively in her ear, tempting her with its practicality.

As she climbed the stairs to her apartment, the scent of pine and damp earth rose to meet her, grounding her in the familiar. Her eyes flicked to the second-floor window, and with a soft whisper, as if willing the universe to listen, she murmured, "Tonight will be a good night. It will be a good night..."

Inside, she made a beeline for the shower, the scalding water streaming over her and washing away the grime and tension of the day. She closed her eyes, letting the hot cascade envelop her, soothing her tired muscles. As she scrubbed away the previous day's weariness, her gaze fell upon her pale skin. Her fingers traced the scar that ran down the center of her chest, the faint pink hue of the healed wound glistening under the water. She continued to explore the others—two on her arm, another on her inner thigh, and another on her leg—each marking a different chapter of her past. The hot water made the scars shimmer like delicate ribbons of light across her skin, a subtle reminder of battles fought and endured.

Once finished, she hastily dressed, her thoughts drifting to the impending visit. Max, the handyperson who had become like a surrogate uncle, was due to arrive soon to tackle the leaking pipe in the basement. She glanced at the clock, noting the time with a mix of urgency and relief.

Max had always been more than just a handyperson; he was a comforting presence. His visits were like seeing an old uncle rather than her dad's friend. Retired from the coal mines, his rough hands and lined face told stories of hard labor. She recalled how Max and her dad would sit at the bar, discussing football with passionate gestures and booming laughter. Those memories were a comforting backdrop to her current worries.

When Max arrived, he used his key, and Doodle barked twice, rushing to greet him. After a brief exchange, Max followed LuLu down to the basement, his presence a reassuring constant in her life. As Max worked on the pipe, LuLu stood awkwardly beside him. Max's visits, though comforting, were becoming even more crucial as she navigated a shifting town landscape. There were things that the internet could not teach her.

Max looked at the pipe and smiled. LuLu watched him work, always impressed by his ability to fix anything. She went back upstairs followed by Doodle and thought about what she saw Max do. But she observed for another reason too—she needed to learn. She hated depending on anyone, even Max, who she knew enjoyed helping. Within 15 minutes, he was done and packed up. He left without a word, being a man of few words.

With Max's work done and gone, LuLu headed back to the bar to prepare for the evening. The neon signs buzzed softly, and she turned on the TV to pass the time. A murder documentary provided a chilling backdrop until she switched to a lighter Austin Powers' movie to lift her spirits. With a swift motion, she took her help wanted sign and placed it in the window. She needed to live her life. She can't devote her entire life to work.

By seven, the bar had taken on a warmer glow. LuLu was wiping down the counter when the door creaked open, and a customer strolled in. LuLu froze, her breath catching in her throat.

Her body tingled at the sight of him. Standing tall and commanding attention, he wore a bespoke suit that perfectly complemented his rugged yet refined features. His dark, wavy hair fell in effortless waves, framing a chiseled face with high cheekbones and a strong jawline that spoke of both mystery and strength. His piercing dark brown eyes, deep and intense, held an air of quiet confidence and depth, reminiscent of a stormy sea beneath a calm surface.

A perfect combination of classic sophistication and modern edge defined the suit. The rich charcoal fabric hugged his broad shoulders and sculpted physique, tailored to stress every contour of his athletic build. The sharp lines of the jacket, combined with the slightly unbuttoned collar of his crisp white shirt, created a look that was both polished and effortlessly cool. His posture, relaxed yet commanding, added to the aura of self-assured charisma that seemed to follow him like a well-fitted cloak.

As he moved, the subtle sheen of the suit's fabric caught the light, highlighting the power and grace in his every stride. His overall appearance combined the rugged allure of a modern warrior with the timeless elegance of a gentleman, making it clear to LuLu that this was a man of both extraordinary allure and undeniable sophistication. LuLu almost didn't notice he was

carrying a laptop bag. He sat in the far corner of the bar, close to an outlet.

"Hi. Here is a menu of what we have." She slid a small square menu at him. "We don't serve food, but you can order from the dinner across the street."

"I will take a…" He looked at the menu and the bottles behind LuLu. The door swung open and Max walked in, pulling her attention.

"I will give you a minute." She smiled, automatically reaching for a pint glass. She poured his usual with practiced ease, the golden liquid settling just right.

"Hey, Max," she greeted, sliding the beer across to him.

"Thanks, LuLu," he replied, taking a long sip. They chatted about this and that—local gossip, the latest sports scores, the unpredictable weather—until the door burst open again, this time admitting a loud group of fraternity brothers.

"I take what he got." Said the man in the corner. LuLu smiled and slid the drink to him. "Thanks." The man then opened his laptop and got to work.

The noise level in the bar instantly spiked. LuLu, Max, and the suited gentleman all turned to look. LuLu deduced they were from a local frat for two reasons: she observed some guys wearing polos with Greek symbols, while she assumed the pledges were dressed in garish 1980s prom dresses and bad wigs.

The boisterous group commandeered the two large tables near the center of the bar, laughter and chatter filling the space. LuLu sighed, grabbing a tray and heading over to check IDs. The smell of cheap cologne and the rustling of taffeta filled the air as she moved through the group.

"Alright, gentlemen," she said, her voice cutting through the din. "Let's see those IDs." One by one, they handed over their identification, and she scrutinized each one carefully. Satisfied, she handed them back and took a deep breath.

"What can I get for you all?" she asked, pulling out her notepad.

The orders came fast and loud—beers, shots, a couple of mixed drinks. She scribbled them down, her hand moving quickly across the paper.

"Be right back," she said, flashing a professional smile before heading to the bar to prepare the drinks.

As she worked, LuLu felt a moment of gratitude for the small routines that kept her grounded amidst the chaos. She expertly mixed drinks, poured beers, and arranged them all on her tray. Glancing over, she saw Max chatting with the suited man, both observing the frat boys with amused expressions.

Balancing the tray in her hand, she made her way back to the tables, distributing drinks and dodging the over-excited gestures of the fraternity brothers. She felt the familiar hum of energy in the bar, the kind that signaled a busy night ahead. Despite the noise and the crowd, this was her element, and she thrived in it.

The gentleman at the end of the bar glanced up and noticed the dusty bottle of 25-year-old scotch on the top shelf. "I'll switch to that," he said, pointing when he had LuLu's attention.

"Neat or on the rock?" She asked.

"Do I need to answer that?" He joked with her.

LuLu's eyebrows raised slightly in approval. She had no problem serving a $50 glass pour. She retrieved the bottle, wiping away a layer of dust before expertly pouring the amber liquid into a crystal tumbler. The scotch settled with a gentle swirl, and she slid the glass across to him.

LuLu grinned. "I'm impressed," she replied, leaning soon. "You drink it the right way."

"There are only two ways to drink scotch," Max inter-jected with a chuckle, nursing his beer. "Both are fine. At least that is what I hear, anyway."

"See, that's my point," LuLu laughed, raising her voice over the growing commotion of the frat boys. "There is a right and wrong, and he's doing it right."

The three shared a laugh, the camaraderie of a pleasant contrast to the rowdy noise from the back. LuLu floated from customer to customer as the night progressed, her steps light and efficient. The bar gradually filled, a mix of regulars and newcomers creating a lively atmosphere.

As the night wore on, she noted the frat boys were getting louder, their laughter and shouts rising with each round of drinks. They drowned out the TV, which was still playing Austin Powers, with their boisterous revelry. LuLu kept a watchful eye on them, knowing that a group like this could either keep the energy fun or tip into chaos.

She moved back to the bar, where Max and the suited gentleman were still deep in conversation. "How's that scotch treating you?" she asked, wiping down the counter near them.

"excellent," he replied, lifting his glass in a small toast.

LuLu nodded absently, her gaze flicking back to the rowdy cluster of frat boys. The cacophony of the bar swelled around her—voices jostling for dominance, laughter echoing sharply off the walls, and the constant clinking of glasses punctuating the din. A heavy bassline from the jukebox throbbed through the floorboards, vibrating up through her shoes and into her bones. She felt in total control of the night.

Amid the chaotic swirl, LuLu sensed a shift—a subtle undercurrent of unruliness. It was like watching a tidal waveform in the distance, its cresting edge promising turbulence. She drew a steadying breath, pushing the unease to the back of her mind, and turned her attention back to her drink.

Couples drifted in and out of the bar like ghosts, their movements blurred by the dim lighting and the haze of cigarette smoke hanging in the air. Yet, through it all, Max, the sharply dressed man in the corner seat, and the boisterous frat boys remained a constant, their presence anchoring the night in its familiar chaos.

As the evening wore on, the atmosphere grew denser,

the air thick with the scent of spilled beer and sweat. At the stroke of midnight, the mood shifted abruptly. The bar door swung open with a creak, and a chill breeze swept in, carrying with it an ominous silence that momentarily hushed the crowd. Four men and a woman strode in, their silhouettes stark against the neon glow outside.

LuLu's heart skipped a beat. Her hand tightened around the glass she was washing, the condensation slick under her fingers. She knew these faces too well—an unwanted chapter from her past. The sight of them was like a needle scratch across a record, jarring and unwelcome. The bar seemed to hold its breath, waiting for what would come next.

The five newcomers sauntered to the bar, their presence casting a palpable shadow over the room. They settled onto the stools with an air of entitlement. Max, nursing the last sip of his beer, watched them intently. His eyes narrowed as he surveyed the group, his fingers tapping a quiet rhythm on the countertop. He knew the stakes better than anyone else in the bar, knowledge that weighed heavily on his decision to linger instead of paying his tab and leaving.

The woman among them, blonde and willowy with striking blue eyes, clung to the arm of a rugged man. Her gaze darted around the room, sizing up the crowd with a practiced disdain. LuLu's stomach tightened as she approached, her steps measured. All the color drained from her face as her eyes shot from person to person. She could feel the electric crackle of impending trouble in the air. While it was the girl that called attention to everyone, LuLu could not take her eyes off the smirking blonde haired man and the other standing next to him. Her eyes stared into his.

The man with the woman glued to him, Greg, leaned

forward with a smug grin, his voice slicing through the bar's ambient noise. "Busy night, huh?"

LuLu looked from each person and looked him directly in the eyes, her eyes flicking briefly to the woman before locking onto Greg. "Get out. All of you." LuLu growled at them, locking eyes with one man behind Greg. Sweat formed on her forehead.

"Four beers and a vodka cranberry," he said, his tone casual but eyes gleaming with a hint of challenge. LuLu didn't move. LuLu's gaze remained fixed.

LuLu's gaze bore into the group as the blonde woman's voice cut through the clamor, amplified by an almost theatrical tone as she boasted about her sparkling ring. Her hand glittered under the dim lights, waving it around for all to see, the men murmuring their admiration.

LuLu's hands clenched into fists, nails digging into her palms as she fought the urge to lunge at them. The woman pulled LuLu's attention, a sly smile twisting her lips. "I guess not everyone gets to wear things this nice, huh?" she taunted, her words like venom in the air.

Feeling the sting of the jab, LuLu kept her composure, her voice steady but edged with tension. "Greg, why would you come here? Annie, you made your point." She questioned, stepping back to glance at the others.

"We wanted a drink, and we are looking for a new local place. I moved back. I got a job at the college. So, it is the old crew again." Greg explained with a smirk. "Who would have thought all of us were in the same town again, for good?"

"Plus, you know you missed us," one other said.

Annie's laughter followed her retreat, sharp and mocking, echoing in the tense silence that followed as LuLu stared at the man.

"You are a fucking joke, Liam. Everyone knows without your daddy, you would have never even gotten a job." LuLu snapped.

"You're just jealous." Liam slid back. Venom dripped from his tongue. "I have a daddy that loved me from the start."

"Please, you fail at everything you do." LuLu retorted, not backing down. She hated him. This was her place.

"I don't fail at everything, do I, Lu?" He sneered at her and rage took over her.

"GET OUT, NOW!" LuLu shouted. Despite not intending to lose her temper, she couldn't control herself. She hated him. She hated all of them.

The frat boys in the back, already a few beers deep, leaned forward in their seats, eyes gleaming with anticipation as the tension in the bar escalated. A few of them, feeding off the energy, started chanting, "Fight, fight!" Their voices grew louder, egging each other on.

LuLu's glare cut through the noise like a blade. She shot them a warning look, sharp enough to make them freeze mid-chant. Silence fell over their corner. A couple of them stood anyway, not ready to back down entirely—those types always wanted to be close to action, eager to jump in once fists started flying. LuLu knew their kind all too well.

"Don't act like you didn't enjoy it. You know I'm the best you ever had," Liam retorted with a smirk, prompting the gentlemen next to him to erupt in laughter.

"Shut up, Ryan." Greg snapped, face red and rigid.

"Wait, what? You two," Annie sneered. "Gross." Annie looked at Greg and sighed.

Max's protective instincts surged as he watched LuLu retreat to the safety of the bar's far end. With a sudden slam of his fist on the counter, he broke the escalating tension in the room. "You all need to leave. Now," Max commanded, his voice cutting through the laughter.

"Make us, old man," Liam challenged, stepping forward with his friend Ryan at his side. Liam glared at Liam. He stepped back.

"Be careful. Do not threaten him. I will destroy you. I will kill you. Get out!" LuLu growled, leaning across the bar.

"Oh, no. All of that 5'6" height and 120 pounds is coming at me. What will I ever do?" Liam cruelly joked. LuLu saw red.

In the corner, the well-dressed man observed the group with a keen eye, sensing the thickening tension in the air like a gathering storm. His expression betrayed nothing as he took in the brewing conflict, a silent spectator to the impending clash. He picked up his phone and texted quickly. LuLu did not notice the large man that entire the bar right away, but the others did.

Annie tried to break the tension. With calculated precision, she angled her hand to flaunt the glittering ring—a three-carat pink diamond that shimmered in the dim light. "Isn't it beautiful?" she declared, her gaze locking onto LuLu's with a challenge.

A wry smile tugged at LuLu's lips, barely concealing the turmoil beneath. "Oh, I remember that ring," she quipped, her tone light but tinged with bitterness. "Same one Greg gave me before he broke it." Recycling, Greg? "Classy."

Annie's smile faltered, replaced by a flicker of anger that she quickly masked with a forced laugh. The air grew thick with tension, each word a carefully aimed dart in this silent battlefield.

"What did you say?" Annie's voice crackled with anger and contempt, slicing through the charged atmosphere.

LuLu met her glare with a defiant smirk. "Do you want me to shout it at everyone?" Her voice dripped with sarcasm, challenging Annie to escalate.

"It is a family ring. You know that," Annie said through her teeth.

Annie's retort was swift and cutting, her words aimed to wound. "Just because you're a frigid- cold-bitch doesn't mean everyone is. I mean, that is why he always found my bed. "Maybe someone who is a good match for him should have this ring," she spat, thrusting her hand towards Greg.

Laughter erupted from the men, a chorus of mockery that grated on LuLu's nerves. The frat boys, sensing the tension, fell silent, their ears perked for the next verbal blow.

Suddenly, a well-dressed man's voice sliced through the mounting hostility. "Did you just call my girlfriend a frigid-cold?" His tone was cold and dangerous, cutting through the tension like a knife.

Annie faltered, surprised by the challenge. The entire group turned to the man. "Excuse me?" Her bravado wavered under his icy glare.

Ryan's laugh was low, a nasty edge in his tone. He leaned in closer, his phone practically shoved in LuLu's face, the lens catching every flicker of discomfort. "Please," he sneered, his voice dripping with mockery.

LuLu flinched, her hand shooting up instinctively to shield herself from the intrusive camera. Her heart raced, the sting of humiliation burning in her chest.

Ryan's smirk widened as he lowered the phone slightly, his eyes glinting with a cruel amusement. "LuLu doesn't date. She's a prude," he continued, his voice laced with derision. "But get a little spice in her, and then... well, you might as well bring a friend. It's a party."

His words hung in the air, ugly and twisted, as LuLu's hand trembled in front of her face, trying to block out both the lens and the venom behind his words. Ryan finally pulled the phone away, giving up the chase, but the damage was done.

"Shut up, Ryan," LuLu snapped, her patience wearing thin.

The well-dressed man's gaze hardened, his jaw set in steely determination. "What I was saying was that 'frigid' and 'cold' are synonymous; you don't need both to make your point. And if you utter another word about her, you're out the door," he warned, his authority unmistakable. "This is my friend and driver, Christopher Heath. I'm sure he'd be more than happy to show you out." He gestured toward the door with an imperious flick of his hand. Unbeknownst to anyone in the room, he had discreetly texted someone, and now they had entered the bar.

Heath was the largest man LuLu had ever seen, towering over 6 '5 " with a formidable presence. His deep black beard framed a face set in a permanent scowl, adding to his intimidating demeanor. Two blue eyes hung in the air, glaring through the black thickets of hair. He loomed in the doorway with his arms crossed, a silent, unyielding sentinel.

Annie bristled at the challenge, her entitlement on full display. "How dare you talk to us like that? Do you know who I am?" she seethed, her voice rising with indignation.

"I don't give a shit," the gentleman in the corner shot back, his voice unwavering. "You do not get to walk into her place and treat her like shit. Only pigs throw shit."

Annie's face flushed with rage, her eyes ablaze with fury. "Are you going to let him talk to me like that? He just called me a pig!" she shrieked, her voice echoing through the now-silent bar.

"If the shoe fits," the man retorted, his tone cutting like a knife.

"I think you mean trough." LuLu slides in. Max's laughter rang out like a bell, a sharp contrast to the tense atmosphere.

Greg's anger radiated from him. He was the only one that surveyed the bar and realized the scene they were causing. He knew better than to escalate things here, especially with his father being the president of the college.

"Let's go," he said firmly to the group, motioning towards the door.

"Are you going to let them speak to me that way?" Annie protested, stomping her foot dramatically.

"Shut up. Let's go," Greg commanded, grabbing her arm and ushering her out of the bar. Annie continued to protest with profanity until the bar door closed behind them. Michap followed them out, ensuring they found their way away from the bar. As Greg and his companions left, leaving behind a wake of chaos and resentment, LuLu couldn't help but chuckle at the absurdity of it all. The frat boys' raucous laughter filled the air, a cacophony that served as a bittersweet symphony of victory.

Max's concern was evident in the gentle tone of his voice as he inquired, "Are you sure you're okay to close up by yourself?" His gaze flicked towards the rowdy group of boys in the back, a silent acknowledgment of the potential trouble they could cause.

LuLu offered him a reassuring smile. "I'll be fine, Max.

Don't worry about me," she replied, her voice steady despite the lingering tension in the air. For the first time that night, Doodle, the old bar dog, stirred from his spot and padded over to Max, seeking a farewell pat. Max obliged, giving the faithful companion a few affectionate pats before bidding them both goodnight and disappearing into the night.

As the door closed behind Max, LuLu turned her attention back to the remaining patron at the bar. "Name's LuLu Pillar. Thought I should introduce myself since we're apparently dating," she quipped, a playful glint in her eye.

"Silas Heartly," he replied simply, his tone measured and composed.

LuLu furrowed her brow, a flicker of recognition crossing her features. "Silas Heartly... Where have I heard that name before?" she mused aloud, racking her brain for the source of her familiarity.

Silas leaned forward, his expression guarded. "I'm the founder of the fashion app, Style Me Up," he began, but before he could continue, LuLu's eyes widened with sudden realization.

"Of course! The app that revolutionized the way we dress! Everyone's been buzzing about it," she exclaimed, her excitement bubbling over.

Silas shot her a cautionary glance. "Keep it down," he cautioned, his tone low but firm. "I've just set up an office here in Evy. San Francisco's become too expensive for my employees to afford. With the college, we thought we could recruit easier, too. Plus, my partner and I are moving into the medical field that will help patients when they have to go from hospital to hospital. I cannot say more about it now, but there are a few practices in town we are going to or have contracts with."

LuLu nodded eagerly, her enthusiasm undiminished. "That's fantastic news!" she exclaimed, unable to contain her excitement at the prospect of Silas's venture. "Great for the town and local business."

As LuLu and Silas chatted, a frat brother in a polo shirt swaggered up to the bar, clearly looking to order more drinks. LuLu, still reeling from the earlier commotion, turned to fill his order.

"So, since we're dating now, does that mean I get to take you out?" Silas asked, his smile playful and his eyes twinkling with mischief.

LuLu raised an eyebrow, a smirk forming on her lips. "I don't really date," she said, her tone light but teasing.

The frat brother, catching the exchange, was quick to jump in. "Oh, come on, give the guy a chance!" he urged, grabbing a few of the drinks as LuLu carried the rest back to the table.

As LuLu returned, Doodle decided he'd had enough for the night. He pulled the chain to the apartment, opened the door with surprising dexterity, and disappeared inside.

"Did that dog just open a door, or am I just really drunk?" a pledge asked, eyes wide with amazement.

LuLu chuckled. "He's a therapy dog. Very smart. It reminds me of last call."

She turned to leave when the frat brother grabbed her wrist. "Guys! See that dude at the bar? He just asked her out. What do you think?" he exclaimed to his group.

They erupted into a chant, "Do it! Do it!"

LuLu's face turned dark and cold in an instant. "Let go. Do not touch me."

The kid threw up his hands, obviously drunk. "Sorry,

sorry. No offense. Just trying to get an answer for my man here."

"To make it clear, I am not his man," Silas jokes, eyeing the scene.

LuLu gave a curt nod. "Yes, okay, yes," she said, then raised her voice. "Last call!"

The group settled their tab and trickled out of the bar, their earlier rowdiness replaced by a sullen quiet. Silas packed up his laptop and approached the bar to pay his bill.

"So, about that date..." Silas began, leaning in closer, his voice low and inviting.

LuLu tilted her head, a playful glint in her eyes. "You're persistent, aren't you?"

"I just know something interesting when I see it," Silas replied smoothly. "How about I pick you up here at 7:00 tomorrow? Nothing crazy. Let me take you to dinner. That was quite a show, and I would at least love the story behind that. How about I pick you up here at 7:00 tomorrow?" He opened his wallet and left 500.00 on the bar and walked out.

"Wait, what?" LuLu called after him, but he was already gone. She stood there, realizing that when she had said "yes," he had taken it as an agreement to go out. Even worse, she didn't have his phone number to call and cancel. Despite herself, she felt a flicker of intrigue. Maybe this wasn't a bad thing after all.

Two

The next morning, LuLu woke up with a start, her heart pounding as the realization hit her—she had agreed to a date. Or, at least, she sort of agreed to one. She hadn't been out with a man since her engagement had fallen apart, and the memories of that disaster flooded her mind.

Sitting up in bed, she rubbed her eyes and stared at the ceiling, the remnants of her dream mingling with the harsh reality of the morning light. Her engagement had been a major train wreck in her life, a whirlwind of broken promises and shattered dreams. The final blow came during the darkest time of her life and she needed someone, even her cheating fiance. But he left her for Annie.

She remembered the day she discovered the truth. It was as if the world had tilted on its axis. The whispers, the suspicious glances—all of it crystallized into a harsh reality when she found out that Greg had been sleeping with one of her best friends, Annie, for nearly the entire duration of their relationship. LuLu would not sleep with him unless he was faithful, so they entered an unhealthy loop. She had thought Annie was her friend. When he proposed, he promised it would only be the two of them. Then there was the night of the party...

Her mind wandered back to that dreadful night. Greg had ended their relationship while she was in the hospital, barely conscious and grappling with the shock of her accident and her parents' deaths. The cold, clinical smell of antiseptic still lingered in her nostrils, the sterile white walls closing in on her. She could still hear the beeping of the heart monitor, the soft murmurs of the nurses, and then Greg's words—merciless, final.

"It's over, LuLu."

It didn't matter that he chose that moment, when she was at her lowest. What truly haunted her was what they didn't know. It was her fault that her parents were rushing to the hospital.

She shook her head, trying to dispel the haunting memories. It was a heavy burden, this guilt she carried. She felt responsible for their deaths, for the wreckage of her life that followed. The hospital bed, the funeral, Greg's betrayal —it all blended into a nightmare she couldn't wake from.

But as she stood in her kitchen, the morning sun filtering through the curtains, she realized she had a choice. She could let the past define her, or she could try to move forward, one tentative step at a time.

She poured herself another cup of coffee and took a deep breath. The aroma filled her senses, grounding her in the present. Doodle, sensing her distress, nuzzled her leg gently.

"Thanks, buddy," she whispered, scratching behind his ears. His unwavering companionship was a balm to her soul.

Tonight, she will meet Silas. Maybe it wouldn't be a date, or maybe it would. Either way, it was a chance to step out of the shadows of her past, to see if she could find a glimmer of hope amid her pain.

She thought about the date—tonight, 7:00. The idea of stepping back into the world of dating felt daunting, a step into the unknown. But there was something about Silas, something intriguing. And he is a current successful entrepreneur. If anything, maybe he could give her advice about the bar. Maybe this was a chance to start fresh, to move beyond the mess in which her life had become.

As she stood there, contemplating the possibilities, a small, determined smile crept onto her lips. "Maybe it's time to take a chance," she whispered to herself, feeling a flicker of hope ignite within her.

Doodle followed her around through her chores in the morning. He wasn't much help, like normal, but she enjoyed his company. She mostly pushed him around the bar with the broom. He was a friendly dog. She smiled down at him as he lounged on the floor, his tail wagging lazily. After cleaning up the bar, it was off to do laundry. She crooned to herself, finding a strange sense of peace in the rhythm of her routine. By the time she cleaned up the bar and counted the inventory, it was almost two. She marveled at how a boring day could pass so quickly.

She called her vendors to make their weekly orders and then headed to shower and get ready for her date. As the warm water cascaded over her, she felt a mix of anticipation and nervousness. Two more calls than it would be time for LuLu to over think the date for the evening. She needed to talk to Dr. Clover first. She had her weekly appointment at 3:00.

LuLu's fingers flew over her phone screen, sending a quick text to her therapist. She mentioned the date and within moments, Dr. Clover had set up a video call link. They talked for an hour, dissecting every detail of the date, unpacking its highs and lows. They discussed what happened with the group.

"I am proud that you are doing this." Dr. Clover urged gently through the screen, her voice a steady anchor in LuLu's stormy thoughts. "You know, the steps we set up for you to feel safe."

Nodding with determination, LuLu said, "I'll have Sasha swing by as soon as we're done here." Her voice was steady, though a thread of vulnerability wove through her words.

"We should discuss what happened with Liam and the group." Dr. Clover pointed out. For the rest of the hour, that is exactly what they did.

When the call ended, LuLu paused just long enough to catch her breath before dialing Sasha's number. The phone rang twice before Sasha's familiar voice, warm and comforting like a hug, answered.

"Hey Sasha, I need your help," LuLu began, striving to keep the tremor out of her voice.

"What's going on?" Sasha's tone was serious, curious, her interest clear.

"I have a date tonight and... Sasha's excited interruption swallowed" LuLu's words up.

"A date?! LuLu, that's amazing! Who's the lucky guy? Did you talk to Dr. Clover?"

A laugh bubbled up from LuLu as she responded to Sasha's infectious enthusiasm. "Yes, I did. She thinks it's a good thing. His name's Silas. He's new in town. We met last night at the bar."

Sasha's excitement crackled through the phone. "Tell me everything! What are you wearing? Where are you going?"

"That's why I'm calling. I need help to pick out what to wear," LuLu admitted, her cheeks warming with a hint of shyness.

"Say no more. I'm on my way," Sasha declared, her determination as clear as a bell. "We're going to make sure you look absolutely stunning."

A wave of gratitude washed over LuLu. "Thanks, Sasha. I owe you one."

"You can repay me by having an amazing time tonight," Sasha replied with a chuckle. "I'll be there in twenty."

As LuLu hung up, a sense of relief eased her tension. She glanced at Doodle, who sat with his big, soulful eyes fixed on her. "Looks like we're in expert hands, buddy," she said, offering him a reassuring pat.

True to her word, Sasha arrived twenty minutes later, bursting through the door with an array of clothes and accessories spilling from her arms. "Alright, let's work some magic!" she announced, her eyes twinkling with enthusiasm.

The next hour was a whirlwind of fabric and laughter. Sasha and LuLu sifted through outfits, trying on different combinations until they settled on the perfect ensemble— The dress was a stunning shade of deep amethyst, the kind of purple that shimmered in the light, enhancing the richness of her hair and the striking color of her eyes. It featured intricate lace detailing along the bodice, the delicate patterns drawing the eye up to where the fabric met at her collarbone and tied gracefully behind her neck in a halter style. The neckline dipped just enough to be alluring without feeling too revealing, and the lace extended down her back, leaving a small keyhole opening between her shoulder blades.

The dress flowed effortlessly from her waist, the fabric cascading down in soft, ethereal layers that swirled with every step she took. It was light and airy, the perfect blend of elegance and ease, as if the dress had been made for her. The hem brushed just above her ankles, showing off the strappy silver heels Sasha had picked out, which sparkled subtly with each movement.

When she turned in front of the mirror, the dress moved with her, the lace catching the light while the flowy material swayed like water. It was simple but sophisticated, with a timeless elegance that made LuLu feel like she was floating. She ran her hands over the smooth fabric, the softness against her skin adding to the sensation of confidence.

While LuLu was amid her wardrobe transformation, Sasha dove into a new task. Fingers flying across the keyboard, she delved into the mystery of Silas Heartly. LuLu watched as Sasha's face lit up with disbelief and excitement.

"Holy shit! You're going out with Silas Heartly, the app developer? He's a billionaire. Not just a millionaire, but a billionaire! Look at this photo of him!" Sasha exclaimed, her eyes wide with awe as she held up her phone.

"Why does that even matter?" LuLu asked, her voice tinged with frustration. "I am not even sure if he was serious. He might not even show up. He was pretty drunk. His driver was there too."

"Driver! That is insane! Well, he asked you out in front of everyone," Sasha shot back. "And look, here's a picture of him with the president—the good one!" Sasha's voice carried from across the room.

"He only did it because Greg, Annie, and the others

showed up. He was just being polite. Or just trying to help." LuLu insisted. "Plus, it doesn't matter how much money he has. I can take care of myself." She made air quotes as she said, "taking care of myself."

"It's still really cool, and... And wait, what did you say about Greg and his entourage?" Sasha's phone nearly slipped from her grip. "They had the audacity to come in here? Liam, of all people? I will kill him. If he even looked at you..."

"It's fine. I handled it. They want to bother me, but I'm not about to let them see they've gotten under my skin."

"Next time, text me. I'll put a stop to it real quick," Sasha said with an unwavering seriousness her eyes set.

LuLu stepped out and did a little twirl to show off her dress. This was the first time in a long time that she had the opportunity to dress up. Sasha's face beamed with satisfaction.

"You look amazing," Sasha said, stepping back to admire their handiwork. "Silas won't know what hit him."

"You can't see them, right?" LuLu asked, referring to her scars.

"No, the shirt covers them perfectly," Sasha assured, picking up her phone. "It's almost seven. He should be here soon. I guess I'll have to give him the 'if you hurt her, then I'll hurt you' talk."

LuLu laughed, looking at her petite friend. "I'm sure he'll be terrified."

Sasha was terrifying when she wanted to be. She stood at only five feet tall, but alway felt awkward. A former gymnast, she still practiced regularly, maintaining her intense athleticism. Her wild curls of hair only added to her fierce demeanor, accentuating her intensity. Despite her formidable nature, she was one of the most beautiful people LuLu had ever seen.

"Good," Sasha said with a wink. "Because you deserve someone who treats you right, billionaire or not."

Just then, the doorbell buzzed. LuLu's heart skipped a beat as Doodle barked excitedly. Sasha gave her a reassuring nod.

"Go get him, tiger," Sasha teased and smacked LuLu on the ass.

LuLu took a deep breath and opened the door to find Silas standing there, looking dapper and holding a bouquet. Silas stepped inside and looked at the other girl in the room.

"Hi, LuLu," he said with a warm smile. "These are for you."

LuLu blushed, accepting the flowers. "Thank you, Silas. They are so pretty." They just stood for a moment, looking at each other.

"I'm Sasha, by the way, the best friend," she said, stepping forward and shaking his hand. "If you hurt her, I will kill you," she added, pulling his hand closer before releasing it. She turned and smiled at LuLu. "I'll take those and put them in water."

"Got it," Silas replied with a chuckle. "You're the muscle, and he's the lover." Silas patted Doodle on the head, but Doodle quickly lost interest and trotted off to lie down somewhere.

"What's the plan for the evening?" Sasha asked, getting on LuLu's nerves. She was behind the bar, trying to find a vase.

"Dinner," Silas replied simply.

"HMMM... mysterious...Have fun, you two," Sasha said,

heading up the apartment steps. "LuLu, see you when you get home."

"Wait, what?" LuLu asked, surprised.

"You really think I was going to leave? No way. I want to hear all about this, and if you don't come home, I'll know you're dead or the date went really well."

LuLu laughed, shaking her head. "Alright, alright. I'll fill you in when I get back. You have your keys. Can you make sure you lock the apartment?"

"Locked? I am going to be right here. I will wait up, you too," Sasha yelled as they left.

As they headed out for their date, LuLu felt a sense of optimism she hadn't felt in a long time. This was her chance to start anew, and she was ready to embrace whatever the night had been in store. Silas opened the car door for her, and as she settled into the backseat seat, she glanced at him, feeling a mix of nerves and excitement as he sat next to her. The driver started the car, and they were off.

"So, dinner," LuLu said, breaking the silence as Silas started the car. "Any hints on where we're going?"

Silas smiled, a hint of mystery in his eyes. "I thought we'd start with a place that has the best view of the city. It's a bit of a surprise. It is my favorite place."

LuLu felt her curiosity piqued. "I love surprises."

"Good," Silas replied, his smile widening. "I promise you'll love this one."

As they drove through the city, the conversation flowed easily. They talked about everything from their favorite books and movies to their childhood memories. Silas was charming and attentive, making LuLu feel at ease. He reached over gently and touched her fingers. Electricity shot through her body, and she realized no one had truly touched her in a very long time.

When they arrived at the restaurant, its elegance took aback LuLu. As soon as they walked in, the host took them directly to their table. Silas didn't need to say a word. The view from their table was breathtaking, with the city lights twinkling below them. The conversation continued to flow effortlessly, and LuLu laughed and smiled more than she had in a long time.

"So, what's your story, Silas Heartly?" LuLu asked, her eyes twinkling with curiosity. "How did you end up making a successful app?"

Silas leaned back, his expression thoughtful. "I needed a change. San Francisco was getting too hectic, and I wanted to find a place where I could actually live, not just exist. Plus, it's easier to recruit talent with the college nearby. I have family trying to make their mark here, too. I want to help support them."

LuLu nodded, understanding the sentiment. "It sounds like you've found a good balance."

"I hope so," Silas replied, his gaze softening as he looked at her. "And what about you, LuLu? What made you stay here?"

LuLu hesitated for a moment, then was honest. "It's home. I've thought about leaving, but this place, the people here, they're my family."

Silas reached across the table, taking her hand in his. "I'm glad you stayed."

LuLu let Silas take her hand, her fingers intertwining with his. The moment their skin touched, a surge of warmth radiated from him to her, like a spark igniting a long-dormant flame. Her stomach fluttered with a mix of nervous excitement and yearning. She felt a flush spread across her cheeks, the intensity of the sensation making her heart race uncontrollably. It jumped into her throat, making it hard to breathe as she absorbed the depth of the connection they were sharing. Each touch seemed to awaken a part of her that had been asleep for too long, and she realized, with a jolt, just how much she had missed the simple, electric thrill of being close to someone.

The waiter arrived and handed them menus. This restaurant, situated just outside of town, was a far cry from the places her family frequented. The elegant ambiance, complete with candles and actual tablecloths, was a rarity for her. Typically, their dining experiences involved drive-thru windows or the diner next door—simple, homey places that were comfortable but far less sophisticated.

As LuLu scanned the menu, Silas ordered a bottle of wine. The lack of listed prices made her uncertain about what to choose. She glanced around the room and noticed that all the women were eyeing her. She realized she had dressed significantly under the dress code for this upscale venue. The other guests, clad in tailored suits and elegant dresses, seemed in attire that cost more than everything she was wearing.

Silas noticed LuLu's discomfort as the waiter brought the wine, and he tasted it. He nodded to the waiter, and he filled both of their glasses. LuLu drank her in one swallow. Silas filled her glass again, and she did the same.

"Keep drinking like that. I'll need to order a bottle for each of us," Silas joked.

"Sorry, this is new for me, and it's pretty fancy," LuLu admitted, feeling embarrassed. She gestured toward her empty glass and then around the room. "I'm wearing $50 jeans, and that woman's handbag probably costs more than my bar," LuLu sighed. "I date a little, as you might have guessed from the other night and from Sasha. Sorry about that."

"I understand. She just wants the best for you, and that's a good thing," Silas replied, taking a sip of his wine. "I actually like what you're wearing."

"She's great. Annie, Sasha, and I have been friends since kindergarten. Annie and Sasha's parents are from the higher end of town. I had a scholarship to their school when I was young. We were so excited to go to college together, and now we've all ended up back here," LuLu explained.

"What brought you back here?" Silas asked.

"That's a story for date two," she teased.

Silas chuckled, leaning back in his chair. "Alright, fair enough. So, there's going to be a date two?" He raised an eyebrow.

"It's your turn. Why don't I tell you what I know about you, and you can fill in the gaps?" LuLu said, turning the tables.

She grinned. "So, you're a billionaire who created an app that made you a lot of money. You're single, thirty, and on the list of most eligible bachelors."

Silas raised an eyebrow, smirking. "Not bad. Now it's my turn. Your LuLu Pillar. You own and run that bar we were at last night. You have a dog named Doodle who I saw at the bar last night. Parents both passed. I am sorry, by the way. That had to be hard."

LuLu's smile softened. "That's quite a bit you know there. But I guess it's my turn to go deeper."

Silas nodded. "Go for it."

"You moved to this town to escape the chaos of San

Francisco, to find a place where you could live, not just exist. You're looking for something real, something meaningful." LuLu finished her third glass of wine, feeling a bit more confident.

Silas stared at her. "That's not fair. I told you that," he replied, making LuLu blush. She glanced at the menu, which was mostly in French. Despite knowing a bit of Spanish, the French dishes were foreign to her.

"Umm, what would you recommend?" LuLu asked, glancing at the elegant script on the menu. Silas closed his menu with a decisive snap and grinned, about to respond when a familiar, A grating voice cut through the air.

"Well, look who it is! LuLu and her new boyfriend," Annie sneered as she and Greg swaggered up to their table. "I never thought I'd see you here."

LuLu's jaw tightened. "Are you fucking kidding me? Are you stalking me?"

Annie smirked, her eyes flicking over LuLu's outfit. "Like I care what you do. Do you really think you interest me that much?"

"I actually do, or you'd just move on," LuLu pointed out.

Greg's laughter echoed Annie's mockery, a sound that made LuLu's blood boil.

"I actually owe you a thank you," Annie said with an insincere smile.

"Oh?" LuLu asked, her guard up.

"Now that Greg knows you slept with his best friend, he doesn't feel bad about us. You've set us free."

"Okay. So you can go now?" LuLu shot back, her voice rising. She turned her back to them and her eyes settled on Silas, who was eyeing the couple. He and Annie chuckled, but Silas's face remained stone cold, his gaze fixed on Greg.

Annie's smirk turned into a sneer. "You always were a drama queen," she said.

"At least I'm not a whore who slept with my best friend's boyfriend for years," LuLu whispered, her voice icy.

"What did you say?" Annie demanded, her voice rising to a shrill pitch.

Forks clinked against plates, conversations lulled, and all eyes turned toward the growing tension in the room. A few diners exchanged disapproving glances, their hushed whispers cutting through the once pleasant hum of the high-end restaurant.

"Well, this is more than I ordered," someone muttered dryly, the hint of a smirk in their voice.

LuLu caught the comment, but her spine straightened. She wasn't about to fold under their judgmental stares. With a slow breath, she stood her ground, her eyes locked on the source of the conflict, refusing to let the whispers or the weight of the room silence her.

"You heard me," LuLu said, meeting Annie's gaze steadily. "It's impressive how you've turned betrayal into an art form. You have no respect for friendship or boundaries. Just remember, when I said no, he found you. What will happen when you're the one saying no, Annie?"

Before anyone could react, the palm of Annie's hand collided with LuLu's cheek. A sharp sting radiated through LuLu's face, her head jerking to the side from the force of the slap. The searing pain lingered, and for a moment, it felt as if the entire restaurant had collectively held its breath, stunned by the sudden eruption of violence.

Silas's eyes blazed with fury. He stood up so abruptly that his chair toppled over. "From where I'm sitting, it's you two making the scene," he said through gritted teeth.

Without hesitation, he walked up to Greg and delivered a sharp knee to his groin. Greg's eyes crossed as tears streamed down his face, and he crumpled to the floor, gasping in pain.

Turning back to LuLu, Silas's tone softened. "You know what? I see nothing on this menu that jumps out at me. I'm in the mood for a burger. Know any good places in town?"

LuLu's eyes brightened, the tension momentarily lifting. She began enthusiastically listing off a few local diners, her excitement and suggestions effectively drowning out the presence of Annie and Greg. Silas, intrigued by her recommendations, waved for the waiter.

"Excuse me, we're not done here," Annie said sharply.

"Oh, we are," Silas replied coolly. "I won't sit here and let you speak to her like this, let alone assault my date."

"What's going on, sir?" the waiter interjected, sensing the escalating tension.

"We're leaving," Silas said firmly, his gaze fixed on Greg. "Please inform Annalisa I was here; I didn't have time to stop in the kitchen to say hello. And as for these two, they're insulting my date. They need to find somewhere else to eat this evening." He stood, taking LuLu's hand. "If you touch her like that again, you'll regret it. I'm more than happy to continue this conversation with your boyfriend outside."

"Is that a threat?" Greg spat, trying to compose himself.

"It's a promise," Silas growled. He turned and walked to the waiter's station, leaving LuLu and the others to watch him.

"I paid. Are you well?" he asked, ignoring the other two now standing awkwardly.

"Burgers?" LuLu said with a smile. Silas offered his hand

to help her out of her seat. They walked out, but Silas shouldered Greg as they left, earning a laugh from LuLu.

As they exited, they overheard the waiter addressing Annie and Greg firmly, "We're going to have to ask you to leave."

"Excuse me? You know who my father is, right? And his!" Annie shouted, stomping her foot and pointing aggressively.

"Greg, take care of this," she demanded.

"Who the hell does he think he is?" Greg fumed, pointing to the couple as they left.

"His sister owns the restaurant," the waiter said simply, turning away and leaving Annie and Greg standing, red-faced, in the middle of the dining room.

Silas and LuLu walked to the car, and the driver, Heath, promptly opened the door for them. They settled in, and soon, Milcap was pulling up to a drive-through, ordering cheeseburgers, fries, and a large soda. LuLu made sure Milcap got what he wanted as well.

Silas then asked for a cup of ice and gently pressed it to LuLu's cheek where Annie had slapped her. She winced at first, but then let the cool ice numb the sting. When she reached for the cup, their fingers brushed for an instant, making LuLu catch her breath. A blush crept up her cheeks as Silas lowered his hand.

They sat in the car, munching on their fast food. The informal atmosphere made LuLu feel more at ease, and she chatted animatedly with Silas, the tension from earlier slowly melting away. Suddenly, she noticed Silas looking at her with an amused expression.

"You have ketchup on your cheek," he said with a laugh. She tried to wipe it off, but missed it entirely.

"Here, let me," Silas said softly, stroking his napkin against her cheek.

LuLu blushed, her heart racing as she caught the scent of sandalwood. Her breath hitched in her throat. When he finished, he tenderly moved a strand of hair out of her face, his face lingering close to hers.

For a moment, LuLu thought he might kiss her, and panic surged through her. "I think we should get back," she said, glancing at the clock and noting that it was past midnight.

"Oh, yeah," he agreed, settling back in his seat. "Heath, can you take us back to the bar?"

"Yes, sir," Heath responded, rolling up the partition between the front and back seats.

"Thank you," LuLu said, turning to him with genuine appreciation. "I really appreciate you driving us tonight." Silas watched her interact with Heath, intrigued by how easily she engaged with his staff. He had dated no one who connected so naturally with his people.

As they drove home, Silas gently placed his arm around her. LuLu felt a warm, comforting sensation spread through her, her entire body tingling with a newfound excitement. Maybe this was the beginning of something new, something good. She felt more hopeful than she had in a long time, ready to embrace whatever the future held.

When they arrived back at the bar, Silas walked her to her door. "I had a wonderful time tonight, LuLu," he whispered. "Even with the craziness. I haven't kneed someone in the balls for a really long time."

"Me too," LuLu replied, feeling a blush creep up her cheeks. "Minus the ball stuff. But thank you for dinner."

Silas smiled, leaning in to kiss her cheek. "Give me your

phone." LuLu complied. Silas punched a few things in and handed it back. "You have my number now, and I just texted myself with your number."

"Thank you for not asking me about Greg and Annie." LuLu said and smiled.

"I reserve the right to ask you at a later date," Silas said as LuLu watched him walk away, a smile on her face. Tonight had been more than she could have hoped for, and she couldn't wait to see what tomorrow would bring. "I will text you tomorrow."

Silas walked back to the car, and Heath opened the door for him. Silas settled into the backseat, thinking about the evening. It had been a long time since he felt this good, yet something was weighing on him. LuLu had baggage, and baggage followed her even into this small town. He needed to know what he was getting into.

"Heath, what do you think?" Silas asked, breaking the silence.

"Of what, sir?" Heath responded, keeping his eyes on the road.

"Don't play dumb," Silas joked lightly. "Really?"

"She's the first girl you've taken through a drive-thru. I actually enjoyed that. I don't think you've ever eaten in this car," Heath laughed.

"Very true," Silas replied, a smile playing on his lips.

"She invited me to eat with you. You've never dated a girl who acknowledged me, let alone included me," Heath said more seriously.

Silas nodded, appreciating Heath's candor. "Thank you for your honesty. I need you to do something for me," he stated intensely.

"Yes, sir," Heath replied, his tone returning to a professional edge.

"Look up everything on LuLu Pilar. I want a complete background check. Everything you can find on her and a man named Greg. I don't have his last name, but if you find out enough about her, you'll find information about him."

"Yes, sir. Are you sure you want everything?" Heath asked.

"Everything," Silas confirmed, his voice firm.

As they drove through the quiet streets, Silas gazed out the window, the flickering street lights casting shifting shadows inside the car. He knew that delving into LuLu's past might reveal more than he bargained for, but he needed to be prepared. He needed to protect himself—and perhaps protect her, too.

Three

LuLu's cheek throbbed with warmth from where Silas's lips had lingered. Her heart fluttered in a way she hadn't felt in years. She gently pushed open the creaking door to the bar, exhaling softly as she closed it behind her. Climbing the stairs to her apartment, she took deliberate, steadying breaths.

The sound of the door opening startled Doodle, who barked sharply. Sasha, engrossed in whatever was playing on LuLu's TV, jerked upright at the noise.

"You didn't need to wait for me, really." LuLu said, setting down her bag as she entered the room.

"I can't use your Netflix password anymore, and I'm way behind on Bridgeton. Soooo, spill! How did it go?" Sasha asked eagerly.

LuLu smiled, settling onto the couch beside Sasha. "It was... interesting. Dinner started off nice, but then Annie and Greg showed up."

Sasha's eyes widened. "No way. Are you serious? They are really back, aren't they? What happened?"

LuLu recounted the evening, how Annie had mocked her, and Greg's insults. "Silas stood up for me. He didn't let them get away with it," she said, feeling a surge of appreciation for Silas. "He decided we should leave, and we ended up getting burgers instead."

Sasha grinned. "Burgers? That sounds more fun anyway. What else?"

LuLu blushed, feeling like a high school girl. "After we finished, he walked me to my door and kissed me on the cheek. Goodnight."

Sasha squealed, hugging a pillow. "He sounds perfect! Standing up for you, burgers, and a sweet goodnight kiss? Not too pushy, no expectations! I will wait to make my final decision."

LuLu felt a warm glow inside, a mixture of excitement and hope. She looked at Sasha, her friend's enthusiasm contagious.

"Yeah, it felt... good. Fantastic." LuLu replied.

Sasha nudged her playfully. "You deserve this, LuLu. It's about time you had someone who treats you right."

Doodle, sensing the shift in the mood, trotted over and placed his head on LuLu's lap. She scratched behind his ears, feeling the comfort of his presence.

"Maybe this is the start of something new," LuLu whispered, more to herself than anyone else. For the first time in a long time, the future didn't seem so daunting.

Sasha threw a pillow at LuLu's head and laughed, a lighthearted sound that filled the room. She wanted and needed something good to happen to LuLu. The past two years had been too much, even for her as a friend, let alone for LuLu. Sasha had broken up with Ryan because of the whole mess with LuLu. She didn't regret it, but she desperately wanted something better for both of them. It actually worked out better for Sasha because she met Rebecca.

LuLu changed into her pajamas and joined Sasha on the bed. Sasha had made it clear she was staying the night. They settled in and watched their favorite Shanda original until sleep overtook them.

Late the next afternoon, Sasha and LuLu finally woke up. On Monday, Sasha called in and mentioned that she could easily reschedule a few appointments. She was the best realtor in all of Envy. They dressed and chatted as they walked across the street for breakfast at Max's wife's diner, the best spot in town. With the bar closed again tonight, LuLu didn't have to worry about prepping too much.

Nina, Max's wife, took their order. She was an older woman whose once-red hair now danced with silver and gray. She was always at the diner, a comforting presence. Max sat at the counter, drinking his coffee and chatting with the locals.

"So, tell me more about Mr. Billionaire, now that you had time to sleep on it?" Sasha asked, winking as she sipped her coffee. "It seems like you actually like him."

LuLu laughed, her eyes twinkling. "I do. He was nice."

Sasha grinned. "Nice. That is all I get." What you told me last night sounded like a scene straight out of a rom-com. But if Annie thinks she is going to get away with hitting you, she has another thing coming. I cannot believe those two. They are ridiculous. I wish I would just wrap my hands around all of their throats. "All of them, all four."

Nina approached with their breakfast plates, setting them down with a warm smile. "Here you go, girls. Enjoy!"

As they dug into their meals, LuLu couldn't help but feel a sense of contentment. The night before had been a roller-coaster of emotions, but now, sitting in the cozy diner with her best friend, she felt hopeful about the future.

Max strolled over, refilling their coffee cups. "How's everything tasting?"

"Delicious as always, Max," Sasha replied with a grin.

Max nodded, satisfied. "Good to hear. You girls have a great day."

After breakfast, they lingered over their coffee, savoring the moment. LuLu felt grateful for the stability and warmth that places like Max's wife's diner and friends like Sasha brought into her life. It was a reminder that, no matter what challenges lay ahead, she had a strong support system to help her through. She still had doubts, though. While the date went well for her, she can never tell what he was thinking.

LuLu stared at her phone, the screen dark and silent. Her fingers drummed against the coffee cup, her mind racing. "He said he would call today. If Annie and Greg didn't scare him away," she murmured, her voice tinged with uncertainty. She took a sip of her coffee, her eyes clouded with doubt. "Maybe I'm making more out of this than I should. Maybe he was just being nice."

"You do like him. You are hoping he calls, like a girl with a crush. I love it." Sasha reached across the table, her hand warm and reassuring as it enveloped LuLu's. "Hey, you put yourself out there. That's huge, especially after everything," she said, her voice gentle but firm. "You've been through so much. You deserve to let your guard down a little. The shit with your birth dad. I mean, you almost died, and with Greg and your parents..."

LuLu's eyes flickered, her lips pressing into a thin line. She nodded, but the gesture was perfunctory, her mind already seeking an escape from the painful topic. "Yeah, anyway..." she trailed off, desperate to change the subject. There was no bill, like every other time they ate at the dinner. Max and his wife would take offense if they tried.

As they strolled back to the bar, the dim streetlights casting long shadows on the pavement, Sasha pulled LuLu into a tight hug. "Don't forget to call me if Silas reaches out," she murmured, her voice filled with concern. With a last squeeze, Sasha turned and walked away, her silhouette gradually blending into the night.

LuLu hesitated at the bar's entrance, taking a deep breath. It was her day off, yet the uncertainty of how to spend it loomed over her. Laundry seemed like a good start, a mundane task to keep her grounded.

Inside her apartment, the sudden ring of the wall phone interrupted the rhythmic hum of the washing machine. LuLu's heart skipped a beat, anxiety creeping in as the shrill sound echoed through the room. The bar's phone line, rushing into her apartment, was a lifeline for the business, separate from her personal cell. Doodle followed her to the phone.

She picked up the receiver, trying to steady her voice. "Pour Decision," she greeted cheerfully.

"Hello. I am calling for the owner of this pub, Ms. L-u-L-u P-ill-la-r," a formal voice responded, saying each letter of her name.

"That's me. LuLu Pillar," she replied, her curiosity piqued.

"My name is Audrey Lane. I'm the premier party planner

for the area. I'm sure you've heard of me." Audrey paused, waiting for recognition.

"Oh, of course!" LuLu lied, forcing recognition into her voice. "What can I do for you?"

"I have a client who wants to host an event at your bar this Friday," Audrey said smoothly.

LuLu frowned. "Unfortunately, Fridays are the second busiest night for us." I can't close. I don't normally do events. The short notice...

"We understand the inconvenience. We're prepared to offer $10,000 for the night," Audrey countered.

All the color drained from LuLu's face. She clutched the phone tighter, feeling lightheaded. Ten thousand dollars was more than she made on a weekend.

"That can't be right." LuLu asked, her skepticism sharpening her tone. This sounded too good to be true.

The woman responded with equal surprise, "They are dead set on hosting at your establishment."

"What do you need for the event?" LuLu asked.

"Just the usual setup and help with serving drinks. Basically, a normal night for you," Audrey will be at the bar in 15 minutes. Thank you so much. Annie and Greg were dead set on having their engagement party at your bar. Audrey said, "Well, anyway, see you in 15," and hung up before LuLu could respond.

LuLu stood frozen, the phone still pressed to her ear as the dial tone buzzed. Her heart sank, and a wave of anger washed over her. Annie and Greg. The names echoed in her mind like a bitter curse. Greg, her ex, and Annie, her former friend. They were doing this to spite her, to flaunt their happiness in her face.

LuLu's foot tapped restlessly against the barstool, her

eyes scanning the rows of empty chairs that seemed to mock her. The place wasn't sinking, but it sure wasn't thriving either. Every bill paid felt like balancing on the edge of a cliff. She chewed at her thumbnail, her thoughts racing. This party wasn't something she wanted to take on—the people, the vibe—it all felt wrong. But then again, their cash could change everything. With that money, she could finally hire someone who wasn't just scraping by, maybe even build a buffer for the slow months. She swallowed hard, knowing she didn't have the luxury to be picky. Their money would keep the lights on

She went up to her apartment to clear her head with Doodle. She glanced around her apartment, the laundry momentarily forgotten. She had to prepare, not just for a busy night at the bar, but for the emotional storm that was sure to follow.

With a deep breath, LuLu squared her shoulders and headed downstairs. This was her bar, her sanctuary. She wouldn't let them take that away from her, no matter how hard they tried. SHe quickly texted Sasha, who replied that she would be there to help. LuLu could tell in her text that she was livid.

With her cellphone in hand, another text message pinged through, making LuLu glance down. The sound of Doodle's annoyed grumbling filled the room as he shifted uncomfortably, clearly disturbed by the constant interruptions. LuLu stifled a laugh, her gaze fixed on the new message from an unfamiliar number.

"I had a great time last night. Is it too soon to do something again on Saturday night?" the message read. "Oh, this is Silas, by the way, in case I read the night wrong and you block my number or something."

LuLu chuckled as she typed her response. "I had fun too. Sorry again about Annie and Greg. I'd love to get together with less drama, but the bar is open until two on Saturdays."

Silas responded quickly, "Perfect. Right after then. I can help you clean up if you need. How about I pick up food and you supply the wine? We can eat and watch a movie at the bar or at your place if I'm not overstepping."

LuLu paused, her heart racing as she considered his offer. She wanted to say yes, but a wave of anxiety washed over her. The bar had always been her sanctuary, a personal refuge from the chaos of dating and relationships. For two years, she had kept her distance from romantic entanglements and brought no one into her "fortress of solitude."

Taking a deep breath, she tried to channel Sasha's fearless approach to life. What would Sasha do?

LuLu typed back, "I have a dog. But sure, it sounds like fun."

Silas's reply was swift: "It's a date."

She stared at the screen, her heart fluttering with a mix of excitement and apprehension. After a moment of contemplation, she fired off a message to Sasha detailing the exchange. The response took a while to come through—Sasha was at work—but when it did, the excitement practically burst from the phone. Sasha reassured her that she would be just a call away if needed and reminded her it was high time to hire a part-time bartender.

LuLu nodded to herself, knowing Sasha was right. The thought of leaving the bar in someone else's hands made her uneasy, but the help wanted sign went up in the window. Maybe it was time to take a step towards change, even if it meant opening up her sanctuary a little.

She texted on and off with Silas and Sasha most of the

day. It was a good day for LuLu. There were no problems at the bar at the moment. She was putting herself back out there. Doodle and she went for a long walk around the town. Something was changing. She didn't know what, but something was changing.

Four

LuLu and Silas texted on and off for the rest of the day, their messages a lifeline of distraction. The bar was closed on Sunday, Monday, and Tuesdays, which were her days of solitude. But today, the phone call from Audrey echoed in her mind, an unwelcome intruder.

She sat on her couch, staring at the laundry she had yet to fold. Annie and Greg. Why wouldn't they leave her alone? Their engagement party at her bar felt like a cruel joke. She wasn't the one at fault, yet they seemed determined to paint her as the villain. LuLu sighed, picking up her phone to reread Silas's last message.

She stood up, walking to the window and looking out at the quiet street. The stillness outside contrasted with the turmoil inside her. She wished she could shake off the frustration, but it clung to her like a shadow.

"Why can't they just let me be?" she muttered to herself, the question lingering unanswered in the quiet room. Doodle barked a small, playful response, making her laugh despite herself. With a resigned sigh, she turned away from the window and forced herself to focus on folding the laundry. She decided she would wait for Audrey, the premiere party planner, to arrive with her contract.

Almost on cue, the doorbell buzzed, and a well-dressed woman walked in. From her polished appearance, LuLu immediately assumed it was Audrey. Her heels clicked sharply on the wooden floor as she approached the bar, exuding an air of confidence.

LuLu straightened up, putting on her best professional smile. "You must be Audrey," she greeted, extending a hand.

The woman smiled back, her grip firm and businesslike. "Yes, that's right." And you must be LuLu. Finally, meeting you in person is a pleasure.

"The pleasure's mine. Can I get you anything?" LuLu asked, gesturing to the array of bottles behind the bar.

Audrey shook her head. "No, thank you. I just wanted to drop by and complete the details for Friday."

"Of course," LuLu replied, leading Audrey to a quiet corner table. As they sat down, LuLu felt apprehension knowing who the party was for. In order for both the financial boost and the chance to reclaim a bit of control over her life, she needed this night to go smoothly. She needed them to know that she was fine. She cannot give into this bullying.

As they discussed the arrangements, LuLu's mind drifted back to the roses from Silas and the support from Sasha. She felt a renewed sense of determination. No matter what happened on Friday, she would face it head-on, with the strength of her friends behind her.

LuLu reviewed the paperwork carefully, her eyes scanning each clause and condition. Satisfied, she signed the documents and handed them back to Audrey, who responded by giving her a check for $5,000.

"This is the deposit," Audrey explained. "You will receive the second half at the end of the party, on the condition that there are no violations of the general clauses," Audrey explained.

Audrey raised an eyebrow. "You might need additional help. I can supply a few, but that will come out of the total cost."

LuLu shook her head. "I'll let you know. I think I might find a few."

"Well, let me know if that falls through," Audrey remarked, organizing the paperwork. They shook hands, sealing the deal. Audrey took a moment to look around the bar, her gaze both critical and curious.

"Cute place," Audrey commented. "But I'm not sure it's worth $10,000 for an engagement party. No offense."

LuLu chuckled, a hint of irony in her smile. "None taken. I feel the same way."

With the business concluded, LuLu returned to the bar to finish her night. She felt a mixture of relief and anticipation. The check in her hand was a tangible reassurance, yet the thought of Annie and Greg's party still gnawed at her.

As she resumed her tasks, she caught Max's eye. "Everything sorted?" he asked, taking a sip of his beer.

"Yep, all set," LuLu replied, slipping the check into her pocket. "Big night ahead, but we'll get through it."

LuLu grabbed Doodle's leash and called for him. The big dog bounded over, tail wagging with enthusiasm. Although she had a small fenced-in area that Max maintained for her, Doodle needed more exercise.

They walked their usual route, LuLu smiling and

exchanging brief greetings with a few familiar faces. Doodle trotted happily beside her, his excitement infectious. At the small dog park, she let him off the leash, watching as he raced around with a few other dogs. She cherished these moments, the simple joy of seeing Doodle so carefree.

On their way back to the bar, LuLu noticed something unusual at her door. Her steps slowed as she approached cautiously. A vase of twelve red roses sat on the doorstep, their deep crimson petals vibrant against the gray sidewalk.

Her heart raced as she picked them up, a mix of curiosity and apprehension swirling in her mind. She stepped inside the bar, Doodle obediently following her. As trained, he trotted up to the apartment, leaving LuLu alone with the flowers.

She brought the vase inside and set it on the counter. Who could have sent these? Her thoughts immediately flickered to Annie and Greg, but that made little sense. A pang of unease struck her as unanswered questions gnawed at her. Taking a deep breath, she resolved to find out who was behind this unexpected gesture.

LuLu carefully opened the card tucked among the roses. As she read the note, a smile spread across her face.

The note read: I hope this isn't too much. I had a great time and look forward to seeing you again. Silas.

She felt a flutter in her stomach, the familiar yet exhilarating sensation of budding romance. With a soft sigh, she placed the flowers in the center of the bar and moved the others by the register, where their vibrant color brightened the room. The bar looked like a florist.

Gently, she traced the petals with her fingertips, feeling their velvety texture. Her thoughts drifted to Silas, replaying their time together. The roses were a sweet, unexpected gesture, and they brought a warmth to her heart that she hadn't felt in a long time.

LuLu picked up her phone and dialed Sasha's number. When it went to voicemail, she left a message, her voice filled with excitement. "Hey Sasha, it's me. I just wanted to tell you about something amazing that happened today. He got me more flowers, roses. Call me back when you get a chance. Love you!"

After hanging up, she sighed, feeling a mix of relief and longing. Since her breakup with Ryan two years ago, Sasha had been her rock. Sasha had found happiness with Rebecca, and LuLu genuinely wished the same for herself. She knew Sasha worried about her, often complaining about her solitary life.

LuLu glanced at the flowers on the bar, a symbol of new possibilities. She wished she didn't feel like such a burden to her only friend. Despite Sasha's reassurances, the guilt lingered. She wanted to share her happiness without the weight of her past dragging her down.

LuLu moved through her day with a focused determination. She busied herself with various tasks around the bar, finding solace in the routine. Tuesdays were her deep-cleaning days, a ritual she relished. It was a chance to clear her mind, to ground herself in the familiar rhythm of scrubbing, polishing, and organizing.

She moved effortlessly from one task to another, her hands working with practiced ease. She had been part of this bar for longer than she could remember, each nook and cranny as familiar as the lines on her palms. Cleaning was therapeutic, a way to pull her head out of the clouds and anchor herself in the present.

Just as she was finishing up, her phone buzzed on the

counter. Seeing Sasha's name on the screen, LuLu's heart skipped a beat. She answered eagerly, barely getting out a "Hello" before pulling the phone away from her ear as Sasha's excited scream echoed through the speaker.

"Roses!" Sasha shouted, her voice brimming with excitement.

"Yes. Flowers. No diamonds, so just calm down." LuLu said, but could not hide her excitement.

"He likes you." Sasha replied with a singsong voice.

"Stop it. It was one date so far," LuLu replied, a playful note in her voice.

"So far?" Sasha questioned, her tone teasing.

"We're having dinner at my apartment on Saturday after the bar closes," LuLu informed her. As she paced around the bar, she made her way up to the apartment. Doodle glanced at her from the living room, then went back to bed with an air of indifference.

"Seriously though, are you okay with that? Have you talked to Dr. Clover?" Sasha asked, a hint of concern creeping into her voice.

LuLu continued, "I'm actually okay with it. I feel... good about this. I'm excited, actually. But no, I don't have an appointment with Dr. Clover until next week. Then, I will give her an update. If I need to, I promise I'll reach out. I have a lot on my plate this week, and I'll probably need to connect with her. I want to see if I can manage on my own for now."

"What does that mean?" Sasha asked, her concern deepening.

"Greg and Annie had their party planner call, and they offered me $10,000 for the bar this Friday. It covers the space, alcohol, and servers. They want me to work there too," LuLu complained. "I can't turn it down. It's so much money, more than I make in an entire weekend. I've already signed the contract, so you can't talk me out of it. I might hire someone with the extra income."

"Well, Rebecca and I will be there to help. You need servers or extra help, right?" Sasha offered. In the background, someone with a vague voice asked why they mentioned her name.

"Actually, that would help me a lot, but I don't want to put you both out," LuLu protested.

"You're not. I'm offering. Actually, I'm insisting," Sasha said firmly.

"Well, if you insist," LuLu replied, a smile tugging at her lips. "How is Rebecca?"

"I think she's going to propose," Sasha whispered. "I found a ring in her makeup drawer."

"OH MY GOD, Sasha! And you let me go on about my problems," LuLu exclaimed.

"Shhhh... She has hearing like a bat even with the phone. She hasn't done it yet, but I hope you

know you're my maid of honor," Sasha whispered.

"You know it," LuLu replied, her heart swelling with happiness for her friend.

"I have to go. Rebecca just finished dinner. I want to eat while it's hot," Sasha said.

"Talk soon," LuLu said.

"Brunch this week? If not, I will see you on Friday. Love you!" Sasha replied before hanging up the phone. "

LuLu slipped her phone into her pocket and glanced. Her stomach growled loudly, reminding her she hadn't stopped to eat dinner, let alone lunch. She walked to the fridge and opened it, only to laugh at the sight. It looked like a scene from a cartoon she remembered from her youth—empty except for a lone ketchup bottle, minus the cobwebs.

She usually ate at the diner, but today felt too odd for that routine. The thought of walking over there didn't appeal to her. Instead, she rummaged through her freezer and found a frozen pizza. "This will have to do," she muttered to herself, preheating the oven.

While the pizza was baking, LuLu reflected on the day. The phone call from Sasha, the roses from Silas, and the impending confrontation with Annie and Greg—it all swirled in her mind like a chaotic dance. She was grateful for Sasha's unwavering support and the unexpected kindness from Silas, but the upcoming party weighed heavily on her. She fed Doodle with a piece of pizza and dog food. He was happy. LuLu finished her laundry and called it an early night. She called it an early night and fell asleep watching a murder documentary on HBO.

Wednesday came and went without incident. Good old Max stopped by for his usual couple of beers, settling into his favorite spot at the bar. A few tourists wandered through, their curious gazes taking in the rustic charm of Pour Decision. Overall, it was a boring night for LuLu. Normally, she hated slow nights, but tonight she welcomed the quiet. She needed the time to clear her head and prepare for the chaos ahead.

As she wiped down the bar, she chatted with Max, filling him in on the news. "The bar's going to be closed this Friday," she mentioned casually, not missing the surprised look on Max's face.

"Closed? Why?" Max asked, his eyebrows shooting up.

"Got an offer I couldn't refuse," LuLu replied with a small smile. "Ten grand to host a private party." LuLu left out it was Annie and Greg reserving for the night. He didn't need to worry.

Max whistled appreciatively. "That's a lot of money, Lu. Good for you." Max gave her an encouraging nod. "You'll be fine, Lu. You've handled worse."

She smiled, grateful for his support. The rest of the evening passed uneventfully, and for once, LuLu appreciated the monotony. It gave her time to prepare herself mentally for what lay ahead.

As she closed up for the night, she glanced at the flowers Silas had sent, their vibrant red petals a reminder of the good amidst the chaos. She felt a spark of hope, knowing that no matter what happened on Friday, she had friends who had her back.

Five

The bar was quiet again on Thursday. Max sat in his usual spot, nursing his beer, while a couple in the back booth engrossed themselves in each other, largely forgetting about their drinks. LuLu exchanged amused glances with Max, shaking her head at the sight.

"Times sure have changed," Max chuckled. "That was the backseat of the car stuff when I was their age."

LuLu laughed with him, enjoying the moment of levity. The bar door swung open, drawing their attention. Silas walked in, accompanied by Heath, his imposing bodyguard and driver.

"Hey there," Silas greeted, his smile lighting up the dimly lit bar.

"Silas! Heath!" LuLu exclaimed, her face breaking into a wide smile. Heath gave a curt nod, his expression as stern as ever. She caught herself, not wanting to appear too excited.

"Mind if we join you?" Silas asked, gesturing to the barstool next to Max.

"Not at all," Max replied, motioning for them to take a seat. "What brings you in tonight?"

"Just thought we'd stop by and see how you're doing," Silas said, settling in. "Needed to stretch our legs and figured we'd kill two birds with one stone."

Max grinned, tipping his hat to Silas. "Good to see you, Silas. And you too, Heath. LuLu told me about you. I'm Max. My wife owns the diner next door."

Heath gave a small, respectful nod, his watchful eyes scanning the bar, and then extended his hand. Max stood and shook it before returning to his drink. As LuLu poured Silas a drink, she felt a warmth spread through her. Despite the looming engagement party and the tension it brought, moments like this reminded her of the good things in her life.

"So, how have things been?" Silas asked, taking a sip of his drink.

LuLu sighed, leaning against the bar. "Busy. Got a big event coming up tomorrow that's got me a bit on edge."

"Oh? An event?" Silas asked, raising an eyebrow.

"It's an engagement party," LuLu said, her voice tinged with weariness. "For my ex, Greg, and a former friend of mine, Annie."

Silas's expression hardened, his disdain clear. "Greg? That guy? Why would you set yourself up like that?"

LuLu's eyes met his, and she could see the concern mingled with anger. "The money. Why else? Plus, they're doing this party just to get under my skin. This will be a good chance for me to show them I do not care, and we can end this bullying once and for all."

Silas leaned forward, his tone firm. "If there's anything

you need, LuLu, ask. Heath and I are ready to step in if things get rough."

"Thanks, Silas," LuLu said, feeling a surge of relief. "I might just take you up on that." She laughed uncomfortably.

As the night went on, the three of them chatted and laughed, the easy camaraderie making the quiet evening feel warm and comforting. Even the amorous couple in the back booth couldn't dampen LuLu's spirits. For the first time in a while, she felt a glimmer of hope that everything would be okay. Max and Silas reminded her of the good days when her father ran the bar and she watched him while she was supposed to be doing her homework.

At last call, LuLu called Max's wife to pick him up. He had been having a bit too much fun with Silas and Heath. When Nina appeared in the doorway, Max swayed slightly as he stood and stumbled over to her. He extended his hand, and Silas shook it firmly, clapping him on the back with a hearty farewell. Nina guided her husband out to the car with a mixture of exasperation, humor, and affection.

After Max and the amorous couple departed, Silas, LuLu, and Heath remained in the bar. Heath, ever vigilant, excused himself and stepped outside, his presence hinting at a protective nature rather than mere curiosity. LuLu appreciated his discretion. Silas walked around the bar and picked up a rag. He picked up a few glasses and started drying them and putting them under the bar.

"Thanks." LuLu said. "It goes much faster with help."

"Can I ask you a question?" Silas said as LuLu washed the few glasses left from the night.

"Technically, that's a question," LuLu jokes, glancing over her shoulder with a smirk.

"Ok, grandma," Silas laughed, teasing her.

"Shoot," LuLu replied, focusing on the glasses as she rinsed them.

"LuLu. It's not a name you hear every day. Is it a family name?" Silas asked, curiosity clear in his voice.

LuLu took a deep breath, the question bringing a wave of memories. She walked around to the other side of the bar and started wiping it down. They were now in the opposite position. "So, Lou was the name of my real birth father, and Laura was my mother's name."

Silas looked thoughtful. "I thought your parents were Frank and Laura."

LuLu froze, surprised. She had never shared her parents' names with him, but he had been chatting with Max for a while. She felt a pang of discomfort, but blew past it.

"Divorced," she whispered. "My stepfather, Frank, adopted me. He was the best man I ever knew. Taught me everything I know today. He's the one who opened this bar, actually."

Silas's expression softened, and he nodded appreciatively. "Sounds like he was a great guy. And I can see his influence in how you run things here."

LuLu gave a small, genuine smile. "He was. It's not always easy talking about him, but if this is going somewhere, I guess I have to."

Silas nodded understandingly. "I appreciate you sharing that with me, LuLu."

LuLu nodded with a smile. She needed to open up, but it was so hard. This was still new, and she was not sure even how to act. Every time she did, that person betrayed her, well, almost everyone. She had and will always have Sasha.

As they continued to chat, the warm camaraderie

between them felt like a balm to LuLu's nerves. Even though the upcoming event loomed large in her mind, moments like these provided a sense of reassurance and connection.

"This might be the best second date I've ever had," Silas said, his eyes twinkling.

"It's not really a date if I'm working," LuLu laughed back.

"Being a bartender makes dinner dates a little difficult," he quipped.

"Okay, I'll let this one slide," LuLu flirted, her face burning with a mix of embarrassment and excitement.

She walked around the bar, her gaze lingering on Silas as she approached. Stopping beside his bar stool, she looked down at him; her smile widening. She studied his handsome face—his deep brown eyes, his perfectly styled dark hair, half pulled away from his face, and the warm, sandalwood scent that surrounded him.

"Thank you for the flowers," she said, glancing at the vase on the bar as he joined her on the other side of the bar.

"You're welcome," he replied, looking up at her with a mixture of admiration and longing. "I really want to kiss you. Would that be alright?"

"Yes," she whispered, surprising herself with how easily the word came.

Silas nuzzled his stool back and stood, towering over her by just a few inches. He lifted her chin with his thumb and forefinger, his touch sending shivers down her spine. LuLu closed her eyes and pressed her hands on his chest, feeling the warmth radiate through his shirt. She could feel his heart beating under her hand. Her heart raced as their lips met.

The kiss was soft and gentle at first, a tentative exploration, but as he pulled her closer, it deepened, growing more intense and urgent. His arms wrapped around her waist, pulling her flush against him. He pulled at the back of her shirt, pulling him closer to him. The heat and electricity of the moment were unlike anything LuLu had ever experienced. She felt the rapid beat of his heart, matching her own racing pulse.

Time seemed to stand still as Silas's tongue softly brushed her lips, coaxing her mouth open. LuLu allowed herself to be carried away by the sensation, enjoying the heat and tenderness between them. He tasted like scotch and mint, a combination that sent a shiver down her spine. The kiss grew more fervent, their breaths mingling as they lost themselves at the moment.

When she finally pulled away, she bit his lower lip gently, their breaths hot and mingled. He wrapped his arms around her waist, the muscles in his biceps flexing as he lifted her effortlessly. Silas picked her up and placed her on the bar, his eyes never leaving hers. The cool surface of the bar against her thighs sent another thrill through her.

LuLu looked at him, running her hand along the stubble on his jaw, the rough texture contrasting with the softness of his lips. She pressed her forehead against his, their breaths intermingling, her fingers tracing the contours of his face.

Silas gazed at her with a mix of awe and desire, their faces inches apart. The connection between them was palpable, an electric current that made her heart race even faster. They were both trying to catch their breath, the intensity of their shared moment leaving them dizzy and exhilarated. He rubbed his thumb on her lower lip.

She bit his lip gently, a tease that made his breath hitch.

Without a word, he leaned in again, his lips capturing hers in a searing kiss. His hands roamed over the curve of her back, pulling her closer with a desperate need. LuLu responded with equal fervor, her hands sliding up to tangle in his hair, pulling him even closer. She could feel his arousal pressing against her, igniting a fire within.

The world outside faded away, leaving only the two of them and the undeniable chemistry that burned between them. For the first time in her life, she wasn't sure if she could stop. She breathed him in, the scent of cedar and mint intoxicating her senses, and let herself melt into his kiss. Her body pressed against his, every touch and movement stoking the flames of desire between them.

Silas's kisses trailed down her neck, leaving a path of heat that made her shiver. He whispered her name against her skin, his voice a low, sensual growl that sent a thrill through her. She arched into him, her hands exploring the hard planes of his back, feeling the rapid beat of his muscles beneath her fingertips.

Their breaths came in ragged gasps as they clung to each other, lost in the moment's intensity. LuLu's mind was a whirlwind of sensations, each kiss and caress driving her closer to the edge. She had never felt this alive, this consumed by desire. The sensation of his arousal pressed against her, large and hard, sent a surge of heat through her. She knew they should stop, but she couldn't bring herself to pull away.

Silas's hands roamed over her body, his touch both urgent and reverent, igniting fires everywhere he touched. He kissed her deeply, his tongue exploring her mouth with a possessive hunger. LuLu responded with equal fervor, her hands sliding under his shirt, feeling the taut muscles of his back flex under her touch.

He groaned softly against her lips; the sound vibrating through her and heightening her arousal. She could feel his desire, the hard length of him pressing insistently against her thigh, making her ache with need. She wrapped her legs around his waist, pulling him even closer, their bodies melding together in a feverish embrace.

Silas pulled back slightly and gently, his eyes dark with longing. "You are so beautiful," he murmured, his voice thick with passion. He brushed the palm of his hand on her cheek.

LuLu's heart raced at his words. She pulled him back to her by the collar of his shirt, her lips finding him in a kiss that was both tender and demanding. She knew she was crossing a line, but at that moment, she didn't care. All that mattered was the heat between them, the way he made her feel alive and desired. She kissed him again gently, still holding him so close she could smell him.

He pulled away to catch his breath. "Well, I'm going to say it again," Silas said, still gazing into her eyes. "This was the best second date I've ever had. I should head out. I'll call you tomorrow." She set her forehead against his and breathed him in.

"I need to close up," LuLu replied, catching her breath from their intimate moment and let him go.

"See you tomorrow." He said slyly.

Silas leaned in to place one more gentle kiss on her cheek before turning and walking out of the bar. The moment the door closed behind him, LuLu collapsed onto a barstool, her knees weak. She waved her hand in front of her face, trying to cool the warmth that still lingered from their kiss.

Confusion and exhilaration swirled inside her. She had thought she loved Greg, but this was something entirely different—something she hadn't felt before. LuLu's heart raced as she thought about Saturday, and the anticipation made her almost giddy. She could hardly believe how quickly things had changed, and she looked forward to what was to come.

With the last kiss from Silas still lingering on her cheek, LuLu collected herself and locked the bar door. Turning off the open sign, she couldn't help but smile at the irony. She quickly sent a text to Sasha, letting her friend know about the evening's events before climbing the stairs to her apartment.

Doodle greeted her with his usual exuberance, his tail wagging furiously. LuLu let him outside for a bit, watching as he trotted around the fenced area with boundless energy. Once she had settled him in, she jumped into the shower, embracing the warm water as it washed over her like a baptism of anticipation.

As she stood under the stream, she pressed her fingers to her lips, recalling the vivid image of Silas standing before her. His deep brown eyes, his smile—it all made her heart race faster. She smiled at the memory, her hand resting on her chest as she felt the rapid beat of her heart. Leaning against the shower wall, she took a deep breath, trying to steady herself. She opened her eyes, turned off the water, and stepped out of the shower, wrapping herself in a towel.

In the bedroom, Doodle waited eagerly with his tail wagging. As she entered, he jumped up, showering her legs with affectionate kisses.

"Doodle, stop that," she said with a laugh, though her voice was gentle. He immediately sat down, looking up at her with a disappointed expression. She patted him on the head, despite knowing she should be more firm. His adorable face made it hard to resist.

After dressing, LuLu sat on the edge of her bed, talking to Doodle as if he were a confidant. "I have to be careful. Things are going too well. I keep worrying that the other shoe will drop."

,

Doodle tilted his head, his eyes full of innocent curiosity. LuLu chuckled at his cluelessness and shook her head. She knew she was procrastinating going to sleep, her mind preoccupied with thoughts of the party and the day ahead.

She finally settled into bed, Doodle curling up beside her. As she closed her eyes, she felt a mix of nervousness and excitement for the next day. Despite her concerns, she couldn't help but look forward to what was coming, the promise of something new and hopeful lifting her spirits. Once again, thoughts of the kiss occupied her. She touched her neck where he kissed her. She ran her fingers down the spots he touched.

Six

LuLu's eyes fluttered open, and she blinked around the room, disoriented. Grabbing her cell, she saw with a jolt that it was already eleven o'clock. In the whirlwind of last night, she'd forgotten to set her alarm. They were because they started setting up at two, and she still needed to get the bar cleaned.

She jumped out of bed, letting Doodle outside as he did his pee dance, clearly relieved to be out. LuLu threw on her old clothes and dashed down to the bar, still in her pajamas.

In a burst of energy, she immersed herself in cleaning mode, diligently scrubbing the bar, bleaching the floor, and tending to every nook and cranny. She knew that with the high stakes of tonight, she couldn't afford to leave any room for complaints. She even cleaned and polished the dusty top-shelf bottles. With just minutes to spare, she texted Sasha to let her know what time to arrive.

Exactly at two o'clock, there was a knock on the bar door. LuLu unlocked it to find Andrea standing there with four other adults—Greg and Annie's parents. LuLu's stomach dropped when she saw them.

"LuLu?" Greg's mother, Mrs. Leverline, greeted, and LuLu realized she was still in her pajamas.

"Hi, Mr. and Mrs. Leverline," LuLu said, trying to sound upbeat. "Sorry, I know I look a bit like Deb from Napoleon Dynamite, but I was cleaning to make sure this place would be perfect for tonight. I figured why mess up good clothes, right?"

"No, no. Your hair is different. I love it." Mrs. Leverline stated.

The Leverlines smiled politely, but Mrs. Topher's eyes scrutinized the bar. "I don't think all the cleaning in the world will make this place look nice."

Mr. Topher grumbled, "I don't understand why they picked here. The college cafeteria would be better and cheaper."

"This is what the kids want," Mr. Leverline replied diplomatically. "Plus, we're giving back to the community. We're showing that the college and the town can coexist." LuLu understood now; the Leverlines were using this opportunity for good publicity, leveraging their sympathy for her situation

"Well, I'll let you set up," LuLu said, trying to keep her voice steady. She excused herself and made her way to the apartment door, feeling the urge to flee. But she forced herself to stay composed, not wanting to give in to her nerves.

Taking a deep breath, she slipped into the apartment and leaned against the door for a moment. She kept thinking about the money. She was doing this for the money. Despite the uncomfortable situation, she knew she had to focus on getting through the evening. She reminded herself of the good things: Sasha was coming to help, and Silas had left her with a sense of hope and excitement that she wasn't ready to let go of just yet.

LuLu took a quick shower, letting the hot water wake her up and refresh her. Afterward, she spent some time on her makeup, carefully applying foundation and a touch of mascara. She curled her hair, letting it cascade around her shoulders. Tonight, she wanted to look her best.

She selected a top that was lower cut than her usual style, aiming to balance stylish and appropriate. The top covered all of her scars, and she paired it with a tight pair of jeans that stressed her figure.

As she inspected her reflection in the mirror, she couldn't help but frown. No matter how much effort she put into her appearance, she felt like she fell short compared to Annie. Annie was a model, and LuLu had always felt frumpy in her shadow. She compared her own reflection to the idealized image of beauty she held in her mind, feeling a pang of inadequacy.

"You can put lipstick on a pig," LuLu said to Doodle, who sat at her feet looking at her.

LuLu sighed and shook her head, trying to push away the negative thoughts. She reminded herself that she had more to offer than just looks. Tonight was about more than just appearances—it was about showing confidence, professionalism, and that she could handle this challenging event with grace.

She took a deep breath and gave herself a last look in the mirror. "You've got this," she breathed, trying to boost her own morale. With one last glance, she headed back to the bar, determined to make the evening a success despite her insecurities.

She played around in the apartment for about an hour, and then Sasha texted her; she and Rebecca were there. Sasha greeted her with a hug and noted that they needed to talk about her text last night, playfully hitting her on the shoulder. LuLu smiled at Rebecca and thanked her for coming.

"Anything for Sasha, and since she considers you family, I do too," Rebecca said with a smile. "Plus, how often do you get to see a lawyer and a realtor serving drinks?"

LuLu smiled. "Thank you, just the same."

"Excuse me, girls. We are paying good money for this place. Do you mind helping?" Mr. Topher interrupted.

"Yes, sorry, I wasn't aware that you needed help to set up. I was told it was for the place and for serving drinks."

"Well, you're here now. You might as well help," he scoffed and walked away.

"Wow, he's still a piece of work, isn't he?" Sasha said, shaking her head. She looked at Rebecca. "Annie's dad. We were not rich enough to be her friend, so she had to sneak around to hang out with us. Her dad only wants high-class people around his daughter."

"Wow. Okay. Now I see why we are here. We've got you, LuLu," Rebecca said and moved to help. The two others followed her lead.

Everyone set to work setting up the bar for the Roaring 20s theme. LuLu took care to align and make sure every-thing was easily accessible while arranging the beer options. Andrea walked up to the bar with her clipboard, methodi-cally checking boxes with a pen while muttering, "Check," under her breath.

"LuLu, everything looks great," Andrea began briskly. "The bride-to-be requested a few changes," Andrea stated briskly. She wants a signature cocktail—vodka cranberry—and she wants everyone to dress as flappers. I have your costumes here. Annie gave me your size, but I have others if needed. "I just need the sizes for the others," she said, while glancing at Sasha and Rebecca.

Sasha and Rebecca quickly provided their sizes, and Andrea returned almost immediately with dresses for all of them. "Go change soon."

"I am not dressing up," Sasha shot back, crossing her arms defiantly.

"You will if you all want to get paid," Audrey stated coldly. "They were very specific about what they wanted, even though they waited until the last minute."

"My daughter knows what she wants," Annie's mom shouted, overhearing the conversation. "Plus, LuLu and Sasha, you will look adorable as flappers. I'm not sure who the other one is."

"The other one is Rebecca, my girlfriend," Sasha corrected firmly.

"Oh, I didn't know you were one of those. How nice," Mr. Topher commented awkwardly, before returning to her work.

"Excuse me." Sasha shot her face and turned red.

"We'll go change now. Give me my dress. Thanks," LuLu said, grabbing the bag and heading up to her apartment.

As LuLu examined the costume, she couldn't help but feel a twinge of apprehension. No matter what she did, Annie would likely find something to criticize. The dress was a glamorous flapper number with a fringe that shim-mered under the light.

Sasha and Rebecca had opted to change in the living room. Sasha was busy adding the final touches to her costume, adjusting the fringe and feathers with a critical eye. Rebecca was expertly pinning up her long braids to create a convincing 1920s bob, her movements precise and practiced.

LuLu emerged from her room, the dress hugging her figure and the fringe swaying with each step. She gave a small twirl, trying to ignore her lingering worries about the night ahead.

"Wow, you both actually look great," Rebecca said, surprised. "I was sure we would look ridiculous."

"Well, the night is young," Sasha joked, twirling a feathered headband around her finger.

LuLu smiled, feeling a bit more at ease. She slipped into her flapper dress, a black number with shimmering sequins and fringes that swayed with every movement. The dress was a perfect fit, hugging her curves in all the right places. She added a pearl necklace and a feathered headband, completing the look. LuLu looked at herself in the mirror and instantly realized why Annie wanted her to wear this dress. Three large scars shown against the dress. The scar on her shoulder, arm, leg, and chest almost glitter against the black dress since she was so pale.

"I can't wear this. I can't go down there. Not like this," LuLu said with tears in her eyes.

"It's ok. It's ok. You have a black tights and a cardigan, right?" Sasha suggested while Rebecca just looked at LuLu. LuLu was used to this. That is why she wore long sleeves and pants most of the time.

Rebecca went into LuLu's bedroom. She brought tights and a cardigan for her. "Put these on. It will help." LuLu complied and looked in the mirror. She wiped the tear from her cheek and nodded. He added the items to the costume.

"How do I look?" LuLu asked, doing a little spin.

"Like a million bucks," Rebecca said, giving her a thumbs-up.

Sasha nodded in agreement. "Yeah, the 20s look good on you."

"Thanks, guys. Let's do this," LuLu said, feeling a renewed sense of confidence.

All three walked downstairs together. Rebecca and Sasha grabbed trays and put a few drinks and beers on each as well-dressed guests began trickling in. LuLu knew some and chatted while she served. It wasn't until Liam arrived that LuLu's blood boiled. As Liam smirked and made his way to the bar, Sasha intercepted him.

LuLu forced a smile as she approached Liam, offering a drink. "Beer?" she suggested, trying to keep her voice steady.

Liam took the bottle from her tray, lifting it to his lips. "Hmmm... I never thought I'd see you serving drinks, Sasha," he said, misnaming her deliberately. He took a sip and then grimaced. "This one's stale. I think I might need to get one from the bar." With that, he carelessly put the bottle back on the tray and sauntered over to LuLu.

LuLu barely registered Liam's approach as Silas caught her attention entering the bar, deep in conversation with Audrey. As Audrey checked her clipboard and welcomed him to the party, LuLu felt a rush of relief, confusion, and antici-pation. Ignoring Liam's snide comments, she walked to the edge of the bar to meet Silas.

Silas's eyes lit up when he saw her, a warm smile spreading across his face. "What are you doing here?" LuLu asked, her voice tight with the mix of anger and attraction swirling inside her. Twice he had intruded into her sanctuary. Twice. This was her bar, her territory, and he didn't get to take it away from her.

"The more important question is, what are you wearing?" Liam interrupted with a mocking tone, reaching for the beer LuLu had just slammed on the bar.

"Fuck off," LuLu snapped, her eyes fixed on Silas, the anger bubbling up inside her.

Liam leaned in closer, his voice low and serious. "Someday, LuLu, you're going to let go of all this anger. It's been two years. How's it working out for you?"

LuLu's gaze remained locked on Silas, her expression a mix of defiance and vulnerability. "I don't need to listen to you," she shot back, her tone firm. "Not tonight, never."

Silas stepped closer, his presence a comforting contrast to Liam's provocations. "You look amazing in that costume," he breathed, his gaze steady and sincere.

"What are you doing here?" LuLu asked, turning to Silas, her confusion clear as she tried to understand how he kept showing up in her life.

Silas's eyes softened. "I donate to the university. I am paying for the new engineering building," he replied. "That gives me invites to all kinds of parties."

LuLu took a moment to really look at Silas. He wore a sharp black suit, and his dark eyes sparkled in the evening light. He had shaved, and she wasn't used to seeing him without his usual stubble. She reached out, touching his smooth cheek, a smile tugging at her lips. Silas leaned into her hand, his smile mirroring hers, the warmth between them palpable. Liam's throat clearing interrupted LuLu and Silas. LuLu frowned, glaring at Liam.

"I'm I interrupting something?" Silas asked, his gaze now focused on Liam, his smile gone.

"No," LuLu replied firmly, turning her back on Liam. "Liam was just leaving. Let's talk at the other end of the bar."

Silas's gaze remained steady, unyielding. "I'm here for LuLu. I think you've made your point. Maybe it's time for you to go."

Liam's eyes flashed with irritation, but he didn't argue further. With a final, resentful look at LuLu, he turned and walked away, leaving Silas and LuLu in a quieter corner of the bar.

Silas turned back to LuLu, his expression softening. "Are you alright?" he asked gently.

LuLu took a deep breath, her tension easing. "I am now," she said, offering him a grateful smile. "Thank you for doing that."

Meanwhile, Sasha kept a watchful eye on Liam and his interaction with LuLu. Her gaze narrowed as she noticed him lingering near her friend. Determined to keep him away, she approached him with a defiant stance. "Need any help?" she asked, her tone sharp and unyielding.

Liam smirked, leaning closer to Sasha. "What's your problem, Sasha? Just trying to get a drink."

"My problem is you," she shot back, her voice icy. "Why don't you find someone else to bother?"

Liam's smirk faltered, and he stepped back. "I'm just here to enjoy the party. No need to be so hostile."

Sasha didn't relent. "We both know why you're here. Stay away from LuLu, or you'll regret it. You've gotten away with too much already. Why?"

Annoyance flickered in Liam's eyes, but he took a step

back. "Fine. Enjoy your little party. I'm bored anyway," he muttered, turning away.

Sasha watched him leave, a satisfied but worried frown on her face. She then returned to LuLu and Silas, ensuring her friend's night remained as stress free as possible. With one last glance, Sasha noticed LuLu's smile.

LuLu continued to blush, feeling a warmth spread through her chest. "I'm glad you're here," she said to Silas.

Silas leaned in closer, his voice lowering. "Me too. I couldn't stop thinking about our date."

Before LuLu could respond, Sasha approached them, her protective instincts still on high alert. "Can I get you something?" she asked defensively.

"Sasha, this is Silas. Silas, this is my best friend, Sasha. I know you two met before. I just wanted to make sure you remembered each other since Sasha is so important to me." LuLu said, introducing them. It was a little early for them to meet, but what was she going to do?

"Nice to meet you again, Sasha," Silas replied, sensing the tension.

LuLu glanced between them, her smile faltering slightly. "Sasha, is everything okay?"

Sasha nodded, giving Silas a pointed look. "Just making sure everything's running smoothly."

LuLu caught the unspoken message and sighed. "It's fine, Sasha. Really."

Sasha hesitated, her eyes flicking between LuLu and Silas. She finally nodded, though the tension in her posture remained. "Alright. Just let me know if you need anything."

"Thanks, Sasha," LuLu said, trying to ease the situation. "We'll be fine."

As Sasha walked away, Silas turned back to LuLu, his expression softening. "I didn't mean to cause any trouble."

"You're not," LuLu assured him. "Sasha's just being... Sasha. She is, well, protective."

Silas chuckled. "I get it. She's looking out for you."

LuLu smiled, feeling grateful for her friend's loyalty. "Yeah, she is."

Silas reached out and gently took her hand. "How about we make the most of tonight? I really don't know anyone here, so I think I might hangout back here with you."

LuLu's heart skipped a beat as she squeezed his hand. "I'd like that."

For the rest of the evening, LuLu and Silas stayed close, sharing stories and laughter amidst the clinking glasses and lively chatter. Sasha kept a watchful eye on Liam, ensuring he stayed away from LuLu. The night went smoothly, with LuLu finally feeling a sense of hope and happiness she hadn't felt in a long time.

As the party wound down, Silas leaned in and whispered, "How about a dance before the night ends?"

LuLu's eyes sparkled with excitement. "I'd love that."

LuLu was about to leave the bar when Mr. Topher walked up, his steps unsteady. He slapped Silas on the back, causing him to turn around. Silas shook the man's hand, noting the overly pleased expression on Mr. Topher's face that hinted he might have had a few too many drinks.

"Mr. Heartly, I'm thrilled you could make it. Didn't think you'd come to a thing like this," Mr. Topher said, his voice loud and cheerful. He reached out and shook Silas' hand. He slapped his back with merriment. "I'd love to introduce you to a few people. Better company than the barmaid, I'm sure."

LuLu maintained her professional smile, her grip tightening slightly on the glass she was holding. "Well, gentlemen, let me know if you need anything else." She turned to make herself look busy.

As she moved away, her ears caught Mr. Topher's next words. "You should meet my younger daughter. She's just graduated. She has a lot of interest in the tech world."

Silas's voice was firm but polite. "I'm actually seeing someone right now."

LuLu's heart skipped a beat, her steps faltering momentarily. She glanced back and saw Silas's eyes meet hers briefly, a reassuring smile on his lips.

Mr. Topher's face reddened as he looked from Silas to LuLu, shaking his head in disapproval. He then glanced at the empty, dirty glasses on the bar and frowned. "Are you going to do something about that? It looks like a mess. Shaking his head in disapproval, he glanced at the empty, dirty glasses on the bar and frowned. Corrected: "Are you going to do something about that?"

LuLu explained, "Sorry, sir. I will..." when Annie strolled up to her father, her eyes narrowing as she assessed the situation.

"What's going on over here?" Annie asked, picking up one drink on the bar. She eyed LuLu up and down, her disdain clear. Sasha and Rebecca got lost in the crowd, leaving LuLu feeling exposed. "Daddy, she is all wrong."

Mr. Topher and Silas exchanged confused glances, but LuLu knew exactly what Annie was trying to do. She closed her eyes, silently praying Annie might show some kindness on a night meant to celebrate her and Greg. Just then, Greg appeared, wrapping his arms around Annie's waist and resting his head on her shoulder.

"What?!" Mr. Topher asked, his confusion amplified by the alcohol.

"The sweater and the tights. It isn't part of the costume, Daddy. Make her take it off," Annie demanded.

"I'm just cold," LuLu lied, hugging herself tighter and pretending to shiver.

"We are paying good money. Take it off," Mr. Topher echoed. Silas looked from person to person, not believing what he was witnessing.

"Please," LuLu pleaded, her face burning with embarrassment. She avoided Silas's gaze, looking at the ground instead. "It's not that big of a deal. Please, I've done everything else. I'm wearing this stupid costume. Isn't that enough?"

"LuLu," Greg said sternly, and she reluctantly complied, her hands shaking as she removed the sweater. Tears streamed down her face as she looked down, not wanting them to see her anger and humiliation. She slammed the sweater on the bar and stood there, exposing her scars, which glistened in the light on her pale skin.

Annie grabbed the cardigan off the bar, walked over to the trash, and threw it in. She then walked calmly back and put her arm around Greg.

"So this is how the head of the university treats people in the community," Silas yelled, taking off his suit coat. The group turned to him in surprise; they had forgotten he was there. He walked around the bar and draped the coat over LuLu's shoulders. LuLu looked down, not out of shame, but rage. She was angry.

"Who the fuck do you think you are? You keep popping up like LuLu's personal jinn." Annie screamed, her anger boiling over at his defiance. "What are you even doing here, anyway?"

Before Silas could reply, Sasha pushed through the crowd and joined them behind the bar. She looked confused, but knew something was wrong. LuLu marveled at having such a loyal friend.

"You can only push someone so far, Annie." Sasha grunted through clenched teeth. Sasha stood behind LuLu. Sasha's eyes glared at the group.

"Excuse me." Annie said, turning her attention back to her original prey. LuLu's face burned with anger and rage. LuLu looked up and stared Annie in the eyes. "I think you heard me."

"Annie, this is Silas Heartly. He runs the software company that funded the new engineering department at EU," Mr. Topher interrupted nervously. Annie's eyes darted between Silas and LuLu as Greg straightened up beside her fiancée. Her father grabbed her by the arm.

"I was considering donating to the new sports center, but I may need to reconsider where my donations go this year. I think your barmaid might need a minute," Silas said through gritted teeth, glaring at Greg. "I warned you about this, didn't I?"

"What does he mean by that?" Mr. Topher asked, observing the tension between the two men. "What is going on here?"

"This is boring. Let's go dance," Annie said, tugging at Greg's arm. He didn't move. The two men stood like marble statues, neither willing to back down. Annie kicked Greg, causing him to swear and glare at her before they disappeared into the dancing crowd.

"I'm so sorry for this, Mr. Heartly..." Mr. Topher started.

"Come on. Let's go upstairs for a break," Sasha suggested, trying to guide LuLu toward the apartment.

"We need to work. We can't leave Rebecca down here by herself," LuLu protested, but Sasha stopped her.

"Silas, take her. I'll finish up down here," she said, glancing at her phone. "There's only an hour left before they need to clean up."

Silas had enough. He scooped LuLu up like a groom carrying a bride, heading toward the door marked "Private." She felt the strength of his muscles and the comforting scent of his cologne.

She protested, kicking her legs like a child. "I can walk by myself."

Silas let her down, and she marched to the door, climbing each stair with him following close behind. She heard others call for Silas, but he ignored them, shutting the door behind him.

LuLu sat on the floor, and Silas took a seat on the couch in front of her, shifting uncomfortably. She knew what he was going to ask. Everyone always did.

"I need to talk to you about something," Silas said, his tone serious. "I was going to wait, but I think I should just get it out there. We are, well, seeing each other, correct?"

LuLu smiled at that, the tension easing slightly. She nodded. "Seeing each other," she repeated, making air quotes as she wiped the tears from her face. He laughed, and the sound was comforting.

Silas looked away, a shadow crossing his features. "I haven't dated in a while," he admitted. "People treat you differently once they know you have money. They always need something from you. You never know who likes you because of who you are or because of your wallet."

LuLu glanced around her modest apartment, then back at Silas. "Look at my life. I have everything a billionaire would be jealous of," she joked, waving her hands to show her humble surroundings. He smiled, but his eyes remained serious.

"You think you're joking, but you have authentic things," he said, leaning closer, his eyes locking onto hers. "Sasha cares about you because of who you are, not because of your stuff or what you can do for her. I just need to be smart, too."

LuLu's smile softened. "I can't say I understand exactly how you feel, but I empathize. It must be hard, always wondering if people want to use you for something."

"That's it," Silas said, his voice laden with a weariness that seemed to drain the room of light. "Used for everything. For anything." His words were heavy, like stones sinking into still water, creating ripples of exhaustion and disillusionment. His gaze was distant, as if he were staring through layers of his own tumultuous past. "It's relentless, this feeling of being consumed. I've become a commodity, a means to an end."

He paused, the silence thick with unspoken hurt. "I once overheard my last girlfriend confiding in a friend, revealing that she planned to marry me for my money—like it was just another transaction. That my wealth somehow made me more appealing, more bearable. Since then, I haven't dared to dive into anything genuine." His eyes, shadowed with the weight of past betrayals, met hers with a steely resolve. "I need to know what's happening now and I need honesty. That I'm not just another asset to be exploited. I am the public face of my company. I have to be cautious to protect myself from being just another pawn in someone else's game. SO there you go."

LuLu just looked at him, surprised by his confession. This was not what she expected when he brought her up here. She closed her eyes and faked a smile.

He took a deep breath, and she could feel the weight of his next words before he spoke them. "I need to ask you about Greg and Annie. I need to know what I'm getting into. Can you please tell me what happened?"

LuLu's smile faded. As she gathered her thoughts, she looked down and traced patterns on the couch with her fingers. She jumped up from the couch and paced back and forth in front of Silas. She started ringing her hand as she paced.

"Greg and I were together for a long time. We were engaged, planning a future, the whole thing. Annie was my best friend, the person I trusted the most. But... they betrayed me. I found out they were seeing each other behind my back."

Silas's expression darkened, his jaw tightening as he absorbed her words. "That must have been devastating."

"It was," she admitted, her voice barely above a whisper. She cleared her throat, but her eyes glistened with unshed tears. "But he promised he would end it with her and proposed to me." She paused, her voice catching in her throat. "I don't know why I said yes. I think it was my parents. They really liked him, and our families were close."

Silas leaned forward, his elbows digging into his thighs as he clasped his hands together, looking down. "And then what happened?" he asked softly. "Tell me only what you want."

She took a deep breath, her hands trembling as she

wrung them together. She stood up and began pacing, each step heavy with the weight of her memories. "He and I dated on and off in high school and college. Annie was in love with him forever, so every time we fought, she was there for him. I refused to sleep with him until he would stop messing with her. I needed a commitment. He proposed and promised it would just be us. At first, he kept his word. He was really loving and worked hard to regain my trust. But at some point, they were seeing each other behind my back again. Every time we fought, he found solace in her bed. I thought she was my friend, but she knew he would not leave me, so she tried to make me leave him."

Her breath hitched, and she paused, fighting to maintain her composure. "We went to Greg, Liam, and Ryan's frat graduation party. Sasha was dating Ryan. The party was fine until Annie cornered me. She had this smug look and told me they were still sleeping together."

Silas's eyes narrowed, anger simmering beneath his calm exterior. Doodle, sensing the tension, trotted into the room and paced at LuLu's feet. Silas reached down and patted the dog absentmindedly.

"I was so furious," LuLu continued, her voice trembling. "I confronted him." He admitted it and said he loved her. I threw my drink in her face and ran. I found an empty room to hide in and tried to collect myself. Liam and Ryan found me there. Ryan said Sasha had sent him to check on me, and Liam brought me a drink. They seemed genuinely concerned.

LuLu's breathing grew shallow. She stopped pacing and sat on the floor, pulling her knees to her chest. Her chest rose and fell rapidly as she rocked back and forth. "The next thing I knew," she whispered, her voice trembling and tears spilling over.

The drink I had tasted different—sweeter, almost as though it had a chemical aftertaste. I felt dizzy, and everything around me became a blur. I tried to call out, but no sound came out. It was like I was sinking into a thick fog.

Then, it all became horrifyingly clear when I saw Liam. He was on top of me, his weight pressing down so hard I could barely breathe. His hands were everywhere, groping, violating—I couldn't move. I just froze, like my body had betrayed me, refusing to respond, heavy and useless.

And then there was Ryan, just standing there at the edge of the room, like a shadow in the corner of my eye. I could feel his gaze, cold and relentless, like he was pinning me down with just his eyes. His presence was this dark, unsettling thing, just hanging in the air. I saw something small and gleaming in his hand—no idea what it was, but it felt like a threat, like a promise of something worse. The entire room was spinning with this suffocating sense of dread, each breath a struggle. I could barely focus through the haze of fear and confusion. It was like he was enjoying it, savoring my pain, watching me suffer.

Then suddenly, everything went black. I remember little after that—just a void, like nothingness. When I finally woke up, I was in this dimly lit room, completely naked, shaking like a leaf. I felt so exposed, so vulnerable. My clothes lay scattered everywhere, and my hands trembled so badly that I could barely button my shirt. I just had to get out of there—had to escape.

My vision was all blurred with tears and whatever the hell they'd given me that I could hardly see. Everything went black again, and when I came to, I was at the bottom of some stairs, broke the banister and fell into the glass bar. A wooden pole pierced through my arm, glass cut my chest, and someone had sliced open my leg. I must've looked like a damn pin cushion—that's what the paramedics said later. Then the cops showed up, people got arrested, and somehow, they pinned the whole thing on me.

Later, I found out that Ryan's father is the Head of medicine. He treated me for the accident, and that's where the scars came from. His family used their influence to protect him and control the situation. Dr. Lief made it clear what would happen if I went to the police. They told my parents I was in an accident. I felt shattered and confused after everything that happened. Sasha stayed with me the entire time, practically living in my hospital room.

The worst part came when I learned my parents had been rushing to see me and didn't see a deer on the road. The car flipped, and they both died. I missed graduation because I was recovering and ended up moving back here. Greg and Annie came to the hospital to break up with me and take his ring back. They did not know what happened at the party. Greg sent me an apology text later, but it felt empty and insincere. They would never have believed me, anyway. I tried to explain, but Greg was not interested. I was left feeling lost and confused."

"Have you talked to anyone about this?" Silas asked, his brow furrowing deeply. The darkness in his eyes was unmistakable, his gaze burning with a smoldering intensity. His knuckles cracked in the silence, his fist tightening before he pressed it firmly against the ground. LuLu felt her jaw clench involuntarily, her lips pressing into a thin line as she fought to keep her emotions in check. She took a slow, deliberate breath, forcing herself to hold his gaze without flinching, though her pulse thudded in her ears.

LuLu nodded, her voice trembling. "I have a therapist, Dr. Clover, and Sasha. I've been seeing Dr. Clover since I was ten years old. Sasha left Ryan as soon as I told her. She's with Rebecca now, so at least something good came out of it. I was just so stupid... so stupid." She began patting herself on the head with the palms of her hands. Silas gently caught her hands, his touch firm but comforting, grounding her.

"I know you're from their world, not exactly one of them, but connected to it. When I was in the hospital, I felt so lost. I had no one and was terrified to speak out. Eventually, I told Sasha, and she believed me. She wanted me to go to the police, but honestly, what's the point? Liam's dad is an attorney. He knows everyone. So, I did the smartest thing I could think of: I confided in Sasha and started therapy. I get it; it's not my fault. But you don't understand. No one really does unless they've been through it themselves. And it's my word against his. Here I am, a jinx, my car accident leading to my parents' deaths. All of this is my fault. Who would believe me if I came forward? Look at them, look at me. I have anxiety and PTSD. That's why I see the doctor and take medication. They'd dredge up my past and my dad. I just can't handle that. But I will not let it define me. Dealing with mental health is a lot. So, here's your chance if you want to leave..."

Silas's grip tightened around LuLu's hands, the pressure firm but not painful. His gaze bore into her, warm yet intense, the kind of look that promised unwavering support. His lips parted, his voice gentle but edged with something darker, almost vibrating with restrained emotion. "I'm here for you, LuLu. I see your strength, not your past. Thank you for trusting me with this." But beneath the softness of his words, there was a simmering anger, like a storm waiting to break.

LuLu glanced up, her vision blurred with unshed tears. "Silas, I won't be seen as a victim." Her voice was steady, even as emotion surged within her.

"I'm a survivor. I need you to understand that. I'm not ashamed. That's why I'm telling you now, like this." She paused, gathering herself.

"I don't show my scars because it's no one's business, and people always ask. But I'm done hiding. After tonight, I won't keep running. I can't handle it anymore. No one will ever abuse me again."

Her words hung in the air like a vow, her resolve palpable, pushing through the vulnerability. The fire in her voice didn't flicker, it blazed.

Silas nodded and pulled her into a comforting embrace. "I see you, LuLu. You shouldn't have to hide. I am here for whatever you need. I like you." LuLu could feel his body shake with rage.

Silas's eyes flashed with fury. LuLu shook her head, pulling away. "But I trusted them, Silas. I trusted them, and they betrayed me. I should have known better. So, I don't trust anyone, really, either."

"You couldn't have known," Silas said, his voice hard as steel but quiet, as if speaking to himself. The anger in his voice was palpable. "They're the ones who did this to you, not the other way around." His face burned with rage, his jaw clenched tightly. "They deserve punishment. If this happened to my sister, I would probably be in jail and not with you right now."

LuLu looked down, her breath coming in ragged gasps.

"Since the recent additions to the college, Annie and Greg have moved back, and that's when all of this started. They constantly terrorize me. I can't escape them. I tried for a restraining order and—"

"They are not threatening you, and you did not report," Silas interrupted. He reached out to pull her into a tight embrace, but she pushed him away. "You did everything you could. The people you trusted hurt you most. That's not your fault. You're strong, LuLu, and you're going to get through this."

LuLu hung her head, bringing her knees to her chest, her body shaking with sobs. "This is a lot, so I am giving you a way out."

"What?" Silas responded, confusion and hurt flashing across his face as she pushed him away.

"You can leave and forget this. Go back to your life with them. I will be fine," LuLu said, wiping her eyes with the back of her hand. Silas reached into his pocket and handed her a piece of fabric. She took it without looking at him and wiped her eyes. "I have a lot of baggage. It's not fair to you. I'm not one of you. I'm just a piece in a game. I don't know the rules either," LuLu said, rocking herself back and forth, still clutching her knees. "I'm strong. I can take it if you leave." She closed her eyes, bracing herself for his departure.

Silas stood up, and for a moment, LuLu thought he was leaving. Instead, he moved behind her, sitting on the floor and wrapping his enormous arms around her. "I'm going to hold you," he whispered in her ear, his breath warm and steady. "I believe you, and I'm not going anywhere. What type of man would act like that? Boys, immature boys act like that. Greg is not a man, and Liam and Ryan are scum. And that's an insult to scum. I do not resemble them."

"Thank you for believing me." She whispered through her own erratic breaths.

LuLu could sense the raw power emanating from his taut muscles, knowing he was serious in every word. She couldn't believe it, but she felt secure and protected in his embrace. His fiery rage only added to the intensity, but his warm breath on her neck calmed her own erratic breathing.

"You are completely safe with me," he huskily whispered in her ear.

"Thank you, Silas. It means a lot to hear that. I just want to feel safe." She could feel his heart beating against her back. He rested his head on top of hers, his presence a protective shield around her. Without letting go, he shifted slightly, so he was facing her.

"You're safe now," he murmured into her hair. "I promise you, you're safe with me."

LuLu felt enveloped by his warmth and strength. His scent, a mix of cedar and amber, surrounded her, and his touch sent a comforting thrill through her. For the first time in a long while, she allowed herself to believe in the promise of safety and the possibility of healing.

"I want to trust, but it's so... terrifying," LuLu sobbed, hanging her head.

He slid his finger under her chin, lifting her gaze to meet his. "Don't look down. You're stronger and braver than anyone I know." He leaned in and carefully took her hands.

"I would like to kiss you, if that's okay?" he asked softly. LuLu nodded. Silas kissed her forehead, then the tip of her nose. She took a deep breath and pressed her lips to his, craving the intimacy.

He pulled away to catch his breath, and LuLu noticed fresh tears in his eyes. She hadn't realized he had been crying too. He wiped his face with his suit coat and kissed her gently on the top of the head.

"I think if I go downstairs now, I might hurt someone, and that might not be best for your bar. You should get some rest. I don't think you should be alone, but I don't think I should stay in your room. I'll take the couch if that's okay with you?" he asked gently. LuLu nodded in agreement. "I need to make a call, but if you need anything, I'll be out here." He traced a finger gently over a scar on her chest, making her blush. "You're beautiful, and I enjoy the feel of your skin. I cannot get out of my head the way your body moves." he murmured.

"I need to know you much better for that," LuLu said, her voice trembling slightly. Silas stood to leave, but hesitated. LuLu wanted him to stay but wasn't sure how to ask.

"I'll see you tomorrow?" he asked, still facing away.

"Yes," was all he needed to hear. LuLu went and locked her apartment door, knowing Sasha had a key if needed. She made her way to her room and lay down on the bed. She texted Sasha to let her know she was okay. As she heard Sasha calling last call for the party, LuLu let her eyes close, feeling a small sense of peace for the first time in a long while.

Seven

The next morning, LuLu woke uncomfortably in her 1920s costume, the fabric itching against her skin. She rolled over, squinting against the morning light streaming through her bedroom window. The events of last night replayed in her mind, a whirlwind of emotions and revelations. With a deep sigh, she forced herself to get up.

Doodle trotted alongside her to the living room, his tail wagging energetically. LuLu opened the back door, letting him into the small yard. He pranced around, sniffing the grass until he found the perfect spot. She watched him for a moment, finding a slight comfort in his routine, before letting him back inside and rewarding him with a treat.

With a groan, she peeled off her costume; the sequins catching the light as she discarded it on the floor. She rummaged through her clean laundry basket, pulling out a pair of somewhat clean gray sweatpants and a T-shirt. After dressing, she made her way to the kitchen, her bare feet padding softly on the floor.

She pressed the button on the coffee machine, the familiar gurgling sound offering a sense of normalcy. As the coffee brewed, she took her morning medication and quickly typed out an email to Dr. Clover, contemplating whether she might need an extra appointment.

Feeling slightly more prepared for the day, LuLu unlocked her apartment door. With Doodle trotting by her side, they descended the stairs to the bar, bracing herself for the mess she was sure awaited her.

But when she opened the door to Pour Decision, she stopped in her tracks. The bar was spotless — not just clean, but sparkling. The surfaces gleamed, every glass looked polished to perfection, and the aromatic scent of bleach filled the air. She took a deep breath, savoring the smell of cleanliness, and a large, toothy smile spread across her face.

She walked up to the bar, still in awe of how pristine everything looked. There, in the center of the bar, was a check for $10,000, double what they owed her. A note was paper-clipped to it, the handwriting neat and precise. She picked it up, curiosity piqued.

The note read:

LuLu,
Thank you for the use of your establishment. The party decided that an additional $5,000 would be appropriate for the misunderstanding last evening and for the help of your additional servers.
Sincerely,
Mr. Topher

LuLu couldn't help but giggle, the sound bubbling up from a place of unexpected joy. She had made $15,000 in one night—something that had never happened before. The thought of how concerned they must have been about Silas's opinion made her smile. She knew they wanted to stay on his good side, but she didn't want to exploit that connection for money. She resolved to tell Silas about the check when they talked later.

Realizing she didn't need to prepare the bar for the evening, LuLu felt an unusual lightness in her chest. She allowed herself to savor the quiet morning, taking in the sparkling cleanliness of the bar. The sight of every glass shining and the lingering scent of bleach filled her with an unexpected sense of peace.

She poured herself a cup of coffee and sat at the bar, Doodle settling at her feet. Absentmindedly stroking his fur, she thought about the previous night and Silas's comforting presence. The warmth of the coffee seeped through the mug, grounding her at the moment.

A knock at the door pulled her from her reverie. Sasha stood there, her eyes widening as she took in the pristine state of the bar.

"Morning, Lu. Wow, they really went all out cleaning up, huh?" Sasha remarked, looking around in amazement. "Because we did not do this. Sorry, I help, but I do not clean."

"Yeah, I don't know how they did it, but they did and they left this," LuLu said, holding up the check with a grin, the paper slightly crinkling in her fingers.

Sasha's jaw dropped. "Fifteen thousand? They must really want to stay on Silas's good side."

"What, this beautiful place isn't worth it for a Friday night?" LuLu joked, and Sasha laughed. "But in all honesty, probably," LuLu agreed, the corners of her mouth still turned up. "But I don't want to use him like that. I'll have to tell him about it when we talk later."

Sasha nodded, her eyes narrowing. "You really like him, don't you?"

"It's new, and he is really great. I don't want to rush things," LuLu responded, her face burning with embarrassment. She felt like a middle school girl with a crush.

Sasha smiled. "So, what now?"

LuLu stretched, feeling the tension of the past few days melt away. "Well, since the bar's already clean and we're unexpectedly flush with cash, how about we cash this bad boy and maybe do something fun for a change?"

A grin spread across Sasha's face. "I like the sound of that. What do you have in mind?"

LuLu paused, considering. "How about we take Doodle for a walk by the river and then grab breakfast at that new cafe downtown?"

"Perfect," Sasha agreed enthusiastically. "Let's go."

As they stepped out into the morning sun, LuLu felt a wave of optimism wash over her. Despite the challenges of the previous night, people who cared about her surrounded her. With that comforting thought, she felt ready to face whatever came next, her heart lighter than it had been in a long time.

As Sasha and LuLu strolled along the riverbank, their conversation flowed effortlessly. LuLu recounted her late-night talk with Silas, each detail drawing a thoughtful nod from Sasha. When they reached the bank, Sasha stayed with Doodle, giving LuLu a moment to cash her check at the nearby bank. The transaction was quick, but the significance of the check made LuLu feel like she was on the brink of something extraordinary. She felt a happiness she hadn't experienced in a long time.

Returning to the apartment to drop off Doodle, Sasha then drove them to the new cafe, Drip. Upon entering, the hostess scrutinized them with a gaze and noted their casual attire.

"Is there a problem?" Sasha snapped, matching the hostess's stare with one of her own.

"Uh… no. No. Inside or outside?" The hostess stammered, attempting to regain her composure.

"Outside," Sasha answered curtly, and they followed her to the patio. As they settled at their table, Sasha rolled her eyes dramatically, prompting a laugh from LuLu.

Once Sasha was seated, she couldn't help but comment, "I guess we don't meet their dress code."

"Sasha," LuLu said in a mild rebuke, noticing the hostess hesitating but not turning back. Sasha chuckled, and LuLu's laughter soon joined hers, dissolving the tension.

The waiter arrived to take their order. LuLu opted for her usual pancakes, while Sasha chose an omelet. They continued their light-hearted chat as they waited for their food, the morning sun warming the surrounding air.

"So, tell me everything! He stayed the night last night." Sasha leaned in with a playful wink, her eyes twinkling with mischief.

"Nothing happened," LuLu said, her tone betraying a hint of stubborn pride. She adopted a straight-faced emoji expression, her attempt to mask her emotions. "We just talked. I told him everything, Sasha."

Sasha's eyes widened with anticipation as the waitress set down their steaming cups of coffee. "Well?" she pressed, her voice filled with curiosity.

"Thank you," LuLu said to the waiter, her voice soft as she watched him retreat. The clinking of cups and the low hum of the cafe created a backdrop of warmth.

"Honestly," LuLu began, stirring her coffee, "it was the first time I've ever felt really heard. And not just in the way where someone listens, but doesn't really understand. He listened, and he didn't judge. He just... supported me. I think that's the most important thing right now."

Sasha nodded thoughtfully, her expression softening. "It sounds like he really cares about you, Lu. That's a good sign. You deserve someone who makes you feel that way."

"Yeah," LuLu said, a small smile playing on her lips. "I think I believe that, too."

Their food arrived, and they shifted their focus to enjoying the meal, the conversation drifting to lighter topics. As they ate, LuLu felt a renewed sense of hope and contentment, her heart full from both the conversation with Sasha and the unexpected kindness from Mr. Topher. The day was shaping up to be better than she'd dared to hope.

Sasha's gaze was sharp, waiting for a clue in LuLu's expression. "So, what's the verdict?" she asked, her tone a mix of excitement and concern.

"Well, he didn't run, so that's a good sign," LuLu began, her cheeks tinged with a rosy blush. Her mind drifted to the moment Silas had kissed her knuckles, the touch lingering like a spark against her skin. The memory made her face flush with heat. "But I'm worried. He's been so... nice. I keep expecting something to go wrong."

Sasha's excitement bubbled over. "Oh my god, you really like him!" She clapped her hands together, her eyes dancing with delight. "This is a good thing, right?"

LuLu nodded slowly, her thoughts tangled in uncertainty. "Yes, I just..." Her phone beeped, interrupting her train of thought. She glanced at the screen, the moment of contemplation broken by the new message.

Suddenly, the distinct sound of notifications echoed around the cafe. LuLu and Sasha's phones chimed simultaneously, joined by a chorus of other devices. LuLu glanced at Sasha, whose eyes had widened in surprise.

"Holy shit!" Sasha exclaimed, her gaze fixed on her phone screen. Her shock piqued LuLu's curiosity, prompting her to check her own phone.

Breaking News

** CEO and creator of Heartly Technology Corporation, Silas Heartly, has released a statement: **

The Heartly Technology Corporation will no longer be doing business with the Steins Group and the Baker Medical Group. All new contracts have been terminated and all ongoing contracts will be wrapped up. Employees will be merged into the Heartly Technology Corporation.
The CEO has stated he will release a formal statement in the next few days.

LuLu's heart raced as she processed the news. Silas had severed ties with the Steins Group, the very company owned by Liam and his father. She felt a mix of shock and awe at the extent of Silas's influence and the decisive action he had taken. The bold move spoke volumes about his commitment to integrity and his willingness to stand up against the very people who had wronged her. It was both exhilarating and daunting, knowing she was now deeply connected to someone with such significant power and influence.

Sasha's eyes met LuLu's, a knowing smile spreading

across her face. "Looks like Silas is making a statement, and not just in your life. This is huge."

LuLu nodded, still processing the magnitude of the news. "Yeah, it is. I guess it's a good sign that he's serious about standing by me."

Sasha reached across the table, giving LuLu's hand a reassuring squeeze. "You're lucky, Lu. But remember, it's not just about what he can do for you. It's about how he makes you feel and how you feel about him."

"True," LuLu agreed, her voice steadying. "I guess this is a lot to take in. But for now, I'm just going to focus on enjoying the moment."

As they continued their breakfast, LuLu felt a renewed sense of optimism. The news about Silas was a powerful affirmation of his commitment and support. She was determined to embrace this new chapter with cautious hope, taking things one step at a time.

Putting down her phone, LuLu glanced at Sasha, whose expression mirrored her own astonishment. "I did not know Silas had his hands in so many pots," LuLu said, shaking her head in disbelief.

Sasha nodded, still processing the news. "This is huge. Lu. Silas just cut them off completely. He's not messing around."

LuLu took a deep breath, feeling a mix of empowerment and apprehension. She realized Silas's actions could have significant repercussions, not only for the Steins Group but potentially for her as well. Yet, for the first time in a long while, she felt like she had someone powerful in her corner. With that thought, a new sense of resolve formed.

The waiter brought their food, and as they ate, the weight of the news lingered in the air. LuLu found each bite more enjoyable, the meal enhanced by the swirling emotions inside her.

"Sasha, I don't believe in revenge, but…" LuLu hesitated.

"I do," Sasha interrupted with a sip of coffee, her eyes twinkling with mischief.

LuLu continued, "I don't believe in revenge, but karma is real. I believe that. But things are moving so fast, right? Who knows? After everything last night, he might even cancel tonight."

"You get into your head too much," Sasha said, rolling her eyes. "But seriously, what did you tell him last night?"

"Do I need to remind you I told him everything about Greg, Annie, Liam, Ryan, and you?" LuLu stated, and Sasha nodded thoughtfully.

"He will not cancel. He just ended his business with Liam and his dad. If that isn't a romantic gesture, I don't know what is," Sasha pointed out with a smile. "Plus, isn't this your third date?" She wiggled her eyebrows. LuLu's face turned a bright crimson red.

"It doesn't count as a date if I'm working, so it's our second," LuLu corrected, still blushing at the thought of a third date. She recalled Silas's arms around her as he carried her up the stairs and how his embrace felt as he held her close.

Sasha snapped her fingers in front of LuLu. "I think making out at a bar counts as a date," she said with a victorious sip of her coffee. "You really do like him, don't you?"

LuLu nodded and hid her smile behind her napkin. She hadn't considered it from that perspective, but Sasha was right. Silas's decisive action was more than just a business move—it was a declaration of support and protection. As they continued their meal, LuLu's heart felt lighter. For the first time in a long while, she sensed a glimmer of hope that maybe, just maybe, things were looking up.

They finished their breakfast, lingering over their coffee and enjoying the rare moment of peace. LuLu smiled more freely, the burden of the past night's revelations eased by Sasha's unwavering support and Silas's unexpected actions.

As they left the cafe, the sun was shining brightly, casting a warm glow over the city. LuLu took a deep breath, feeling the warmth seep into her bones. She looked at Sasha, who was already planning their next adventure, and felt a rush of gratitude for the people in her life who stood by her side.

"Let's make today count," LuLu said, her voice filled with determination.

Sasha grinned. "Absolutely. Let's show the world what we're made of."

With renewed energy, Sasha and LuLu set off, ready to face whatever challenges lay ahead. The sun shone brightly as they wandered through the shopping district, the streets bustling with activity. It felt like a world of possibilities had opened up to LuLu, and she was eager to explore it.

As they strolled through the shops, LuLu marveled at the variety of clothes and accessories. For the first time in a long while, she had a little extra cash to spend, and the idea of treating herself to a new outfit was too tempting to resist. They meandered through a few stores, LuLu trying on dresses and skirts, savoring the thrill of retail therapy.

She spent a couple of hours and filled her shopping bags with new finds. The day had been a refreshing escape from her usual routine, but it was time to return to reality. They made their way back to the bar, LuLu's mood still buoyant from their earlier adventure.

As she approached Pour Decision, LuLu noticed a tall, thin woman standing outside. The woman had long blonde hair and was scrolling through her phone, lost in thought. Her presence was unfamiliar, and LuLu approached with cautious curiosity.

"Can I help you?" LuLu asked as she neared.

The woman looked up, her gaze shifting from her phone to LuLu. "I'm looking for LuLu Pillar. She's the owner of the Pour Decision?" Her voice was smooth but carried an edge of impatience as she scanned LuLu's casual attire with a discerning eye, clearly unimpressed.

"Yes, that's me," LuLu replied. "I'm Matty, from the local temp agency. Mr. Heartly contacted my firm and hired me for the night," Matty said, her tone showing she was used to being the center of attention.

LuLu's eyebrows furrowed. "Okay, I'm not sure what's going on, but come inside, and we'll figure this out." She opened the door and led Matty into the bar. Once inside, LuLu pulled out her phone and dialed Silas's number. The call connected on the first ring.

"Heartly," Silas's voice came through, brisk and confident.

"Silas, there's a woman here claiming she's been hired to work the bar tonight," LuLu said, trying to keep her tone neutral.

"Surprise!" Silas's voice sounded cheerful. "I figured you could use a night off. Better than flowers, right?"

LuLu paused, her mind racing as she walked to the restroom and closed the door behind her for privacy. "That's really kind of you, but I don't know her."

"She is from a temp service we use at work." I've done all the background checks; she's got bartending experience. I already paid her and told her all tips were hers. I thought it would be a good way to give you a break. Didn't I do well? Silas's voice conveyed genuine concern.

LuLu took a deep breath, the weight of the day beginning to lift. She could hear the sincerity in Silas's voice, and it made her smile despite her initial confusion. "You did. I appreciate it, really. But I need to make sure everything's in order here. Just next time, ask me first, okay?" Silas agreed, and they confirmed the plans for the evening.

LuLu connected with Matty, and to her surprise, Matty quickly proved herself to be a natural behind the bar. Once she grasped the system and the flow of the evening, she had a genuine talent for bartending. LuLu watched with growing confidence as Matty handled orders and managed the crowd with ease.

Feeling a wave of relief and gratitude, LuLu decided it was time to get ready for her date. She made her way upstairs, her thoughts swirling about the day's events. Although Silas's generous gesture had been thoughtful, it left her with mixed feelings. The idea of Silas solving problems with money unsettled her. She was used to working hard for what she wanted, and while his gesture was kind, it felt somewhat alien. She had always valued effort and perseverance over financial solutions and wondered if her discomfort stemmed from a fear of not being valued for who she was, but for what she could receive.

She shook her head, dispelling the self-doubt. Silas had shown her kindness and interest in her as a person, not just as a recipient of his generosity. If there were any concerns or misunderstandings, she realized it was her responsibility to address them honestly.

After her shower, LuLu wrapped herself in a towel and

walked into her bedroom. She spread out her new clothes on the bed, the vibrant hues of the fabric promising a fresh start. Her phone buzzed with a notification, and she pulled up Silas's app, carefully choosing the perfect accessories to complement her outfit.

Taking her time, LuLu meticulously styled her hair, using a curling iron to create soft, cascading curls that framed her face. She applied her makeup with care, each brushstroke enhancing her features while reflecting her inner resolve.

When she finally dressed, she paused in front of the mirror, admiring the new blue and teal dress that clung to her figure as if it were tailored just for her. The sweetheart neckline highlighted her best features, while the sash delicately covered her scar, allowing her to feel both elegant and confident. For the first time since her accident, she chose not to cover her arms, embracing her body as it was.

Spinning slowly, LuLu saw herself anew in the mirror. The dress fit perfectly, and her reflection seemed to radiate newfound confidence. She wasn't just putting on a new outfit; she was shedding layers of insecurity and fear. Tonight, she vowed to embrace who she was without hiding or feeling diminished.

With a deep breath and a final glance at her reflection, LuLu felt ready to step out and face the evening. She was no longer hiding from her past or her present. Tonight, she would be fully present and true to herself, ready to meet whatever came next with courage and grace. Before she took one last look, Matty called her from downstairs. She had just realized she didn't check her phone. She grabbed it and had it on, silent by mistake. Sasha called. No message.

Sasha:

Call me asap.

Lulu was just about to text her when a voice called to her. "Ms. Pillar...Ms. Pillar?" Matty's voice echoed up the stairs.

"Yes," LuLu responded. Slipping her phone into her pocket.

"There is someone down here to talk to you. They are—" Matty stopped, listening to the other person. "Alright, alright. He's insistent."

LuLu hurried down the stairs two at a time, still barefoot. She burst through the door, her mood shifting instantly when she saw the person waiting.

In the middle of the bar stood two formidable figures, a storm personified. Liam, a towering presence at over six feet tall, was a wall of raw anger and sheer size. Ryan standing beside him with his arms crossed. Liam's face was flushed crimson, veins bulging on his neck like angry worms beneath the skin. His blonde curls, unkempt and wild, mirrored the chaos he brought with him, each strand defying order just as his emotions defied control. Ryan's black hair looked like it hadn't been washed for days. His eyes were wild and looking for someone to blame.

His broad shoulders and muscular frame, accentuated by a tight shirt, exuded a brutish force. When he shouted, his voice cracked through the room like thunder, causing Matty to flinch and take an involuntary step back. Liam's eyes, blazing with fury, locked onto LuLu with an intensity that threatened to scorch. His very presence seemed to fill the space with an oppressive heat, clarifying that his anger was a force to be reckoned with.

"What the actual FUCK did you do?" Liam demanded, stepping closer to LuLu.

"Sir, I really think you both should leave," Matty suggested, realizing the mistake she had made by letting them into the bar. LuLu froze in place.

Liam stood in the center of the bar like a human storm, his towering frame casting a long shadow across the dimly lit room. With a fiery shade of crimson, his face displayed bulging veins on his neck, resembling angry worms beneath his skin. His wild blonde curls writhed with his rage, each strand a testament to the chaos inside him. His fists were clenched, knuckles white with the strain of his fury.

Matty, sensing the impending violence, took a cautious step back, her eyes darting nervously between Liam and LuLu. The tension was palpable, like the air before a thunderstorm. Liam's voice thundered through the bar, each word dripping with venom. "What the fuck did you tell him, you... you... CUNT!" Ryan moved behind her.

LuLu's composure cracked under the pressure. Her normally steady hands trembled as she faced Liam. Her heart pounded in her chest, a fierce counter-rhythm to the raging storm before her. She stood her ground, anger flaring in her eyes like a wildfire. "There never was an 'us,' you rapist! Get the fuck out of here."

"I know what I saw," Ryan commented with a sneer.

LuLu had enough. This was her place. These men would not push her around. Not anymore.

"Fuck you, you rapist." She yelled at Liam and turned to Ryan. "You are almost worse. You know, and you did nothing. I cannot believe Sasha ever let you touch her."

Liam reeled back as if struck, his face a mask of disbelief and fury. Ryan's face hardened. The impact of LuLu's words seemed to physically stagger him. Neither of the men realized Matty was on her phone. In a split second, he lunged forward, his grip iron-clad around her arm, pulling her roughly. The pain shot through LuLu, sharp, as Liam spun her around with brutal force.

"Get the fuck off me, you piece of shit!" LuLu roared, her voice raw with fury. She slapped Liam across the face, the sound of skin meeting skin echoing through the bar. LuLu smirked at him and turned to Ryan. Liam's grin twisted into a gnarled sneer, his fingers touching the stinging spot on his face.

"Get out." She said, pointing to the door.

"This is how you want to play?" he growled, his rage crackling around him like an electric storm. His face contorted into a mask of sheer fury. As LuLu stared into his blazing eyes, she barely registered the deadly arc of his fist.

The punch landed with a sickening thud, a brutal collision of flesh and bone that sent a jarring shockwave of pain through LuLu's face. Stars exploded behind her eyes as the force of the blow blurred her vision and made her balance falter. Her feet tangled, causing her to crash into Ryan, who let her fall to the floor. The impact jolted through her bones, leaving her gasping as her cheek throbbed with a relentless, pulsing ache.

"You two are pathetic. It takes both of you to gang up on a woman? Proud of yourselves?" LuLu shouted, her voice strained but defiant.

Liam's leg drew back, muscles coiled and ready to strike, but before he could make contact, a hulking figure charged into the bar. Silas stormed in like a force of nature, his massive frame filling the room with his presence. He grabbed Liam with one hand, easily lifting him off the ground like a rag doll. With a ferocious yell that shook the walls, Silas slammed Liam onto the hard floor with brutal force.

The sound was deafening as Liam hit the ground, the impact reverberating through the air like thunder. Silas wasted no time in delivering a series of powerful punches to Liam's face, each blow landing with bone-crushing intensity. Ryan watched in shock as Heath joined in, his fist connecting with Ryan's face and sending him sprawling to the ground. Heath stood over him, his hand flexing as he rubbed his knuckles, his expression unyielding and fierce like a battle-hardened warrior. The bar was filled with chaos and violence, screams and grunts mingling together in a chaotic symphony.

Liam's eyes widened in astonishment as Silas, with raw, primal intensity, delivered a series of punishing blows. LuLu, still dazed and aching, struggled to rise and shuffle toward the bar. Matty's urgent voice slicing through the chaos punctuated the harsh reality of the scene.

"Hey, dickheads. You're on camera. Leave, or I will call the police," Matty shouted, her voice ringing with authority from behind the bar. LuLu's heart pounded as she sprinted behind the bar and grabbed the soda gun, unleashing a torrent of ice-cold water on the two men.

The threat of exposure snapped Liam back to reality. He scrambled to his feet, wiping blood from his swollen mouth, his face a twisted mask of bruises and fury. Heath appeared, ducking into the doorway, covered in sweat, as if he had run all the way there. He rushed to Silas, grabbing him around the waist and holding him back as LuLu continued to spray the intruders.

"LET ME GO! I AM GOING TO KILL THIS MOTHER-FUCKER!" Liam screamed. "I WILL KILL YOU!"

"Sir, enough," Heath commanded, his large, menacing presence casting a shadow over the scene. He held onto Silas with a firm grip, restraining him like a father holding back an enraged child. Silas struggled to break free, his eyes burning with protective rage.

"Fine! Fine! Fuck it! I'm leaving," Liam muttered, staggering to his feet. He spat blood and a tooth onto the floor, ran a hand through his soaked hair, and stumbled toward the door. He paused, glaring back. "This isn't over. Tell your boyfriend he won't like me when the gloves come off, LuLu."

Silas surged forward again, fury radiating from him. Heath held firm, but his eyes quickly scanned the room, landing on the bruise swelling on LuLu's cheek. A darkness settled over Heath's face.

"I will kill you if you ever touch her again," Silas growled.

"I'm going to let him go," Heath said, locking eyes with Liam. Locking eyes with Liam, Heath's voice carried a hint of anger. He released Silas, whose shirt clung to his muscles, slick and wet. LuLu could see every sinew through the fabric, but instead of thrilling her, the sight intensified her fear for him.

Liam's face contorted into a malicious grin as Silas stepped forward. He didn't notice LuLu moving directly behind him, her anger boiling within her. For the first time, she realized it was okay to be angry. Both men moved toward each other, oblivious to her next action.

With all her might, LuLu lifted her leg and kicked Liam squarely between the legs. Both men stopped in an instant, grimacing as Liam's eyes crossed and his mouth opened in silent agony. He collapsed, doubling over and vomiting. Instinctively, both men shielded themselves.

"GET THE FUCK OUT OF HERE, YOU MICRODICK SON OF A BITCH!" LuLu's voice cut through the tension, raw and fierce. Silas let out a deliberate, mocking laugh as Liam stood and grabbed his friend who was just coming too, and they both made a hasty, defeated exit. Heath stood silently, giving a casual wave as Liam vanished through the door.

Silas pulled LuLu into a tight embrace, his arms enveloping her protectively. The pressure of his hold sent sharp reminders of her bruises, but the warmth and safety she felt outweighed the discomfort. She rested her head against his chest, feeling his heartbeat and the steady rise and fall of his breath. He breathed in the scent of her shampoo and skin. She panted, trying to control the burning tears. Silas simmered in this moment, thinking about his sister and knowing that if anyone treated her like LuLu, he would be in jail.

LuLu winced at his touch, feeling the sting of her split lip and the throbbing ache of her injuries. "Do you want me to call the police?" Matty asked, her voice soft with sympathy as she leaned across the bar.

LuLu shook her head, the pain mingling with a newfound resolve. "No point," she murmured, clutching the ice to her cheek. Standing there with Silas's arm around her, she felt a mix of emotions churning inside her. The pain was sharp, the anger simmering beneath the surface. Fear lingered, yet an unexpected sense of liberation washed over her. She had finally stood up to Liam. Despite the physical agony, a small spark of strength and control kindled within her, flickering to life amidst the chaos.

"I'm so sorry for this," LuLu whispered, her voice barely audible. "For dragging you into my mess. If you want to walk away, I'll understand. I wouldn't blame you."

Silas's gaze softened, his protective instincts still on high alert as he looked at her. He remained by her side, his presence a comforting shield against the aftermath of the violence.

Silas inhaled deeply, his eyes locking onto hers. His normally calm demeanor was stormy, his brows drawn tight in frustration. He released her chin, shedding his dress coat and wrapping it around her shoulders. The scent of cedar and grapefruit enveloped her, grounding her at the moment.

"I'm not going anywhere. Please stop trying to push me away," he said firmly, his voice a low growl. "This isn't about you. My partner and I have been planning to cut ties with the Stein Group for a while. You were just the catalyst. I need you to know that I would never betray your trust."

LuLu shook her head, tears spilling over. "But I brought you into this. You can still walk away. I'd understand."

Silas pulled her closer, the warmth of his embrace battling, the icy fear gnawing at her. "I'm not leaving," he repeated. "But we should get you upstairs. The bar is open, and Max doesn't need to see you like this."

She glanced around, realizing for the first time the curious glances from patrons. Silas scooped her up effortlessly, cradling her against his chest. As he carried her up the stairs, she buried her face in his shirt, the fabric dampening with her tears.

Heath and Matty exchanged a nod, silently taking over the bar duties. LuLu felt a flicker of guilt but pushed it aside, focusing on Silas's steady heartbeat against her ear. For the first time that night, she allowed herself to believe that maybe, just maybe, things could be okay. Silas gently set her down on the couch.

"Do you have a zip-lock bag?" Silas asked, striding into the kitchen with determination. "You need a proper ice pack for your eye, or it's going to swell. The ice in the rag isn't enough. And do you have any antiseptic for your lip?" He started rummaging through drawers, the sound of them opening and closing with urgency. LuLu got up and joined him.

"Center drawer," she pointed out. Silas grabbed the bag and scooped a handful of ice from her small ice maker on the counter. "Ice maker," she added, pointing to the counter.

"You have an ice maker?" he remarked, breaking the tense silence.

"I like ice in all my drinks. It's a habit I picked up from my mom," LuLu said softly.

"That's interesting," he commented.

"No, it's not," LuLu replied. "What else do you need?"

"Antiseptic?" he asked, moving swiftly.

"Bathroom the cabinet," she responded.

"Okay. Go sit down. You've been through enough. Let me help. Let someone take care of you for a change. You don't need to do everything yourself." His voice was gentle but firm, leaving no room for argument. LuLu, feeling a mix of gratitude and reluctance, returned to the couch.

Silas followed, pressing the ice pack gently against her cheek. He poured a bit of antiseptic onto a cotton ball and carefully dabbed her bottom lip. LuLu winced and pulled away at the sting, but he held her chin steady, his touch both tender and insistent.

She glanced down at herself, noticing the ripped dress and bloodstains. "I'm a mess. Look at me. We can't do this tonight."

"Look at me. I look like I just lost a wet t-shirt contest, so I think we're even." Silas unbuttoned his shirt and shook it out a few times, the fabric making a soft swishing sound.

LuLu couldn't help but study his perfect chest, her eyes tracing the defined lines and curves of his muscles. She had to stop herself from reaching out to touch him, her fingers itching to feel the warmth and firmness of his skin. Flashes of a high school trip to Italy flickered in her mind, where she had marveled at the chiseled marble statues of ancient art, their beauty and perfection mirrored now in the living man before her.

The light caught on the contours of his chest, casting shadows that emphasized his sculpted form. Each movement he made seemed deliberate, almost artistic, and she felt a growing heat within her, a longing that was both thrilling and terrifying.

"We don't need to go out. We can stay in. I can cook," Silas said, heading back to the kitchen. Before LuLu could protest, he opened the fridge and quickly shut it. "If this were a cartoon, a moth would have flown out."

"I don't cook," LuLu admitted, watching Silas try to make sense of her sparse kitchen. "But I can throw your shirt in the dryer. I have a few of my dad's old bar t-shirts around. He thought college parents might want to buy a shirt from a local bar. Didn't really take off."

LuLu grabbed his shirt, feeling the damp fabric between her fingers, and tossed it into the dryer in her tiny laundry closet. Above the dryer was a box of soft gray t-shirts. She pulled one out, noting the small "Pour Decision" logo on the front and the phrase "But the best decision you ever made" emblazoned across the back.

She threw the shirt to Silas, who caught it effortlessly

and slid it on in an instant. The soft cotton hugged his frame perfectly, emphasizing his broad shoulders and lean torso.

"There you go," she said, trying to ignore the flutter in her stomach as she watched him adjust the fit.

Silas looked down at the shirt, a small smile tugging at the corners of his lips. "Not bad," he said, running a hand over the logo. "Feels like it was made for me."

"I'll be right back." Silas ran down the stairs, the door closing behind him. LuLu heard voices and the faint sound of a TV from the bar below.

Carefully, LuLu stood up. They never tell you that getting punched means bruises form on every part that hits the ground. She gingerly made her way to her bedroom and peeled off her dress, wincing at the pain. In her drawer, she found a simple white dress and pulled it out, slipping it on to find a slight comfort in the soft fabric against her battered skin. She tied her hair into a bun on top of her head.

Stepping out of the room, she caught her reflection in the mirror. Her entire left eye had swollen and turned purple, making it barely able to open. She had a split lip, and a scab was already forming. A handprint bruise marred her arm where Liam had grabbed her, and the side of her head was tender from hitting the ground. This was a different girl from the one in the blue dress. She shook her head, fighting back tears, and returned to the couch just as the door opened and Silas reappeared, carrying two bags of groceries.

"I'm cooking tonight," he declared with a broad grin.

LuLu managed a small smile, her heart warming at his determination. "You don't have to do this, you know."

"I want to," he replied, setting the bags on the counter. "You've had a rough night. Let me take care of you."

She watched as he unpacked the groceries with deliberate precision, his movements smooth and practiced. The crinkling of plastic bags and the clinking of glass jars punctuated the quiet kitchen. Despite the lingering ache in her body and the weariness in her soul, LuLu felt a flicker of optimism. Perhaps, just perhaps, tonight could be a turning point.

LuLu drifted into the kitchen, her gaze following his purposeful stride. He rummaged through the cabinets, his hands brushing against the cool metal and warm wood. She pointed with a playful smirk. "The pan and one pot are in that cabinet."

"I'd be grateful for a cutting board," he said, his tone light and appreciative.

"Oh, I have one of those. I'm a bartender, after all." She opened a drawer and retrieved a small, sturdy cutting board, handing it to him. As their fingers brushed together, a jolt of electricity sparked between them, causing her cheeks to flush a soft pink. She glanced down at his hands, noting the angry red knuckles swollen from his confrontation with Liam.

"Your hand is hurt," she said, gently taking his hand in hers and pressing the ice from her cheek against his raw skin. He flinched slightly, a pained hiss escaping his lips as the ice met his injury. LuLu looked up into his eyes, feeling the intensity of his gaze and the warmth of his breath brushing against her face. He withdrew his hand, handing the ice back.

"You need this more than I do," he said with a reassuring smile. "Go relax. I can't cook with you hovering around."

"Yes, sir," she replied with a mock salute, returning to the couch. She settled in, turning on a streaming show but barely focusing on it. The ice melted against her cheek, its chill gradually fading as she became more engrossed in the culinary performance unfolding in the kitchen.

The rich, savory aroma of garlic and herbs filled the living room, a fragrant promise of the meal to come. Each scent—roasted garlic, simmering tomatoes, freshly baked bread—wafted through the air, enveloping the space in a comforting warmth. LuLu's mind wandered back to her mother, who, despite her lack of culinary skills, always poured her heart into every dish she made. The aroma was a nostalgic embrace, reminding her of simpler, warmer times.

Silas emerged from the kitchen wearing an apron that Sasha had gifted her as a gag—a bright apron with the bold declaration, "If this cook is cooking, you better be running." He chuckled as he adjusted the apron. "I hope you don't mind if I borrow this. I had a slightly different outfit planned for the evening," he said with a laugh. "You know what they say about the best-laid plans."

"Are only for mice and men," LuLu replied, a knowing smile curling at her lips.

"Few people know that part," Silas said, clearly impressed.

"I'm sorry for causing all this trouble and getting you hurt," LuLu said, her gaze dropping to her bare feet, feeling the weight of her apology.

"Nothing to be sorry for. I have a feeling you're used to handling everything on your own. From experience, I can say that while independence is great, sometimes it's nice to have someone take care of you," he said with a soft, understanding look. "Oh, and dinner is served." He gestured to the small table in the corner, usually cluttered with mail, now elegantly set with two mason jars repurposed as wine glasses.

He escorted LuLu to the table and pulled out her chair with a flourish. She admired the simple yet elegant spread: perfectly cooked pasta bathed in a rich, red sauce, crispy garlic bread with a golden-brown crust, and a fresh, vibrant salad. Silas had even placed the wine bottle next to LuLu, the label glinting under the kitchen light.

"If you'd do the honors," he said, passing her the bottle opener. As she uncorked the wine, the dry, fruity notes of grapes and cherries burst forth, mingling with the heady aromas of the meal. The conversation flowed as smoothly as the wine, and LuLu found herself drawn into Silas's stories of family and food.

"This is delicious," LuLu said, savoring the last bite of her meal. "Where did you learn to cook like this? From your mom?"

"No, actually," Silas said, his eyes brightening. "My sister. The restaurant we went to on our first date is hers. She's passionate about French and Italian cuisine. The sauce is actually her recipe. When she was in culinary school, she practiced at home, and I was the annoying little brother always trying to hang out with his cool older sister." He smiled at the memory. "She's part of the reason I'm here— to support her and to find a more affordable base for my business than Silicon Valley."

LuLu listened intently, struck by the contrast between their lives. Silas's story was one of close-knit family bonds and shared dreams, a stark contrast to her own fractured past.

As they sat together, their casual conversation gradually faded into the background. The way he spoke about his family, his eyes lighting up with every memory, drew her closer to him. She felt a magnetic pull, the dim light casting soft shadows that danced across his face, enhancing the intimate glow of the moment.

After their meal, as they shared a last glass of wine, Silas reached across the table, his fingers whisking hers. The touch was electric, sending shivers up her spine. Their eyes locked, and the connection between them was palpable, thickening the air with anticipation.

Silas leaned in, his breath warm against her skin. "There's something I've been wanting to do," he murmured, his voice low and husky. His hand cupped her cheek gently, his thumb brushing softly across her skin.

LuLu's breath caught in her throat as he slowly closed the distance between them. The world outside seemed to fall away as his lips met hers. The kiss started slow and deliberate, a tender exploration that made her heart race with exhilarating speed.

His lips brushed against hers, sending a wave of warmth through her. The initial touch was soft, almost teasing, but quickly deepened into something more fervent. As their lips moved together, the kiss grew more insistent—a silent conversation of longing and desire.

A shiver of excitement rippled through LuLu as his lips pressed firmly against hers, the pressure building with a sweet intensity. Her fingers, almost instinctively, tangled in his tousled hair, drawing him closer, feeling the heat of his body against hers. The scent of the wine they'd shared mingled with the rich aroma of his skin, creating a heady blend that made her senses whirl.

Their breaths intertwined in a heated rhythm, each exhale blending with the next in a symphony of pleasure.

Silas's tongue traced a delicate path along her lips, a gentle coaxing that made her heart race. As he parted her lips with a soft, deliberate motion, LuLu responded eagerly, her own tongue meeting his in a dance of exploration and intimacy.

The kiss was a fusion of warmth and urgency, each touch and caress a promise of more. His tender guidance stirred a deep, primal desire within her. LuLu felt an unfamiliar, thrilling heat pooling between her thighs, her body aching with anticipation.

Every brush of his lips, every flicker of his tongue, heightened her senses, leaving her breathless and yearning. Their bodies pressed together, perfectly aligned, as if trying to merge into one. The world outside seemed to dissolve, leaving only the intoxicating electric connection they shared.

LuLu's entire being was consumed by the moment, her desire for him a tangible, pulsating force. For the first time in her life, she felt an intense, all-encompassing need, an urgent longing that quickened her pulse and made her breath hitch. The kiss—a blend of passion and tenderness— left her yearning for more, her body betraying the depth of her desire.

When they finally pulled away, their foreheads pressed together, both panting softly. The room buzzed with palpable heat, which made their skin tingle and their hearts thud loudly in their chests. Silas's eyes searched hers, his expression a mix of desire and tenderness.

"That," he said breathlessly, "wasn't in the plans."

"Plans change," LuLu replied, her voice a soft whisper against his lips. They stayed like that for a moment, wrapped in the afterglow of their kiss, savoring the intoxicating closeness.

"Let me tidy up a bit, and then we can hang out if you're up for it," Silas said, his voice still warm from their earlier embrace. "Maybe watch a movie? I'm not quite ready for this night to end yet. But if you're tired…"

"Movie it is!" LuLu exclaimed, her excitement bubbling over. She practically sprang to her feet, her eyes sparkling with enthusiasm. Movies had always been her escape, a passion that never waned. "Scary works?"

"Perfect," he replied with a grin that made her heart skip a beat.

As Silas cleared the remnants of their meal, LuLu darted into the living room. Her fingers danced over her streaming service apps, her mind racing through her favorites. The soft glow of the television illuminated her face as she scrolled through titles, her pulse quickening with anticipation.

She settled on it, a nod to Stephen King's eerie genius. A small, knowing smile curled her lips as she thought, A little Stephen King to set the mood. It wasn't just a joke—it was her idea of a perfect date movie, a thrilling escape that mirrored the spark of excitement she felt.

LuLu adjusted the couch cushions with a nervous flutter, her fingers trembling slightly. As she clicked play, the screen lit up with the eerie opening credits of it, casting flickering shadows across the room. She stole a quick glance at Silas, the air thick with a new, exciting tension.

Silas entered the living room. His presence filled the space, and as he settled onto the couch beside her, he draped his arm over her shoulders. A small wince escaped LuLu, and she instinctively pulled away.

"Sorry. I forgot. You need more ice," Silas said, rising. LuLu reached out, her hand closing around his wrist, and shook her head. He relented and settled back beside her. She eased his arm around her again, curling up against his side. The warmth of him seeped through her, the scents of amber and cedar mingling in the air.

He leaned over and placed a soft kiss on the top of her head. LuLu turned her face up to him, their gazes locking.

"I will do nothing with you tonight. Not here, and not like this," Silas said gently but firmly. The words took LuLu by surprise, causing her to sit up with confusion clouding her expression.

"What?" she asked sharply, instinctively pulling the afghan tighter around herself.

Silas threw up his hands, frustration crossing his face. "No, no, no. You've got it all wrong."

LuLu's eyes widened, a wave of unease washing over her. Despite being in a position that most guys would be thrilled about, LuLu was uncertain about what she had done wrong.

"I'm enjoying tonight, and I really like you. But today was a lot. You're a walking bruise, and I don't want to risk hurting you more. And honestly, as much as I want to be close to you, sex isn't the priority for me right now," he explained, his voice trailing off as he searched for the right words. "I'm not saying it's off the table forever, but I want to make sure you're comfortable."

LuLu reached out, her fingers brushing gently against his stubbled cheek. She guided his face toward hers; her smile was soft and reassuring. Her lips brushed his in a tender, innocent kiss that spoke volumes more than words ever could.

"I like you too. I'm okay with taking things slow," she said, her voice barely above a whisper. She reached to pause the movie, only to realize she hadn't even started it yet.

"Isn't that what we're doing?" Silas teased, attempting to lighten the mood.

LuLu nodded, her gaze dropping as she took a deep breath. "I told you about my past," she began, a shadow flickering across Silas's face. She took his hands in hers, her touch gentle and earnest. "I never slept with Greg because of Annie. So Liam was my... first. I just don't want to disappoint you."

Silas pulled her into a tight embrace, his arms wrapping around her with protective intensity. The pressure of his hold made her bruises throb sharply, but the enveloping warmth and sense of safety he provided were comforting enough to make the pain fade into the background. She nestled her head against his chest, the steady rhythm of his heartbeat a soothing counterpoint to the tumultuous thoughts swirling in her mind.

He breathed deeply, the subtle, familiar scent of her shampoo mingling with the softness of her skin. Each inhale was a blend of floral notes and something uniquely her—a mix that stirred a fierce, protective urge within him. The urge to whisk her away to a more private setting conflicted with his resolve to respect her boundaries. He fought to contain his instincts, determined to offer her the care and tenderness she deserved, far beyond mere physical comfort.

As he held her, his thoughts briefly drifted to his own sister. If anyone dared to treat her with such disregard, his rage would be a force to be reckoned with. The thought of anyone inflicting pain on someone he loved ignited a deep sense of justice within him. He held LuLu closer, his emotions simmering with a mixture of protective fury and compassion.

Slowly, he released her, his touch still tender. "You won't disappoint me," he whispered. "Let's just watch the movie."

LuLu smiled, her heart easing as she turned back to the TV. She hit play, and Silas wrapped his arm around her, drawing her close. He took a deep breath, savoring the comforting presence of her. They watched the movie together, the tension of the day slowly melting away, while Silas's heart ached with a mixture of anger and compassion.

"You'll never disappoint me," he whispered into her ear as the film played, his voice a soothing promise in the darkness. He took a deep breath, breathing her in. She looked up at him and smiled.

"I have an idea," LuLu said, jumping up from the couch and disappearing into her room. Silas paused the movie, curiosity piqued. A few minutes later, she returned, her arms full of blankets, with Doodle, her dog, trotting behind her. Doodle bounded up to Silas, sniffing his hand enthusiastically. His tail wagged furiously as he started jumping.

"Can you let him out quick?" LuLu asked, pointing to the back door. Silas quickly complied, letting Doodle out, and then returned to the living room to find LuLu hard at work. She had transformed the floor into a cozy nook with pillows and blankets, creating a nest of comfort and warmth. Every pillow in the house seemed to have been used to create a soft top layer, with comforters and blankets providing a cushioned base.

Silas smiled, feeling a surge of affection for her. Doodle, overjoyed, leapt into the makeshift bed and nestled beside his master. LuLu patted the free side, inviting Silas to join them. He took a seat next to her and instinctively pulled her into his arms. A grazing bruise made her wince, and he froze in response. She got up and pulled the Doodle into her bedroom. He was not normally happy about being in there, but she figured a few hours would not hurt him.

She looked up at him and kissed him gently, a soft, sweet peck that sent a shiver down his spine. Instead of pulling away, she nipped his bottom lip, making his body stiffen. He let out a low moan, pulling her closer. She could feel his desire, sensing how much he wanted her. This was fresh territory for her; she had never felt this in control before, but she felt like she was losing control. Her head swam with the taste and smell of him.

"I don't want to hurt you, and I hate to say this again, but you are a walking bruise," Silas said, his voice a mix of concern and longing. "You don't know what you do to me."

She smiled softly, her fingers tracing his jawline. "I think I have a pretty good idea," she whispered, leaning in to kiss him again. He pressed into her, and although pain shot through her cut lip, she ignored it, letting her body take the lead. She slipped on top of him, straddling him, and looked down at him with an intensity that mirrored his own.

His hands instinctively moved to her hips, steadying her, and he let out a soft gasp as she leaned in closer. Her fingers brushed through his hair, and she felt his breath quicken beneath her. Silas's eyes burned with a mix of desire and restraint, his grip on her hips tightening slightly, but not enough to hurt.

"You drive me crazy," he murmured, his voice husky. He lifted a hand to cup her cheek, his thumb gently grazing her bruised lip. "But I want you to be sure."

LuLu's heart raced, every beat pounding in her ears. For the first time, she felt powerful, in control. "I am sure," she breathed, leaning down to kiss him again. This time, the kiss was deeper, more urgent, their lips moving in a heated dance. She could taste the remnants of wine on his lips, mingling with the raw sweetness of the moment.

Her movements grew bolder as she ground her hips against him, feeling his response beneath her. His hands roamed her back, careful yet eager, sending shivers down her spine. Every touch, every caress ignited something primal within her, a hunger she had never felt before.

Silas's self-control wavered, his breaths becoming ragged. "LuLu," he whispered, his voice a mix of plea and promise. She silenced him with another kiss, her hands exploring the contours of his chest through the thin fabric of his shirt.

Their world shrank to just the two of them, a tangle of limbs and shared breaths, the outside world forgotten. In that moment, beneath the soft glow of the television and the warmth of their makeshift haven, LuLu felt a spark of bravery she had never known.

LuLu's breath was warm against Silas's neck as she trailed kisses down to his clavicle. She shifted, her body brushing against his, and her fingertips found his belt. With deliberate slowness, she kissed his navel, eliciting a low, feral growl from Silas as his eyes fluttered closed.

She deftly unbuttoned his pants, drawing out the moment as she inched the zipper down. His breathing quickened, his body thrumming with anticipation at her touch.

"Please," he whispered, his voice raw.

LuLu's newfound confidence surged within her. She tugged down his pants and boxer briefs, her movements languid and teasing. Silas lifted his hips to aid her, his desire palpable. She paused, taking in the sight before her. Though she'd never liked the word "cock," Silas's was unlike anything she had experienced before. Her hand hesitated, momentarily overwhelmed by its size. Realizing she was losing the moment, she shook off the distraction and focused on what she wanted.

In an instant, she was on him, her mouth caressing the head of his shaft with her tongue, swirling around the sensitive tip. "LuLu," he grunted, his control slipping.

"Do you want me to stop?" she teased, her eyes flicking up to meet his.

"No, please." His voice was almost a beg, stirring something primal within her. She took him deeper into her mouth, her lips stretching to accommodate his size. She pushed him as far as she could into her throat, her body reacting instinctively to his need. Her hand joined in, wrapping around the base and providing a rhythmic pressure as her mouth worked with a deliberate, practiced skill.

His moans grew louder, each one a desperate plea that fueled her determination. She could feel his muscles tense beneath her touch, his pleasure palpable in the way he gasped and shivered. She grazed him gently with her teeth, a teasing caress that elicited a fresh wave of shudders from him. His escalating moans excited her, urging her to increase her pace. The sound of his pleasure, combined with the heat of her own desire, made her movements more urgent and fervent, every stroke and touch a testament to her newfound control and confidence.

"I'm going to cum," he said, his fingers tangling in her hair. But she didn't relent. She quickened her pace, taking him as deep as possible. "Oh, fuck!" he cried out, his body convulsing as he released. Warm liquid filled the back of her throat, and she swallowed, feeling every pulse of his climax.

"How was that?" she asked, her voice tinged with satisfaction.

"Not disappointing," he panted, struggling to find the right words. "The opposite of disappointing, but I can't think of the word."

Her seductive smile was still plastered on her face as she laid down next to him, his pants barely clinging to his hips. Her body was tense with anticipation, the unfinished business between them only adding to the excitement. But before she could fully give into her desires, LuLu knew she had to check on the bar - after all, she had an employee now thanks to him.

As she got up to grab a glass of water from the kitchen, her mind was still buzzing with arousal. The evidence of their passion was clear in her disheveled clothes and dampness between her legs. She wanted him badly, but tonight wasn't about quick satisfaction.

"I'll be back to finish the movie," she purred before walking away. However, he wasn't ready for her to leave just yet. He grabbed her waist and pulled her back onto the bed, kicking off the rest of his pants and showing his eagerness.

With a sly grin, he turned off the TV and focused all of his attention on her. Pulling her close, he began kissing her neck and making his way down her body. Every touch sent shivers through her spine and drove her wild. She couldn't resist as he explored every inch of her, caressing and teasing until she was moaning in pleasure.

"Tell me if I do anything you don't want," he whispered with respect for her boundaries. She nodded eagerly and he continued, slipping his hand under her bra and expertly massaging her breasts.

The sensation was almost too much for LuLu to handle

as he positioned himself on top of her, removing her top and bra with ease. His lips found their way to her nipples, gently sucking and biting until she arched in ecstasy. She wanted nothing more than to surrender herself completely to him, but she knew tonight wasn't the night for that.

With a heavy moan, he unbuttoned her pants but she quickly stopped him with her hands. "Can we, I mean...should we wait? I just don't know if I'm ready after everything..." Her face flushed with embarrassment at how quickly things had escalated. But he simply took her hand in his and showered her with sweet kisses.

"Don't worry, there's no rush. We can take our time and go as fast or slow as you want," he assured her with a loving smile.

Feeling relieved and content, they snuggled up and turned the movie back on until Silas dozed off peacefully. LuLu decided it was the perfect time to head downstairs and check on the bar.

LuLu danced down the stairs to the busy bar. Matty was pouring beers, moving seamlessly among the patrons. Heath stood at the door, checking IDs as people came in. Watching the scene, a warmth spread through her chest, reminiscent of her childhood. For the first time in a long time, she felt genuinely happy.

She approached Matty at the bar, catching Max's eye. He raised his beer in salute, but froze when he saw her face. She shook her head, reassuring him she was fine. He nodded, though she knew a bigger conversation was coming.

"Hey, boss. Everything's been going smoothly. I need to make a drop if you want to take this to the safe." Matty handed her a blue bank envelope.

"Thanks, I'll take that." LuLu slipped the envelope under

her arm, aware that she was the only one who knew where the safe was. "If you need to make a drop and I am not here. You can put it under here." She pointed to a small safe with a slit on top.

"Can you cash out my tips, or will they come with my check from the temp agency?" Matty asked. Before LuLu could respond, a patron waved her over. She smiled at Heath, who was watching her intently.

She walked up to Heath, nudging him with her elbow. His face showed confusion.

"What?" he asked.

"Matty isn't just some random temp agency worker Silas found for me, is she?" LuLu asked, already suspecting the answer.

"We went to high school together. I knew her when she had a dead name. We stayed in touch for a long time. She had it rough. Couldn't pay for school. Took 10 years to get here. When Silas needed someone, I might have recommended her a bit more strongly than I should have," he explained carefully.

"Oh, I see." LuLu's smile widened into a full grin. She was on top of things tonight. "The day might start out as hell, but it's up to you to turn it into heaven."

"What?" Heath asked.

"Something my mom used to say. It meant to make the best of things."

"I'll think about it," he replied. LuLu returned to Matty, who had just finished closing out a customer. He gently caught her arm.

"Between us, please? I don't want Silas to think I'm using him. It was really for her..." Heath started.

LuLu raised her hand to stop him. "Secret between friends," she said with a smile.

She walked back to Matty, feeling a renewed energy.

"Matty, instead of going through the temp agency, how would you like to work here a day or two a week? I can offer fifteen an hour, and you keep your tips. If you're a college student, you can study during the slow times."

Matty's eyes lit up, her excitement practically bursting out of her. "Yes! I'm dying to leave the temp agency. Saturdays and Wednesdays work perfectly. I'm taking business classes at EU, so if there's any downtime to study, that would be amazing," she said, her voice brimming with enthusiasm. LuLu exchanged a glance with Heath, who chuckled softly and shook his head in amusement.

"Alright, consider it done," LuLu replied, extending her hand with a firm, confident gesture. "You'll work from 4 to 2 on Wednesdays, Thursdays, and Saturdays. I can be flexible with the times if you need adjustments."

Matty eagerly grasped LuLu's hand, sealing the agreement. LuLu then reached into a drawer and pulled out a stack of forms, setting them on the counter with a precise, practiced motion.

"Here's the I-9 and the other paperwork. Fill these out and bring them back on your first shift. I'll handle the rest." LuLu explained.

"Thank you!" Matty said, her voice full of gratitude. She glanced at the clock and then back at LuLu. "I should get back to closing up for the night, boss. Last call!"

LuLu handed her a key with a serious expression. "This is for the main door only. Keep it secure." Matty nodded, her face determined as she pocketed the key.

Max finished his beer, gave LuLu a reassuring pat on the

back, and headed out the door. She exhaled deeply, feeling the weight of his unspoken concerns linger in the air, though she knew they were beyond her control. A small smile played on her lips as she watched him leave.

"Here's the number to the bar and my personal cell," LuLu said, handing Matty a small card. "In case you ever need anything when I'm not around. But I've got to say, I'm impressed with you already."

"One last thing," LuLu added, her tone shifting to something more serious. She gestured toward a black lockbox on a shelf, its keypad gleaming faintly. "There's a loaded .22 in here. It was my dad's. We've never had to use it, but it's there if you ever need it. The code is easy to remember, just in case."

Matty's eyes widened slightly, but she nodded, quickly taking notes on her phone. She understood the gravity of the situation, but she also understood her determination to live up to LuLu's expectations.

LuLu took the blue envelope to the apartment steps, unlocked the door, and went up three steps. She pressed a board to reveal a hidden safe, quickly typed in the code, placed the envelope inside, and restored everything to its place.

Quietly, LuLu returned to the apartment. Silas was still on the floor, his arm draped over his eyes. He was wearing his bar t-shirt, with his pants neatly folded beside him. His chest rose and fell gently, accompanied by soft snoring. He had fallen asleep. LuLu curled up against his chest and let sleep take her.

She awoke suddenly, feeling herself being lifted. Silas was carrying her. She stirred, letting him know she was awake.

"I'm heading out. You should sleep in your bed," he said, placing her gently on her mattress and pulling a blanket over her. "I'll call you tomorrow. I really had a good time." He bent down, kissed her softly, and left the room through the side door, avoiding the bar.

As soon as she heard the door close, she walked over and hit the lock with a click. She turned and slid down the other side of the door, laughing to herself.

Eight

LuLu slept heavily through the night, her body sinking into the mattress as if she were in a deep, untroubled slumber. She awoke to the persistent, wet slaps of Doodle's paws on her face, a rhythmic nudging that broke through her dreams. Blinking groggily, she noted the dim light filtering through the curtains, the hour far beyond her usual waking time.

She dragged herself from the bed, Doodle's eager whines guiding her through the familiar motions of the morning. The air was still and quiet in the apartment, save for the faint shuffle of Doodle as he darted outside to relieve himself. He returned with a happy trot, his tail wagging as he pranced past her.

In the kitchen, LuLu methodically prepared her coffee, the aroma of brewing beans gradually stirring her senses. She carried her steaming mug to her room, where her phone lay on the nightstand. The screen glared up at her, blinking with a frenzy of notifications. Her heart skipped a beat as she scrolled through the messages, her eyes widening at the string of missed calls and text alerts from Sasha. The last message stopped her cold.

> **Sasha:** Ryan was shot in his dad's office parking lot at the hospital early this morning. He was found in his car. They think suicide. CALL ME ASAP!

The message on her phone seemed to pulse in the dim light, each word a piercing echo in LuLu's mind. Her fingers tightened around the coffee mug, the porcelain growing warm and heavy in her trembling grip. The kitchen felt suddenly small, the silence pressing in around her as the message's meaning settled, a chill creeping over her.

Her gaze fixed on the screen, disbelief warring with the stark reality of Sasha's words. She had harbored a deep-seated resentment for Ryan, and yet the news of his death felt surreal, like a plot twist in a story she couldn't quite believe. Her heart pounded, her breath coming in short, sharp bursts as she tried to reconcile the news with the reality she knew.With unsteady hands, LuLu fumbled with her phone, her thumb grazing the screen to dial Sasha. The line clicked and then Sasha's voice burst through, raw and frantic.

"Thank God, LuLu! I just had a bad feeling." Sasha said. LuLu could hear tears in her voice. "I know he and I broke up. I know he was so shitty to you, but... he is dead."

LuLu's voice came out in a hushed whisper, barely above a breath. "What happened?"

The words tumbled out of Sasha's mouth in a rush, each sentence colliding with the next. "Rebecca is on the phone with her police contacts. He was shot once in the head in his car at his office. They think it happened early this morning, but they're not sure. The morning cleaning crew found him."

As Sasha spoke, LuLu felt a cold numbness seep through her veins, dulling her senses. The words buzzed in her ears, each syllable a heavy weight that sank deeper into her mind. Her thoughts swirled, fragmented and disjointed, as she struggled to piece together the reality of the situation. The devil she had known was gone, and the gaping void he left behind felt like an uncharted chasm.

"I just saw him yesterday," LuLu murmured, her fingers instinctively brushing the bruise beneath her eye, as if the touch might ground her.

Sasha's voice cut through the fog, tinged with confusion. "Wait, what? What do you mean you saw him yesterday?"

"It's not a big deal," LuLu replied, her voice wavering. "There was a sort of fight at the bar yesterday. Liam and Ryan were here causing trouble, but nothing that we didn't handle. It's a long story. I'll tell you later." She tried to sound nonchalant, but the strain in her voice betrayed her unease. "I'm fine, and he seemed fine when he left."

Sasha's voice cracked as she spoke. Tears streamed down her face, and her hand trembled as she held the phone to her ear. "I...I loved Ryan," she said, her voice barely above a whisper. "We were together for so long, but then I met Rebecca, and everything changed. I know now what real love feels like." She let out a bitter laugh. "I can't believe I wasted all that time with someone who didn't truly love me."

LuLu reached over and gently took Sasha's hand in hers. "Mistakes are part of life," she said softly. "But they're also learning experiences."

Sasha paused for a second and said, "I have to take this,"

she said, wiping away her tears before answering the call with urgency in her voice. The conversation abruptly ended as she hung up to speak to Rebecca.

LuLu stood alone in her empty apartment, the silence amplifying her confusion. Doodle's eyes met hers with a curious tilt of his head. Her temple throbbed with a dull ache, and in a daze, she grabbed her car keys, driven by an instinct she couldn't quite name.

She drove to Ryan's office, the familiar route now shadowed by a sense of foreboding. As she approached, the parking lot was cordoned off with yellow tape, police cars flashing their blue and red lights. Officers waved traffic away, their voices muffled by the distance.

LuLu craned her neck, trying to take in the scene. The sight of Ryan's car, its door ajar, sent a chill through her. The absence of an ambulance and the flurry of police activity suggested that they had already removed his body.

A loud knock on the car window startled her from her daze. A police officer stood outside, motioning for her to move her car. She slowly rolled down the window and craned her neck to see the commotion on the street - a crowd had gathered around a store window with shattered glass and a missing merchandise display.

The drive back to the bar was a blur, and she parked her car, sitting in the driver's seat for what felt like an eternity. The weight of yesterday's events pressed heavily on her. She stared blankly ahead, knowing that the police would likely come around with questions. A gnawing sense of inevitability overshadowed the feeling of liberation from her troubled past. Here she was, caught in the aftermath of a life she thought she had left behind.

LuLu got into her apartment and pulled out her phone.

She shifted through her messages. Most of them were from Sasha. Then she hit a message that made her stop.

Silas:Hey, gotta head to SF for a few days with my partner to wrap up some stuff. Back in 3 days. Leaving right after work today. I can't stop thinking about last night. Can I see you when I'm back?

LuLu looked at the message. She texted Silas about Ryan, but deleted it. If he didn't know, there was no point in bothering him right now. She could always text him if she needed to. Plus, she didn't want to talk about her feelings. She was still reeling from last night, and now Ryan.

"Why can't my life just be normal?" she said out loud to herself. Doodle barked in response. LuLu laughed at her little dog, who promptly decided to starfish in the middle of the floor. She typed into her phone:

LuLu:Sounds great. See you when you get back.

There was nothing LuLu could do now. To gather her thoughts, she needed to think and talk to Sasha. She jumped into the shower quickly, the hot water burning the cut on her chin. She winced as she noticed the large bruise on her arm and the swelling around her eye. Though she could still see out of it, it looked rough. After dressing, she applied makeup as best as she could to cover the bruises. She texted Sasha a few times and tried to wait patiently for a reply. To LuLu's surprise, it was Rebecca's number that showed up.

"Hello," LuLu answered.

"It's Rebecca. We all need to get together. Nina's place, an hour?" Rebecca asked in a hurried tone.

"I'll be there," LuLu responded, slipping her phone into her pocket.

She grabbed her laptop and headed over to Nina's place, deciding to arrive early to check the news. The drive felt surreal, her mind racing with thoughts of last night and Ryan.

Once at the cafe, she slid into a booth and ordered a coffee. She opened her laptop, her fingers trembling slightly as she navigated to the local news website. Nina shot over to her table and gave her a hug, offering a moment of warmth in the chaos. Nine filled her cup and looked at LuLu's face. She opened her mouth to ask, but she could see in LuLu's face that she was not talking. She left LuLu for her business.

LuLu's fingers shot over the keyboard. As soon as she entered his name, article after article popped up. LuLu read through a few articles, not much information. She clicked around and found one piece of information.

Local News Article Excerpt:
The victim was found with a single gunshot wound to the head, sparking an ongoing investigation. While authorities have yet to confirm the exact circumstances, sources show they are exploring all possibilities, including suicide. However, the police have ruled nothing out at this stage. An inside source reports the scene raised questions, with some evidence suggesting the possibility of a struggle before the fatal shot was fired. The investigation remains active as detectives work to piece together what led to this tragic incident.

LuLu's breath hitched, her eyes scanning the word "beaten." The memory of the fight from the previous day flashed in her mind, and an icy dread crept over her. Her hands trembled slightly as she wondered if the police might suspect her involvement. Before she could spiral further,

Sasha slid into the seat beside her, her arrival as abrupt as her usual demeanor. Rebecca followed, her movements fluid and composed. Sasha's eyes caught LuLu's bruised face, and her expression twisted into a fit of anger.

"What the hell happened to you?" Sasha demanded, her voice low but fierce.

LuLu's hand instinctively went to her swollen eye, the touch gentle as if to soothe the throbbing pain. "It's nothing," she mumbled. "Just some trouble at the bar."

"Nothing? You call that nothing?" Sasha's voice was incredulous. "Who did this to you?"

LuLu glanced at Rebecca, whose calm gaze was filled with concern. She sighed, feeling the weight of the night pressing down on her. "Liam and Ryan," she whispered. "There was a fight."

Rebecca's eyes widened slightly, but she remained silent, waiting for LuLu to continue.

"They... they attacked me," LuLu admitted, her voice trembling. "Silas and Heath stepped in. It was a mess. I thought it was over, but now with Ryan... and the news..."

Sasha's anger softened into protectiveness as she reached out, gripping LuLu's hand tightly. "We'll figure this out," she said, her voice firm and steady. "You're not alone in this."

Rebecca nodded, her expression calm and reassuring. "We'll understand it. But first, let's make sure you're safe. So, give me a dollar."

LuLu managed a small smile and reached into her pocket, pulling out a crumpled five-dollar bill. She slid it across the table. "I'm fine, but I need to know what's going on. Do you know what happened?" she asked, her voice trembling slightly.

Rebecca took the bill, her gaze serious as she leaned in closer. "I'm now your attorney. Anything we talk about is confidential. You understand that?" she asked, her voice low and firm.

LuLu nodded, her expression tense.

Rebecca lowered her voice to a whisper, forcing LuLu to lean across the table to hear her. "Did you do it?"

"No!" LuLu's shout drew the attention of others in the diner. Anger surged through her, a hot flush rising to her cheeks. She had thought about it from time to time, but she could never do it, no matter how much she hated him.

Rebecca's eyes bore into LuLu's bruised face, the evidence of the recent fight glaringly obvious. "Understand how this looks. They came to your bar. There was a clear fight."

Sasha nodded, her hand squeezing LuLu reassuringly. "If you say you didn't do it, I believe you."

"Good, because I didn't do it," LuLu insisted, trying to convince Rebecca. The attorney nodded thoughtfully.

"I need your alibi," Rebecca said, pen poised over her notepad.

"After the fight, they left. I had a new girl working the bar..." LuLu began.

"New girl?" Sasha interrupted, her eyebrows raised.

"Yeah, Silas called a temp agency so we could have an actual Saturday date," LuLu explained.

"What?!" Sasha exclaimed.

"Stay on topic, baby." Rebecca said to Sasha. "And?" Rebecca prompted, signaling LuLu to continue with a wave of her hand.

"Silas and I were together until about 4, maybe 5 a.m. He left, and I've been home alone until now," LuLu finished.

Rebecca nodded, jotting down notes. "I will not lie. It doesn't look great. The police are going to want to talk to you for sure." She paused, turning to Sasha. "They're going to talk to you, too."

"Why me?" Sasha asked, her voice tinged with anxiety.

"Because you're his ex. Plus, I was at my mother's last night, so they'll want to make sure all loose ends are tied up," Rebecca pointed out, her tone matter-of-fact. She put her arm around Sasha. "It's going to be alright."

The three ate their breakfast in a heavy silence, the clinking of cutlery the only sound breaking the tension. LuLu could feel Sasha's curiosity radiating from across the table, her eyes occasionally flicking towards her, clearly eager to ask about her night with Silas. LuLu's heart raced with the urge to spill every detail, but the timing felt off.

Rebecca's presence was imposing, her demeanor radiating an effortless authority that made LuLu shrink slightly in her seat. There was something about Rebecca that commanded respect, her confidence and poise, a sharp contrast to LuLu's own insecurities. Rebecca had been out since middle school and owned every aspect of her life with unapologetic pride. She exuded a strength that both intimidated and inspired LuLu.

LuLu watched as Rebecca gently squeezed Sasha's hand, the subtle gesture filled with affection. Despite her tough exterior, Rebecca's kindness shone through, and LuLu admired her for treating Sasha so well. Determined to rise to the occasion, LuLu made a silent vow to herself to be stronger, to try harder, to emulate some of the courage and assurance that Rebecca embodied.

Watching Sasha and Rebecca share a quiet moment, LuLu felt a pang of longing for Silas. She glanced at her phone, but the screen was empty. She sighed, feeling ridiculous, like a high schooler hoping for a text from her boyfriend. The realization struck her—was Silas even her boyfriend? The uncertainty made her throat tighten. She coughed, reaching for her water, and noticed both Sasha and Rebecca looking at her.

"Chew. No one is going to take it away from you, LuLu," Rebecca teased, breaking the tension.

LuLu tilted her head, a small smile forming. "Was that a joke, Rebecca?"

Rebecca's lips curved slightly. "Don't get used to it." Their shared laughter lightened the mood briefly, but Rebecca quickly steered them back to the seriousness of their situation. "You said Silas left somewhere between four and five, right?" Rebecca asked, her tone turning professional again.

"Yes," LuLu replied, choosing her words carefully.

"It might be good for me to talk to his counsel as well. When the time comes," Rebecca suggested.

Lulu said, "He had to wrap up closing the San Francisco offices. He should be back in three days."

Rebecca's fork paused in mid-air. "He left town?"

"It's business," LuLu shot back, defensive.

Rebecca's gaze sharpened, her tone calm but firm as she leaned in slightly. "I get it, LuLu, but the optics aren't great," she said, lowering her voice. "From now on, no more texts about this. We can't afford to leave a trail that could lead back to either of you. Face to face only—nothing in writing. Got it?"

LuLu nodded, but the tension in her shoulders didn't ease. "Silas had nothing to do with this," she fired back, her voice tinged with frustration. Her hands clenched in her lap, the conviction in her words leaving no room for doubt. Even though her relationship with Silas was just beginning, her trust in him was solid as a rock. She met Rebecca's gaze with unwavering resolve, certain that once Silas returned, everything would be clear.

"No one is saying he had anything to do with this," Sasha interjected, her words slightly muffled by a mouthful of food. "I think what Rebecca is trying to point out is what the police might see. We just want to be ready."

Rebecca nodded, her expression softening slightly. "Exactly. It's about being prepared for how things might look to the authorities. We need to cover all our bases."

LuLu exhaled, her frustration ebbing. "Now I understand. I just... I wish things were simpler."

Sasha reached across the table, giving LuLu's hand a reassuring squeeze. "We'll get through this. Together."

LuLu hesitated, her words catching in her throat. "Who could have done this? Ryan was an asshole and a—" She cut herself off, a mix of anger and confusion flashing across her face.

Sasha's voice was calm, but her words cut through the tension like a knife. "It could be anyone. He wasn't exactly winning any popularity contests. Everyone had a reason to hate him."

LuLu's gaze dropped, her thoughts spiraling inward. "It's not just anyone," she murmured, almost as if speaking to herself. "This was personal. My sources... they're certain of it. And now, the story's catching fire. Where's Liam?"

Rebecca's eyes locked onto LuLu's, her unwavering confidence radiating like a beacon. "He's missing. For now, no one knows where he is. But don't worry. We'll handle this. I'll do everything in my power to keep you safe. But you've got to stay sharp."

The reality of the situation settled over them, heavy and suffocating. Yet beneath it, something new sparked—a flicker of hope. With Rebecca and Sasha by her side, LuLu felt the weight lift slightly, ready to confront whatever lay ahead.

As she left, her thoughts swirled in a chaotic dance of fear and resolve. But for the first time in what felt like ages, she didn't feel completely alone.

Nine

As the days passed, life seemed to slip back into its usual rhythm. Max stuck to his routine, steady as always, his presence a constant LuLu could rely on. But beneath his calm exterior, there was a tension in the way he watched her, a silent acknowledgment that he knew more than he let on. Ryan's name never came up, nor did the gruesome details of his murder, but the unspoken truth hung between them like a thick fog.

LuLu spent most of the day glued to her computer, digging through articles and reports, trying to piece together what had happened. The headlines were stark and unforgiving:

Prominent Doctor's Son Found Dead in Parking Lot of Medical Office By Tilda Line
In a shocking incident, Ryan Caldwell, 24, son of the esteemed Dr. Henry Caldwell, was found dead in the parking lot of Envy Medical late last night. Ryan, who was in his second year of residency at the pres-

tigious medical facility, was discovered with a single gunshot wound to the head, sparking an ongoing investigation.

Authorities have not ruled out the possibility of suicide, but Ryan's parents strongly disagree with this theory. They have emphasized that their son was in a happy relationship with his girlfriend and thriving in his work as a doctor. In their only statement to the press so far, they stressed their belief that Ryan would never take his own life. The investigation remains open, with detectives exploring all potential leads.

As the community grapples with the loss of a promising young doctor, Ryan's colleagues at Envy Medical have expressed their shock and sorrow, describing him as a dedicated and compassionate professional. The Caldwell family is receiving an outpouring of support as they navigate this devastating time, and the police are urging anyone with information to come forward as the search for answers continues. A girlfriend, that word stuck in her head. Girlfriend. LuLu knew Ryan was not the guy that would and/or could stay single for very long. LuLu figured if anyone would know anything, it would be her.

But as much as the thought gnawed at her, she pushed it away, forcing herself to focus on something else, anything else. She snapped her laptop shut, shaking her head to clear the tangled thoughts inside. Her phone was in her hand before she even realized it, and within seconds, she was staring at Silas's message for the hundredth time. It was absurd how her heart raced just seeing his words, like she was a teenager with a hopeless crush.

Frustration welled up inside her, mingling with a deep, aching longing. She wanted him there, right then, to pull her into his arms and make everything else disappear. Her fingers hovered over the keyboard, eager to type a reply, but nothing felt right. Each word she tried seemed to fall flat, failing to capture what she really wanted to say. With an exasperated sigh, she deleted the half-typed message and tossed the phone aside, feeling more restless and alone than ever.

She exhaled sharply, sinking back into her bed as her mind raced. The urge to text him was overwhelming. She wanted to pour out everything—how lost she felt, how she couldn't stop replaying their night together, how much she needed him right now. Her heart quickened, the thoughts tangling in her head. How could someone like him be interested in her? The doubt gnawed at her. He could have anyone, so why choose someone as broken and poor as she was?

LuLu shook her head, trying to scatter the thoughts that clung to her like a heavy fog. She sat up abruptly, the sudden movement causing Doodle to lift his head and bark, clearly annoyed at having his sleep interrupted. His sleepy eyes glared at her as if demanding an explanation.

"Oh, I'm sorry, Lord Doodle," she cooed, reaching out to pat his head, her tone light despite the turmoil inside. She was just about to lie down again when her phone buzzed, the screen lighting up with a message.

She grabbed it, her heart skipping a beat as she saw Silas's name. The text was brief, as usual, but she realized with unexpected force.

Silas: I saw the news. I hope you're okay.

Her breath caught in her throat, a mix of relief and

longing flooding her chest. Without overthinking, she quickly typed a response, her fingers hovering over the send button for a moment before she hit it.

LuLu: I'm okay. Miss you too.

As soon as LuLu sent the message, a rush of nerves hit her like a tidal wave, her pulse quickening as she waited for Silas's response. Her fingers hovered over her phone, feeling the weight of anticipation mingled with a warm comfort from his words.

Silas: I cannot stop thinking about the other night. What do you think about next time, it being my turn?

Her cheeks flushed, warmth spreading from her neck to her face. A shiver of excitement ran through her, making her hands tremble slightly as she began typing a reply. She hesitated, her usual "ok" feeling too simple, too flat. She recalled Sasha's playful, teasing advice and allowed a mischievous smile to tug at her lips.

LuLu: What do you have in mind? ;)

There was a brief pause before Silas's response appeared on the screen, each word like a spark igniting her curiosity.

Silas: It's a surprise. Do you trust me?

The word "trust" lingered in her thoughts, heavy and profound. Her mind flashed back to the other night, the intimacy they had shared. She felt a mix of vulnerability and hope, her fingers trembling as she typed her response, each letter deliberate and charged with meaning.

LuLu: Yes.

Silas: I have to go to bed, so I'm ready for tomorrow. I'll be in and out of meetings, but I'll be back the day after. Think you can ask Matty to pick up a shift?

LuLu's lips curled into a smile. Matty was already scheduled to work, so it would just be her shift alone. She reassured herself with the thought of Max overseeing things, ready to step in if needed.

LuLu: Sure. But we need to talk about that.

Silas: Did I do something wrong?

LuLu: I appreciate what you are trying to do, but my business is my business. It is very important to me that you understand that. You wouldn't want me to mess with your business.

Silas: Understood. I am sorry. Unless you ask, I will not help. Fair?

LuLu: Yes.

Silas: I'll pick you up at 6:00 on Wednesday. I have a gift coming for you. Hope you like it. Sasha helped. Digital, of course.

A soft laugh escaped her as she read his message. She typed back quickly, trying to keep the mood light.

LuLu: No more people as gifts. I can hire my staff.

Silas: Understood. I shouldn't have interfered, but she's pretty great, right?

LuLu: Yes, but that's not the point.

Silas: You're right.

LuLu paused, staring at the screen. Silas's message was straightforward, but the combination of "you're right" and the mention of Sasha's involvement left her with lingering questions. She had heard nothing from Sasha about the gift, and with the recent chaos, she wondered if Sasha had simply forgotten. She resolved to follow up with her soon, feeling a mix of curiosity and concern.

LuLu: Go to bed.

Silas: I will dream of you.

A soft smile curved LuLu's lips as she read his message. She settled back onto her bed, her feet lifting slightly as she adjusted her position. Doodle, disturbed by the motion, let out a huff and leaped off the bed, his tail flicking in irritation. LuLu's usual composure felt shaky tonight; she couldn't remember the last time she'd been so unsettled by a simple text.

LuLu: Cheesy.

Silas: But it is true.

LuLu sank back into her bed, her smile spreading across her face. The warmth of her happiness was a stark contrast to the chill that had settled in her chest. Her thoughts, however, quickly darkened, and the smile faltered. Guilt gnawed at her as she stared up at the ceiling. How could she permit herself to experience this joy when she had lost someone she knew? The conflicting emotions swirled inside her, leaving her caught between the fleeting happiness and the heavy weight of her conscience. She took a deep breath and let sleep take her.

In the pitch-black void, LuLu felt a suffocating pressure around her, a crushing weight of fear and dread. Faces materialized out of the darkness—Ryan's sneering, Liam's menacing glare. Their expressions twisted and warped, as if mocking her. The darkness surged, swallowing their faces, and she spiraled deeper into the abyss. Shadows clawed at her, closing in with an oppressive force, and her breaths came in ragged gasps. Her heartbeat thundered in her ears, a relentless reminder of the terror she couldn't escape. The darkness seemed endless, wrapping around her, isolating her in a nightmare where she was both prisoner and spectator.

LuLu shot upright, gasping for air, her body trembling uncontrollably. The remnants of the nightmare clung to her like a heavy fog. Doodle, sensing her distress, bounded onto the bed and pressed his warm body against her. His soft fur was a grounding presence in the chaos. She clutched him tightly, her fingers sinking into his fur as she buried her face in his neck. Her skin was damp with sweat, and her breaths came in shuddering waves. Doodle nuzzled her gently, offering silent comfort as she clung to him, trying to shake off the lingering terror.

LuLu lay back down, her heart still racing from the nightmare. She reached for her phone with trembling hands, her fingers brushing over the screen as she typed out an email to Dr. Clover. Each word was deliberate, her resolve steady despite the lingering dread. She needed an appointment, a chance to untangle the knots of fear and confusion that twisted inside her.

As she hit send, she exhaled slowly, trying to calm her racing thoughts. The room was still dark, the early morning light not yet breaking through the curtains. She closed her eyes, letting the weight of exhaustion pull her into a deep, dreamless sleep, hoping for a reprieve from the night's shadows.

The buzz of LuLu's phone pulled her from a restless sleep. She squinted at the screen, seeing a missed call and an email. The email from Dr. Clover offered two appointment slots: one in two hours and another tomorrow. LuLu quickly tapped out a reply, opting for the sooner slot. She set the appointment for 10:00 AM at the doctor's office, hoping the one-on-one conversation would bring some clarity.

Next, she saw the missed call from Sasha. LuLu dialed her number, listening to the familiar voice on the voicemail. "This is Sasha Baker. I am not here right now, but leave a message and I will phone you back when I can. Thank you for calling."

LuLu sighed and left a message. "Sasha, I saw your call. I hope everything is okay. I have an appointment with Dr. Clover at 10:00, but I should be free after." As she was about to hang up, she added with a slight smile, "Silas mentioned you helped him with a gift? Looks like there's a story there. Talk soon." She ended the call, feeling a mix of curiosity and amusement.

LuLu followed her usual morning routine, humming to herself until the abrupt buzz at the door startled her. Her steps were light with anticipation, but the moment she opened it, her cheerfulness evaporated. Two men stood there, their faces set in grim lines.

The first man, stocky and bald, looked like he belonged in a shadowy underworld rather than a suit. The fabric seemed to absorb all the light, making him appear more imposing. His face was a blotchy red, and his glare bore into LuLu with an unsettling intensity. The second man stood tall and gaunt, his suit hanging loosely from his thin frame. His bug-like eyes darted around the room, never settling in one place for too long.

LuLu kept her stance firm, her grip on the door tight. "We're closed on Tuesdays, gentlemen," she said, not budging an inch.

The bald man's voice was a gravelly command, cutting through the air. "Envy Police, ma'am. We need to talk." There was no question in his tone, only expectation.

LuLu's eyes narrowed, her voice sharp. "I'll need to see your badges first."

With a flick of their wrists, both men revealed their badges. The bald one, Detective Lee, let his credentials linger in the air as LuLu scrutinized them, her smile slipping into a cautious frown. She stepped aside, allowing them into the bar with a wary glance.

Once inside, Detective Marc, the skinny one, began surveying the room with a calculating gaze. His movements were deliberate, like he was sizing up a crime scene. Lee, less interested in the surroundings, drifted further into the bar, his eyes skimming the decor with disinterest. LuLu took a deep breath, feeling the weight of their presence.

Marc settled onto a bar stool, his gaze fixed on LuLu. "Coffee?" LuLu offered, trying to keep her voice steady despite the tension in the air. Both men declined with curt shakes of their heads.

"Ms. Pillar," Marc started, his tone as sharp as his eyes. "I'm sure you know why we're here."

"Ryan's suicide?" LuLu's voice was steady, though her eyes betrayed a flicker of something else.

"Murder, actually," the bulkier detective corrected from across the room, his voice carrying a hint of something darker. Lee remained close to LuLu, flipping open his notebook with a snap, ready to document every word.

"Yes, murder," LuLu echoed, her tone resigned as she met Marc's unyielding stare.

Marc sifted through his notes, his expression tightening. "We're here to speak with anyone who had contact with Ryan Caldwell. That includes you." He paused, waiting for her to respond. LuLu, without a word, texted Rebecca: Police. Bar. Now. The message sent. She placed her phone face down on the bar, frustration simmering just beneath the surface.

Marc took a seat directly across from her, his gaze probing. "Tell us about your relationship with Dr. Caldwell."

"No relationship," LuLu replied, her voice clipped.

Marc's eyes narrowed as he consulted his notes. "We have a witness who saw him leaving your bar the day before his death. He wasn't alone. They said both men looked like they'd been through hell." He stared at her, his gaze demanding answers.

LuLu's eyes flicked to the other detective, who was carefully bagging something from the floor. He handled it with the precision of someone well-versed in collecting evidence.

"What's that?" LuLu's voice held a note of irritation as she glanced at the detective handling the item.

Marc's sharp tone redirected her attention. "Let's stick to the matter at hand. What about the day when someone saw Ryan and Liam here, both beaten?" His gaze dropped to the bruise on her face, his expression hardening. He reached out, fingers brushing the bruise before he quickly pulled back, as if remembering his place.

"Officer?" LuLu's voice wavered, surprised by the sudden intimacy.

"Apologies. I can't stand seeing a woman hurt. Call it old-fashioned." He explained, but the door to the bar burst open with a loud bang, cutting him off.

Rebecca entered, her presence commanding the room. "Please tell me you're not questioning my client without her lawyer," she said, her voice cold and authoritative.

"We're just talking, Ms. Tyme. No need to get defensive," Marc replied, irritation seeping into his voice.

"Yes," added the other detective, dismissing Rebecca with a wave.

Rebecca moved behind LuLu, her presence a reassuring anchor. "If it's just a conversation, I should have no problem being here," she stated firmly.

Marc leaned in closer to LuLu, his gaze unwavering.

"Someone observed Ryan leaving here with Liam Stein. They both looked like they'd been in a fight. That's not a coincidence, is it?"

Rebecca's eyes met LuLu's, silently urging her to stay calm. LuLu took a deep breath and recounted the recent events—the contract Silas had pulled from Liam's company, the subsequent altercation, and Silas's intervention. Rebecca nodded, satisfied with LuLu's explanation.

Marc's next question cut through the tension like a knife. "Boyfriend, huh? Why would he pull those contracts? Is that what led to this?" He pointed at the bruise on LuLu's face, his tone accusatory.

Rebecca's composure never wavered. "That's Silas's business, not LuLu's. And don't refer to my client as 'this.'"

Marc's gaze hardened, but he didn't press further. "Interesting. Mr. Stein hasn't been seen since leaving here. His phone is off, and no one's heard from him. Any ideas?"

Rebecca's eyebrow arched ever so slightly, her voice cutting through the tension like a blade. "Perhaps your time would be better spent finding him rather than harassing my client."

Marc's jaw tightened, a flicker of irritation crossing his face as he stood. His movements were deliberate, controlled, but there was no mistaking the displeasure simmering beneath the surface.

"We're done here for now," he said, his tone clipped. He extended his hand, offering LuLu his card, but his gaze remained locked on Rebecca, the air between them crackling with an unspoken challenge.

LuLu kept her expression calm, her voice unwavering as she spoke. "Thank you, detectives. I'll reach out if anything comes to mind." Her words were polite, but there was a firmness beneath them, a quiet resolve that hinted at the strength she was holding onto.

As the detectives turned to leave, the heavy atmosphere in the room seemed to ease, the oppressive tension lifting with their exit.

But just as the door closed, Detective Lee paused, his hand on the handle. "One last thing," he said, his tone deceptively casual. "Do you own a gun?" He asked

LuLu met his eyes without flinching, her reply coming quickly, her words firm. "Yes. My dad's .22. It's locked in the gun safe at the bar. Barely touched, only ever used at the firing range."

Lee's face remained impassive, a flicker of something unreadable passing through his eyes. He nodded, a small, almost imperceptible gesture, then turned back to the door. The room seemed to hold its breath as he stepped out; the door clicking shut with a finality that left the air thick with unspoken tension.

But just as the silence settled, the door creaked open again, and Lee's voice sliced through the quiet. "Mind if we see it?"

LuLu stepped towards the bar, but Rebecca stopped her. She didn't miss a beat, her voice cold and cutting. "Do you have a warrant?"

"Not yet, counselor," Lee responded, his words laced with an edge of challenge. Without waiting for a response, he exited, leaving the door to swing shut with a soft thud. The heavy atmosphere lingered long after their footsteps faded. The bar was now a quiet space filled with unspoken questions.

Once they were gone, Rebecca's concern was understandable. "Did you say anything before I got here?" she asked softly.

LuLu recounted the conversation, including the detective bagging the mysterious item. Rebecca listened intently, her expression thoughtful.

"I'll find out what that was," Rebecca promised, her voice steady. She pulled LuLu into a comforting hug, offering a reassuring squeeze before heading out, leaving LuLu alone with her thoughts in the now-quiet bar.

LuLu stared at the card, her heart pounding so hard she could feel it in her throat. Her hands trembled as she opened her phone, typing in Marc's number with shaky fingers, labeling it "Copper" as if the nickname could shield her from the panic swelling inside. She flipped the card over repeatedly, her mind racing with the relentless certainty that Ryan would never have committed suicide. The thought that the police might actually suspect her was suffocating.

Her breath hitched as a wave of tightness wrapped around her chest. The anxiety was unbearable. As she checked the time on her phone, a jolt of panic shot through her—she was almost late for her therapy appointment. Grabbing her anxiety medication, she shoved it into her bag and bolted out the door, her mind fixated on reaching her therapist. She needed to talk through this insane week, to get the grounding her therapist always provided.

Each step toward the office felt frantic, her thoughts a chaotic whirlwind. She didn't take the medication yet, focusing instead on reaching her therapist, where she hoped to unpack the fear and confusion consuming her. The city moved around her in a blur, her panic ebbing and flowing with each hurried step, but the appointment was the only thing anchoring her to reality.

Finally, the familiar building came into view. A small measure of relief washed over her as she pushed open the door and walked inside. Therapy was her safe space, the one place where she could let go of the chaos and breathe. She knew she needed this—she needed to talk, to process, and to find her way back to calm.

Dr. Clover's office was as unremarkable as LuLu had imagined—off-white walls, a few chairs arranged neatly, the obligatory potted plants, and a desk with a computer. But as LuLu stepped inside, she couldn't help but notice the absence of the stereotypical therapy couch she'd expected. Instead, she sat across from Dr. Clover in a simple chair, the room feeling more clinical than comforting.

As LuLu talked, the words spilled out of her in a steady stream. She had learned the hard way that therapy only worked if you will be completely honest, and over time, she'd broken down the walls she'd built around herself. Dr. Clover listened intently, her pen scratching furiously across her notepad. By the time LuLu finished, the doctor's eyes were wide with the weight of what she had just heard, her hand momentarily pausing as if to absorb it all.

"That's... quite a lot for anyone to carry, especially given your history," Dr. Clover finally said, her voice tinged with concern. LuLu nodded, acknowledging the truth in her words.

Dr. Clover set her pen aside, leaning forward, her gaze softening with genuine interest. "Tell me about this new person in your life, LuLu. Over the years, we've watched others move on—Sasha, Annie, Greg—and through it all, you've seemed... stuck. But now..."

LuLu felt a flicker of warmth in her chest as she met Dr. Clover's eyes. "I'm finally living my life, leaving the baggage behind," she said, a small but hopeful smile forming on her lips. Dr. Clover's nod was slow and reassuring, a gentle push toward something brighter.

"It's good to be cautious, but shutting yourself off from everyone isn't the answer. That you're opening up, even carefully, shows actual progress. I'm proud of you, LuLu," Dr. Clover's words were like a balm, and LuLu's smile grew a little wider.

"Thank you," LuLu replied, the sincerity in her voice palpable.

Dr. Clover's expression shifted slightly, her tone becoming more serious. "Now, we need to discuss the situation with the suicide... or murder."

LuLu's eyes darkened, the earlier warmth quickly dissipating. "I didn't do it," she stated firmly.

Dr. Clover gave a reassuring nod. "I know, but I have to ask. You mentioned the police visited you?"

"Yeah. They suspect murder, but Sasha and the news reported it as a suicide, so I'm confused. And... I had a strange dream," LuLu added, her voice tinged with uncertainty.

"Let's explore that," Dr. Clover encouraged. "You haven't had nightmares in six months. What do you think the dream could mean?"

LuLu shrugged, a hint of frustration seeping through. "I don't know. That's why I'm paying you."

Dr. Clover chuckled softly. "Fair enough. I think your subconscious is trying to tell you something, and only you can unlock what that is. But I know someone who specializes in hypnotherapy. If you're open to it, I'd like to refer you."

LuLu nodded, a mix of reluctance and hope in her eyes. She was ready to try anything that might help her move forward. Dr. Clover opened her laptop and typed swiftly, emailing.

"Dr. Blackwood will reach out to you," Dr. Clover informed her. "Same time next week, but I suggest twice a week until we resolve the situation with Ryan," Dr. Clover informed her.

"I'll think about it," LuLu said, standing up. With a deep breath, she left the office, the weight of the session lingering as she made her way home.

Ten

After therapy, LuLu grabbed Doodle's leash and stepped outside, the crisp air a welcome change from the tense atmosphere inside. She fastened the leash and headed down the street, her thoughts a jumble of worry and confusion. She slipped her earbuds in, the familiar strains of Taylor Swift's new album easing some of the knot in her chest. Each song seemed to offer a temporary escape from the gnawing anxiety that clung to her.

As she made her way back to the bar, the familiar façade seemed to offer a momentary reprieve. She noticed a small package on the doorstep, nestled against the threshold. With a furrowed brow, she picked it up, her curiosity piqued. Doodle, now free from his leash, darted excitedly around her legs.

Inside the apartment, LuLu set the package on the counter. She untangled the leash from Doodle and watched him scamper off before returning to the package. Her fingers trembled slightly as she untied the bow on the black box, the pink ribbon slipping away with deliberate slowness.

She lifted the lid, and her breath caught in her throat. Inside was a dress unlike anything she had ever seen—a stunning shade of teal blue that seemed to pulse with a life of its own. The fabric shimmered softly as it caught the light, casting a gentle glow that was nothing short of mesmerizing.

An artist's hand crafted with such delicate precision that it appeared to embrace the curves of the dress as if the sweetheart neckline sculpted it. The tea-length hem flowed gracefully, its fabric falling in soft, elegant waves that spoke of timeless sophistication. Each fold and drape of the material seemed to dance with an ethereal quality, highlighting a level of refinement that was both captivating and enchanting.

The dress was a vision of pure beauty, its every detail radiating an effortless grace. The dress appeared to have been crafted not just for adornment, but to transform, creating a magical aura that felt both intimate and grand. At that moment, LuLu could scarcely believe that such a breathtaking creation was meant for her.

LuLu unfolded the note, her eyes scanning the words:

> LuLu,
> I could not find the dress that was destroyed, so I hope this one will make up for it.
> Silas.
> P.S. I know you want to be more out there. I hope this helps.

She stared at the dress, her frown deepening. It was beautiful, but unavoidably revealing. The scars she had worked so hard to hide would be visible, but perhaps this was an opportunity to face them. The dress, with its elegant design, seemed to challenge her to step beyond her comfort zone.

Sasha's influence was obvious to LuLu as she recalled Sasha's encouragement and the perfectly sized dress. This gesture wasn't just about the dress; it was a nudge to embrace change and confront her fears. With a deep breath, LuLu decided. She would no longer shy away from the scars that told her story.

Determined, she headed to the bathroom to try on the dress. As she slipped into the fabric, she felt a strange mix of apprehension and anticipation. The dress fit perfectly, the color stressing her features in a way that felt both empowering and vulnerable.

Standing in front of the mirror, LuLu took one last look, a sense of acceptance settling over her. Most of her scars were on full display and for the first time in a long time, she didn't care. The dress was more than just fabric; it was a step toward embracing who she was.

She slipped out of the dress with careful movements, as if afraid to crease the delicate fabric. With a gentle touch, she hung it on the outside of her closet, where its vibrant teal still gleamed softly in the muted light.

Her fingers danced over her phone screen, sending a quick thank you to Silas before she tapped out a message to Sasha, her excitement palpable. A heart emoji blinked back almost instantly, filling her with a warm sense of approval.

LuLu's mind drifted to the thought of the police. She wondered if they had already spoken to Sasha. The question lingered at the edge of her thoughts, but she hesitated to voice it, unsure of how to navigate the growing web of uncertainties. LuLu completed the inventory at the bar with a steady rhythm, her mind preoccupied. After LuLu finished she headed over to the diner for something to eat. As she settled into a booth at the diner, she saw Nina slide into the seat across from her. There was a noticeable shift in Nina's demeanor—more guarded and tense than usual.

"The police stopped in and asked about you and those boys," Nina said, her eyes rolling slightly at the term "boys." A concerned edge replaced the casual air she usually carried.

LuLu met Nina's gaze with a nod. Nina continued, "Sarah saw them leaving your bar a few days ago. I can tell something's up." Her voice took on a sharper note as she leaned in. "Tell me you didn't do it."

The question hit LuLu with unexpected force, leaving her momentarily stunned. The weight of Nina's doubt felt like a betrayal. They had known each other for years; she hadn't expected this.

"I did not kill Ryan," LuLu said firmly, her voice steady despite the sting of Nina's suspicion.

Nina's expression shifted from worry to relief, and she quickly stood up.

"Good. I'll grab your dinner," she said, leaving LuLu alone at the booth.

As LuLu waited, she pulled out her phone and scanned the latest news articles. The headline about Liam's disappearance caught her eye. Annie and Greg quoted Liam as a close friend and a key figure in their wedding plans. LuLu scoffed, knowing the truth—Liam was much closer to Ryan than to Greg. Greg had only kept him around because of his connections and as a party favor. None of that mattered to LuLu now; she had her own concerns.

The hum of the diner and the rhythmic tick of the wall

clock seemed to blur into the background as LuLu's mind churned with worry. Her food arrived, and she ate swiftly, her gaze darting around the room. The chatter of nearby tables faded into a muted buzz as she noticed curious glances and hushed conversations directed her way. The whispers, though indistinct, felt heavy and invasive.

Unable to shake the feeling of being under scrutiny, LuLu paid her bill quickly and retreated to the safety of her apartment. Once inside, she booted up her laptop with urgency. The glow of the screen illuminated her face as she began her search for information on Ryan.

Her investigation quickly revealed a seemingly mundane social media presence—photos of meals and casual snapshots of him with a striking blonde. LuLu clicked on the woman's profile. Heather Lamb. The name rang unfamiliar, but a quick search confirmed she was a former model turned nurse at the same hospital where Ryan was interning. LuLu's eyebrows arched in surprise; she hadn't known Ryan had a girlfriend, though it made sense in hindsight.

Driven by a mix of curiosity and a need to connect the dots, LuLu sent Heather a friend request. She continued her search late into the night, the click of her keyboard the only sound as she delved deeper into the digital trail Ryan had left behind. She was so into her research that she never noticed her phone buzz. Exhaustion eventually overcame her, and she fell asleep at her desk, the laptop still glowing softly in the darkness.

The soft, rhythmic thud against her cheek pulled LuLu from sleep. Blinking groggily, she found Doodle's bright, eager eyes inches from her face. A burst of laughter escaped her as she swatted playfully at him. He wagged his tail furiously, his excitement palpable.

After a quick walk with Doodle, LuLu fell into her usual morning routine. Yet, beneath the surface of her everyday tasks, a flutter of anticipation danced in her chest. Tonight was the night she'd see Silas, and the thought of it brought a mix of thrill and nerves.

She stole a glance at her phone. A text from Silas brightened her screen: a simple, cheerful "Hello" and a reminder about their date tonight. He mentioned he was back, and the words made her smile. Her fingers danced over the keyboard as she replied, her excitement barely contained.

As she typed, she wondered if she was overstepping by showing too much enthusiasm. But then, memories of their last encounter, the electric connection they'd shared, reassured her. She chuckled to herself, thinking that perhaps it was too late to worry about coming on too strong. The anticipation of the evening made her heart race, and she couldn't wait for the night to unfold.

LuLu flicked through the TV channels absentmindedly, her gaze barely registering the images as she straightened up the bar. The anticipation of the night ahead made every second drag. The clock's hands move at a snail's pace. Despite the restless energy bubbling inside her, she kept busy, wiping down counters and rearranging bottles until there was nothing left to do but wait.

Finally, the clock signaled it was time. She headed to her small bathroom, where she carefully applied her makeup, each brushstroke precise and deliberate. She scrutinized her reflection, pleased to see that her black eye had faded from deep purple to a mottled green, the foundation doing a decent job of concealing it. Her lip, once split, was nearly healed, just a faint pink line remaining. Satisfied, she turned her attention to her hair, curling each strand until it fell in soft waves around her face.

Slipping into the black thong and strapless bra, LuLu felt a mix of excitement and nerves flutter in her chest. It had been so long since she felt like this—sexy, desirable, and genuinely beautiful. As she smoothed the teal dress over her body, the way it hugged her curves sent a wave of confidence through her. For the first time since the assault, she felt pretty, sexy, and truly beautiful, like she was reclaiming a part of herself she thought she'd lost forever. The anticipation was there, but something new joined it—a readiness to embrace the night, to feel something good again.

Matty, already setting up behind the bar, greeted her with a nod. LuLu handed her a list of instructions for Doodle. "Can you let him out at least once before you head home? He can stay here until I come back."

"Sure thing, boss lady," Matty responded with a reassuring grin. Just then, Heath appeared in the doorway. LuLu looked up in surprise.

"Mr. Heartly got held up with something at work and asked me to pick you up. I hope that's alright?" Heath's voice was warm and respectful.

LuLu's nerves eased a bit as she smiled and nodded. Heath opened the car door for her, and she slid inside. The car ride filled LuLu with excitement and nervous energy, and when they arrived, she was taken aback. They had pulled up to the very restaurant where they'd tried to eat on their first date.

She glanced down at her dress, taking a deep breath. This was it. No one would focus on her scars tonight; she reminded herself that this was her moment. Heath opened the door with a wide smile.

"I hope you don't mind, Ms. Pillar, but you look absolutely lovely tonight," he said.

LuLu's cheeks flushed with a rosy hue. "Just LuLu, please. And thank you. Be honest, how bad are the scars?"

Heath's gaze softened. "Don't be self-conscious. Everyone has a past. Some scars are on the inside, others on the outside. Wear yours with pride."

With that encouragement, Silas guided LuLu into the restaurant, her breath hitching as she stepped inside. The room was bathed in soft candlelight, casting a warm glow over the space, except for Silas standing at a small table set with wine and an air of undeniable charm. His impeccably tailored suit made him look more dashing than ever, his presence alone filling the room with magnetic allure.

"What's all this?" LuLu's voice quivered, a mixture of awe and excitement tingeing her words.

Without a word, Silas crossed the room with deliberate strides. He enveloped her in a warm embrace, the rich scent of sandalwood and vanilla mingling with the heat of his body. As he leaned in to kiss her, their lips met with a fierce, desperate intensity. The kiss was a fervent dance of passion; LuLu nipped at his bottom lip, their tongues swirling together in an exploration that left them both breathless and yearning. Her pulled her in closer and harder and as their lips intertwined the heat and electricity between the kiss grew.

Her pulse quickened, each touch igniting a shiver that coursed through her. Silas's hands roamed over her back, his touch sending waves of electric desire through her. The thought of their bodies intertwined, the primal dance of intimacy, consumed her thoughts. She had never imagined such a deep yearning, never considered opening herself up to someone in this way. Yet now, every kiss, every touch, heightened her craving, leaving her gasping for more.

Silas's hands slid down to her waist, pulling her flush against him. The firm press of his arousal against her inner thigh made her heart race, her body instinctively arching toward him. When he finally pulled back, both of them panting, his eyes danced with a teasing, wicked glimmer.

"You do not know what you do to me," he murmured, his voice low and laden with desire. LuLu's cheeks flushed crimson as she glanced away, her gaze dropping to the floor. Silas gently cupped her chin with his thumb and forefinger, tilting her face up to meet his. His touch was both tender and commanding, sending a shiver down her spine. "If we keep this up, we might not get to our dinner," he said, his thumb brushing away a smudge of her lip gloss from his cheek. The simple, intimate gesture only heightened the charged atmosphere between them.

He led her to the table, pulling out her chair with a flourish. As LuLu settled into her seat, Silas took the one opposite her, his gaze locked onto hers with a heat that made her pulse race. She fought the urge to leap across the table, instead letting her foot trace along the inside of his leg.

Their waiter appeared, refilling their glasses with wine. As they began their meal, Silas regaled her with tales from his trip and updates on the business. LuLu listened, captivated by his every word, struggling to keep her focus on the conversation while her desire for him simmered just below the surface.

LuLu considered bringing up Ryan and his murder, but pushed the thought aside. This moment was for them, for connecting and enjoying each other's company. As Silas spoke, she hung on to his every word, captivated by the sound of his voice and the way his eyes lit up when he talked. The evening unfolded like a dream, course after course arriving at the table, each more exquisite than the last.

She tasted dishes that were almost too beautiful to eat, their vibrant colors and intricate presentations making her hesitate before taking a bite. She didn't recognize half of what she was eating, but each morsel was a revelation, the flavors dancing on her tongue in a way that made her forget everything else.

When dessert arrived, it wasn't the waiter who delivered it, but a tall, slender woman with skin the color of warm sand and sleek black hair tied back. Silas's face broke into a wide smile as he stood up to hug her.

"LuLu, this is my sister, Ara. Ara, this is LuLu," Silas introduced them, his tone filled with warmth.

LuLu felt a rush of nerves as she took in Ara's confident demeanor. The two women exchanged smiles, and Ara extended her hand, the warmth of it surprising.

"It's nice to meet you, LuLu. Silas has told me so much about you," Ara said, her grip firm but friendly. "Sorry, chef hands—anything but soft."

LuLu laughed softly, the tension easing slightly. "I've heard great things about you too," she replied, trying to keep her voice steady despite the unexpectedness of meeting Silas's family.

"You've got to bring her to Mom and Dad's," Ara teased, nudging Silas playfully.

Silas shook his head, a smile tugging at his lips. "You're just lucky because you own this place," he retorted.

"Everything was amazing," LuLu blurted out, her appreciation genuine. Ara's grin widened at the compliment.

Ara exited the room with a theatrical flair, her exaggerated double thumbs up aimed squarely at Silas. The moment left LuLu both flustered and charmed, especially when she noticed Silas's face flushing a deep strawberry-red.

"Sorry about that," Silas mumbled as he sat back down, trying to distract himself by diving into his dessert. His sudden shyness only made LuLu's smile widen.

"I love how close you are to your family," LuLu said softly, her eyes warm with admiration. "I've never really seen that before."

"I'm lucky," Silas replied, his voice sincere, though a smudge of chocolate betrayed his otherwise composed demeanor. Without thinking, LuLu reached across the table, her fingers brushing his cheek as she wiped the chocolate away. Before he could react, she playfully slipped her finger into her mouth, her smile turning mischievous.

Silas's eyes darkened slightly, his gaze locked on her in a way that made her pulse quicken. The air between them shifted, charged with a sudden, palpable lust that neither could ignore. The simple gesture had ignited something deeper, something both thrilling and irresistibly magnetic.

The drive to Silas's apartment was charged with anticipation. When he asked, "Would you like to have a drink at my place? I'm not ready for the night to end. What do you think?" LuLu's heart raced. She smiled, nodded, and took his offered hand. Walking hand in hand to the car, the air between them crackled with unspoken desires.

As the car glided through the night, LuLu leaned into him, her head finding its place on his shoulder, where warmth and strength seemed to radiate from his body. The steady rhythm of his breath matched the gentle sway of the vehicle, a quiet, calming presence that she wanted to lose herself in. Silas reached over, his finger pressing a button that raised the divider between them and the driver, sealing them in their own private world.

Without a word, his hand found her thigh, the touch firm and possessive. A jolt of electricity shot through her, igniting every nerve ending in her body. Her breath hitched, the air around them thickening with unspoken desire. The heat of his hand seeped through the fabric of her dress, setting her skin on fire. She didn't think—she just reacted.

Her lips found his neck, each kiss slow and deliberate, as if she were tasting the very essence of him. His pulse thrummed beneath her lips, a steady beat that quickened with each kiss she planted along his skin. His breathing grew heavier, more ragged, the sound a fuel to the fire burning inside her. She let her lips trail up to his ear, her teeth grazing it gently, sending a shiver through his entire body.

The air between them crackled with intensity, the space suddenly too small, too charged. Her heart pounded as she felt him respond, his body tensing, the undeniable hardness pressing against the confines of his pants. The realization sent a surge of pride and desire coursing through her, the power of his reaction amplifying her own need. His restraint only fueled her hunger. Each touch and kiss a dance on the edge of control, a silent agreement that neither wanted to break.

Silas turned his head toward her, his face inches from hers. His eyes were dark with want, but gentle as they lingered on her bruised eye. He leaned in and pressed a tender kiss on it, a gesture that made her heart squeeze with emotion. His hand slid further up her thigh, fingers grazing the edge of her panties. The tension in the air was thick as he pulled away slightly, his gaze locking onto hers.

"Tell me to stop, okay?" His voice was low, rough with restraint. "I'll stop."

The intensity in his eyes made her heart pound. Instead of answering, LuLu crashed her lips against his, the kiss deep and desperate. She was trembling with want, feeling the wet heat pool between her thighs. Silas's hand slipped under the fabric of her panties, his fingers finding her slick core with practiced ease.Her skin became sensitive under his touch, and sent shock waves of heat and yearning and lust racing through her body.

Her breathing grew heavy, every flick of his fingers pushing her closer to the edge. The tension in her body built, coiling tighter and tighter until she was a trembling mess of need. The pleasure became overwhelming, crashing through her in a tidal wave that left her gasping for breath. She bit down on his shoulder, trying to muffle the scream that threatened to break free, her body shuddering as she rode the intense waves of her orgasm, feeling more alive than she had in years.

Silas pulled her close, wrapping her in a hug that felt both protective and possessive. She leaned into him, resting her head against his chest, breathing in his scent—a mix of something woodsy and clean. She felt him inhale deeply too, like he was memorizing the way she smelled, the way she fit against him. It was a moment of quiet connection, the kind where words were unnecessary.

When the car came to a stop and the door opened, LuLu's breath caught in her throat. They had arrived at the newest apartment complex just outside of town, a place she'd only seen on the news. It was touted as the pinnacle of luxury, with state-of-the-art amenities and a price tag to match. That Silas lived here was another reminder of how different their worlds were, yet it didn't feel intimidating—just exciting.

Stepping into the elevator, they filled the quiet with unspoken anticipation, each lost in their thoughts. The elevator's ascent seemed to stretch out, their shared excitement palpable. When the doors finally slid open, LuLu's eyes were drawn to the sleek, modern hallway that awaited them—a narrow stretch of polished floor and clean lines leading to a single, unobtrusive door. Silas produced a key, its metallic click breaking the silence as he unlocked the door.

As LuLu crossed the threshold, her breath caught. The penthouse was a marvel of understated luxury—silver and black dominated the palette, creating a minimalist elegance that made the space feel expansive. Every piece of furniture and tech was a statement of refined taste: a massive flat-screen TV loomed over the room, flanked by a high-end sound system that promised a cinematic experience. The space was undeniably modern, each detail meticulously chosen, but it didn't feel cold or unwelcoming. Instead, it was a stylish, high-end retreat.

Silas gestured for her to follow, leading her through the apartment. The small office, with its sleek silver desk and black chair, was immaculate. The art on the walls was striking, clearly curated by someone with a keen eye—either a designer or perhaps his sister, LuLu thought.

The dining room was elegantly simple, featuring a single vase in the center of the table, which somehow made the room feel more intimate. The kitchen, however, told a different story; it was well-used, with a few dishes left in the sink. LuLu couldn't help but smile at the domestic touch, and Silas noticed her amusement, offering a sheepish apology.

He continued the tour, showing her the two guest rooms —spacious but plainly furnished, set up for visits from his parents and sister. When he finally opened the door to the bedroom, its simplicity struck LuLu. The bed was enormous, the largest she had ever seen, draped in a gray comforter and black sheets. A black dresser and a closet completed the room, all understated yet luxurious.

She sat down on the edge of the bed, her cheeks flushing as she felt herself sink into the plush surface. The softness enveloped her, contrasting with the sleek, minimalist design of the rest of the apartment.

He smiled, his gaze lingering as he said, "You look good on my bed." LuLu's laughter was a soft, playful sound that filled the room. "You want a drink?" he asked, and she nodded.

As he left the room to fetch something for them, LuLu felt a surge of determination. This was her moment to be bold. She unzipped her dress and carefully folded it on the dresser, revealing her bare skin. She then settled onto the bed, striking the most alluring poses she could muster. Her scars, once hidden, were now on full display—a raw testament to her past but also an invitation for him to truly see her.

The anticipation was palpable. Her breath caught in her throat as she heard his footsteps returning.

He walked into the room, his presence commanding attention as he carried two glasses and an unopened bottle of scotch. The sight of her lying provocatively on his bed left him momentarily breathless. His eyes roamed over her, a mixture of surprise and desire flickering across his face. For a brief, anxious moment, LuLu moved, her hands instinctively reaching to cover herself.

"Sorry. I thought maybe..." LuLu started, her voice trembling as she sat up.

"Wait. Stop." He said firmly, placing the drinks on the dresser. He turned back to her, his eyes blazing with an intensity that made her heart race. He strode over to the bed and drew her into his embrace with a possessive pull. "You are beautiful," he murmured, his voice a deep, velvety rumble. "You just surprised me. In a good way." He pressed a soft, lingering kiss to the top of her head.

She looked up at him, her eyes smoldering with desire, and kissed him back with a fierce passion. Their mouths moved together, the heat between them palpable. He responded with equal fervor, his body pressing hers into the mattress as he gently laid her back. His hands roamed over her curves with a reverent touch, exploring every inch of her body.

As he unbuttoned his shirt, LuLu's fingers traced over his rock-hard abs, feeling their steely strength beneath her touch.

"What?" he teased, his lips curling into a playful grin.

"You're built like a Ken doll," she teased, her eyes sparkling with mischief.

"Not quite. I have a few more parts," he whispered, his lips crashing against hers with fierce hunger. His kiss was urgent, demanding, as his hands slid lower, finding her breasts and cupping them with a possessive grip. The heat of his touch set her aflame, her moans escaping in breathless, ecstatic gasps. Her hand drifted down, feeling his rigid erection pressing hard against his pants. The knowledge of his arousal only fueled her own, igniting a deep, primal need.

His lips traced a slow, deliberate path down her neck, lingering on the scar on her inner arm with a reverent touch before descending to her breasts. He paused, his breath coming in ragged, uneven bursts as he took in the sight of her flushed, eager form. "Beautiful," he murmured, his voice raw with need.

His hands roamed with purpose, molding her breasts with a teasing pressure that elicited shivers of pleasure. His touch was a seductive promise, each caress a delicious torment. With fervor, his lips located her right nipple, as his tongue skillfully intertwined gentle, playful nibbles with fervent, deep sucks. LuLu's back arched in response, her body surrendering to the waves of ecstasy that rippled through her. She was drenched in anticipation, her skin a canvas of flushed desire.

As his kisses trailed down her body, he shifted his position, moving from above her to between her legs. His lips brushed against the scar on her inner thigh, a tender kiss that ignited a desperate yearning within her. Slowly, she slid off her panties, her movements languid and filled with a quiet, eager anticipation.

"You're soaked," he groaned, his voice dripping with lust. Lulu's cheeks flushed in a delectable blush, her chest heaving as desire coursed through her body. "I want to devour you." He gripped her legs firmly and drew closer, leaving a trail of hot kisses along her inner thighs until reaching her core. With expert strokes of his tongue, he explored every inch of her, leaving her gasping and quivering. It was an erotic feast that he indulged in with insatiable hunger, driving her to the brink of ecstasy.

He paused, lifting his head to look at her with a satisfied smile. "You taste like spring rain," he whispered, before diving back in. His tongue moved in slow, deliberate circles, each stroke driving her wild with pleasure. Her breaths came faster, her body trembling with the overwhelming sensation.

With a deliberate, slow motion, he slid his long, slender finger into her, the movement eliciting a moan from her lips. He worked his finger in and out, her muscles tightening around him, causing him to growl with pleasure. The soft hum of his voice accompanied the rhythm of his actions, the vibrations sending shivers up her spine and curling her toes.

"Silas," she cried out, her voice a mixture of desperation and ecstasy. The pleasure became too much to bear; her back arched off the bed as her body convulsed in a powerful climax. She clutched at his hair, holding him close, her eyes squeezed shut as waves of intense pleasure washed over her.

Silas finally withdrew, kissed her thigh softly before standing to pour himself a drink while he watched LuLu, flushed and breathless, lying on the bed. He joined her, laying down beside her and pulling her into his embrace. LuLu felt an overwhelming sense of exhaustion, as if she hadn't slept for weeks, but the comfort of his arms eased her into a peaceful state.

Her fingers fumbled with the buckle of his belt, her heart racing as she assumed he was expecting something in return. She understood the unspoken quid-pro-quo, but before she could pull it off, he gently removed her hands and shook his head.

"No," he said softly, placing a tender kiss on top of her head. "Let's just make tonight about you."

She looked away, feeling overwhelmed and grateful at the same time. "Thank you," she said, the words spilling out without thought.

He turned her to face him, concern etched on his features. "Why?" he asked, his hand reaching up to wipe away a tear that had escaped her eye.

"For everything," she replied, her voice barely above a whisper as she turned away again, unable to face him fully in that moment.

"Wait, what's happening here?" he asked, gently turning her back towards him. "This is how men treat women. You dated boys before. I'm not a boy; I'm a man."

She kissed him, not sure how to respond or what to say. The warmth and security of his embrace made her feel safe for the first time in a long time, and as sleep pulled her under, she let it envelop her.

The darkness curled around her like a living thing. After first what had felt like calm and peaceful darkness had suddenly become dense and suffocating. A voice echoed through the void, whispering her name, and she felt a cold shiver slide down her spine. A spotlight snapped on, casting a harsh, unforgiving light over an empty chair. Then, out of the shadows, Ryan emerged, his face pale, and his eyes hollow. The bullet wound in his head was a grotesque, gaping mark, still fresh with blood trickling down. He moved with an eerie, unnatural grace, taking the chair without a word.

Another spotlight flickered to life, illuminating a second chair opposite him. His lifeless eyes met hers, and he gestured for her to sit. She knew she was dreaming, the oppressive weight of it pressing on her consciousness, but something stronger than fear pulled her forward. Her steps were heavy, deliberate, as if the dream itself was dragging her to that chair.

She sank into the seat, unable to tear her gaze away from him. The wound in his head was too vivid, too real, as if this was how he existed now—broken, bleeding, caught in a loop of torment. His skin was mottled with bruises, the purple and black splotches creeping up his neck, and blood dripped steadily from the wound, pooling at his feet. His eyes, once bright, were now sunken and empty, staring at her with an expression that made her chest tighten.

She didn't need to be told; she felt it in the marrow of her bones. This was her nightmare taking form, twisting reality into a macabre vision. The air was thick with the metallic scent of blood, and the silence pressed down on her like a weight. She studied him, every detail searing into her mind. There was something here, some dark truth hidden within the dream, and it clawed at the darkness smothered LuLu like the cloak of a demon, thick and choking, as if it were alive and intent on dragging her into the abyss. The air was heavy with the stench of sulfur and decay, burning her lungs with every breath. Somewhere in the void, a voice slithered through the blackness, a twisted echo of her name that sent a chill racing down her spine. Then, as if commanded by a force beyond her control, a spotlight pierced the void, illuminating a single chair.

Ryan emerged from the shadows like a grotesque monster, his once handsome features twisted and distorted beyond recognition. His hollow eyes held no trace of humanity, instead seeming to hold an endless void of torment and agony. With each step, the bullet hole in his forehead pulsated and oozed a thick, black liquid that seemed to seep from a dark, otherworldly source. He moved with an eerie grace, as if being controlled by some malicious entity. As he slumped into the chair and beckoned her closer, another chair appeared as if by magic. His hand reached out like a claw, his elongated fingers beckoning her towards him with a chilling aura. His skin was pulled taut over his emaciated frame, covered in bruises and wounds that spoke of unimaginable suffering even in death. And still, the wound on his head continued to bleed, casting a foreboding air over his corpse-like appearance.

LuLu tried to resist, trying to wake herself from this hellish nightmare, but her body Resisted her desperation to wake up and moved forward as if the floor itself were alive and pulling her in. The metallic stench of blood mixed with the foul scent of rotting flesh filled her nostrils, making her gag as she took her seat. Every detail of his tortured appearance became etched into her mind, a horror too real to be just a dream.

"Why did you do this to me?" Ryan's voice slithered out, but it was warped and grotesque, as if spoken through a throat full of bile. The tone was sickeningly sweet, almost cartoonish, yet dripping with venom, a cruel mockery of his suffering.

"I didn't," LuLu choked out, her voice trembling as she struggled to hold on to her sanity.

Ryan's head tilted at an unnatural angle, his lips curling into a smile that was more a sneer, revealing teeth that were yellowed and cracked, like tombstones in a forgotten graveyard. "I know," he whispered, his voice laced with dark amusement, "but everything you touch dies, LuLu. Pain follows you like a shadow, poisoning everything in its path."

"Go to hell," she spat, though she laced her words with

terror rather than defiance. She could feel the darkness tightening around her, suffocating her.

"I'm already there," he hissed, his smile widening far beyond what was humanly possible, stretching his lips until they cracked and bled. Fear shot through LuLu's spine like a bolt of lightning, freezing her in place. Her body locked in place, her limbs became as rigid as the dead man before her.

A sudden, jarring ding cut through the oppressive silence, its sound sharp and dissonant. Ryan's eyes, voids of nothingness, flickered with something dark and malicious as he raised a bony finger, signaling her to wait. Slowly, with deliberate cruelty, he reached into his tattered pocket and pulled out a cell phone, the screen glowing with an eerie light that seemed to seep into his mutilated face, highlighting every bruise, every crack in his decaying flesh. His fingers, skeletal and elongated, danced across the screen, tapping out a message with sickening patience.

"What do you want?" LuLu whispered, her voice barely audible over the pounding of her heart.

Ryan's eyes bore into hers as he waved the phone, the glow casting shadows that twisted and danced across his disfigured face.

"I wonder if they found this," he murmured, his voice dripping with malevolence.

"Why would I care?" she shot back, her voice trembling as she tried to suppress the panic clawing at her insides.

He shrugged, a casual gesture that made her blood run cold, as if her fear was nothing more than a trivial amusement to him. Then, without warning, the darkness lunged at her, wrapping around her like chains made of shadow. She felt a yank backward, as if an invisible rope was pulling her, and the world around her dissolved into a whirlpool of black and red. The abyss swallowed her whole, pulling her down into an endless void, until—

A gentle hand brushed across her forehead, coaxing her from the depths of a twisted nightmare. The warmth of his touch contrasted with the icy terror that had gripped her moments before. His eyes, filled with concern, searched her face as he softly murmured, "You were having a nightmare." The tenderness in his voice pulled her back to reality, anchoring her in the safety of his presence.

But the remnants of fear still clung to her, and she pulled away from him, her movements hurried and shaky. She reached down, grabbing her underwear, and slipped it on with practiced speed. The cool fabric of her dress followed, a familiar barrier between them.

"Are you leaving?" he asked, his voice low, laced with something deeper than just concern. He remained on the bed, his gaze tracking her every move.

"I have to get home to take care of Doodle," she lied, her voice steady but her heart racing. The truth was too complicated, too raw to share.

He nodded, his expression unreadable as he picked up his phone. His fingers moved swiftly, sending a message. "Heath will drive you home. He's downstairs."

"I can take a Lyft," she began, trying to reclaim a sliver of control, but he raised his hand, silencing her.

"Please." The word hung in the air between them, heavy with unspoken emotions. His eyes locked onto hers, a silent plea burning in their depths as he rose from the bed, closing the distance between them. His arms wrapped around her, his lips finding hers in a kiss that held both urgency and tenderness. She let herself melt into it, the intensity of the moment overwhelming her defenses.

"Okay," she whispered, the word barely audible as she accepted his offer, feeling the weight of his affection in that simple, loaded exchange.

He walked her downstairs to the waiting car, his hand a steadying presence on her back. As she slid into the backseat, Heath nodded in acknowledgment, offering a polite, "Good night, Miss LuLu," before driving off into the quiet night.

LuLu stared out the window, her eyes tracing the outlines of trees and buildings as they blurred past. Each landmark became a focal point, something to distract her from the turmoil inside. She couldn't afford to think, not now, not with so many emotions vying for her attention.

When Heath finally pulled up to her building, LuLu stepped out, the cool night air a welcome relief. She let herself into her apartment, the familiar scent and sight of her home grounding her. Doodle trotted over, tail wagging, and she let him out, her movements automatically.

After a quick shower, she took her medication, and she slipped into bed, exhaustion pulling her into a deep, dreamless sleep, the darkness now peaceful and welcome embrace.

<h1 style="text-align:center">Eleven</h1>

The shrill alarm cut through the quiet morning, jolting LuLu awake. She reached out, half-asleep, and accidentally knocked her phone off the nightstand. The clatter startled Doodle, who barked in response, his tiny form scrambling into her chest. His enormous eyes, framed by floppy curls, peered at her with concern, eliciting a smile despite the rude awakening. She ruffled his fur, feeling the warmth of his little body against her.

With a sigh, LuLu pushed herself out of bed and opened the door to let Doodle outside. He trotted back in moments later, content, and promptly curled up on her pillow as if reclaiming his spot.

LuLu picked up her phone, noticing the missed call and a text from Sasha, asking about their usual Sunday brunch plans. But it was the other message that made her freeze mid-motion. An unfamiliar number had left a voicemail. Her heart raced as she played the message, the voice on the other end breathless, scared, and desperate.

"LuLu, I didn't do this, and he didn't kill himself. I know

you don't trust me, and you shouldn't. But if you meet me, I will tell you everything. The old mall meets in the parking lot outside where Sears used to be. It should be safe. I'll be there at midnight on Friday. Please. It will not stop. I know you don't trust me, and you shouldn't. You need to know the truth. I can't live with myself anymore. Midnight Friday. Please. I just need to get the proof and you will understand everything."

LuLu's fingers trembled above her phone, her pulse quickening as the message echoed in her mind, each word lingering like a sinister whisper that the monster in her dream will not let her forget. "It will not stop." An icy shiver crawled down her spine, the unease settling into her bones, tightening her chest. The voice on the recording seemed to grow more desperate with each replay, a plea laced with fear and urgency. Her breath hitched as she listened again, the weight of the situation pressing down on her. She hesitated for a moment, her thumb hovering over the screen, before she finally forced herself to delete it, her stomach twisting with unease.

She quickly texted Sasha, her fingers moving automatically, meeting at Nina's at 11:00. Sasha's confirmation buzzed back almost instantly, but LuLu barely registered it. The tension coiled in her muscles was a little eased by the hot water from the shower, and by the time she dressed and left the door, her mind remained ensnared by the ominous words.

At Nina's, LuLu placed her phone on the table, staring at it as if it might betray some hidden clue. The message was like a dark cloud hanging over her, every detail of the voice's panic etched into her thoughts. Her gaze was distant, lost in the endless loop of fear and uncertainty playing in her head.

She didn't even notice when Sasha plopped down across from her, only snapping back to reality when she practically jumped out of her skin at the sudden movement. Sasha shot a look at LuLu that only read with concern.

"How are you doing with everything?" Sasha asked as Nina brought them coffee. They both told Nina what they wanted before LuLu answered.

"I'm ok. Well, as ok as can be expected." LuLu said, taking a sip of her coffee.

"Lu, Rebecca said the police came to see you," Sasha said with a sense of frustration.

LuLu forced a steady breath, the words catching in her throat before she said, "I didn't do it, so if I'm just honest, everything will be okay."

Sasha's expression tightened, her voice trembling as she replied, "It's not always that simple. Rebecca told me innocent people end up in jail all the time." Her eyes shimmered with unshed tears, and LuLu's resolve softened at the sight.

"You're right," LuLu said gently, her tone more cautious now. "I'll be careful, I promise. I texted Rebecca as soon as they showed up."

Sasha's lips curled into a faint smile, though worry still lingered in her gaze. "That was smart. I just don't get why they're pushing this so hard. Everyone's saying it was a suicide." The frustration in Sasha's voice was palpable.

LuLu offered a wry smile, trying to lighten the mood. "Sometimes this big brain of mine comes in handy." But beneath her playful tone, she kept quiet about the message from Liam, deliberately holding that detail back.

Sasha's mood shifted quickly as she leaned in, a mischievous glint in her eye. "Now, spill the tea—how's everything with your new LLLOOOOVVVEERRRR?" She drew out the word with exaggerated enthusiasm, making LuLu cringe.

"Gross," LuLu muttered, but the faintest hint of a smile tugged at her lips. "But..."

"But what?" Sasha's eyes widened with eager curiosity, leaning in even closer. LuLu knew that look all too well; Sasha was practically buzzing with interest.

"We've been on a few dates. It was... nice. He's nice. I like him," LuLu admitted, her voice trailing off.

Sasha's face scrunched in dissatisfaction. "That's not enough detail. Come on, I need to live vicariously through you! I'm practically a married lady over here."

LuLu seized the opportunity to shift the focus. "Speaking of which, has she proposed yet?"

But Sasha wasn't so easily deterred. "Not yet, but we're talking about you right now." Just then, Nina arrived with their food, momentarily pausing their conversation. As soon as Nina walked away, LuLu leaned in, lowering her voice as she shared every steamy detail from the past few weeks.

Sasha fanned herself dramatically, her eyes wide with excitement. "Oh my God, that is what I call hot. So, are you going to sleep with him?"

"Maybe," LuLu replied with a sly smile.

Sasha's eyes sparkled with determination. "Okay, we're going shopping right after breakfast."

True to her word, Sasha dragged LuLu through every store in Town Square until LuLu finally made a purchase. After saying goodbye, LuLu strolled back to the bar, idly scrolling through her phone. She noticed a new Facebook message from Heather, Ryan's girlfriend, who had just accepted her friend's request.

Heather:

I know your name from Ryan. Are you his friend from college?

LuLu hesitated, her fingers hovering over the keyboard before she typed her reply.

LuLu:

Yes. I'm so sorry for your loss.

Almost immediately, the three dots appeared, showing that Heather was typing.

Heather:

I'm having a small gathering at our house next Wednesday. The address is 8403 Line Lane. You're welcome to come between 12:00-3:00. His parents will be there too.

LuLu's fingers hovered over the keys, her mind spinning with possibilities before she finally typed a quick thank you, adding that she'd try to make it to the gathering. As she hit send, a thought gnawed at her—talking to Heather might be the key to finally putting all of this to rest.

LuLu spent the rest of the day moving through the bar with a quiet precision, ensuring everything was just as it should be. Her new employee seemed competent, but LuLu's instincts kept her watchful. Trust wasn't something she gave easily. Every bottle was checked, every supply counted, as she worked through the inventory with a sharp eye. Once everything was in order, she tucked the Saturday envelope into her personal safe, the cash ready for Monday's deposit.

Business had been booming since the engagement party, an irony that wasn't lost on her. She couldn't stand Greg and Annie, but had they inadvertently done her a favor? Was this Greg's twisted way of apologizing, driving customers her way to make up for his betrayal? The thought made her scoff, but a flicker of doubt nagged at her—Greg's expression the night he'd heard about Liam still lingered in her memory.

'

She shook her head sharply, trying to rid herself of the lingering thoughts. She needed to stay focused. There was no excusing their behavior, no justifying the pain they'd caused. Still, something gnawed at her, an unease she couldn't shake.

Despite her desire to leave the day behind, an insistent voice in the back of her mind compelled her to check instead of going upstairs. She hadn't done this, but she needed to make sure everything was secure. She had to protect herself.

The police's question about the gun echoed in her mind, refusing to be silenced. Why had they asked about it?

The thought wouldn't leave her alone, so she made her way to the gun safe, each step weighed down by a growing sense of dread. Her heart raced as she punched in the code, the sound of the lock disengaging louder than usual. The door swung open, and LuLu's breath caught in her throat.

The gun was gone.

LuLu's hands flew to her face, her fingers trembling as she reached into the gun safe, searching frantically as if the missing weapon might magically appear. But it was gone. The realization hit her like a punch to the gut. The room spun, her vision narrowing as her breath came in short, desperate gasps. She couldn't breathe. Her chest tightened, a crushing weight bearing down on her lungs. Her legs buckled, and she collapsed to the floor, her phone slipping from her grasp.

She started coughing, gagging as she crawled toward her phone, her vision blurring with each ragged breath. Her fingers shook uncontrollably as she typed in her password, the screen refusing to unlock with her face. Panic surged through her as she paused, gasping for air, unsure who to call. She dialed Sasha's number, her heart pounding in her ears. Voicemail. She couldn't bring her into this. Her breath hitched, and she hung up, her breaths coming faster, each one more painful than the last.

Sweat poured down her face, mixing with the tears that burned her eyes, streaking down her cheeks in fiery trails. Gasping for breath, her body betrayed her as she was on fire. She needed air; she needed her emergency meds—but she couldn't think, couldn't focus. In a blind panic, she dialed Silas.

He answered on the first ring, "Hello?"

"Help. I..." LuLu choked out before the darkness closed in, swallowing her whole. Her body went limp, and the last thing she heard was Silas's frantic voice, yelling her name, "LuLu, LuLu, talk to me..."

But she couldn't. The world faded to black as she fell unconscious, her body giving in to the overwhelming terror.

The darkness surrounded LuLu as she stood in the black room, the only light coming from two spotlights illuminating a pair of chairs. She could hear footsteps echoing in the void, her heart pounding as a figure emerged and sat down. Ryan—or at least what remained of him—emerged and sat down. He waved her forward, and despite the gnawing fear, she felt an irresistible pull to approach.

As she moved closer, the stench hit her like a wall—an overpowering miasma of rotting flesh, bile, and excrement.

It clung to the air, thick and choking, as if the very essence of decay had taken on a life of its own. Flies buzzed around his decomposing form, their wings flickering in the dim light as they swarmed the gaping, festering bullet wounds that marred his grotesque body. The suit he once wore was now a grotesque second skin, fused with his decaying flesh, oozing a sickly yellow pus that dripped in slow, nauseating rivulets. His skin sagged and split open in places, revealing raw, maggot-riddled flesh beneath, as if his entire body was slowly liquefying into a pool of putrid slime. The sight of him was a living nightmare, a creature born from the deepest pits of hell, a twisted, melting abomination that defied all reason and sanity.

"What do you want?" LuLu demanded, her voice steady despite the revulsion twisting her gut. She forced herself to stare at the grotesque creature before her, refusing to look away from the nightmare that had crawled out of some unspeakable corner of hell. Ryan, or what had once been Ryan, let out a chilling laugh, exposing rows of rotting yellow teeth.

He stopped laughing abruptly, his dead eyes locking onto hers. LuLu's gaze narrowed, the tension between them thick in the air.

"Looking for this?" he rasped, lifting LuLu's father's gun in one slimy hand. Her eyes darted to the weapon, then to the cellphone in his other hand.

"Seems like you're losing it, LuLu. Losing it, LuLu, Losing it, LuLu," he chanted, his voice a sinister echo.

"You're just a dream," LuLu shouted, defiance flaring in her chest. The monster cocked his head to the side, confusion briefly clouding his decayed features.

"Am I?" he taunted, his voice dripping with malice. "If

I'm not, then I ask again, what do you want?" LuLu sneered, her fear turning to anger.

"I want you to think. I want you to think," he hissed, pointing a bony finger behind him toward a door that hadn't been there before. Compelled, LuLu walked to the door, her hand trembling as she grasped the handle. Just as she turned it, Ryan opened his mouth, but instead of words, a loud beeping noise filled the air.

Beep, beep, beep. LuLu's eyes fluttered open. She felt strange, disoriented. Her arm was heavy, and when she looked down, she saw an IV line snaking from it. They hooked a nasal cannula around her face, delivering oxygen to her lungs. The beeping continued, coming from a monitor beside her.

She wasn't in a hospital bed, but the softest bed she'd ever laid in, surrounded by walls adorned with tasteful art in shades of gray, black, and silver. The bed was massive, easily as large as her entire bedroom. Beside her, Silas slept in a chair, his body slumped awkwardly half on the bed, half off.

As she shifted, he stirred, his eyes snapping open. The moment he realized she was awake, he shot up, rushing out of the room. He returned quickly with an older man dressed in a lab coat and scrubs.

"Am I in the hospital?" LuLu croaked, her throat dry.

"No," Silas replied, his tone firm. "You're at my house. I have a private doctor on staff. He's been taking care of you here." Silas glanced at the doctor, a silent command to explain further.

"You had a severe anxiety attack, Ms. Pillar," the doctor began, his voice calm and measured. "I reviewed your medical history and consulted with your regular physician,

Dr. Clover. We believe a few adjustments to your medication, along with more rest, will help. I'm prescribing some changes and recommending bed rest for at least 24 hours. Do you understand?"

"Yes, once I'm home..." LuLu started, but Silas cut her off.

"You'll stay here until you're well," Silas's voice was firm, brooking no room for protest.

LuLu opened her mouth to object, but the intensity of his gaze made the words die on her lips. She felt a heavy knot form in her stomach; the realization dawning that Silas was not just concerned—he was angry, and this was not a battle she was going to win. The air in the room thickened, charged with unspoken tension. Sensing the shift, the doctor quietly excused himself, leaving the two of them alone.

Silas lingered for a moment, his eyes never leaving her. Then, with a sigh, he crossed the room and sat on the edge of the bed beside her. The mattress dipped slightly under his weight, the closeness of his presence both comforting and disconcerting.

"How are you?" he asked, his voice softer now, but still carrying the weight of his earlier command.

"I'm... okay," LuLu answered, her voice a faint echo of its usual strength. "How did I get here?"

Silas' voice was calm but firm as he began explaining, his eyes holding LuLu's gaze steadily. "You called me, sounding like you were in a dangerous place. I came over with Heath, and luckily, Max and Nina were just across the street. They let us in, and we got you into the car. Max called Sasha, and she picked up Doodle."

LuLu nodded, her voice soft with gratitude. "Thank you. I didn't mean to worry you."

Silas acknowledged her words with a nod, though the serious expression on his face didn't waver. "It's okay," he replied, his tone measured but carrying a weight of concern. He paused, taking a deep breath before continuing. "Here's the deal: we're going to have a fight, but not now—not while you're recovering. We'll revisit this tomorrow. For now, you need to focus on resting."

He ran a hand through his hair, the tension clear in the way his fingers lingered, pulling slightly before he placed his head in his hands, rubbing his temples. Frustration etched itself into the lines of his face, but he kept his composure. "I know the bar is your responsibility, but Heath filled me in. Matty's going to cover for you. I paid her first paycheck out of my pocket. You can pay me back once we've had our talk tomorrow. Not that you need to, but I know how you are—you'll insist."

LuLu opened her mouth to apologize, guilt washing over her. "I'm sorry for all of this..."

Silas leaned in before she could finish, pressing a gentle kiss to her lips, a gesture that silenced her more effectively than words. When he pulled back, his expression was tender but serious. "Don't be sorry, but we need to talk about ourselves."

The words hung in the air long after he left the room, like a heavy cloud that refused to dissipate. LuLu's heart sank, dread pooling in her chest. She couldn't shake the feeling that this conversation might lead to him leaving her. The fear gnawed at her as the doctor re-entered, bringing her new medication.

He explained the changes, his voice calm and professional, as he removed the IV and handed her the pills. LuLu swallowed them, trying to push down the rising tide of anxiety. The exhaustion was overwhelming, and despite the turmoil churning inside her, she allowed herself to drift into sleep, clinging to the last threads of hope as the darkness claimed her until morning.

Twelve

When LuLu awoke the next morning, the unfamiliar surroundings reminded her of the events from the day before. The oversized T-shirt she wore hung loosely on her frame, the fabric soft against her skin as she slowly eased herself out of the bed. Her stomach growled, a sharp reminder that she had eaten nothing since brunch with Sasha.

She padded quietly across the room in her bare feet, the cool floor beneath her soles as she stepped into a large, sparsely decorated living room. The space was minimalistic, yet everything exuded an air of understated elegance. Curiosity led her to explore further, her gaze taking in the carefully curated art on the walls and the sleek, modern furniture.

Then, a scent hit her—rich, savory, and irresistible. The smell of bacon wafted through the air, pulling her like a magnet towards its source. She felt almost like a cartoon character floating toward the scent of a freshly baked pie cooling on a windowsill. Following the aroma, she made her way to the kitchen, where she found Silas sitting at a table, focused on his laptop with a plate of food in front of him. A middle-aged man, unfamiliar to her, stood at the stove, his back turned as he expertly flipped bacon.

Stepping into the room, LuLu's presence immediately drew both men's attention. Silas looked up from his work, and the man at the stove turned to greet her.

"Hello," she mumbled, feeling a bit out of place.

"Come and sit. Are you hungry?" Silas rose from his chair, pulling one out for her.

"Yes," LuLu replied, her voice tinged with relief. The warmth of his gesture made her feel slightly more at ease.

"I'm making eggs and bacon now, but I can get you something else if you prefer…" the cook offered, his tone friendly and accommodating.

"That sounds great," she replied with a smile. "I'm LuLu, by the way."

"I'm Chase," the man responded, returning her smile before turning back to the stove. "I work security. Heath and I switch off—two weeks on, two weeks off. Mr. Heartly takes wonderful care of us."

As Chase busied himself with the final touches on breakfast, LuLu couldn't help but feel a twinge of guilt. "I didn't get to say goodbye to Heath," she mumbled, glancing at Silas.

"He lives right downstairs," Chase said over his shoulder. "All security lives in the building. Mr. Heartly covers our room and board."

LuLu looked at Silas, who merely shrugged in response, as if to say it was no big deal. Chase placed a plate in front of her, and without hesitation, she ate, her hunger overriding any self-consciousness. The food was delicious, and she devoured it as if she hadn't eaten in days. Chase nodded respectfully to Silas before leaving the kitchen, giving them some privacy.

"How are you feeling?" Silas asked, closing his laptop and folding his hands, his gaze steady and focused on her.

"Better," LuLu said between bites, her mouth still full of food.

Silas watched her for a moment, then leaned forward slightly, his tone shifting to one of concern. "Are you feeling up to talking?"

LuLu paused, setting down her fork. She took a deep breath, meeting his eyes. The weight of the previous day's events hung between them, but she nodded, signaling that she was ready, even though she did not want this to end.

LuLu opened her mouth to speak, but the words caught in her throat. She took a deep breath, trying to steady herself. "I know what you're going to say, and I understand. I will be..."

Before she could finish, Silas cut her off. "I'm not breaking up with you." His tone was firm, leaving no room for misinterpretation. His eyes, usually warm, now narrowed with concern.

"LuLu, what's going on? The police came to my office yesterday. They were asking about you and Ryan." His gaze pierced through her, searching for answers. "I knew he was dead—it was in the papers—but why didn't you tell me they were investigating you?"

The question hit her like a jolt, knocking the wind out of her. LuLu's mind raced, replaying every word he'd just said. She had never been in a relationship where she could be completely honest, where she didn't have to hide parts of herself. But now, faced with Silas's unwavering stare, she knew she couldn't keep it all bottled up.

Her chest tightened as she took another deep breath, preparing herself for what came next. The words tumbled out, each one heavy with the weight of her confession. She told him everything—well, almost everything. She left out the part about the message from Liam and friend Heather, not yet ready to reveal those secrets.

Silas listened intently, his face a mask of concentration. When she mentioned the gun, she noticed him stiffening, his breath hitching slightly. But he didn't interrupt; he just sat there, absorbing every detail she shared.

When she finally finished, the silence that followed was thick with tension. Silas sat motionless, his eyes searching hers as he processed everything she had said. The air between them felt charged, the unspoken words hanging in the balance as they both waited for what would come next.

"You don't know where the gun is? Are you sure you didn't move it?" He asked. She shook her head. "Who knew the code?"

LuLu stared down at her empty plate, her fingers nervously tracing the edges as she quietly confessed, "Me, Sasha, Greg, my parents, and if Greg has it, then probably Annie and Matty, too. And I did something stupid." Her voice faltered as she admitted the last part. Silas, who had been listening intently, sat up straighter at her words. "My mom put the code on a Post-it and kept it under the register. I never threw it away."

Silas exhaled deeply, his head falling into his hands. His face flushed with a mixture of frustration and concern, making it difficult for LuLu to gauge his emotions. She kept her gaze downward, too scared to meet his eyes, her heart pounding in her chest.

After a moment that felt like an eternity, Silas lifted his head, his voice carrying a sharp edge. "You're my girlfriend, LuLu. You need to tell me these things—everything. We can't take care of each other if we're not honest. Start understanding that." His voice grew louder, almost a yell, but instead of cowering, LuLu smiled.

His frustration momentarily broke, replaced with confusion. "Why are you smiling? I'm mad at you."

"You called me your girlfriend," LuLu replied softly, her eyes finally meeting his, a glimmer of warmth in them.

Silas blinked, clearly thrown by her response. "What? Of course you are," he said, still processing.

"We never had 'the talk,'" LuLu added, her voice tinged with a teasing lilt.

"We're not twelve, LuLu. But yes, you're my girlfriend. I'm not seeing anyone else, and I hope the same for you." His tone was firm, but there was a softness in his words that made LuLu's heart flutter.

"Of course," she answered, her voice barely above a whisper.

Silas stood and walked over to her, placing a tender kiss on the top of her head. His scent, a mix of sandalwood and leather, enveloped her, making her want to reach out and pull him closer, but she knew this wasn't the moment.

"I had Chase pick up a few things for you to wear home when you're ready," Silas said, his tone shifting to something more practical. "I have to go to work. Chase will drop you off." He left, but paused at the door. "Don't worry about Heath, by the way. I believe he'll be at your bar on the nights

Matty works." A playful grin tugged at his lips before he turned and left the room.

LuLu watched him go, her mind swirling with thoughts. She walked back to the room she had awoken in and found a pair of sweatpants and a few shirts laid out for her. Slipping into them, she felt a strange mix of comfort and apprehension.

When she emerged, Chase was already waiting by the door. Their conversation during the drive home was light, filled with casual small talk that helped ease some of her lingering anxiety. Once home, LuLu thanked Chase with a nod before stepping inside, the door clicking shut behind her, sealing in the stillness of her apartment. The silence felt almost suffocating, wrapping around her like a heavy blanket. She moved to the couch, sinking into it as if the weight of the world had finally settled on her shoulders. Her phone rested in her hand, the screen glowing softly as she stared at it, heart pounding in her chest. She knew what she had to do, but that didn't make it any easier.

With a deep breath, her thumb hesitated over a contact, her resolve wavering for just a moment before she pressed it. The name "Copper" flashed on the screen, a name she had hoped she would never have to call. Bringing the phone to her ear, she listened to the ringing with a sinking sense of dread, each tone like a drumbeat in her chest. When the line finally clicked, a voice on the other end answered, calm and cool.

"Marc," came the voice, devoid of emotion.

"Detective Marc?" LuLu asked, her voice betraying her nerves.

"Yes. What can I do for you?" His response maintained

the same measured tone as before, but LuLu could sense a shift, a quiet intensity on the other end of the line.

"This is LuLu Pillar. I... I needed to talk to you about something," she started, trying to steady herself.

"Ms. Pillar, yes. What can I do for you?" His tone remained professional, but she could hear the faint rustle as the call switched from the receiver to speaker. More ears were listening now.

"You asked about my .22 before you left the other day. It got me thinking... I don't remember the last time I checked the gun safe. When I opened it up, I realized my .22 was not there. I wanted to report it as soon as possible," LuLu explained, her words tumbling out in a rush. "I just wanted to make sure you knew."

There was a pause on the other end before he responded, "Thank you, Ms. Pillar. I'll make a note of that. You'll need to file a report on the missing gun. Your lawyer should be able to assist you." He paused, his breath audible over the line. "Does Tyme know you're talking to us right now?"

"No. I was going to call her after I spoke with you. I know it's backwards, but I felt it was more important to tell you about the gun than to protect myself," LuLu confessed, her voice small but determined.

Another pause, longer this time. "Ms. Pillar, if you're ever interested in coming down and having a conversation with us, we'll be here."

"Thank you," LuLu replied, though discomfort lingered in her tone. There was an implication in his words, something she couldn't quite grasp.

"Well, thank you, Ms. Pillar. We'll be in touch soon," he

said, his voice final before the line went dead, leaving LuLu staring at her phone, the dial tone echoing in the silence.

Pushing aside the unsettling call, LuLu quickly messaged Matty, letting her know she was home and that the bar would be open as usual. With a deep breath, she called Max and Nina next, her voice steady as she brought them up to speed on everything that had happened.

Soon after, Sasha and Rebecca arrived, Doodle bounding into the apartment with the enthusiasm only a dog could muster. His tail wagged furiously as he found his usual spot on the couch, curling up with a contented sigh. The sight of him, so blissfully unaware of the surrounding chaos, brought a brief, fragile smile to LuLu's lips.

As they all settled in, LuLu hesitated, her stomach knotting as she prepared to tell Sasha and Rebecca about the gun. Rebecca's expression darkened, her tone firm as she gently scolded LuLu, "Next time, you tell me before you do something like that."

Sasha's eyes locked onto LuLu's, her brows knitting together as if the weight of the conversation was too much to bear. Her mouth opened slightly, but no words came out at first—just a shaky breath as she tried to make sense of it all. "I can't believe this is happening," she finally murmured, her voice barely above a whisper, tinged with a mix of disbelief and fear. The question hung in the air between them, unspoken but heavy: "How was it stolen?"

LuLu's shoulders sagged as she shook her head, her voice thick with uncertainty. "I don't know. I don't even know if it's the gun that was used." The admission hung between them, an unsettling truth neither of them wanted to face.

Rebecca's lips pressed into a thin line, a flash of something unreadable crossing her face. The silence that followed was tense, loaded with the weight of unsaid words. LuLu and Sasha turned to Rebecca, both sensing that she held back more than she let on.

Finally, Rebecca exhaled slowly, her voice steady but laced with caution. "He was shot with a .22. The police think it was murder, and they're looking closely at you, Lu. Just... be smart about this." Her eyes bore into LuLu's, as if willing her to understand the gravity of the situation.

LuLu gave a small nod, feeling Sasha's arms wrap around her in a comforting embrace.

"Rebecca's the best lawyer in town. You have nothing to worry about, right, babe?" Sasha's voice was soft, reassuring, but it was clear she was seeking reassurance herself. Rebecca offered a small, tight-lipped smile in response.

The three of them grabbed dinner at the diner across the street, a temporary distraction from the storm brewing around them. But even as they shared a meal, LuLu's mind remained miles away, tangled in thoughts that refused to untangle. After parting ways with Sasha and Rebecca, she found herself alone in her apartment once again, the quiet amplifying the gnawing unease in her gut.

Something wasn't right. The phone. The gun. Every piece of the puzzle felt deliberately placed, yet out of reach. The more she tried to piece it together, the more elusive the answers became. Why was she so fixated on that phone? The question haunted her, circling in her mind like a vulture waiting to descend. LuLu knew one thing: there was someone with answers. And she was going to meet that someone on Friday at midnight.

Thirteen

The week sped by in a blur of activity and distraction. At the bar, Matty quickly proved herself indispensable, her deft handling of the shift and effortless charm making her a hit with the regulars. LuLu couldn't help but marvel at how seamlessly Matty fit into the role—she was exactly the bartender LuLu had hoped for. The thought of Silas being behind this perfect match lingered in the back of her mind, but she firmly pushed it aside. She needed to maintain her boundaries.

Text exchanges with Silas were sporadic, just enough to keep the lines of communication open, but never too personal. His busy schedule meant he was often tied up at the office late into the night, leaving brief visits to the bar as his only respite. When he stopped by, it was usually to drop off work or catch up, his presence a fleeting but welcome distraction.

Heath had carved out a niche of his own among the locals, particularly Max, who had taken a liking to the body-guard's company. The two of them had settled into a routine of playing cards, their laughter and competitive banter adding a dimension to the bar's atmosphere.

Amidst the steady hum of daily life and the comfort of new routines, LuLu pushed thoughts of Ryan to the periphery of her mind. The intensity of the past weeks faded into the background, replaced by the comforting rhythm of bar life. If it hadn't been for her planned rendezvous on Friday, Ryan might have slipped entirely from her thoughts.

He wasn't even haunting her dreams. LuLu thought that might have something to do with meeting with Dr. Clover an extra day and the new medication dosage. Dr. Clover still wanted her to reach out to her hypnotherapist friend. LuLu decided she would after the get together at Ryan's on Wednesday. She had to go. She didn't know why, but she did.

When Friday rolled around, Silas was eager to whisk LuLu away for a night out, but she had to turn him down. For the first time since they'd started seeing each other, she had to tell him she had prior plans. The disappointment in his voice was palpable, but he quickly masked it with an offer for Saturday, encouraging her to stay the night.

LuLu accepted the invitation, though her mind was a whirlwind of thoughts. The idea of spending the night with Silas brought a mix of anticipation and dread. Despite her readiness for this next step, the thought still triggered a wave of anxiety. Silas was everything she wasn't—wealthy, worldly, and experienced. She knew he was confident in their relationship, often reassuring her she could never disappoint him. Yet, her own insecurities loomed large, making her question if she could ever live up to his expectations.

As she considered the upcoming Saturday, she couldn't

shake the feeling that Silas might be just as apprehensive as she was. This relationship was unlike anything she'd experienced before, even more so than with Greg. For once, the thrill of uncertainty mingled with the comforting embrace of what could be.

At 11:00 p.m., LuLu emerged from her apartment, shrouded in all black. Her hair was twisted into a tight bun, a look she'd seen in countless movies depicting midnight rendezvous. The darkness of her outfit and the tightness of her bun were her attempts to blend in with the shadows, to slip past unnoticed. Knowing that the police might have their eyes on her, she moved with purpose, aware that her every move could be scrutinized.

Navigating the backstreets, she relied on her childhood familiarity with Envy's labyrinthine alleys. She darted through familiar paths, the same ones she'd raced through as a child, when freedom extended until dusk. By 11:45, she reached the old Sears building, her pulse quickening.

She glanced around nervously, wishing for the comforting weight of her gun. The sense of vulnerability gnawed at her. As the clock struck midnight, a car rolled into the empty parking lot, its lights off, a specter in the dark. The vehicle glided to a stop in front of LuLu, and the window slid down.

The face that greeted her was one she vaguely recognized, but the transformation was startling. Liam, usually the picture of calm composure, appeared deranged under the moonlight. His hair was a tangled mess, his clothes disheveled and stained from the day's fight. His eyes, wide and unsteady, flickered with fear and something far more primal.

"I'm here. What do you want?" LuLu's voice was steady, though her insides twisted with apprehension.

"I didn't kill him." Liam said. "You do not know. Ryan was an evil man."

"I think I do." LuLu said.

"No, you don't. You need to find his cell phone before the police." He said. "I have been looking, but there is a USB drive too." He was talking so fast and LuLu was getting confused. "You don't understand. He had stuff on all of us. Even you, but he couldn't use it."

"What are you talking about?" LuLu shouted at him and slapped him through the window. His eyes shot wide with shock and pain.

"He had folders on all of us. Why do you think we are all still connected to one another? Annie, Greg, me, Sasha, and you. He has been using it to get things from us for a year. I literally paid every student loan he had."

"Ok. What did he have on me?" LuLu asked, unsure of what she was asking.

"There is a video. That is all I am saying. If you find the phone or the USB drive, it will make sense. Don't trust anyone. He knew who killed him." Liam said.

"How do you know that?" LuLu asked.

Liam flung open the car door and stepped out, his movements frantic. LuLu instinctively took a step back, unease prickling at her skin. As Liam lunged toward her, reaching out with an urgent desperation, she recoiled further, her heart racing.

"Come with me. We have to find it," he yelled, his voice a mix of panic and command.

"I'm not going anywhere with you," LuLu shot back, her voice sharp with defiance.

"If the police find it, everyone's screwed—especially you and your pet. You need to come with me now! You're not the target. I will be safe if you are with me." His frustration boiled over as he closed the distance and seized her arm with a grip that made her cry out involuntarily.

The words burst out of LuLu, her voice shaking with a blend of fury and terror. "Let go of me! I'm not going anywhere with you. I don't even know if I believe you!"

Before Liam could respond, the sharp crack of a gunshot shattered the air, blasting through the car window. The deafening sound reverberated in her skull, leaving her ears ringing. In a heartbeat, Liam's grip loosened, and they both crashed to the ground, the jagged rocks beneath her scraping against her skin, reminding her just how real the danger was.

The sudden sound of approaching headlights made them both jump. Liam's eyes darted to the source, his face contorted with alarm.

"Fuck. Who did you tell?" Liam's voice cut through the night, sharp and frantic.

"No one!" LuLu lied and her shouts reverberated across the empty parking lot, filled with a mix of fear and defiance. Liam's face twisted in frustration as he jerked the car window up with a harsh slam. The engine roared to life, and the tires squealed in protest, spewing a cloud of dust and rubber as he barreled away into the darkness.

LuLu stood alone, the headlights of an approaching car washing over her like a floodlight, making her squint against the brightness. The vehicle came to a halt with a low rumble, and the door creaked open. Heavy footsteps approached, each step echoing ominously against the silent night. Silas's silhouette emerged, his features etched with a fierce scowl.

"What the fuck are you doing here?" Silas's voice, strained with a mix of anger and concern, sliced through the tense air.

"You followed me?" LuLu's voice wavered with shock and frustration, the words tumbling out before she could stop them.

"Thank God I did," Silas responded, his tone thick with relief and irritation.

"I can take care of myself!" LuLu screamed, her voice cracking as the tears she fought to hold back pooled in her eyes.

"You don't have to anymore," Silas yelled back, his voice softening as he hurried towards her. In an instant, he was pulling her into his arms, his embrace wrapping around her like a shield. LuLu's defenses crumbled as she hugged him back, drawing him closer with a desperate grip. The warmth and solidity of his presence overwhelmed her, and the tears she had fought so hard to keep at bay streamed down her face, soaking into his shirt.

Silas guided LuLu to the car with a steady hand, his presence a comforting anchor in the silence that enveloped them. The drive home was quiet, punctuated only by the hum of the engine and the occasional flicker of streetlights through the windows. With no need to ask, Silas navigated the familiar route to her apartment, his intuition guiding him.

When they arrived, he walked her to the door, the weight of the night's events hanging between them. Gently, he wiped the remnants of her tears from her cheeks with his thumbs, his touch tender and reassuring. He pressed soft kisses to both of her cheeks, a gesture of warmth and care.

"Do you want me to stay?" he asked, his voice low and steady.

"No. I'm okay. I think I want to be alone," she replied, her voice trembling slightly as she tried to maintain her composure. Silas nodded, a trace of concern in his eyes.

As he turned to leave, he paused, his expression serious. "Can I see you next weekend? I have a crazy week and I just need to catch my breath with things. I think we need to talk."

LuLu's heart sank at his words. The familiar weight of the phrase pressed down on her, stirring a deep-seated unease. Silas must have seen the change in her expression because he quickly added, "I'm not breaking up with you. I just think we need to have an open conversation about what's really going on. I like you a lot, LuLu, but I don't want to be constantly worried that you're going to get yourself hurt or worse."

LuLu nodded, a lump forming in her throat. Silas leaned in and placed a gentle kiss on her lips before turning to leave. As he walked away, the sound of his footsteps fading, LuLu was left alone at the door. The solitude felt heavier than usual, the sting of disappointment mingling with the quiet. It was a loneliness she knew well, but tonight, it was deeper, sharper—marked by the ache of letting Silas down.

As LuLu stepped into her apartment, the silence seemed to amplify her thoughts. The door clicked shut behind her, and she stood there, staring into the dimly lit space, feeling as though she were drifting through a fog of confusion. She couldn't shake the question that looped through her mind: Why hadn't she told Silas what she was doing?

She had rationalized it to protect him, to keep him out of the mess she was tangled in. But that logic felt thin now, especially when she considered the police involvement. Silas was already entangled in her world, whether she liked it.

Her mind drifted to the patterns of her past, the familiar rhythm of handling things on her own, with no one else's interference. It had always been her way, a solitary path she walked with a stubborn sense of independence. But Silas wanted something more—something different from what she was used to. The realization hit her with an unexpected force.

She leaned against the wall, her breath catching in her throat. The weight of her feelings for Silas pressed down on her, a revelation both thrilling and terrifying. Her heart pounded in her chest, a steady, relentless beat that echoed through her entire being. She was falling for him. Not just a fleeting crush or infatuation, but a deep, consuming feeling she had never experienced before.

In the quiet of her apartment, LuLu stood still, overwhelmed by the enormity of it. The realization was both exhilarating and daunting, a stark contrast to the solitary life she had always known. For the first time in her life, she was facing the raw, vulnerable truth of falling in love.

The sharp buzz from the bar door snapped LuLu out of her thoughts. She sighed, her feet dragging slightly as she walked to open it. Her heart skipped a beat when she saw who stood there, flowers in hand.

Greg. Of all people.

Suppressing a groan, she leaned against the doorframe, her eyes rolling in exasperation. "What do you want, Greg?" she asked, the irritation clear in her voice.

"Just to talk. Nothing more, I swear. Coffee, please?" His voice was almost pleading, but LuLu was having none of it. She shook her head and closed the door, but his hand shot out to stop it. "Five minutes, LuLu. Just five. I need to say this." He put his foot in the closing door.

With a reluctant sigh, she opened the door wider and gestured him in. He thrust the flowers toward her, and she took them with a roll of her eyes, tossing them carelessly onto the bar. She moved behind it, flipping on the coffee machine with a huff.

"Five minutes. Go," she said, crossing her arms.

Greg tried to offer a smile, leaning casually on the bar. "You've changed, LuLu," he said, with a teasing lilt that only made her roll her eyes harder.

"Four minutes and thirty seconds," LuLu shot back, her finger pointing to the timer on her phone.

Greg's apology hung heavy in the air, his voice thick with guilt. "I'm sorry, LuLu. This whole Ryan thing... it made me realize how I used you when I really loved Annie." His words stumbled out, laden with regret.

LuLu's brow furrowed, the uncertainty creeping into her tone. "Okay..." She wasn't sure where this was going, but something about his demeanor unsettled her.

Greg ran a hand over his face, as if trying to wipe away the shame. "I didn't want to. I was stuck in a dangerous situation," he muttered, his voice barely above a whisper.

Her eyes narrowed, suspicion taking root. "Is this about the videos?" she asked, watching as the color drained from Greg's face. His reaction was immediate—like she'd hit him in the gut. He looked stricken, his eyes wide with panic.

"How did you know about those? You were never supposed to know." His voice cracked, desperation lacing every word. "After your parents... after everything, it was the least I could do."

LuLu's confusion deepened. What was he talking about? Liam had mentioned videos, and Ryan had something on them, but this—this was different. "What did he make you do?" Her voice was steady, but her pulse raced as she pressed him.

Greg's eyes filled with tears, his hands trembling. "Please don't ask me that," he whispered, his face crumpling with sorrow.

LuLu's gaze hardened. "What did you do?" she demanded, her voice now cold and unyielding.

Tears streamed down Greg's face as he looked at her, utterly broken. "Please, LuLu. I'm sorry." His voice was hoarse, the words a pitiful plea for forgiveness.

The alarm on her phone blared, its sharp tone cutting through the tense silence. LuLu's expression turned to stone as she pointed to the door. "Get out."

Greg nodded, his face wet with tears as he wiped his eyes. Without another word, he turned and walked out; the door closing behind him with a final, resounding click. LuLu looked up and emailed the hypnotherapist that Dr. Clover recommended.

Fourteen

LuLu typed out an email to the doctor, her fingers moving almost mechanically over the keyboard. But even as she hit "send," her mind was elsewhere, trapped in the loop of her earlier conversation with Greg. His words replayed in her head, each one gnawing at her with a persistence she couldn't shake. He had sounded so sincere, almost desperate in his apologies, but nothing he said seemed to fit together. The more she thought about it, the more tangled everything became.

As she went about the rest of her day, the dissonance of that conversation lingered, casting a shadow over everything she did. Greg's words didn't add up, and the sense of things unraveling grew stronger with each passing hour. It was as if the foundations of her life were shifting beneath her, leaving her unsteady and uncertain.

Her thoughts drifted to Silas. Their relationship had taken on a strange, tense quality lately, the unspoken words between them creating a distance she hadn't expected. The weight of her secrets was becoming too much to bear. If she wanted to salvage what they had, she knew she couldn't keep going like this.

As the day wore on, a decision solidified in her mind. She needed to be honest with Silas, to tear down the walls she had built around herself. It was time to let him in, to show him she could be open and vulnerable. Taking a deep breath, she resolved that the first step toward figuring things out was to start with the truth—no more hiding, no more excuses. It was time to face whatever came next, together.

She sank into the couch, her fingers absently stroking Doodle's soft fur as she stared at her phone. With a deep breath, she finally opened up a text message to Silas. Her fingers hesitated for a moment before she started typing, recounting the unexpected visit from Greg and giving him a summary of their tense conversation.

Once the message was sent, she couldn't help but feel a wave of anxiety wash over her. She held her breath, her eyes glued to the screen, waiting for any sign of a response. The seconds ticked by slowly, each one amplifying the nervous anticipation in her chest. She felt like a teenager all over again, anxiously waiting for those three little dots to appear, signaling that he was typing. Doodle nuzzled her hand, but her focus remained fixed on the phone, her heart pounding as she waited for whatever was going to come next.

Silas's message came through quickly: **Are you ok?**

LuLu's fingers flew over the screen, crafting a response that was both reassuring and honest. To reassure, she sent a series of quick messages, each one conveying that she was fine and there was nothing to worry about. She didn't want him to think she was hiding anything, not anymore. She added one more line, letting him know that she just wanted to be open with him.

Her phone chimed softly, and a single message popped up on the screen—a simple "thank you" followed by a red heart emoji. The small response sent a flutter through her chest, easing some of the tension that had settled there. LuLu stared at the screen, a faint smile creeping onto her lips despite the lingering unease. The doubt gnawed at her, the sense that something was still unresolved between them. But she was determined to show him she could be open, even if it meant shielding him from the darker parts of this mess.

Before heading to bed, LuLu skimmed through her emails, her eyes catching on a new message from her therapist. A list of dates stared back at her, and she quickly settled on the next Thursday morning. It felt like a small step forward, a way to gain some clarity amid the chaos. The lunch meeting was also on her mind—maybe, just maybe, she'd find some answers.

But even as she tried to focus on the positive, Liam's voice echoed in her thoughts, relentless and unnerving. The memory of his hand gripping her wrist flashed through her mind, the sensation so vivid it made her stomach churn. She doubled over, dry heaving, the revulsion nearly overwhelming. There was no escaping it now; the images were too real, too close.

With a shaky breath, she forced herself to climb into bed, pulling the covers tight around her as if they could shield her from the darkness. Sleep came, but it was far from peaceful. Her dreams were plagued with familiar terror, dragging her into another harrowing nightmare that left her tossing and turning in the grip of her fears.

The room was an abyss, swallowing all light except for the door across from her, its outline barely visible in the oppressive darkness. LuLu's breath hitched as she reached for the doorknob, her fingertips trembling. Just as she was about to grasp it, a hand shot out from the shadows, cold and clammy, clamping around her wrist with the strength of a vise.

It was Liam.

But this wasn't the Liam she knew. His face was a grotesque mask of terror, veins bulging hideously under his skin, his eyes sunken and rimmed with dark circles as if he hadn't slept in weeks. His skin clung to his bones, taut and sickly pale, like a corpse pulled from the grave. The stench of decay wafted off him, so potent it made her gag.

His grip tightened, the bony fingers digging painfully into her flesh, sending a jolt of fear through her. "Don't," he rasped, his voice a ghastly croak, as if speaking was tearing his throat apart. "You'll destroy everything."

She tried to pull away, but his strength was inhuman, his fingers like iron shackles around her wrist. "Let me go!" she cried out, panic rising like bile in her throat.

Liam's mouth twisted into a deranged grin, his teeth stained black and rotting, bits of decayed flesh clinging to his gums. He chanted, his voice a horrid sing-song mockery. "It's all falling, falling, falling..."

Her heart pounded as she struggled, but he only pulled her closer, his face inches from hers, his breath rancid and foul. His eyes, wide and bloodshot, wept thick, dark blood, the red streaks carving grotesque paths down his hollow cheeks.

"Let go!" she screamed again, her voice cracking.

But he didn't stop. His chant grew louder, more frenzied, more manic. "It's all falling, falling, falling down. LuLu's broken. Broken down, broken down, broken down..." Blood dripped from his eyes like tears, thick and viscous, mixing with the rot on his face until it seemed like his very flesh was melting away.

"What do you want?" LuLu screamed, her voice shrill with terror.

Liam's grin widened impossibly, the skin at the corners of his mouth splitting, oozing more blood as he whispered, "To protect our poor little LuLu, poor little LuLu, poor little LuLu..."

His voice was a horrific gurgle, wet and thick, as if he was drowning in his own blood. His grip slackened for a moment, and he stepped back, motioning towards the door with a skeletal hand. "I warned you. Wanted you..." he muttered, each word dripping with malice.

Before she could react, blood poured from his eyes, mouth, and ears in torrents. His skin bubbled and hissed, peeling away to reveal raw, bloody muscle beneath. He let out a guttural scream as his body convulsed, twisting in unnatural angles, before collapsing into a writhing, bubbling mass of blood and gore.

The pool of blood spread across the floor, thick and suffocating, the remnants of Liam's form dissolving into it until there was nothing left but the dark, sticky puddle and the echo of his demented song, "Poor little LuLu, poor little LuLu..."

"You protect me?" she spat, disbelief turning to anger.

Sweat streaked with crimson oozed down his face, the droplets trailing over his gaunt, tattered clothes. With a sudden, eerie calm, Liam's grip on her arm loosened, his fingers slipping away as he gestured towards the door. His voice was barely audible, a rasping whisper that sent chills down her spine. "I warned you. Wanted you..."

LuLu's hand hovered over the doorknob, hesitation gripping her as every instinct screamed for her to flee. But before she could move, a grotesque snickering echoed through the room, low and sinister. She whipped around, heart pounding, only to see Liam's body convulsing, then collapsing, as his flesh dissolved into a bubbling pool of blood. It was as if he were melting, his form disintegrating into a thick, dark tide that spread across the floor.

Tap, tap, tap. Liam's decaying hand struck his cellphone with skeletal fingers, his voice twisting into a chilling nursery rhyme, "Time, time, go away. Soon LuLu will be thrown away." His laughter bubbled up from the blood, a sound so twisted and wrong that it reverberated in the suffocating darkness, seeping into her bones.

The pool of blood continued to spread, consuming the remnants of Liam until there was nothing left but the echo of his twisted song lingering in the air like a dark omen.

LuLu's alarm blared, pulling her from the nightmare's clutches. Her eyes flew open and she shot up in bed like a gun went off in her head. Gasping for breath, she rushed to her computer, her fingers trembling as she typed furiously. She had to capture every detail, every horrific image from the dream. There was something there—And she was determined to get as much of it down before her memory failed her.

LuLu's eyes darted over the screen, her pulse quickening with each line she reread. The hurried, jagged words seemed to pulse with a life of their own, the edges of her notes blurring as if they might jump off the page. Her stomach churned with a persistent, gnawing unease that refused to subside. Something hid in the labyrinth of her nightmares—something vital, teetering just out of reach.

She stared at the first set of notes.

Ryan and his cell phone.Need to find the phone.His cloud?

A shiver crawled down her spine. She could almost feel the cold, smooth surface of Ryan's phone in her hand, a puzzle piece that was vital to understanding the picture she was missing.

Her gaze moved to the second dream.

Phone and gun.Find those, you find the killer.

The connection was undeniable. Her breaths grew shallow as she recalled the weight of the gun in the dream, heavy with secret and deadly intent. The phone, the gun—two keys to unlocking the truth.

Finally, her eyes fell on the last set of notes.

The door. I need to go through the door.Time is running out.

The door stood in her mind, looming like a barrier she was terrified of crossing. But the urgency was palpable, pressing against her chest like a ticking clock. She knew, deep in her bones, that whatever was behind that door was crucial, that it held the answers she was so desperately seeking.

LuLu leaned back in her chair, her fingers trembling slightly as they hovered over the keyboard. Her dreams weren't just nightmares—they were a message, a warning. Time was slipping through her fingers, and the truth was buried in the darkness of her subconscious, just waiting to be unearthed.

LuLu's mind was set. Delays were no longer possible because of the lack of time. She took a deep breath and gave the dog a quick pat before heading to her room. She needed to be out early—before anyone else arrived. Even though

Greg had been oddly kind lately, she wasn't willing to risk running into Annie.

Before leaving, she dashed to Nina's cafe, grabbing one of their famous pies. It was a ritual her mother had instilled in her: never show up empty-handed, no matter the reason. With the pie in hand, LuLu hurried back, taking a quick shower and slipping into a simple black dress. She pulled her hair up, glanced at her reflection one last time, and looked up at Heather's address on her phone. The car arrived minutes later, and she was on her way.

When she pulled up in front of the apartment, a strange mix of nerves and determination settled in her stomach. As she walked to the door, she noticed the welcome mat adorned with delicate flowers. It was a slight detail, but she realized it was out of place—something Ryan would never have chosen. She shook off the thought and pressed the bell.

A moment later, the door opened to reveal a stunning woman, every inch of her radiating model-like perfection. The woman's surprise was evident as she took in LuLu's appearance.

"If you're here for the luncheon, you're about two hours early," she remarked, her eyes scanning LuLu from head to toe.

Responding with a polite smile, LuLu said, "I know." "I wanted to come before the crowd. I'm LuLu. Would you mind if I come in?" She held up the pie as a peace offering, hoping it would ease her way in.

The woman hesitated for a brief second before stepping aside and motioning LuLu inside. "I brought a pie," LuLu added, hoping to soften the tension.

The apartment was warm and inviting, filled with an air of cozy luxury. Every item seemed to be the most exquisite and expensive in the market. LuLu couldn't help but notice the artwork on the walls—pieces that were likely worth more than her entire bar. Heather led her to the dining room, offering her a seat before disappearing into the kitchen with the pie. LuLu settled into the chair, her eyes roaming the room, her thoughts swirling as she prepared for what came next.

Heather returned, balancing two steaming mugs of coffee in her hands. She handed one to LuLu, who accepted it with a polite smile, her fingers wrapping around the warm ceramic.

"We take our coffee black here," Heather said, her tone flat and unyielding, as if there was no room for debate.

"That's perfect," LuLu responded, her smile tightening as she tried to match Heather's detached demeanor.

Heather's eyes studied LuLu for a moment before she spoke again, her voice laced with an almost knowing curiosity. "So, what brings you here so early? Trying to avoid someone?"

LuLu shifted slightly in her seat, the question hitting closer to home than she'd expected. "I'm not sure what Ryan told you, but we knew each other in college. I guess you could say I was part of his friend group. I was engaged to Greg." She paused, watching as a flicker of recognition crossed Heather's face. "But you already knew that, didn't you?"

Heather nodded, her expression unreadable. "I've heard them talk about you from time to time. I always thought you were an ex-girlfriend of Ryan's as well as Greg's, but Ryan would never talk to me about you."

LuLu nodded in acknowledgment, sensing the tension thickening between them. She quickly tried to steer the conversation in a different direction. "How are you holding up? With his death, I mean."

Heather's façade cracked slightly, her voice softer, more vulnerable. "I'm not great. I miss him every day. Annie and Greg have been over almost every day. They're helping me clean and organize his things. I'm just not ready to get rid of anything yet."

"That's nice of them," LuLu said, forcing herself to sound sincere as she took a sip of her coffee, the bitterness grounding her. She hesitated, knowing she needed to ask but dreading the answer. "I have to ask, and I'm sorry if this is hard, but... was it suicide?"

Heather froze, the color draining from her face as her eyes grew glassy with unshed tears. "They've declared it a murder. Liam has been missing since. What if something happened to him, too? He was Ryan's best friend." Her voice cracked, and tears spilled down her cheeks.

LuLu reached out instinctively, placing a hand on Heather's shoulder, but Heather quickly brushed it off. She stood, grabbing a tissue from a nearby box, and dabbed at her eyes before forcing a smile, though it didn't reach her eyes.

Heather's voice quivered slightly as she spoke, her words carrying the weight of unresolved grief. "It's just so hard to understand. He was such an amazing man... Who would want to do this?"

A shudder rippled through LuLu, the word "amazing" twisting like a thorn in her mind. The idea of someone describing him that way felt like a foreign concept, unsettling and wrong. She fumbled for something comforting to say, but nothing came to mind. Instead, she forced a small, tight-lipped smile and asked, "May I use your restroom?"

Before Heather could respond, a knock echoed through the apartment, signaling more guests. LuLu noted the subtle tension in Heather's posture as she glanced toward the door.

"Yes, it's the first door on the left," Heather instructed, her finger pointing down the hallway.

LuLu nodded, rising from her seat with an air of nonchalance. She walked down the hall; her steps steady and unhurried, but instead of turning into the restroom, she made a sharp left and slipped into the master bedroom.

The room was a testament to wealth, with a king-sized bed dominating the space, flanked by handcrafted furniture that spoke of meticulous taste and deep pockets. LuLu's gaze swept over the room, absorbing every detail, every clue that might reveal more about Ryan and his life.

She hurried, her heart pounding as she opened the closet. It was perfectly divided, one side filled with Heather's delicate dresses and blouses, the other with Ryan's suits and scrubs. The precision of it all made her uneasy, as if his life had been compartmentalized even in death.

Ignoring the growing sense of unease, LuLu began rifling through the pockets of Ryan's suits, her fingers moving swiftly, methodically. But each pocket came up empty, yielding nothing but more questions. She turned her attention to a few boxes stacked neatly on his side of the closet, her curiosity urging her forward.

LuLu shut the closet door quietly, her mind racing as she crossed over to the dresser. With quick, nimble fingers, she opened each drawer, feeling beneath the wooden bottoms, hoping for something, anything, that might reveal a secret. She didn't know what she was searching for, but the urgency in her gut told her there was some-thing to find.

As she peered under the bed, the absolute emptiness surprised her. Not a single speck of dust, not a stray shoe or forgotten item—just pristine cleanliness. The immaculate state of the room made her feel suddenly self-conscious about her own apartment. She considered herself tidy, but this was a different level of perfection, almost unsettling in its precision.

LuLu scanned the room again, thinking strategically. Ryan wouldn't hide something in an obvious place. He wasn't an obvious person. Her eyes fell on the wood paneling that lined the room, a subtle detail that might have gone unno-ticed by anyone else. Dropping to her hands and knees, she began pressing on each panel, her breath held in anticipation.

Finally, one small section gave way with a soft click. Carefully, she pried the panel loose, revealing a hidden compartment. Reaching into the dark space, her fingers brushed against something cold and metallic. Her nail tapped it with a faint, tinny sound. She pulled it out—a small, unassuming mint tin.

The murmur of voices grew louder in the hallway, making LuLu's heart race. She scrambled to replace the panel and, with a quick glance over her shoulder, slipped into the bathroom attached to the bedroom. She edged the door open just enough to hear, her breath shallow and rapid.

Heather's voice drifted in first, tinged with confusion. "Everyone seems to arrive early," she said, rifling through the dresser.

"Oh?" Annie replied, her tone flat and unengaged.

"LuLu's here too," Heather continued.

"LuLu? Really?" Annie's voice carried an icy edge. The pause that followed was thick with an unspoken judgment. "She was just a tag-along, you know. The poor friend who's always around to keep things grounded."

Heather's response was softer, almost apologetic. "She's in the bathroom now."

"Oh," Annie's reply was curt, dismissive. The sound of their footsteps faded as they left the room.

LuLu waited until she could no longer hear them, then crept out from her hiding spot. She quickly tucked the tin into her pocket and edged toward the door. Pressing her ear against the wood, she listened for any sign of their return. When the hallway remained silent, she cracked the door open, only to find Annie standing right outside, her gaze sharp and accusing.

"Caught you," Annie said, her eyes narrowing with suspicion.

LuLu's pulse quickened, but she forced herself to stay calm. "I thought the bathroom was in here," she said, her voice steady but tight. "I heard you coming, so I just used this one. Annie, I don't want any trouble."

Annie's scrutinizing gaze lingered before a slow, calculated smirk spread across her face. "Listen, with Ryan's death and everything, I just want to put this to bed. Call it waving the white flag. I just hate you. I'm sorry, but I do. You literally had everything I wanted, and you were poor. I just don't get it. But Greg loves me," she said. "I will not blow up your spot, so just leave. Consider it a favor for me being a bitch at my engagement party." With that, she turned and joined Heather.

LuLu's shoulders slumped in relief as she slipped out the door and hurried away, her heart still pounding in her chest.

LuLu didn't need to be told twice. She hurried out of the apartment, her heart still racing, and walked as far as she could before calling for a car. As she sat in the backseat, her fingers wrapped around the tin in her pocket. She gave it a gentle shake, hearing something rattle inside. But this wasn't the time to investigate further.

Back at the bar, she finally allowed herself to open the tin. Inside was a small USB drive, its dull surface unremarkable yet brimming with potential. She held it up, turning it over in her fingers before grabbing her laptop and plugging it in.

The screen flashed, asking for a password to decrypt the files. "Shit," she muttered under her breath, closing the laptop with a sigh. She knew she was out of her depth here and needed help—Silas was the only one she trusted with this.

Determined to regain some semblance of normalcy, LuLu opened the bar for the night. The routine would ground her, at least for a little while. As the evening wore on, Matty walked in with Heath, the two of them laughing and chatting at the bar. LuLu watched them for a moment, wondering if this might actually be a date, though she didn't dare ask. For now, it was enough just to observe, to let the ordinary moments distract her from the extraordinary mess she was entangled in.

Max swaggered into the bar with his usual self-assured grin, sliding into his favorite seat like he was royalty taking his throne. The banter between him and LuLu flowed effortlessly, like a well-rehearsed comedy routine, their laughter punctuated by the clink of glasses. Everything was just as it should be until Silas and Chase entered. Silas, with his commanding presence, seemed to have walked straight out of a magazine cover, causing LuLu's excitement to bubble over, though a small cloud of anxiety loomed because of their recent spat.

Silas slid into his usual seat at the far end of the bar, his gaze locking onto LuLu's like they were in some kind of sappy romance movie. LuLu, trying to appear nonchalant, poured his drink with the precision of a trained bartender. As she slid the glass towards him, Silas grabbed her hand with the smoothness of a practiced magician and yanked her down for a quick, electrifying kiss. The kiss was so sudden it might as well have come with a "Surprise!" banner.

"Hi," Silas said, his voice dripping with charming mischief.

"Hi," LuLu replied, her cheeks turning a shade of red that might have been mistaken for a tomato.

"Get a room, you two!" Heath bellowed from his seat, slapping the table with the force of a drum major. Max's laughter erupted, so explosive it almost made him topple off his chair.

Silas, never one to shy away from a challenge, shot back with a cheeky grin, "Speak for yourself, my friend. I thought this was a bar, not a nunnery." His eyes sparkled with mischief, and Max's laughter doubled, spilling over with unrestrained glee.

As the night wore on, the steady stream of customers dwindled until only LuLu and Silas remained. He packed up, his movements efficient and methodical. LuLu, hovering near the bar, tried to muster the words she needed.

"So, I need..." She hesitated, her mouth opening and

closing like a fish out of water. The word "help" seemed to be stuck in her head.

Silas glanced at her with a knowing smirk. "You need…?" he prompted.

"You're going to make me say it, aren't you?" she challenged, her eyes narrowing.

He nodded, a playful twinkle in his eye. "Yep."

Taking a deep breath, LuLu finally managed, "I need your help."

Silas grinned, his satisfaction clear. "That wasn't so hard, was it?"

LuLu shot him a look that could have frozen lava. "Never mind."

Silas raised his hands in mock surrender. "Sorry, it's just nice to be needed. What can I help you with?"

LuLu walked over to him, reaching into her pocket with a hint of trepidation. She pulled out the small USB drive and placed it on the bar between them. Silas picked it up, turning it over in his fingers with interest.

"Okay, what do you want me to do with this?" he asked, his curiosity piqued.

"Don't be mad," LuLu began, her voice betraying her nerves. Silas's eyes narrowed in anticipation.

"I always love when a story starts with that phrase," he said, leaning in slightly.

"I went to Ryan's apartment and met his girlfriend. While I was there, I, uh, explored a bit. I found a hidden panel in their bedroom. Inside it was a Mentos tin, and in that was this USB. I tried to open it, but it's encrypted," she explained, her words tumbling out in a rush.

Silas's eyebrows climbed. "So, let me get this straight. You went to the apartment of the murdered man, broke into his room, swiped potential evidence, and now you want me to hack the encryption on this drive to see what's on it?" His tone was a mix of disbelief and amusement. LuLu winced at his blunt restatement.

He sighed, taking the USB from her. "Give it to me."

She handed it over, and Silas slipped it into his bag with a practiced ease. As he finished packing up, LuLu watched him, her gaze softening.

Before he left, Silas glanced at her. "Saturday. You're staying over?"

LuLu walked up to him, her resolve firm. She wrapped her arms around his waist, pulling him close. Silas looked down, their faces inches apart. LuLu pressed her lips to his, and a spark of electricity leaped between them. Silas's hands gripped her shirt, pulling her into him with a fervor that made her pulse race.

When he finally let her go, his smile was warm and knowing. "I'll take that as a yes," he said, turning to leave.

LuLu watched him go, a mix of satisfaction and longing in her eyes.

Fifteen

LuLu's phone buzzed, dragging her from the depths of sleep. She groaned, squinting at the screen, which glowed with Rebecca's name. The early hour made her head throb, but she swiped to answer.

Rebecca's voice crackled through the line. No pleasantries in sight. "Care to explain why you were at Ryan's girlfriend's place yesterday?"

LuLu blinked, her mind racing. "I went to pay my respects," she said, her tone as smooth as she could manage. She was getting better at this—too good, maybe.

Rebecca's sigh was sharp, cutting through the silence. "The police didn't buy it. They're not thrilled with your brief visit. LuLu, you need to back off. You're making my job harder."

LuLu's pulse quickened. "So, I'm a suspect now?"

"Yes. Your name has come up as a person of interest," Rebecca replied, her voice steady but edged with frustration. "I've told the detectives they need to go through me for any interviews with you. I need to know what you're doing before you do it, okay?"

LuLu swallowed, her mouth dry. "Okay."

"Good. I'll call you if anything comes up." With that, Rebecca hung up, leaving LuLu staring at her phone, her heart pounding.

The weight of the conversation settled over her like a heavy blanket, suffocating and inescapable. The idea of facing her hypnotherapy session today made her stomach churn, but she knew she couldn't cancel. She needed to push through, to find out what Ryan was trying to tell her in those haunting dreams. She needed answers, and she needed peace. For both their sakes.

LuLu strolled into Nina's cafe, the familiar chime of the doorbell marking her entrance. She slid into a booth, and Nina soon joined her, a welcoming smile on her face. Over a steaming cup of coffee and a generous slice of cake, LuLu reminded Nina about the upcoming Saturday night. "Max and you are dog-sitting Doodle," she said, her voice light with anticipation. Nina's eyes sparkled as she nodded enthusiastically. "We're thrilled to have him. He's a joy."

Leaning forward, Nina's expression grew more sincere. "I'm thrilled for you, LuLu. And don't forget—bring your mystery man around sometime. We'd love to meet him."

"LuLu chuckled, a faint blush coloring her cheeks. "I promise I will."

With the promise made, LuLu made her way to her therapy session. The walk to Dr. Leaks' office was pleasant, the crisp air invigorating. As she approached the building, she was pleasantly surprised. It was a charming brick structure with ivy climbing its walls—a far cry from the sterile, clinical spaces she had imagined.

Inside, the double doors led LuLu into a softly lit lobby, where the subtle aroma of lavender and freshly brewed coffee greeted her senses, soothing her nerves. She took the stairs to the second floor, her footsteps softened by plush carpeting. As she reached Dr. Leaks' office, the cozy, tastefully decorated reception area invited her to relax, its warmth and comfort a stark contrast to the tension swirling within her.

When Dr. Leaks finally appeared, he cut an elegant figure with his tall, slender frame and composed demeanor. His calm smile softened his features, instantly easing LuLu's nerves. His Southern drawl, rich and velvety, wrapped around her like a warm, reassuring embrace.

He guided her into his office, where the soft glow of warm lighting and the earthy palette of browns and greens created a cocoon of tranquility. The faint buzz of a white noise machine, nearly imperceptible, wove a gentle, soothing hum through the room, enhancing the serene atmosphere.

Dr. Leaks took a delicate string and wrapped it around LuLu's wrist with careful precision. "This," he said, "is your lifeline. If you need to return, just pull on this string, and it'll bring you back."

He began speaking in a slow, rhythmic cadence that flowed like a gentle lullaby, walking her through the process of hypnosis with a soothing assurance that felt both professional and comforting. As LuLu reclined on the plush couch, its soft embrace enveloping her, she closed her eyes and focused on her breathing, allowing the room's peaceful ambiance to wash over her.

"Breathe in deeply, LuLu, and then slowly exhale," Dr. Leaks' voice was smooth and even, guiding her into a state of relaxation. "With each breath, let go of any tension in your body. Feel it melt away, starting from the top of your head, down to your toes."

As LuLu followed his instructions, she felt her muscles gradually loosen, her breath deepening as her mind drifted. Dr. Leaks continued to speak, his words becoming a gentle rhythm in her mind.

"Now, I'm going to count backwards from ten. With each number, you'll feel yourself sinking deeper, letting go of the outside world, and drifting into a place of calm and focus," he instructed.

"Ten... nine... eight..." His voice was like a soft lullaby, each number drawing her further away from the present, pulling her into a quiet, inner world. Her breaths became slower, her awareness narrowing to the sound of his voice and the steady beat of her own heart.

"Seven... six... five..." The surrounding room blurred, the edges of her perception softening. She felt as if she were floating, weightless, as though she were gently sinking into a warm, comforting embrace.

"Four... three... two..." Dr. Leaks' voice seemed to come from a distance now, an anchor tethering her to a state of deep relaxation. The sounds of the outside world faded entirely, replaced by the steady rhythm of her breathing and the soothing cadence of his words.

"One..."

The final number seemed to echo, reverberating in the quiet of her mind. And then there was silence. A profound stillness enveloped her, like the calm at the center of a storm. She was aware, yet detached, her mind floating in a sea of calm.

"Now, LuLu," Dr. Leaks' voice came through the silence,

steady and reassuring, "I want you to imagine a door. It can be any color, any shape. This door represents a part of your mind that holds the answers you seek. Tell me what you see."

In the darkness of her mind, a door materialized—a sturdy, brown wooden door, standing alone in a vast, black void. She could feel its presence, solid and tangible, even though she knew it was a creation of her subconscious.

"A door," she murmured, her voice sounding distant and dreamlike.

"Good. I want you to walk towards it, and when you're ready, open it," Dr. Leaks instructed, his voice a guiding light in the dark.

She moved towards the door, but as her hand reached for the knob, an icy grip tightened around her wrist. A shiver ran down her spine as she turned to see Liam's ghostly form, his eyes locking onto hers with a look of sinister intent. Her heart raced, panic clawing at the edges of her mind, threatening to break the calm.

"Tell me what's happening, LuLu," Dr. Leaks' voice was steady, pulling her back from the brink of fear.

"Liam... he's stopping me. He's got me," she whispered, her breath coming in short, panicked bursts.

"He has no power over you here. This is your space, your mind. He cannot hurt you," Dr. Leaks reminded her, his voice firm yet soothing.

She stared at Liam, his grip like ice around her wrist. "You have no power over me," she whispered, the words trembling on her lips. But as she repeated them, her voice grew stronger, more resolute. "This is my mind. You have no power here."

Liam's expression twisted into a grotesque sneer, his

face contorting unnaturally before it liquefied, the skin sagging and sliding off his skull as though melting in slow motion. His features distorted into a nightmarish blend of crimson and shadows, pooling together and collapsing into a thick, viscous substance that clung to the floor. The goo pulsated, throbbing with a life of its own as it slithered toward her, a grotesque, blood-red tide that left a trail of putrid slime in its wake.

The sight of it crawling closer sent a surge of terror through her, every instinct screaming to flee, but she forced herself to focus on the door. Her hand trembled violently as she reached for the knob, the cold metal slick against her sweaty palm. The crimson mass oozed faster, tendrils stretching out to grasp at her feet, the stench of decay filling the air as it closed in.

With a desperate cry, LuLu yanked the door open and threw herself through, the last tendrils of the monstrous goo barely missing her as they recoiled, hissing, from the threshold.

The familiar setting of the Delta Nu house materialized around LuLu, each detail vivid and sharp. She knew exactly where she was: the graduation party. The music throbbed in her ears, a pulsating beat that reverberated through the walls as she moved through the crowded rooms, unseen and unnoticed, like a phantom revisiting her own past.

She drifted through the house, weaving between clusters of people, until she spotted him—Liam. Instinctively, she followed, her movements fluid, almost dreamlike, as though she were gliding on air. It felt surreal, like watching a film of her life, but she was both observer and participant.

"Everyone get together! We need to get a picture!" Ryan's voice cut through the noise, his arm looping around

Sasha's waist as he pulled her close. The memory of herself rolled her eyes, but she joined the group, squeezing in for the inevitable selfie. Ryan's arm extended to capture them all.

As the camera clicked, something caught her eye—a figure lurking at the edge of the scene. Her heart skipped a beat as she noticed the grotesque form of Ryan, but not as she remembered him. He was decayed, bloated, more creature than man, his flesh sagging like melted wax. He leered at her with a sickening grin, and as his gnarled hand beckoned, she felt an icy dread crawl down her spine. Despite the terror clawing at her insides, she found herself compelled to follow.

"You found me," it hissed, its voice like nails scraping over glass. The creature slithered down the hallway, and as they moved, the surrounding party dissolved, the lively chatter and music fading into a haunting silence. They passed open doorways, each one revealing a disturbing tableau.

In one room, she saw Annie and Greg, their bodies contorting and bouncing off each other in a grotesque parody of intimacy. Annie's screams were otherworldly, inhuman, and when they noticed her, their heads twisted unnaturally, eyes locking onto her with eerie precision as she and the creature slid by.

The next room revealed Sasha and Ryan locked in a vicious argument, their voices muted, but their expressions full of rage. Further down, another room showed Heather and Ryan seated on ornate furniture, their eyes following her just like the others, empty and devoid of warmth.

Finally, they reached the last room. The creature halted and gestured for her to enter. She hesitated, hearing Dr.

Leaks' voice, a distant reminder that she wasn't alone, that she was safe. But the pull of the past was too strong, and she stepped inside.

Now outside of her own body, she watched as the scene unfolded before her: Liam was on top of her, his movements brutal and unforgiving as he assaulted her. With pain etched across her face and blood staining the sheets, she watched herself wake briefly. She tried helplessly to fight before slipping back into unconsciousness. She could hear her little cries. The horror of it twisted her insides, and she looked away, repulsed.

But then she saw him—Ryan, in the corner, his phone in hand. He was filming her, a sick voyeuristic thrill clear in his movements. He directed Liam with a disgusting glee, treating her suffering like some twisted film project.

Suddenly, the air was sucked out of the room, and LuLu gasped, struggling for breath as the walls closed in, the darkness thickening around her. Dr. Leaks' voice broke through, counting steadily, pulling her back. The blackness swallowed the scene, and she felt herself being yanked out of the nightmare, dragged back into the safety of reality.

Her eyes fluttered open, and there was Dr. Leaks, his concerned face hovering above her.

"That was excellent. Few can break through their barriers on the first try," he said, his tone gentle but firm. "I'd love to shedu—"

"Thank you, doctor, but I have to go," LuLu interrupted, her voice shaky as she bolted upright, her mind racing. She had to get out, and had to find the answers she needed. Without another word, she rushed out of the office, leaving Dr. Leaks behind. Her only thought on getting to Silas and uncovering the truth he held.

LuLu headed back to the bar to find Matty, hoping she'd be up for running things in her absence. Matty's eyes lit up with eagerness at the prospect, and LuLu felt a weight lift off her shoulders, knowing the bar would be in expert hands.

She stepped out for a moment, dialing the bar's number and firing off a quick text to Silas. She needed answers about the USB drive, the gnawing curiosity turning into a desperate need. His reply was quick and to the point:

Silas: You literally gave it to me last night. Not ready yet.

With a huff of frustration, she tossed her phone onto the couch. The tension in her body was palpable, and even Doodle sensed it, opting to retreat to the bedroom to escape her owner's stormy mood. LuLu's mind raced, trying to piece together the puzzle. Liam was definitely hiding something—his fear of being caught for the rape was clear, but there was a deeper, more intense fear lurking behind his eyes that she couldn't quite grasp.

The phone buzzed again. Silas wanted to know if she was up for spending the entire weekend together. Without hesitation, she shot a text to Nina, asking if she could take care of Doodle for the extra day. Nina's enthusiastic response came almost immediately, her excitement clear. With everything falling into place, LuLu confirmed with Silas, a mix of anticipation and nervous energy coursing through her.

Tonight was going to be the night. The realization hit her with a mixture of nerves and excitement. She was finally ready, and the thought of the new lingerie and nightgown Sasha had practically forced her to buy brought a shy smile to her lips.

The bar hummed with life that night, another successful

evening with the college crowd coming and going. Max and Heath were engrossed in a card game, their banter adding to the lively atmosphere. Despite the noise and the bustle, LuLu's thoughts were elsewhere, on the plans she had for the weekend, and the anticipation of what was to come.

Sixteen

LuLu woke up the next morning with a flutter of excitement in her chest, nerves dancing alongside it. This weekend was going to be different. It was time to take a big step forward with her boyfriend, something that made her feel a mix of anticipation and hope—a rare feeling that maybe, just maybe, things were finally going right in her life. She needed this distraction, something to push the dark thoughts of Ryan and his death far away.

She packed Doodle's favorite toys into a bag, scooped him up, and made her way to the diner. The familiar clink of dishes and the scent of freshly brewed coffee greeted her as she stepped inside. Doodle, as always, became the center of attention, receiving endless pats and treats from the regulars. LuLu watched with a soft smile, feeling a swell of gratitude for the good people in her life who treated her and Doodle like family. She assured them they could reach her anytime, even though she knew she was leaving him in safe hands.

By the time she got back to the bar, she was surprised to see Chase standing outside, waiting.

"Chase?" LuLu called out.

"Yes. Hello. I'm here to pick you up whenever you're ready," he replied, his tone formal. "Mr. Heartly would like to extend an invitation for you to settle into his apartment until he finishes work, if you'd like."

She couldn't help but smirk at his overly polite demeanor. "You don't have to be so formal, Chase. I'll grab my stuff."

After grabbing her bag, she found Chase already holding the door open for her to climb into the car. As much as she appreciated the gesture, the idea of being waited on like this always made her uncomfortable.

When they arrived at the building, Chase led her into the apartment and then quietly excused himself, retreating to the security room. LuLu wandered into the main bedroom, memories of her first night there flashing through her mind. The last time she was here, she'd been so sick she could barely move, holed up in the guest room. But now, exploring the main bedroom felt like stepping into a whole new world.

The bathroom connected to the master bedroom caught her attention, and she couldn't help but gasp. The bathtub was enormous, easily the size of her bed, with a multi-head shower that looked more like something out of a luxury spa. She dropped her bag on the bed and turned on the TV, which nearly covered an entire wall of the bedroom. The living room was equally impressive, with another massive TV and a wraparound couch big enough to seat a dozen people. The dining room and kitchen were equally extravagant, with a cozy breakfast nook that reminded her of the last time she was here.

Deciding to make the most of her time, she headed straight for the jetted tub. Filling it took nearly twenty minutes. The tub was so large, but it was worth the wait. She found a bottle of bubbles under the sink and couldn't help but giggle at the thought of Silas sitting in the tub, surrounded by a mountain of bubbles.

She let the music from the living room TV play softly in the background as she melted into the warm water, the tension of the past days slipping away. What felt like just a few minutes later, a gentle knock on the bathroom door woke her from a peaceful, unintentional nap.

"LuLu?" Silas's voice sliced through the haze of sleep, dragging her back to consciousness. He leaned casually against the vanity, an amused smirk playing on his lips as he looked down at her.

"Shit," she muttered, fumbling to get out of the tub, but her foot slipped on the wet porcelain, sending her splashing back into the water.

Silas chuckled, grabbing a towel and holding it out to her. "Here, let me help you." LuLu carefully stepped out, wrapping herself in the towel, her cheeks burning with embarrassment.

"I just fell asleep like an idiot," she mumbled, avoiding his gaze.

He gave her a reassuring smile. "I'll give you a minute to get dressed. I brought Italian food, but we can go out if you'd rather."

LuLu shook her head, grateful for the outcome. "Eating in sounds great."

"Alright, I'll be in the other room," he said, leaving the bathroom.

As the door closed behind him, LuLu exhaled sharply. "Shit, shit, shit," she whispered, trying to gather her scattered thoughts and regain some composure before facing him again.

As she opened the door, Silas leaned casually against the doorway, his eyes smoldering with desire, a playful grin tugging at his lips. Before she could catch her breath, he closed the distance between them, his arms slipping around her waist with a possessive ease. The warmth of his body pressed against hers, and the thin barrier of the towel felt almost nonexistent as his lips found hers—soft at first, a gentle brush that quickly grew more insistent. His kiss deepened, a raw, hungry need igniting between them, as his fingers traced the edge of the towel, slipping beneath to caress her bare skin, each touch sending shivers down her spine. The heat of his desire pressed against her, making her heart pound with anticipation, the intensity of the moment leaving her breathless.

He finally stepped back, breathless, his eyes dark with longing. "Are you hungry? Dinner's ready."

"Sounds good. Let me get dressed, and I'll join you," she replied, still catching her breath as he planted another quick kiss on her lips before leaving the room.

Once alone, LuLu opened her bag and pulled out the delicate nightgown she had brought. It was more lingerie than a nightgown, but she couldn't bring herself to call it that. The teal fabric was sheer, revealing almost everything except the strategic patches of lace that covered her breasts. It came with matching thigh-high stockings and a robe.

LuLu wrestled with the delicate fabric, her fingers

fumbling as she tried to coax the stubborn stockings into place. Each attempt ended with them slipping down her legs, the silky material refusing to cooperate. With a frustrated sigh, she abandoned the effort, tossing the stockings aside.

As she stood before the mirror, her eyes traced the scars that marked her skin—once painful reminders, now just faint lines etched into her reflection. But tonight, they didn't hold the same power over her. There was something different, a quiet confidence that radiated from within. She tied the rope around her waist, the teal fabric soft against her skin, and for the first time, she saw herself as beautiful, scars and all. Taking a deep breath, she stepped out of the room, heading to the dining area with a newfound sense of self.

As LuLu entered the dining room, Silas froze. His wine glass paused halfway to his lips as his eyes locked onto hers. The air seemed to shift, thickening with tension as she made her way to him, each step deliberate and confident. Without breaking eye contact, she slid into the chair beside him, casually taking his glass and sipping the wine with a playful smile.

"Everything alright?" she teased, noticing his uncharacteristic silence.

"Uh...yeah," he stammered, his usual composure slipping as his eyes widened slightly. "You look...I mean, you look..."

"Thank you," she said, her voice soft as she looked down, a shy smile tugging at her lips, cheeks tinged with a subtle blush. "I'm not really that hungry, but I can keep you company if you are."

He reached for a bottle, pouring her a glass of wine.

Without hesitation, she tipped it back, draining the glass in one swallow.

His brow furrowed with concern as he refilled her glass. "Are you sure you're okay?"

Her sultry gaze burned with fierce desire as she prowled towards him, her body moving with feline grace. Her nails dug into his shoulders, leaving red marks as she pressed herself against his back, her breasts pushing against the hard muscles of his chest. With a predatory smile, she kissed his ear gently.

Without hesitation, he stood and lifted her up into an electric embrace. Every point of skin contact between them was tingling with excitement. carrying her to the bedroom with a determined stride. She let out a throaty laugh as he dropped her onto the bed, her eyes blazing with antic-ipation.

"Silas," she moaned, her voice thick with longing. "I want you."

He growled in response and claimed her lips in a passionate kiss that left them both breathless. As their bodies intertwined, their desire for each other reached a fever pitch, driving them both to new heights of pleasure.

With every touch and caress, they lost themselves in the intensity of their shared desire. LuLu could feel Silas' need for her pulsing against her, igniting a fire within her that only he could quench. As they moved together in perfect rhythm, their connection grew stronger and more primal.

When they finally came crashing down from their climax, they lay tangled in each other's embrace, completely spent but still craving each other's touch. Every moment was filled with an intense electricity that neither of them could deny or resist.

In that moment, LuLu knew that there was nowhere else she would rather be - consumed by Silas' intoxicating touch and giving herself completely to their insatiable passion. Without a word needing to be spoken, they both knew.

She playfully pounced on him, trying to undo his belt with a seductive wink. But as she tugged too hard, the belt flew off and smacked her in the face with a resounding slap.

"Ouch! Shit, I'm sorry!" He exclaimed, rushing to her side and examining her cheek.

"I'm fine, just a little slap-happy now," she laughed nervously, rubbing the red mark on her face.

"Leave it to me to ruin the mood," she joked, but when he planted a kiss on the spot of impact, all embarrassment was replaced by a fiery desire.

"You didn't." He said looking directly into her fiery eyes and with deliberate slowness, he unbuttoned his pants, his intense gaze never wavering from hers. As the fabric slipped away, revealing every inch of his body, she felt her breath catch, her heart pounding in response to the sight before her. All of him stood erect, a testament to his desire, and she couldn't help but let her eyes drink in the sculpted perfection of his form.

Her pulse quickened, every inch of her skin tingling as her gaze traced the contours of his muscles, the smooth lines of his abdomen, and the raw power he exuded. The sheer beauty of him left her awestruck, her body responding with an undeniable, almost primal, need.

Desire pooled deep in her core, a molten heat that spread through her veins like wildfire, igniting every nerve ending. She could feel herself growing wetter, her arousal almost overwhelming as she imagined his touch. Her body ached for him, the need to feel him against her, inside her, becoming an all-consuming hunger.

He leaned down, capturing her lips in a kiss that was all-consuming, filled with a hunger that matched her own. His mouth moved against hers with a fierce urgency, as though he were a man starved, and she was the only thing that could satisfy him. His tongue traced the curve of her lower lip before plunging into her mouth, tasting her deeply as he lowered himself on top of her, the weight of his body pressing her into the mattress in the most delicious way.

His lips broke away from hers, trailing a fresh path down her neck and across her collarbone. When he reached her shoulder, he paused, his breath warm against her skin as he slipped one strap of her nightie off, his lips following the exposed skin. He mirrored the action on the other side, his kisses leaving a trail of heat that made her tremble beneath him. She arched her back, lifting her hips just enough to allow him to peel the nightie away from her body, leaving her bare and exposed to his gaze.

He smiled down at her, a look of pure adoration in his eyes that made her heart skip a beat. "You are so beautiful," he whispered, his voice thick with emotion. The words sent a wave of warmth through her, but it was the way he looked at her, as if she were the most precious thing in the world, that made her feel truly cherished.

His mouth continued its journey down her body, stopping at her chest. When his lips brushed over the scar there, she shuddered, an involuntary pulse of pleasure shooting through her. His hands followed, cupping her breasts, his thumbs brushing over her nipples in slow, teasing circles that made her gasp. His mouth found her left breast, his lips closing around her nipple as he sucked gently, his teeth grazing the sensitive skin just enough to make her moan with pleasure.

Her fingers tangled in his hair, the soft strands slipping through her grasp as she pulled him closer, her hips instinctively rising to meet his. The scent of sandalwood clung to his skin, its earthy, masculine aroma wrapping around her senses and igniting her anticipation. She was enveloped in the sensations of his mouth on hers, his touch reverent and intoxicating, making her feel uniquely cherished.

His hands traveled between her legs, and he whispered into her ear, "You are so wet." His thumb traced slow, deliberate circles around her clit, sending shivers through her body. When his index and middle fingers slipped inside her, she let out an intimate gasp. The sensation was a complex mix of pleasure and discomfort, her body adjusting to the intrusion. His fingers worked with focused intent, each motion heightening the building pleasure to where she felt a wave of almost overwhelming intensity.

As the pleasure swelled within her, it bordered on too much, a maddening mix of pain and delight. Her body trembled, and she called out his name, her voice a desperate plea.

He stood and moved to his dresser, the sound of ripping fabric followed by a soft rustle. When he returned, he lay on top of her, his weight pressing against her, his presence between her legs both comforting and intense. Their kiss was passionate, his lips exploring hers with fervent tenderness.

"Are you sure?" he asked, his voice husky with concern.

"Yes," she whispered, her breath hitching as she let out a deep, shuddering moan. Her hand reached down to touch him, aligning him with her opening. His breath hitched, and he pressed forward slowly.

"I'm going to go slow, okay?" he murmured.

She nodded, taking a deep breath as he entered her. The initial stretch brought a sharp sting, like a brush burn inside her. She gasped, her breath coming in short, ragged bursts, and he halted, allowing her a moment to adjust. She bit into his shoulder, the pain mingling with an anticipatory ache as he continued, inch by inch.

Once he was fully inside, he moved with a slow, deliberate rhythm, each thrust deep and tender. The initial sting of entry gradually softened into a molten warmth that spread through her body like liquid fire. Her breaths quickened as the discomfort melted away, replaced by a tingling, almost electric pleasure that surged with every push. Her body instinctively arched to meet his, drawing him in closer as the heat between them intensified, wrapping her in a cocoon of growing bliss.

"I'm going to move more, okay?" His voice was a deep, sensual rumble against her ear, each word a promise of what was to come.

"Yes," she whispered, her voice trembling with a mix of eager anticipation and vulnerability. His low moan vibrated through her, and he shifted with a steady rhythm. Each thrust grew more confident, igniting a fierce cascade of pleasure that surged through her, building a wave of intense heat with every motion.

He leaned in, his breath warm and heavy on her neck, each exhale sending shivers cascading down her spine. His whispered words were barely audible, yet they carried a promise that made her heart race. "You're so tight. I don't want to hurt you."

"You won't ever hurt me," she murmured back, her voice a breathy promise, her hands gripping him tightly as if to anchor them both. That reassurance seemed to unleash a primal force within him. His pace quickened, each thrust deeper and more intense, filling her with an overwhelming sensation of connection and pleasure.

The pleasure inside her built like a storm, each thrust pushing her closer to the edge. Her moans grew louder, a raw symphony of unfiltered ecstasy. Her body convulsed with intense, shuddering waves of pleasure as she reached the peak, a wild cry escaping her lips.

"Silas!" she screamed, her voice raw and desperate. "I love you!"

"I love you, LuLu," he breathed back, his voice thick with emotion and satisfaction. Moments later, she felt the warmth of his release, and he pulled away, gently removing the condom. He slid back into bed, drawing her close. His touch was tender, his fingers tracing soft patterns through her hair, their bodies entwined in the afterglow of their shared passion.

She rested her head on his chest, his heartbeat steady beneath her ear, his fingers weaving through her hair.

"How do you feel?" he asked softly.

"I'm good," she said with a satisfied, sultry smile, pressing a tender kiss to his chest. "Is that how it's supposed to be every time?"

"I hope so," he said, his voice filled with awe. "It's never been that good before." He rubbed her arm with his knuckles. They held each other until they fell asleep in each other's arms.

Seventeen

LuLu bolted upright, her heart pounding, disoriented by the unfamiliar surroundings. Her eyes darted around until they landed on Silas, peacefully sleeping beside her, his steady breathing grounding her. She slipped out of bed quietly, padding across the room to the bathroom. As she entered, her gaze landed on the shower—a space so expansive it could have easily doubled as a studio apartment. Curiosity piqued, she opened the door, only to be confronted by a panel of buttons.

She stood in front of the control panel, her finger hovering over the button for the shower. The anticipation of a refreshing cleanse filled her, but as she pressed down on the button, she was met with a sharp, high-pitched beep and blinding flashing lights. Panic gripped her as she frantically searched for a more obvious option, finally settling on the "shower" button. In an instant, she was blasted with ice-cold water, causing her to let out a shriek that could rival a banshee's. Her body shivered and goosebumps prickled her skin as she tried to escape the arctic blast. Out of the corner of her eye, she caught sight of Silas in the doorway, a smirk playing on his lips as he stood there nonchalantly in all his naked glory. It was just like him to find amusement in other people's misfortunes.

With a confident grin, he sauntered over to the shower, his fingers brushing lightly against a panel just outside. "Here, let me show you," he murmured, pointing to a small, almost hidden button. With a quick press, the shower roared to life. "This one turns it on. Inside, you can set the water temperature. It's preset to 90 degrees, but you can adjust it once you're in."

She stepped forward, curiosity mingling with uncertainty as she entered the shower. Her fingers fumbled over the array of buttons, frustration tightening her brow. Silas watched her struggle for a moment before stepping in beside her, his presence both reassuring and imposing. Without a word, he reached past her, his hand deftly hitting a button that switched the spray to a gentle rain shower. The water cascaded down in a soothing rhythm, but before he could step away, she caught his arm, a playful glint in her eyes.

"Stay," she whispered, her voice soft yet insistent as she pulled him closer, her body pressing against his. A coy smile curled her lips, and he hesitated for just a moment before allowing himself to be drawn back into the warmth of the shower, the electricity between them palpable.

He pressed the button, and the shower roared to life, jets of hot water spraying from every direction. A wicked smile curved on his lips as he stepped out for just a moment, only to return with a condom in hand, ready for what was to come.

In an instant, he was on her, his mouth capturing hers

with an intensity that left her breathless. He pushed her back against the slick shower wall, his hands roaming her body with a hunger that made her moan into his kiss. The water cascaded over them, heat mingling with heat, as he slid his arms beneath her, lifting her effortlessly. She wrapped her legs around him, pulling him closer, her skin tingling under his touch.

His lips trailed down her neck, teeth grazing her skin in a teasing nibble that made her shiver. He positioned her carefully against the wall, his eyes locking onto hers for a brief, heated moment. Her nod was all he needed. With a powerful thrust, he was inside her, and her scream of pleasure echoed off the tiles, blending with the sound of the water.

He moved within her, grinding, pushing deeper, and she cried out for more, her nails digging into his back. The shower's heat engulfed them, their bodies slick and intertwined, lost in the overwhelming sensation of each other.

Their bodies moved in perfect rhythm, the steam thickening around them as the water cascaded over their entwined forms. Silas's grip tightened, and the intensity of their connection reached its peak, leaving them both gasping as the last waves of pleasure washed over them like the relentless jets of water.

Silas finally stepped out of the shower, peeling off the condom and discarding it with a swift motion. He returned moments later, the cool air mixing with the lingering heat of their passion. Silas handed her the bag, a silent gesture that made her smile as she rummaged through it.

"I will let you finish washing up." He laughed. "Now that you know how." She laughed as he went into the other room.

While she continued her shower, letting the water soothe and cleanse, Silas moved with purpose. When she finally stepped out, wrapping herself in a towel, the scent of freshly brewed coffee and warm toast greeted her. Silas was at the counter, setting down a plate of breakfast, his back to her, the morning light catching in his damp hair.

She smiled at him as she began to eat, her hunger evident in the way she attacked the plate. Each bite was a hurried effort to sate the gnawing emptiness left by skipping dinner the night before. In her eagerness, a piece of food caught in her throat, prompting her to cough. Silas chuckled, shaking his head in amusement as he sipped his coffee, watching her with a mix of affection and mild exasperation.

"I've got some good news for you," he said, his tone casual but carrying a hint of excitement. She paused mid-chew, her eyes locking onto his as curiosity sparked within her. A slow, teasing smirk spread across his lips. "I opened the USB drive."

LuLu's eyes brightened with a mix of surprise and relief. She quickly set her fork down and stood, crossing the space between them in a few swift steps. Without hesitation, she leaned in and kissed him, her gratitude and excitement clear. Her legs slid over his lap as she straddled him, her hands finding their way into his hair. Silas responded, his fingers tangling in her locks, but the sudden buzz of his phone interrupted the moment.

He glanced at the screen, the tension in his shoulders revealing his reluctance. Her lips brushed against his neck, playful and insistent, but he sighed, his focus drawn away. "I have to go to the office for about an hour or two," he murmured, lifting her chin to meet his gaze. "My partner needs to meet about something."

With a resigned nod, she eased off his lap and returned to her seat, the moment slipping away. "I have the USB drive in my office. I'll grab it when I get back," he promised, pressing a kiss to the top of her head before rising to his feet. He walked into the bedroom and changed into one of his tailored suits, the transformation from relaxed to businesslike almost instantaneous.

Once Silas left, LuLu couldn't resist the pull of curiosity. She let the towel slip from her body and reached for one of his shirts, the fabric cool and crisp against her skin as she slipped it on. It draped over her like a dress, his scent lingering in the threads, enveloping her.

She wandered into the kitchen, her fingers grazing the sleek countertops. Opening the refrigerator, she was pleasantly surprised by the well-stocked shelves and the meticulously organized contents—a sharp contrast to her own haphazard approach. Everything had its place, from the neatly aligned condiments to the carefully arranged fresh produce.

As she moved through the apartment, her bare feet padding softly on the pristine floors, she marveled at the cleanliness that seemed to intensify with each room. Not a speck of dust, not a stray item out of place. The space was a reflection of him—controlled, precise, and utterly captivating.

LuLu approached the office door, her curiosity bubbling beneath the surface. Her fingers brushed the cool metal knob, and with a soft click, it turned in her hand. The door creaked open, and she stepped inside, only to come to an abrupt halt. Her breath caught in her throat.

The wall before her was covered in a sprawling mind map—lines and connections linking her name to those of her friends, all circling back to Ryan. Her heart pounded in her chest as she took in the web of thoughts, each thread leading back to her.

Panicked, she dashed to grab her cell phone, snapping pictures of the board, her hands shaking with each click. She couldn't tear her eyes away from the tangle of connections, no matter how hard she tried to piece it together in her mind, every route pointed to her.

Steeling herself, she moved to his desk, her eyes landing on a folder with Sasha's name scrawled across the front. She picked it up, her fingers brushing against another folder beneath it. This one bore a name she hadn't used in years—May, LuLu. Her birth last name. The realization hit her like a punch to the gut, the air thickening around her as the pieces started to fall into place.

She rifled through the rest of the folders, her heart racing as she uncovered documents on everyone—Sasha, Nina, even Max. A sense of urgency washed over her as she quickly grabbed her bag, stuffing all the files inside. Her gaze landed on the USB drive, glimmering in the light. With everything clutched in her arms, she hurried into the bedroom.

She dumped the files onto the bed, pages spilling out like secrets waiting to be unveiled. Her fingers worked quickly as she slid into a pair of jeans, the fabric cool against her skin. With the folders secured in her bag, she tucked the USB drive into her pocket, feeling its weight as a reminder of the danger lurking nearby.

LuLu slid her shoes on with quick, determined movements, her mind already racing. She retraced her steps to the office, her heart pounding in her ears. Reaching for the eraser, she hesitated only a moment before wiping away the intricate web of connections he had meticulously mapped out on the wall. The lines, names, and details vanished under her hand, leaving behind only a faint smudge of chalk dust.

With a sudden burst of defiance, she grabbed a marker and scrawled a single word across the blank space: "Trust?" The letters were bold, stark against the whiteboard, challenging and unmistakable.

She stepped back, taking in the word for a heartbeat before turning on her heel. The office door closed behind her with a soft, deliberate click. LuLu's pulse quickened as she rushed to the front door, pulling it open and slipping outside. Her fingers fumbled for her phone, and she quickly called for a Lyft, her mind whirling with the implications of what she'd uncovered.

When she reached the lobby, Chase was waiting at the desk. His presence startled her, and she nearly jumped. "You need a car?" he asked, his brow raised. She shook her head, "No, I'm good," her voice barely above a whisper as she rushed past him, eager to escape.

As she climbed into the backseat of the Lyft, the driver attempted small talk, but LuLu's mind was elsewhere. She called Max and Nina, her voice hurried as she instructed them to have Doodle back in thirty minutes; they'd be taking him over as soon as she was off the phone.

About ten minutes into the ride, her phone buzzed insistently in her pocket. Silas's name flashed on the screen—she hesitated, then sent it to voicemail. Almost immediately, a text came through, questioning why she'd left. She ignored it, her focus elsewhere.

Questions spiraled through her mind, tangling and twisting into knots. The idea that Silas might have known Ryan before she did gnawed at her. Was it possible he had a hand in Ryan's death? Each connection she made felt like a trap tightening around her. Was this all some elaborate scheme? The unsettling thought that she could be a pawn in his game, manipulated to cover up something far darker, sent a shiver down her spine.

When the car finally pulled up to the bar, LuLu jumped out, the familiar scent of wood and whiskey filling her lungs. Doodle was waiting by the door, tail wagging furiously. She placed the closed sign in the window, the familiar ritual grounding her amid the chaos.

As her phone buzzed relentlessly, LuLu managed to get a call through to Matty. Her voice remained steady, almost too calm, as she informed him the bar would be closed for the week. With her bag still slung over her shoulder, she descended the stairs to the basement, her footsteps echoing in the dim space. She sifted through a clutter of tools until her fingers closed around the one she needed.

Back in her apartment, she dropped the bag on the floor and headed straight for the backdoor that led down to the yard. Without hesitation, she plugged in the electric saw, its mechanical hum filling the quiet room. She positioned it at the bottom of the door and began to cut, the blade gnawing through the wood, leaving behind a jagged square—just big enough for Doodle to slip through.

Satisfied with her makeshift doggy door, she nudged a box over the opening, a temporary shield against the cold. Then, with purposeful movements, she transferred the photos she had taken to her computer, her focus unwavering. Finally, she turned off her phone, silencing the outside world. She needed to think.

LuLu knelt on the floor, her breath catching as she opened her bag and pulled out the stack of folders, spreading them across the floor like pieces of a shattered puzzle. Her hands trembled as she picked up the one with her name, the worn edges betraying how often it had been handled. She hesitated, then flipped it open, her eyes immediately drawn to the lines of text that seemed to bleed from the past.

Her gaze fell on a faded photograph of her mother, the edges curling with age. Next to it, an old newspaper clipping showed a much younger version of her mother, smiling beside her birth father in their wedding announcement. Her throat tightened as she scanned the article, her fingers tracing the inked words as if trying to make sense of them.

She flipped the page, and her breath caught in her throat. The headline blazed across the paper—a detailed article on her father's arrest. The list of charges seemed endless, each offense meticulously documented and clipped together, creating a damning tapestry of his past. Her eyes scanned the arrest record, her stomach churning with every new line that revealed a darker side to the man she barely knew.

Then, something stopped her cold. It was another document, tucked beneath the arrest record—a hospital report, but not from the accident she remembered. This was something different, something she had never seen before. Her hands trembled as she pulled out a social services report that was attached, its contents more disturbing with each word. Her pulse quickened, a sense of foreboding growing with each paragraph she read.

Her gaze fell on a map, folded neatly alongside the papers. Several locations were circled in red, but one stood out—a mark on the map that corresponded to a registry address. Her heart pounded as she realized what she was looking at. Her father was on the sex offender registry, and this location, circled in bold red ink, was where he was currently registered.

The shock hit her like a tidal wave, the implications overwhelming. Silas had known. He had known exactly where her birth father was, had mapped it out, and kept it hidden among the documents he had collected on her life. The betrayal cut deep, a sickening twist in her gut as she pieced it all together. Silas wasn't just aware of her past—he had been digging into the darkest parts of it, the parts she had buried and hoped to forget. And now, staring at the map and the cold, clinical details of her father's criminal history, she realized the full extent of what Silas had uncovered.

The words on the page blurred as her vision clouded with tears, but she kept reading, driven by an unseen force, even as the weight of forgotten memories bore down on her like a crushing wave. Each sentence pulled her deeper into a past she had fought so hard to bury, now clawing its way back to the surface, relentless and unforgiving.

She couldn't take it anymore. The file slipped from her trembling hands, landing with a dull thud on the floor as she bolted to the bathroom. Her stomach churned violently, and she barely made it to the sink before her breakfast came back up. The acid burned her throat as she emptied the contents of her stomach, her body heaving with the effort.

Breathless, she slumped against the cold tile floor, her back against the wall as she stared blankly at the ceiling, searching for answers in the empty, white space above. How did it come to this? What had she done to deserve the constant barrage of pain and betrayal? The questions spun in her mind, but no answers came.

It was then that she noticed she was still wearing Silas's shirt, its fabric clinging to her skin, now damp with sweat. The realization felt like a violation. She peeled it off, her movements jerky and desperate, as if she could shed the feelings of betrayal with the garment itself. She turned on the shower, needing the cleansing ritual she had always turned to after throwing up, the hot water a small comfort as it washed away the remnants of her distress.

Once out, she brushed her teeth, the minty taste cutting through the sourness lingering in her mouth. Doodle, ever faithful, followed her every move, his big eyes filled with concern as he padded after her.

Too exhausted to do anything else, she collapsed onto her bed, the fatigue pressing down on her like a heavy blanket. She didn't bother with the covers; she just lay there, staring at nothing, letting the overwhelming exhaustion take her under until sleep finally claimed her.

In her dream, everything felt off. There was no spotlight, no familiar chair to approach. Instead, LuLu found herself already seated in a cold, metal chair, her wrists shackled to a long, steel table. The dim light above flickered erratically, casting wavering shadows that danced across the black void surrounding her. The only thing she could see clearly was the mirror in front of her.

But the reflection staring back wasn't entirely hers. The gaunt face, the hollow eyes, the stringy hair—these features were hers, but distorted, as if she hadn't eaten in weeks. Her cheeks were sunken, her eyes heavy with the weight of a sleepless eternity. The orange jumpsuit clung loosely to her frame, hanging on her like a cloth draped over a drying rack. She tried to move her hands, but the cold bite of the cuffs reminded her that she was trapped, bound to this nightmarish place.

Detective Marc appeared before her, his face a twisted mask of fury, skin blazing red as if it were about to peel away. But it was his eyes—or lack thereof—that froze her in place. Where his eyes should have been were nothing but black voids, empty and consuming. He leaned in, and his voice, a guttural roar, shattered the silence, "WE KNOW YOU DID IT!" The sound of his fist slamming onto the metal table reverberated through her, making her flinch.

Her voice came out in a rasp, barely audible, "I didn't. Someone is setting me up." The words felt weak, frail against the oppressive weight of the accusation.

Marc's lip curled into a sneer. "If not you, then who?" His hand shot out, pointing into the suffocating darkness. Suddenly, a spotlight pierced the gloom, illuminating Silas. He was running, sweat soaking through his shirt, muscles straining, but he remained stuck in place, as if the ground beneath him had turned to glue. His face was a mask of terror, eyes wide with fear as if he had seen something beyond comprehension, something that stripped away every ounce of courage.

His voice exploded with anger, his face twisted in disbelief. "Worth killing for? You?" He scoffed, his eyes scanning her with a mix of contempt and fury. "Please! Just look at yourself!" The words ripped from his throat, as if the very idea was so absurd it made him want to tear her apart with them. He threw his hands up, shaking his head, unable to comprehend how she could even suggest such a thing..

"No! Please. I don't know!" she screamed, her eyes

locked on Silas, unable to tear herself away from the sight of him desperately running yet going nowhere. Every fiber of her being told her he wasn't guilty, that he couldn't have done it.

"That's right," the detective's voice snapped her attention back to him, to the gaping nothingness where his eyes should have been. He suddenly went silent, his head turning slowly toward the darkness, as if sensing something she couldn't see. "Your lawyer is here," he muttered.

The spotlight flicked off Silas and swung to the opposite side, revealing a grotesque figure that slithered out of the shadows. It was the same suit Ryan had worn in her other nightmares, but now, it wore him. The thing that had once been Ryan crawled toward her, its flesh a sickly, oozing mass that left a trail of decay in its wake. Flies buzzed and danced in the air around it, feasting on the open sores that pocketed its skin.

The creature took the seat beside her, its misshapen face twisting into a mockery of a smile, showing the two front teeth it had left, the rest long gone. Its voice, thick and wet, gurgled out, "My client."

Green bile oozed from its mouth as it spoke, dripping down onto its suit, and the detective vanished back into the shadows, leaving her alone with this horror. The Ryan-thing turned its milky, half-rotted eyes on her.

"What did you find in his office?" The words dripped from its mouth like sludge.

She shook her head, her stomach churning with disgust. "I don't know." She wanted to wake up, to escape this nightmare.

"THINK!" it bellowed, its bloated, rotting form inching

closer, its stench overwhelming. He reached down and grabbed his folder from under the table.

"Map and background research," she whispered, "USB drive."

"Which you gave him," it corrected, its tone accusatory. She nodded numbly. "Not much there," it continued, voice dripping with contempt. She nodded again, her body trembling. "You went through the entire office?"

"Yes," she breathed out, barely more than a whisper. "Was he trying to prove I didn't do it?"

The air around them grew thick, and she looked up to see storm clouds forming overhead, swirling ominously. The creature's gaze followed hers, its voice growing darker. "The clouds," it muttered, "The clouds, USB, and the phone."

Suddenly, she was yanked backward, as if an invisible rope had wrapped around her waist, pulling her with a force she couldn't resist. The next crack of thunder jolted her awake, her heart pounding as she shot upright in bed, gasping for air.

She knew what she had to do. She needed to start with Ryan's folder and work backward. It wasn't about her. It was about a murder.

Eighteen

LuLu slid out of bed, her movements practiced and automatic. She reached for the small bottle on her nightstand, the familiar rattle of pills a constant in her routine. Her fingers deftly tapped out the usual dose, the one she no longer even thought about. But tonight, the lingering edge of panic clung to her, sharper than usual. Without hesitation, she shook out an additional pill, the one marked for emergencies—a low-dose sedative that her doctor had warned her to use sparingly. Dr. Clover's words echoed in her mind: "Only if you need it, LuLu." Tonight, she needed it.

With the pill swallowed, she pushed aside the box that covered the makeshift dog door she'd rigged. Doodle, her loyal companion, darted in and out with unrestrained joy, relishing his newfound freedom to roam between the apartment and the backyard.

LuLu gathered her materials, her thoughts already drifting to the task at hand. She made her way down to the bar, where the quiet solitude awaited her. Behind the bar, she rummaged for her small project—a hidden stash of tools and a dry erase marker. She connected the project to her computer, streaming the mind map from Silas's office onto the screen. The lines and connections spread out before her like a web, each thread a potential clue.

She sank to the floor, spreading out the files in neat columns around her. The marker squeaked as she scrawled names and notes directly onto the floor beneath each file, the information laid out clearly before her. It was a temporary setup—everything could be erased with a mop and bleach, leaving no trace of her work.

Three words from her dream surfaced in her mind: Clouds, Phone, USB Drive. She scribbled them down, the urgency of their meaning gnawing at her. Suddenly, she remembered the USB drive—it was still in her jeans back in the apartment. She decided to review it later, after she combed through the files.

LuLu hesitated, her hand hovering over Ryan's folder before she pulled back, opting instead for a different approach. She reached for the folder labeled "Yeat, Heather," hoping to start with something more manageable. As she flipped through the papers, it became clear that Heather's presence in Ryan's life was fleeting at best. Their relationship had sparked from a dating app, a brief digital connection that quickly blossomed into something more. Yet, despite her status as Ryan's girlfriend, Heather's life was threadbare on paper—unemployed, no significant financial ties, no insurance claims in her name. It all felt too simple, too convenient.

LuLu's brow furrowed as she scanned the documents. The pieces didn't align, like a puzzle with mismatched edges. Heather wasn't the answer, that much was clear. She scribbled a quick note beneath Ryan's file: "Not Heather." The words etched her growing doubt into reality.

Reluctantly, she returned to Ryan's folder, feeling the weight of it as if it were a physical burden. Her breath hitched as she opened it again, finding herself face to face with the sparse details of his life. For someone who had cast such a large shadow over her thoughts, his life was surprisingly insubstantial. His privileged upbringing, his parents' success, the private schooling—all of it amounted to so little in the end. He wasn't the towering figure she had imagined, but rather a man whose life, summarized in these few sheets of paper, felt oddly insignificant.

LuLu stared at the folder, her fingers tracing the edges of the thin stack of papers. It should have felt heavier, filled with the weight of a life that had once cast such a long shadow over hers. But as she sifted through the pages, the story they told was unimpressive, almost trivial. The pedigree, the private schools, the connections—they all seemed so much less daunting laid bare in front of her.

She flipped through the documents again, slower this time, searching for something—anything—that might explain why she had feared him so much. But there was nothing extraordinary, just the mundane details of a life built on privilege and expectations. His achievements, once seemingly untouchable, now read as hollow, bolstered more by circumstance than by merit. Even the note scribbled by Silas—"Nepotism hire"—seemed to mock the idea of Ryan as someone powerful or threatening.

LuLu leaned back, the tension in her shoulders easing as a quiet realization washed over her. The monster she had conjured in her mind was nothing more than a shadow—intimidating in the dark but powerless in the light of day.

She had given him too much, built him up into something he never truly was. And now, with his life laid out in front of her, she saw it for what it was: small, insignificant, and unworthy of the fear she had once felt.

She looked at the words on the floor. Clouds. Phone. USB. She put Ryan's folder down. She was having a hard time trying to understand what her brain was trying to tell her. She knew it was there, she just needed to pull it out. She closed her eyes and repeated clouds over and over again when something hit her.

LuLu's eyes narrowed as the thought hit her like a jolt. "What if he didn't say clouds... what if he said cloud," she muttered, her voice barely above a whisper, the idea unraveling in her mind. His cloud account. That had to be it. That's why his phone was missing—someone knew there was information on it and in his cloud storage. The realization settled over her, the pieces finally starting to come together. The USB drive might just be a backup, but the cloud... that was the real treasure trove.

She flipped Ryan's folder open again, her fingers moving with a newfound urgency. The financials, sparse as they were, stared back at her. No student loan debt. No debt at all, in fact. Every bill was meticulously paid, not a single one missed. But it wasn't the lack of debt that caught her attention this time—it was the numbers on the accounts paying those bills. Each one had different last four digits, none of them matching his own.

Her brow furrowed as she stared at the page, a realization creeping in. Ryan hadn't been footing his own bills. Someone else had been taking care of them, and that someone had gone to great lengths to keep it all under wraps.

LuLu's fingers trembled slightly as she sifted through the papers, her breath catching when she finally found the landlord's contact information. The name stood out on the page, almost daring her to make the call. It felt like a wild gamble, but the gnawing in her gut wouldn't let her ignore it. She had to know.

Crossing the room, she reached for the phone, her hand hovering over the receiver. The memory of yanking it off in frustration the day before flashed in her mind, but she forced herself to steady, slowly setting it back in place. With a deliberate click, she rehung the receiver, then carefully dialed the number, each digit pressed with growing determination.

The line barely rang before a voice crackled on the other end, "Overlook Apartments. Fred Mort speaking."

"Ummm... Hi. My name is Lisa Smith, and I'm a P.I. working with the Bakers," LuLu lied, the words slipping out smoothly despite the knot in her stomach.

"Oh, yeah. Police were here a few weeks ago. Shame what happened," Fred replied, his tone casual, almost indifferent.

"Yes, a real shame, especially since they think it was a suicide," she hinted, testing the waters.

Fred snorted, "Oh, it wasn't, if you ask me."

Her heart skipped a beat. "Why do you say that?"

"He had everything. That beautiful girlfriend, good job, and money coming in from everywhere. I don't know how he did it, but he didn't even have to pay his rent. He had clients do it," Fred explained, the casual revelation hitting her like a punch.

"Clients? He was a doctor, right?" LuLu asked, trying to keep her voice steady.

"Yeah, but I guess he did some other work on the side. I told the police all of this. You should talk to them," he said, sounding almost impatient.

"Do you know which client paid his rent?" she pressed, holding her breath.

"Yeah, give me a second." There was a clatter as Fred put down the phone, followed by the sound of papers rustling and a muffled curse. LuLu's grip on the receiver tightened, her heart pounding in her ears.

"Here we go. A man named... Greg Leverline," Fred finally said.

The color drained from LuLu's face, her breath catching in her throat. The name hit her like a cold wave, freezing her in place. She managed to mutter a quick thank you before slamming the phone down, her thoughts racing.

LuLu's heart raced as she moved swiftly back to her makeshift graph, the urgency in her step matching the intensity of her thoughts. Her eyes locked onto the file labeled "Leverline, Greg," and her hand hovered above it for just a moment before she grasped it, fingers trembling. The once-disjointed pieces now seemed to snap into place, forming a picture that was darker and more complex than she had ever imagined.

For the next two days, LuLu immersed herself in the files, her focus razor-sharp as she sifted through page after page, marking anything that stood out. Doodle trotted in and out through his little door, his presence a comforting background to her intense concentration.

She was deeply engrossed in Liam's file, her eyes scanning each line with determination, when a sudden, forceful pounding on the bar door shattered the quiet. The sound echoed through the empty room, sharp and demanding, sending a jolt through her chest. LuLu's breath caught as she froze, heart racing. With a steadying breath, she edged toward the door, every possible scenario flashing through her mind

She leaned in, peering through the peephole, and felt her pulse quicken. Silas stood on the other side, looking disheveled and worn. His clothes were the same ones she had seen him wear when he left for work on Saturday, though now they were wrinkled and missing the tie and jacket. Dark circles rimmed his eyes, a clear sign of sleeplessness.

Something was wrong—very wrong.

Silas's voice broke the stillness of the night, the desperation clear in his tone as he called out, "I'm not leaving until you talk to me!" The echo of his words bounced off the empty street, raw and pleading. He shifted on his feet, glancing at the glowing windows of the bar, the only signs of life inside. "I know you're in there. I can see the lights on. Please, just let me in."

His voice wavered slightly, but he pressed on, his frustration mounting with every unanswered plea. "I'll live in your parking lot if I have to! I know you turned off your phone, but I'm not giving up!"

He let out a shaky breath, leaning closer to the door, his forehead resting against the cool surface as if willing her to hear him. "And yeah," he continued, his voice softer now, tinged with a sad humor, "I know I probably look like a crazy person yelling out here in the street." He paused as a woman passed by, her eyes wide with curiosity and a hint of concern. Silas offered her a weak, apologetic smile before turning back to the door, his resolve unshaken despite the absurdity of the situation. "But I'm not stopping until you let me in."

The lock clicks with a finality that sends shivers down LuLu's spine, and she retreats into the dark eerie bar, leaving the door open just enough to let in a sliver of light. Her heart races as she stands in the center of the room, arms outstretched, back towards the door. The transformation of the room is laid bare behind her, a silent dare.

Silas steps through the threshold, the door groaning under his weight as he shuts it firmly behind him. He takes in the chaos before him, an intricate web of connections and clues sprawled across every surface of the room. It's his research, his obsession, now on full display. His breath catches in his throat as he realizes the gravity of it all.

But before he can even speak a word, LuLu's eyes lock onto him with a ferocity that makes him freeze. Without hesitation, she grabs her file from the floor and hurls it at him with all her pent-up frustration and anger. The pages scatter like broken glass around him, each one revealing a piece of her life that she had tried so hard to keep hidden.

With trembling hands, LuLu stands before him, her body coiled with rage and fear. She can feel the floor beneath her vibrating in response to her emotions, each tile a painful reminder of her past traumas. Clenching her fists tightly, she confronts him with unbridled fury in her voice.

"What did you hope to gain by exposing my darkest secrets?" she spits out, tears threatening to spill from her eyes. "Did you enjoy seeing how much pain I've endured? How my own father hurt me?" She takes a step closer, daring him to respond. "He did not break me! You will not break me."

Her words are sharp and pointed, dripping with resentment and betrayal. But underneath it all lies a vulnerable plea for understanding and comfort. She had spent so long pushing people away, but he had broken down her walls and made her feel things she never thought possible. And in this moment of raw emotion, she hates him for it.

As tears welled in her eyes, LuLu fought to hold back the raw emotions threatening to consume her. She wanted to scream at him, lash out and make him hurt as much as she was hurting. But seeing the pain in his eyes as he struggled to find the right words only made her heart ache even more.

She could see the conflict in his face - the battle between his own fears and insecurities and his love for her. And it mirrored her own inner turmoil.

In that moment, they were both broken souls searching for some kind of solace. But instead of finding comfort in each other's arms, they found only more pain and confusion.

Silas knew he had messed up - again. He had let his past traumas cloud his judgment and push away the one person who had truly seen through his defenses. And now all he could do was watch as she crumbled before him, unable to reach out and mend what he had broken.

"I never meant to hurt you," he whispered hoarsely, the weight of his guilt crushing him.

LuLu's voice trembled with raw emotion as she shot back at Silas, her eyes blazing with betrayal. "You made me question everything, every moment we shared together."

His heart twisted with guilt and pain, feeling like a monster for causing her such anguish. He could feel his demons clawing at him, taunting him for hurting the one person he loved.

"It's not just about you," he tried to explain, his voice

cracking under the weight of his confession. "I've been hurt before and I couldn't bear to let it happen again."

Her heart ached at the vulnerability in his words, but she couldn't ignore the pain he had caused her. "What about me? Have I ever given you a reason to doubt my love?"

Silas shook his head, regret and longing etched on his face as he met her gaze. "No, but others have." The unspoken reminder of past betrayals hung heavily between them, driving a deeper wedge between their fractured hearts.

In that moment, all they could do was stare at each other with a mix of love and hurt, both desperately wanting to find a way back to each other but not knowing if it was even possible anymore. Slowly, LuLu moved closer to him, taking his hands in hers and searching for any sign of hope in his troubled eyes.

"What happened?" she asked softly, all traces of anger now replaced with genuine concern and confusion.

And as Silas opened up about his past traumas and fears, both of them began to realize that they were more alike than they ever thought - two broken souls trying to heal each other despite their own shattered pieces.

Silas took a deep breath before continuing, his voice trembling with suppressed emotion. "Willa and I met years ago. She seemed perfect - classy, successful, fitting into our social circles seamlessly. But when my company took off and we started making money, she showed her true colors. I found out she was just using me for my wealth."

He paused, his voice breaking as he relived the memory. "I overheard her on the phone with her mother, bragging about how she had found a golden goose and how she would make sure I didn't set up a prenup if I really loved her." The pain in his words was palpable.

LuLu's grip on his hands tightened, trembling with anger and hurt. She could see it all now - the fear, the hurt, the weight of his past that still haunted him. She understood why he had done what he did, but that didn't mean she agreed with it.

"With everything going on, the murder, the uncertainty - I just wanted to protect you, to help," Silas continued, his voice thick with emotion. "I meant every word I said the other night. I have fallen in love with you and I know I have broken your trust. But I needed you to know." He slowly got up from his seat, shoulders slumped as he walked towards the door. "I understand if you don't want to see me anymore."

"Wait," LuLu's voice was a fierce command, halting him in his tracks. "I trusted you with all my heart and you didn't share this with me? You broke that trust." The pain in her eyes intensified, as she reached out to catch his arm before he could leave again.

But she couldn't let him go. LuLu grabbed onto him, her grip tight and determined, her heart pounding wildly in her chest. When he turned to face her, she saw a single tear fall down his cheek. Without hesitation, she leaned in and pressed her lips to his, pouring all of her love and forgiveness into the soft touch. She wiped away the tear with her thumb, a silent gesture of understanding.

He looked at her, torn between longing and uncertainty. "I can't lose you," he confessed in a broken whisper.

"Then stop pushing me away," she demanded, her voice filled with unwavering determination. "Talk to me, let me help you." She kissed him again, more fiercely this time, sealing their promise to each other.

Silas's arms wrapped around her tightly, pulling her close in an embrace that held all the emotions he couldn't put into words. She could feel the tension slowly melt away as he buried his face in her shoulder. "I'm sorry," he murmured against her skin, his tears soaking through her shirt.

"I forgive you," LuLu said firmly, using the power of her love to mend what had been broken between them.

Nineteen

When the morning light filtered into the room, LuLu was surprised to find Silas still there. She had assumed he'd slip out early, but the sight of his overnight bag—tucked discreetly in the corner—suggested he had been prepared to sleep in his car if necessary. He had fallen into a deep, untroubled sleep after his late-night shower, his breathing slow and steady as the sun rose higher.

LuLu left quietly, heading to Nina's to grab some food, hoping to be back before he woke. As she walked across the street, two things struck her. Chase was outside in a black car in her parking lot, the other was a silver car with another familiar face, but this time he had eyes. She walked over and tapped on Chase's window.

"What are you doing here?" she asked, her brow furrowing with concern.

"Security. Gotta protect the big man." he replied, his tone clipped. She shook her head. "Don't worry, my replacement will be here soon.

"At least come into the bar. You don't need to sit in your car all night." He refused with a slight shake of his head. "Well, let me get you something to eat, at least." Before he could protest, she was already walking away, determined to take care of one more thing before heading inside.

She approached the silver car parked across the street, tapping lightly on the tinted window. It lowered slowly, revealing the stern face of Detective Marc.

"Detective," she greeted him, forcing a polite smile. "The bar doesn't open for a couple of hours."

His expression remained cold. "We're just making sure we have all the pieces to the puzzle. Anything you can tell me that I might be missing?"

She met his gaze evenly, though her heart raced. "Nope." With that, she wished him luck and turned on her heel, fighting to keep her composure as she walked into the diner. Her legs felt like jelly, the weight of the police surveillance heavy on her mind.

Sitting at the counter, she ordered breakfast, her thoughts racing as she waited for the food. When her order was ready, she took a deep breath and delivered a breakfast sandwich to Chase, figuring it would be easier for him to eat in the car. Then, she carried the rest of the food back to her apartment, trying to ignore the gnawing anxiety that came with knowing the police were watching her every move.

Inside, she found Silas still asleep, cuddling with Doodle. The sight of them together brought a small, fleeting smile to her face, but the unease lingered as she sat down to eat, her appetite dulled by the tension in the air.

While Silas slept, she crafted a message to Heather on Facebook, trying to keep her tone light and casual despite the real reason for her request nagging at the back of her mind. She asked for an old college photo of their friends, hoping Heather wouldn't read too much into it.

When Silas finally stirred, he emerged looking more like a man who had carried the weight of the world on his shoulders. His hair was tousled, dark circles shadowed his eyes, and though he still looked effortlessly handsome in the T-shirt she'd given him and his boxers, he was clearly exhausted. Without a word, he sat down to the now-cold food, a faint smile tugging at his lips as he began to eat.

"Do you need to go to work today?" LuLu asked, studying his face, noticing the tension he still carried.

He shook his head, releasing a small sigh. "No, I'm taking a few vacation days. My partner and I just finalized a deal to take the company public. It's been a lot of late nights, and with everything else going on... I just need some time."

The weight of his words settled in, and for the first time, LuLu realized just how much he'd been juggling. "So, while dating me with all the drama, you've been working around the clock to get your company public?" Her voice was soft, a mix of guilt and realization.

He just nodded, his gaze dropping back to his plate.

LuLu took in the exhaustion etched into his features. Without a word, she walked over and began to gently rub his shoulders. Silas leaned back into her touch, closing his eyes as he let the tension slowly drain away. He tilted his head back, looking up at her, and she bent down, pressing her lips softly to his.

Silas rose from the bed, his movements slow and deliberate, as if weighing every inch between them. When he reached for her hand, his touch was tender but unyielding. "Don't say that. You're not responsible for any of this," he murmured, his voice a gentle rumble that seemed to vibrate through her.

Before she could respond, she flung herself into his arms, capturing his lips with hers in a kiss that was both urgent and soothing. He caught her effortlessly, holding her against him with the same strength and care that he always did. She pulled back just enough to catch her breath, a mischievous grin playing on her lips.

"I've heard make-up sex is better than regular sex," she teased.

Silas didn't hesitate for a second. With a playful growl, he swept LuLu off her feet, flipping her over his shoulder in one swift motion. She let out a surprised squeal, her laughter echoing in the hallway as he carried her to the bedroom, his pace quick and purposeful, making her heart race with excitement.

As they entered the room, he nudged the door shut behind them, locking Doodle out. The dog barked in protest, his discontent clear, which only made them both laugh at the absurdity of it all. But the laughter quickly faded as their eyes met, a charged silence filling the space between them.

In a blur of movement, his clothes joined hers in a forgotten pile on the floor, leaving nothing between them. His lips found her skin, leaving a trail of heat as they moved down her body, each kiss igniting a fire within her that made her pulse quicken in anticipation of what was to come.

As his mouth moved lower, his hands tugged at the hem of her shirt, peeling it away to reveal her skin. He hesitated at her jeans, but she pushed him back gently, standing up to undress herself. Silas watched, completely entranced, as she shed each piece of clothing, his gaze locked on her with an intensity that sent a shiver down her spine.

When she handed him the condom, he fumbled slightly in his haste to put it on, his hands trembling with barely-contained desire. She straddled him, her breath hitching as she sank down onto him, a moan slipping from his lips as she began to move. Her lips found his neck, leaving a trail of kisses that traveled down to his chest. She bit down on his nipple, earning a sharp intake of breath from him as his body arched beneath her.

Silas reached for her, but she skillfully evade his grasp, maintaining control with a wicked grin. She slid her hand down, cupping his balls, and the other hand guided him, teasing him just enough to make him groan in frustration.

Her voice was a sultry whisper in his ear. "You need to say it. I need to hear it."

He didn't hesitate. "Yes, please," he nearly shouted, the desperation in his voice taking them both by surprise.

Without warning, she slammed down onto him, and his hands flew to her hips, gripping her tightly as she set a rhythm that had them both gasping. He pulled her closer, burying his face in her chest, his mouth finding her breasts as she rode him harder and faster, her movements sending waves of pleasure rippling through both of them.

The sensation of him inside her, hitting just the right spot, combined with the electricity coursing through her veins, was overwhelming. She felt the climax building, her entire body tingling with anticipation until it finally exploded within her, forcing a scream of his name from her lips.

In an instant, Silas flipped her over, his body pressing her into the mattress as he took over. His mouth crashed onto hers, their kiss searing as he thrust deep, his pace quickening until he reached his own release, a low growl escaping him as he finished inside her.

They lay there, breathless and tangled together, the air thick with the scent of sweat and satisfaction. Silas smirked, his chest still heaving. "Make-up sex... not bad," he murmured, his voice laced with a mix of amusement and exhaustion.

LuLu curled up against him, her head resting on his chest. She felt different now, a strange warmth spreading through her that made her feel safe, as if she had finally found a place where she could be normal, whatever that meant. For the first time in a long while, she allowed herself to relax, the worries of the outside world slipping away as she drifted off in his arms.

Silas's eyes twinkled with amusement as he looked at her. "As much as I love having you all to myself, you might want to turn your phone on. Sasha texted me last night— something about you being a terrible brunch partner lately."

LuLu froze, her mind flashing back to when she had arrived home, weary and overwhelmed. The first thing she did was shut her phone off, wanting nothing more than to escape the outside world. She hadn't thought about it since. Now, the weight of reality came crashing back down.

LuLu slipped out of bed with the stealth of a cat burglar, swiping Silas's T-shirt and tugging it over her head as she crept across the room. The moment she cracked open the bedroom door, Doodle was there, his big eyes staring up at her with a mix of impatience and expectation. He let out a dramatic huff and sauntered past her, his mission clear.

With all the grace of a seasoned bed invader, Doodle leaped onto the mattress, immediately launching a full-scale assault of affectionate nuzzles on Silas. Silas's laughter filled the room as Doodle's eager tongue attacked his face.

"Hey, no fair!" LuLu called out, leaning against the doorframe. "The men in my life are not allowed to gang up on me, you know."

Silas, now fully immersed in dog-induced bliss, chuckled through the flurry of licks. "No promises. You're interrupting our bro time. Go call your friend."

Shaking her head, LuLu headed for the kitchen. The phone lay abandoned on the counter, staring back at her like a neglected child. She hesitated for a moment, feeling its weight more than usual as she picked it up. It was like holding a little black box of all the things she had been dodging, but after one last glance at Silas and Doodle, now an inseparable duo, she knew she couldn't avoid it any longer.

With a deep breath, she powered it on. The screen lit up with a flood of notifications—thirty-two missed calls and ten voicemails. She stared at the number in disbelief, a mix of guilt and anxiety swirling in her stomach.

Without a word, she walked back into the bedroom, holding the phone out for Silas to see. His reaction was a lopsided smile and a shrug, as if to say, "What did you expect?"

He got up, stretching lazily as he headed toward the bathroom, leaving her alone with the mounting sense of dread.

She scrolled through the missed calls, her thumb hovering over Sasha's name. With a sigh, she pressed the call button and held the phone to her ear. It rang only twice before Sasha's voice answered, laced with a sarcastic edge. "Look who's alive after all."

LuLu's stomach twisted at the edge in Sasha's voice. She knew it was meant to be playful, but it landed with a dull thud, reminding her of everything she had been neglecting. The weight of guilt pressed down on her chest, and before she could stop herself, the words tumbled out. "I'm so sorry. I've been a shitty friend!"

There was a pause before Sasha sighed, the sound softening into something almost comforting. "Calm down, okay? I'm not breaking off our friendship or anything. Just don't turn your phone off anymore, alright? And we need to keep up our brunches."

"Yeppers," LuLu replied, trying to inject some cheer into her voice. Just then, Silas emerged from the bathroom, dressed in sweatpants and shoes, his hair still damp. His eyes crinkled with laughter as he took in the sight of LuLu on the phone.

"What are you doing today?" Sasha's voice came through the speaker, as Silas crossed the room and planted a quick kiss on LuLu's cheek.

"I need my shirt back," he teased, his grin widening. "You've got all the shirts."

With a playful roll of her eyes, LuLu peeled off his T-shirt and tossed it at him. "I'll be back after my run," he called out as he caught the shirt and headed for the door. "Love you."

"Love you too." She whispered.

"Hello? Still there?" Sasha's voice crackled through the phone.

"Oh, sorry! Silas was just letting me know he's going for a run," LuLu explained, feeling the heat rise in her cheeks.

"Ah, so that's what you've been up to...or should I say who you've been up to?" Sasha quipped, the innuendo clear as LuLu put the phone on speaker and headed into the bedroom.

Doodle barely stirred as she entered, the lazy fluffball content to keep snoozing. LuLu grabbed a pair of sweats, pulling them on quickly as Sasha's words sank in.

"Gross," LuLu shot back, trying to sound disgusted but failing miserably.

"That bad, huh?" Sasha's laughter bubbled through the speaker. "I would've hoped it was better than gross."

"What? No!" LuLu stammered, then caught the joke. "Not gross at all. Actually...really great. I've got so much to tell you. Silas is staying over, but how about we grab dinner tonight? He can hang with Doodle, or we can catch up tomorrow. Plus, Matty's going to work the bar tonight. Oh, I need to call her."

"Matty?" Sasha asked, the curiosity evident.

"My new employee. She's awesome," LuLu said, pulling her hair into a messy bun.

"Look at you, all grown up!" Sasha teased, the affection clear in her voice.

"Thanks," LuLu replied, her tone dry but playful.

"Seriously though," Sasha continued, "Rebecca's been working on some things too. She said she left you a message."

Before LuLu could respond, she heard a familiar voice in the background. Rebecca's tone was unmistakable as she asked if it was LuLu on the phone. A brief shuffle later, and suddenly, Rebecca was on the line.

"Hey, LuLu!" Rebecca's voice was as lively as if she had already had a double shot of espresso, despite the early hour. "I've been trying to get ahold of you."

LuLu's heart skipped a beat. "Is everything okay?"

"Is everything okay, she asks! No, LuLu, everything is not okay," Rebecca's sarcasm cut through the line, leaving LuLu's stomach in knots.

A wave of unease washed over her. "What's going on?" Her thoughts immediately jumped to the pile of research materials sitting downstairs.

Rebecca didn't mince words. "The police have officially declared Liam a missing person. They've contacted me, and they want to talk to you."

LuLu felt her pulse quicken, nausea creeping up. "When?"

"As soon as possible. It's better we go to them rather than them showing up at your door," Rebecca advised, her tone practical but laced with urgency.

LuLu swallowed hard. "Next week. Can you buy me seven days" It wasn't much, but it bought her at least a week to sift through the research.

"I will try. I'll text you the day and time," Rebecca said, her voice softening just a touch. "Until then, lay low. Word is, they've found something."

"Thanks, Rebecca. I'll do my best," LuLu said, trying to keep her voice steady.

Rebecca wasn't having it. "No offense, LuLu, but I've seen your best, and I need you to do better than that." In the background, LuLu caught a faint protest from Sasha, quickly silenced by Rebecca.

LuLu bit her lip, the weight of Rebecca's words sinking in. "I understand." She barely got the words out before Rebecca handed the phone back to Sasha.

"Are you okay?" Sasha's voice was softer, more concerned.

LuLu's eyes flicked around the room, her gaze darting to

the door as if Rebecca might be lurking just beyond it. She leaned in closer, her voice dropping to a near-whisper, "I didn't do this, and if the police can't figure it out, I will."

Sasha let out a long sigh, one that seemed to carry the weight of her worry. "Okay," she said, her tone laced with both concern and determination. "Be ready to talk. Nina's place at 5:00. I know it's early, but I need to hear everything."

"I'll be there," LuLu replied, her voice steadying with resolve. "Love you, Sasha."

"Love you too," Sasha responded, her words warm despite the tension that hung between them.

After the call ended, LuLu dialled Matty's number. Their conversation shifted from casual updates about the bar to more serious matters. Matty's excitement over the bar reopening next week was palpable, but LuLu's focus lingered on something deeper. She listened as Matty talked about the bar's recent success, her pride clear as she mentioned how profits had doubled since she started. But beneath the surface, Matty's concern was evident—she feared the bar might close.

LuLu reassured her, appreciating Matty's dedication, and then shifted gears. "I need you to be more involved in the business side," LuLu suggested, the decision coming from a place of trust and necessity. Matty's enthusiasm for the idea was a small comfort amid the chaos.

As LuLu wrapped up the call, she hurried to change clothes, her mind still spinning with everything that lay ahead. Just as she finished, Silas returned from his run, the sweat glistening on his skin as he moved toward the shower. She caught his arm before he could disappear into the bathroom.

"Wait," LuLu said, her voice holding a note of urgency. She hesitated, searching his eyes for understanding. "Can you help me go through all your research? I really think there's something important there. I closed the bar for the week."

Silas paused, the intensity of her words sinking in. He studied her for a moment, reading the determination in her eyes before he nodded. "Yeah," he said, his voice soft but resolute. "If that's what you want, I'm here to help."

LuLu headed downstairs, the sound of the shower running in the background as she left Silas to his routine. The bar was quiet, almost too quiet, as she flipped open her laptop, the glow of the screen cutting through the dim light. Her fingers hovered over the keyboard, her mind racing with thoughts of what could be lurking in her inbox. When she noticed a new message from Heather, her breath caught.

A glimmer of hope flickered in her chest as she clicked on the email, praying it might hold something that could help banish the nightmares that had been haunting her. But as her eyes scanned the words, that hope quickly turned to a sinking dread.

"LuLu," the message began, the tone cold and distant. "I went into Ryan's cloud account. I was able to get some of his passwords from our safe. The police were here asking about you. I feel there is more here than a visit and a picture. I do not like being lied to. Since this will be our last contact, I looked for the picture. Something weird happened though. Ryan's entire cloud account had been deleted.

Please do not contact me again. Heather"

LuLu's heart pounded as she reread the message, her mind reeling. The words blurred slightly as she blinked, the realization of what Heather had discovered hitting her like a punch to the gut. Ryan's entire cloud account, gone. The weight of it pressed down on her, a new layer of fear settling in her chest. Heather's finality was unmistakable; whatever slim connection they had was now severed, and the truth was slipping further out of reach.

She sat back in the bar stool, the bar's silence now oppressive as the implications of Heather's words sank in. The police were looking at her, and someone had wiped Ryan's account clean. She was being watched, manipulated, and left in the dark, and the feeling of isolation wrapped around her like a vise.

Twenty

LuLu stood in the bathroom, the steam from the shower curling around her as she stared at the email on her phone. Her eyes widened in disbelief, and before she could stop herself, she shouted, "His entire cloud account was deleted!"

Silas, mid-shampoo, blinked through the suds and quickly pulled back the shower curtain just enough to peer out at her, pink-tinted foam sliding down his face. "What?" he asked, rubbing his eyes, trying to process her outburst.

"Someone deleted Ryan's entire cloud account," she repeated, her voice now lower, but the urgency still crackling in the air between them.

Silas frowned, rinsing his face. "Get the USB drive. Let me finish up, and we'll take a look at it. I managed to get it working, but it was really locked down." He let the curtain fall back into place, the sound of water resuming as LuLu's heart raced with the new development.

Without wasting another second, she bolted downstairs to the bar. The familiar glow of Silas's mind map on the wall greeted her, the intricate web of connections and leads he'd been working on. She quickly hooked the projector up, casting the complex diagram onto the wall. The urgency in her movements was palpable as she sprinted back upstairs, rummaging through her jeans from the other day until her fingers closed around the small USB drive.

Returning to the bar, she tried to focus on Annie's file while waiting for Silas, but her eyes skimmed the words without absorbing them. The tension in her shoulders only eased when she heard Silas's footsteps approaching. He entered the room, his hair still damp, and smiled at her with that calm, reassuring presence she needed right now.

Without a word, he took her laptop and the USB drive from her hands. The mind map disappeared from the wall as he plugged in the USB drive, and in its place, a flood of folders appeared, each labeled with something that sent a shiver down her spine.

The list:

1. **Affair Evidence**
2. **Bribery**
3. **Political**
4. **Financial Fraud**
5. **Gambling Debts**
6. **Medical Malpractice**
7. **Sexual Harassment**
8. **Drug Trafficking**
9. **Sex Tapes**

Silas moved the cursor over the folders, each one blinking ominously on the screen. "Every folder has its own encryption," he explained, his voice steady, but with a hint of the weight behind the discovery. "I've managed to unlock a few—gambling debts and medical malpractice. But the rest... they're locked down tight. Ryan wasn't just collecting information; he was building an arsenal, recording every person he ever interacted with."

LuLu's eyes darted over the screen, the names of the folders sending a shiver down her spine. "Which ones did you unlock?" she asked, her voice betraying a mix of fear and curiosity.

"Let me show you," Silas said, opening the folder labeled "Medical Malpractice." A list of names appeared, each one a potential victim or pawn in Ryan's twisted game. He clicked on the name "Baker, Richard." LuLu's breath caught.

"That's his father," she whispered, the realization sinking in like a stone.

Silas nodded grimly. "Yeah. And this is what he had on his own father." He began opening files—videos, emails, charts—each one a damning piece of evidence showing Richard Baker's medical errors and ethical breaches. It was all there, meticulously documented in black and white.

"He kept all this on his own father?" LuLu's voice wavered, her mind struggling to grasp the enormity of Ryan's betrayal.

Silas's expression was hard as he looked at the screen. "Yeah, and if he did this to his father, imagine what he's got on everyone else. You're not the only one who might've wanted him dead."

LuLu scanned through the files, her fingers trembling as she clicked through the evidence. The weight of what Ryan had done was suffocating. If he could blackmail his own father, who else was on his hit list? Greg, Liam, Annie... her heart pounded as she considered the possibilities. And then, her thoughts landed on Sasha. Could Ryan have kept something on her too? She shook her head. No, Sasha was different. Ryan had always claimed to love her, said she was the one person he'd never hurt. But now, with this new knowledge, even that seemed uncertain.

Silas's voice broke through her thoughts. "You should see what he has on his mother," he said, clicking on another folder.

But before LuLu could respond, a soft whining from the stairs interrupted them. Doodle was pacing, eager to go outside. Silas stood up. "I'll let him out. Here, you take the laptop," he said, handing it over.

LuLu nodded, her mind still racing as she clicked through more files. None of the names jumped out at her, but the implications were clear—Ryan's reach was far and wide.

Silas burst through the door, his eyebrows furrowed in confusion. His eyes immediately landed on the giant hole that had been crudely cut out of the wooden frame.

"What the fucking fuck is that?" he cried, gesturing towards the gaping entryway.

LuLu couldn't hold back her laughter at his shocked expression. "Looks like someone's booty call got creative," she quipped, a mischievous glint in her eye.

But Silas was too preoccupied with his phone to join in on the humor. He shook his head and groaned. "You do realize anyone could break into your place now, right?"

With a dismissive wave of her hand, LuLu replied, "Relax dude, I've got it covered. See that box over there? It's my high-tech security system."

Silas just sighed and rubbed his temples. "I swear to

fucking god," he muttered between chuckles at LuLu's antics.

She changed the subject and said, "I'm grabbing dinner with Sasha. Can you work on the USB drive while I'm out?"

"Sure," she replied, watching as he unplugged the laptop and followed her back upstairs, Doodle eagerly trailing behind them. Once in the apartment, Doodle settled beside Silas, wagging his tail as if proud to be part of the team.

Silas smiled, ruffling the dog's ears. "My best friend and I have got this. See you when you get back," he joked, though LuLu couldn't help but feel a pang of jealousy at how quickly Doodle had taken to him.

With a final glance at the two of them, she hurried across the street to meet Sasha, her mind still buzzing with everything she'd just learned. The familiar sight of two parked cars did little to ease her nerves, but when she saw Sasha waiting for her at a booth, the tension eased. They ran to each other, embracing like they'd been apart for years.

"Okay, tell me everything," Sasha said as they sat down, her eyes full of concern.

LuLu took a deep breath, ready to dive into the tangled web of secrets Ryan had left behind.

After LuLu laid out everything that had happened since they last spoke, Sasha just sat there, her eyes wide and her mouth slightly open. For the first time since they were twelve, Sasha was utterly speechless, her usual quick-wittedness nowhere to be found.

LuLu broke the silence, her voice steady and determined. "I know this all sounds insane, but I'm not going to jail for something I didn't do."

Sasha finally blinked, shaking herself out of her stunned

state. "Once they find Liam, this will all get cleared up. I bet he killed Ryan. That's why he's on the run."

LuLu hesitated, her thoughts drifting back to that night in the parking lot. The memory of Liam's face flashed in her mind—he'd looked terrified. She recognized that look, the one of someone cornered by fear. "I thought so too," she began, her voice faltering as she replayed the scene in her head.

"Who?" Sasha leaned forward, her brows furrowed in concern.

"I'm not sure," LuLu admitted, frustration creeping into her tone. "But Greg was paying Liam's rent. Maybe one of those folders has something on him, and he just couldn't handle it anymore."

Sasha nodded slowly, her expression growing more serious. "That makes sense. When I get home, I'll bring it up casually to Rebecca, see if she knows anything."

LuLu's eyes softened as she changed the subject. "Speaking of Rebecca, has she proposed yet?" she asked, reaching across the table to squeeze Sasha's hand.

A blush crept up Sasha's cheeks, and a smile tugged at her lips. "Not yet. I think she's waiting until this whole mess is over. But she's the one, Lu. I know it."

LuLu's chest fluttered with a happiness she hadn't felt in ages, the kind that lifted the weight of the world off her shoulders, even if just for a moment. Seeing Sasha so sure of her future filled LuLu with a deep, contented warmth, a feeling that cut through the chaos surrounding her life.

Suddenly, an idea sparked in LuLu's mind. Her eyes lit up as she grabbed her phone. "I have a crazy idea!" she exclaimed, her fingers already flying across the screen. "I might not be able to text Liam, but what's the bet that he's checking his email? I'm going to email him and tell him I have the USB drive and know everything. I'll lure him out."

Sasha's face was drained of color. She quickly reached out, grasping LuLu's hand tightly. "Wait," she urged, her voice filled with concern. "This isn't safe. You need to let Rebecca take this on."

LuLu hesitated for only a second before gently pulling her hand free, determination hardening her expression. "Sasha, I need you to be with me on this. I need to know I can trust you."

"You can trust me," Sasha whispered, her voice thick with worry. "I just don't want you to get hurt or in trouble. Please, let the police and Rebecca handle this." But LuLu was already typing out the email, her mind set.

```
Liam,
I have the USB drive with the
information. I need to
understand what this is, or
I'm going to give everything
to the police.
Name the time and place.
LuLu
```

She hit send and looked up at Sasha, who seemed on the verge of tears. The tension between them was palpable, but LuLu reached across the table and took Sasha's hands in hers, squeezing them gently. The warmth of Sasha's hands was a silent reassurance, a reminder of the deep bond they shared. LuLu smiled, trying to convey her trust and love for Sasha, who had always been there for her.

"Please be careful," Sasha finally said, her voice soft but laced with an undercurrent of fear. She forced a smile, trying to mask her anxiety, but the worry in her eyes was unmistakable.

Their conversation drifted from topic to topic, weaving through laughter and comfortable silences, yet beneath the surface, an unspoken tension lingered. Sasha's eyes flickered with worry, and LuLu's smile never quite reached her eyes. They were both trying to cling to normalcy, but the weight of everything unsaid hovered between them, pressing down like a storm cloud.

A sudden vibration on the table made LuLu glance down at her phone. A text from Silas: "Might have found something. I need to run home to do something on my own computer. It might take a while. Can we grab breakfast tomorrow?" Her pulse quickened, the words snapping her back to the reality of the situation. She looked up at Sasha, a question in her eyes.

"Do you want to come with me?" she asked, her tone hopeful, though she already sensed the answer.

Sasha shook her head gently, her lips forming a small, understanding smile. "No, you go ahead. I'll be fine here," she replied, her voice steady but tinged with the same quiet concern that had been threading through their conversation all night.

LuLu nodded, the answer making sense, yet leaving a small pang of disappointment in her chest. She reached out, giving Sasha's hand a reassuring squeeze before standing up. "I'll text you later," she promised, trying to keep her tone light, but the undercurrent of urgency was undeniable.

Sasha's smile softened, the warmth in her eyes deepening as if she were silently passing on her strength to LuLu. "Be safe, and text me as soon as you know something," she murmured, her gaze lingering on LuLu as she turned to leave, concern still etched in her features.

LuLu paused at the counter, ordering a few items to take back with her. She added a burger, fries, and a Coke, instructing the server to bag them separately. Sasha waved her goodbye, their parting tinged with unspoken worries, and headed out.

When her food was ready, LuLu left too, but instead of heading straight to the bar, she veered toward the silver car that had become an all-too-familiar presence outside. Approaching the vehicle, she tapped on the window, which slid down slowly to reveal the stocky man, LuLu could not remember his name, behind the wheel, his eyes sharp but unreadable.

Without hesitation, LuLu held up the bag and the drink. "Figured you're not getting many decent meals while watching me. I hope you are not a vegetarian." she remarked, her tone casual as she handed the food through the window. Not waiting for a response, she turned and walked into the bar, leaving the man to stare after her in surprise.

As LuLu opened the door to the bar, she noticed Doodle standing at the top of the stairs, his tail wagging briefly before drooping as if disappointed it was her and not Silas. The sight made her heart sink a little, but she shrugged it off, settling in to watch some TV before heading to bed.

Twenty-One

Silas, his grin stretching wide across his face.

"Guess who cracked the entire USB drive?" he said, flashing a cheeky thumbs-up. "This guy."

Before he could say another word, LuLu darted forward, wrapping her arms around his neck and kissing him with a fervor that spoke of her relief and gratitude. Silas responded by pulling her close, the warmth of his embrace enveloping her as she breathed in his familiar scent. For a moment, the world outside didn't matter. But Doodle's sharp bark pierced the air, snapping them back to reality.

Silas chuckled, gently pulling back. "I'm starving. How about we hit that new spot on the other side of town? Then I can walk you through everything I found."

LuLu's smile wavered, her enthusiasm dimming. "I don't really fit in there," she admitted, recalling her last experience with Sasha. "When we went, they weren't exactly thrilled to see us."

Silas raised an eyebrow and smirked. "Screw them," he declared, grabbing her hand and leading her out to his car, where Heath waited. As they drove, Silas couldn't help but boast about his discoveries on the USB drive, his pride evident in every word. LuLu listened, heartened by his excitement, even as her apprehension about the restaurant lingered.

When they pulled up to the restaurant, they made their way inside, and Silas excused himself to use the restroom. LuLu approached the hostess stand alone, her nerves prickling as she recognized the same hostess from before, now standing with a waiter. The hostess's eyes narrowed as LuLu approached, and a condescending smirk tugged at her lips.

"Table for one today?" the hostess sneered, her gaze sweeping disdainfully over LuLu's sweatpants. "Or should we just bag up some kitchen scraps for you to take home?"

The waiter beside her snickered, and LuLu's cheeks burned with embarrassment and anger. "Excuse me," she said, her voice trembling but firm. "How dare you. My money is just as good as anyone else's."

The hostess's mocking smile only widened. "I'm sure it is."

Before LuLu could respond, Silas appeared at her side, his presence instantly commanding the attention of the two women. "Is there a problem here?" he asked, his voice low and dangerous. Both the hostess and the waiter straightened, their smirks fading.

"No, sir, we were just—" the hostess began, but Silas cut her off, his gaze hardening.

"I think you were insulting my girlfriend," he stated flatly, his tone leaving no room for argument.

The waiter's eyes widened in disbelief. "Your girlfriend?"

Silas didn't bother with a reply. "I'd like to be seated now," he demanded, his voice rising enough to draw the attention of the manager, who quickly emerged to assess the situation. Silas pulled the manager aside, speaking to him in a low, controlled voice. Whatever he said made the manager's face pale.

Turning to LuLu, the manager offered a hurried apology. "I'm so sorry. This is not what we want our restaurant to represent. Your breakfast is on the house." He then turned to the hostess and the waiter, his expression grim. "My office, now."

As they were led to their table, LuLu couldn't suppress the wide grin that spread across her face. "I've never seen anything like that before," she said, still reeling from the unexpected turn of events.

Silas leaned in, his voice dropping to a low, almost secretive tone. "You know," he murmured, "nobody worth a damn cares if you're not wearing thousand-dollar shoes."

LuLu's shoulders relaxed, the tension easing from her body as she soaked in the warmth of his words and presence. Her lips curled into a soft smile as they settled into their seats. The ambient chatter of the restaurant faded into the background as Silas began to explain what he'd uncovered on the USB drive. His eyes gleamed with a mix of triumph and concern as he described the files—everything from tax returns to compromising videos, an overwhelming trove of private information. LuLu listened intently, her brows knitting together in disbelief at how someone could amass such a vast, invasive collection on so many people.

Mid-conversation, Silas's expression shifted as if he'd just remembered something important. "Oh, before I forget," he said, reaching into his pocket. He pulled out a small black velvet box, its surface matte and smooth against his palm. With a flick of his wrist, he slid it across the table to LuLu.

Her breath caught as she opened the box, revealing a delicate white gold heart-shaped locket nestled inside. The locket glinted softly under the restaurant's lights, adorned with a tiny ruby embedded on its surface.

"It's beautiful," LuLu whispered, her fingers brushing over the intricate design. "You didn't need to get me anything."

Silas's gaze softened as he leaned closer. "I had it made, just for you. The locket doesn't open—inside, it has a tiny GPS. If you press the ruby, it sends a signal to my phone. Since you seem determined to find trouble," he teased, a hint of seriousness lacing his words, "this way, if you're in a situation where you can't reach your phone, you can still call for help. But don't worry—it only works if you activate it. I won't track you unless you want me to. Is that okay? It just that you have been off, well, not being so safe. This is just, literally, just if you need me. I swear."

LuLu's eyes sparkled with a mix of gratitude and affection as she fastened the locket around her neck. The cool metal rested against her skin, a comforting weight that spoke of his care for her. "I love it," she said, her voice tinged with emotion, as she looked up at Silas with a smile that held a world of meaning. She hit the ruby on the front and she heard a beep on Silas' phone.

As they shared the meal, their conversation flowed seamlessly, weaving through the chaos surrounding them. LuLu's brow furrowed as she spoke about the urgency of dealing with the police, her voice steady despite the underlying tension. Silas nodded, his eyes narrowing with determination, signaling that he understood the gravity of the situation.

When they returned to the bar, the air around them thickened, the lightness of their earlier conversation evaporating into a tense, focused silence. They moved as one, the weight of their mission clear in every step. Without a word, they made their way to the kitchen table, sitting shoulder to shoulder, their faces set in grim determination as the computer screen flickered to life.

Afternoons blurred into a haze of data and numbers, the monotony of scrolling through endless bank reports only deepening the sense of unease. They waded through file after file, each one a small piece of a larger, darker puzzle. The folder labeled "sex tapes" was left for last, a silent understanding passing between them. When they finally opened it, a cold wave of dread washed over them. Watching the grainy footage, glimpsing people in their most vulnerable moments, left them feeling sullied, yet they pushed through, knowing they had to.

LuLu's eyes caught on a video file labeled with two names that made her blood run cold—"Baker, Sasha" and "Pillar, LuLu." Her heart pounded in her chest as Silas noticed the change in her demeanor. He immediately wrapped an arm around her, his voice low and steady.

Silas's voice was gentle, but firm, as he whispered, "We don't have to watch this." LuLu, however, felt an ironclad resolve settle over her, her mind made up. With a hand that trembled despite her determination, she moved the cursor and clicked on the video labeled with Sasha's name. A deep breath, and then the screen came to life.

The video was raw, unfiltered—clearly filmed without anyone's knowledge. The grainy footage revealed Ryan's room, its familiarity adding a layer of unease. The space remained empty for a few tense moments, filled only with the distant hum of the webcam. Then, the silence was shattered by a laugh, one that LuLu recognized immediately. Sasha stumbled into view, her movements unsteady, clearly under the influence.

The camera caught everything, including the entrance of another figure. A voice followed, one that made LuLu's heart stop—Greg, Ryan's roommate. He stepped into the frame, his presence dark and unsettling. "We can't tell anyone about this," Sasha murmured, her words slurred but insistent, as Greg began to undress her, his hands moving over her with an unsettling familiarity.

LuLu's breath caught in her throat, her chest tightening as the horrific scene played out before her eyes. Her heart pounded in her ears, drowning out the sickening sounds coming from the screen. Time seemed to stretch, each frame of the video an agonizing reminder of a past she had fought so hard to bury. Her fingers twitched, but she couldn't bring herself to tear her gaze away.

Silas's hand, warm and steady, gently covered hers, his touch a lifeline in the overwhelming darkness. His fingers brushed the keyboard, and with a single, quiet motion, he turned off the video, plunging the screen into blackness. The sudden silence was suffocating, wrapping around them like a shroud.

"Let's not watch the other one," Silas murmured, his voice laced with concern. But LuLu's hand moved almost of its own accord, clicking on the video bearing her name. She couldn't explain the compulsion, not even to herself—she needed to see it, needed to confront the monster who had stolen her sense of safety.

The video crackled to life, the sound of static filling LuLu's ears like a warning. Her heart plummeted into her stomach as her worst fears were brought to brutal reality on the screen before her. There she was, sprawled across the bed like a broken doll, her body contorted in pain and terror, her face drained of all emotion.

As Liam burst onto the screen, his movements erratic and fueled by a toxic mix of anger and alcohol, the air in the room seemed to thicken with suffocating dread. The stench of his breath, thick with booze and violence, seeped through the screen, a pungent warning of the horrors to come. His gaze, dark and predatory, lingered on her defenseless form, relishing in the power he held over her.

With every passing moment captured by the camera's mocking lens, LuLu's heart raced with fear. A slight twitch of her hand signaled her brief return to consciousness before she was once again consumed by terror. She tried to fight back against his overwhelming weight but it was useless. Her muffled screams were drowned out by Ryan's maniacal laughter, a sickening soundtrack to her torment.

And then came the strike—Liam's hand crashing down like a sledgehammer, sending shockwaves of agony rippling through her body. It was a brutal blow that silenced her struggles in an instant. As she lay there limp and lifeless, the triumphant laughter continued to ring in her ears, taunting and daring her to defy them again. The cycle would continue until they had drained every last bit of fight from her.

A primal scream tears through LuLu's soul as she watches the nightmare of her past play out on the screen. Each second is like a razor tearing deeper into her psyche, leaving behind a trail of raw and searing pain. She is forced to relive her worst fears in a grotesque and twisted reflection that she can't escape from, no matter how much she longs to break free.

"Those pieces of shit," Silas growls, his voice low and venomous. His hands clenched into fists, knuckles white with restrained fury. "I'll make them pay for what they did to you. And if I ever have another chance at Liam, I will kill him." The intensity in his words resonates throughout the room, a promise of deadly vengeance that sends shivers down their spines.

She could feel his rage boiling over as he reached for the laptop, his movements sharp and decisive. He slammed it shut, yanking the screen away from her as if trying to protect her from the horror it held. But the damage was done. LuLu remained frozen, her eyes locked on the space where the laptop had been moments before.

"I refuse to be broken." She whisper so quite that she hardly heard herself.

Her mind felt as though it had been ripped apart, fragments of memory and pain colliding in a chaotic storm. The weight of the past bore down on her like a crushing wave, drowning her in the relentless flood of emotions she could no longer contain. She sat in a daze, her body unmoving, her thoughts a suffocating blur of anguish.

Silas's hand reached out to her, but LuLu flinched away like a wild animal. Her body coiled tight, ready to strike, as she retreated to the bathroom, slamming the door shut with a resounding thud that shook the entire apartment. The click of the shower knob echoed through the walls, followed by the roar of water at its hottest setting.

She stepped into the scalding stream fully clothed, her clothes clinging to her skin like a suffocating second layer.

The searing water burned against her flesh, but she welcomed the pain, embracing it like an old friend. She curled into herself in the small tub, steam filling every inch of space, suffocating her until she couldn't breathe. And then it happened - the dam broke. A primal scream raged from her throat, ripping through the air and piercing Silas's heart. It was a sound that had been trapped inside her for too long, a sound that demanded to be set free.

"I refuse to be broken!" She screamed so hard her throat felt like a brush burn.

Silas burst into the bathroom, fear and confusion etched on his face as he saw LuLu huddled under scorching water. Without hesitation, he climbed into the tub beside her, frantically adjusting the faucet to cool the water down. But even as the water turned tepid, LuLu remained on fire inside. Silas wrapped his arms around her tightly, trying to hold onto her as she thrashed and twisted in agony. He whispered words of love and comfort in her ear, desperately hoping they could break through the pain and bring her back from the edge of madness.

Her screams muffled against his chest, each one a jagged edge cutting through the air, until they dissolved into sobs. She cried until her voice was hoarse, the tears flowing until there was nothing left, her body trembling in his embrace as the last of her strength ebbed away. The phrase, repeated again and again "I refused to be broken" was her chant. Time passed like the rushing water over her body, in a seemingly endless loop.

When LuLu was ready, Silas gently helped her to her feet, his hands steadying her as they moved toward her bedroom. Without a word, he began to peel off her soaked clothes, his touch careful and deliberate, as if afraid she might shatter. He opened each drawer with precision, pulling out soft, dry clothes, and dressed her with a tenderness that spoke of his helplessness more than anything else.

After finding her emergency medication in the cabinet, he handed her a pill, which she swallowed silently, her eyes distant and vacant. Doodle padded into the room, sensing her distress, and curled up beside her. His little whimpers filled the space as he pressed against her, trying to offer comfort in the only way he knew how. When she rolled over, his body tumbled off her, and he wagged his tail, hopeful for a moment that she might engage with him. But as she remained still, his enthusiasm faded, and he settled down, resting his head on her leg, his quiet presence a small, grounding weight.

Silas slipped into bed beside her, his arms encircling her protectively. He pressed a light kiss to the top of her head, the gesture full of unspoken worry and a deep, aching desire to make things right, even though he had no idea how.

"I don't think you should be alone tonight," he murmured, his voice gentle yet firm. The words seemed to break through her fragile composure, and despite her efforts to hold back, the tears came again, a fresh wave of grief and exhaustion spilling over. She cried softly, the sobs wracking her body until, eventually, the exhaustion overtook her, and she fell into a restless sleep in his arms.

The next morning, Silas brought breakfast to LuLu, hoping she might be tempted to eat, but she remained curled in bed, her back to him. Sleep came in restless waves, a haze that dulled everything. Even the nightmares, once terrifying, had lost their edge—her waking reality had become a far greater horror. Doodle stayed glued to her side, his quiet presence the only comfort she allowed.

Silas lingered by her side, his concern evident in every movement. He stayed another night, but the strain was visible; he needed to go home to gather things if he planned to stay longer. She could see the conflict in his eyes, his hesitation to leave her alone, but she couldn't find the strength to speak. Finally, he brought her phone to her bedside, his voice trembling slightly as he sat down.

"You need to call your doctor," he urged gently, his back turned to her. "Please."

LuLu watched him, noticing the slight tremor in his shoulders. He was fighting back tears, trying to remain strong for her.

Silas' voice broke as he spoke, thick with a mixture of anger and sadness. "I didn't kill Ryan," he spat out, his fists clenching at his sides. "But damn it, I'm glad he's dead. If he were alive now, I don't know what I'd do to him." his eyes burned with fiery intensity. "And if that bastard Liam comes anywhere near you again, I'll make sure he pays for what he did. I'll break every bone in his body and watch him suffer." He took a deep breath, trying to calm himself. "What happened to you is beyond unfair," he said through gritted teeth. "Just tell me what you need from me, and I'll do whatever it takes to make it right." His love and rage for the person before him seemed to want to consume him, pushing him toward a dangerous edge where LuLu might not be able to wheel him back from.

She needed to take care of herself right now. Slowly, she forced herself to sit up, her hand trembling as she reached out and placed it on Silas's back. He turned, pulling her into his arms with a tenderness that made her heart ache.

"What do you need?" he asked softly, searching her face for an answer. "Max is downstairs, if you need anything."

She nodded in response. "I am not going anywhere, but I think you need to go and talk to him. I will give you your privacy." She nodded again, even though she wasn't sure that she wanted to talk to Max. She left Silas and Doodle sitting on her bed and walked to the stairs. She hesitated.

"LuLu! Get your ass down here!" His voice thundered through the walls. She laughed. Of course. At least she wasn't alone.Her feet moved slowly, one stair at a time, her fingers brushing the wooden banister. At the bottom, she saw Max, hunched over the small table. Two beers sat between them. One waited in front of the empty chair.

Without a word, she slid into the seat opposite him. His eyes bore into her, hard and unyielding. She felt the weight of it, the judgment, but stayed silent, waiting.

Max's voice softened, but the weight of his words remained heavy. "Your dad and I go way back, you know that. He was quite the player in our younger days," he said, taking a sip from his beer. She couldn't hide her surprise at this revelation. "Believe me or not, your pops had a different girl for every day of the week. Nina and I were high school sweethearts, but Frank always made fun of us," Max paused momentarily before continuing with a smile, "but then your mother walked into the bar and everything changed." He took another swig of beer before recounting the story of how Frank fell head over heels for her mom at first sight. "I remember it like it was yesterday. She had flowing chestnut hair and bright blue eyes that Frank just couldn't resist," Max said wistfully. "It was like something out of a cheesy romance novel, but it was real." He explained how their lives were forever changed when they met their soulmates, even though both women came with their own complications. But to Frank, none of that mattered once he met her and fell in love with her. The memories hung thick in the air between them as Max took another drink from his beer and she followed suit, feeling like an adult finally being spoken to as one by Max.

"You were in high school, and they couldn't have been prouder. Every damn soccer game, they were there, cheering. Hell, Frank even used the bar for that end-of-year party. Remember that?" His voice caught, and for a second, it seemed he'd stop. But he pushed on. "When you went to college, all they talked about was how their girl was going to make it big. New York, the big city. They were so proud, Lu."

Her heart squeezed as he kept going, the words sinking deeper than she wanted them to. She looked away, but the memories flashed like a film reel in her mind.

Max's voice trembled as he spoke, the deep lines etched into his face making him look older than his years. He took a swig of his beer and stared at her over the rim. "You know, that night you got hurt...we would've moved mountains to get to you. But we couldn't. And then we lost you." His eyes glistened with unshed tears.

He paused and took a deep breath before continuing. "My mom always used to say, the only place where things are fair is in a pie-eating contest or a pig race. Life ain't fair, but we gotta keep going." He reached across the table and gently squeezed her hand.

"I know something happened to you in college, something you haven't told me. And that's okay, you don't have to. But I can see how much it hurts you. You've been working so hard to move past it, but I can see it still haunts you." He leaned in closer and looked into her eyes.

"Don't let them win," he said firmly. "Don't let the bad they did seep into your life and control who you are. You're stronger than that. Show this world who you really are - tough and resilient. Don't let them take that away from you."

LuLu could feel tears prickling at her own eyes as she listened to him speak with such compassion and understanding. Max was right, she needed to stop hiding and start living again. She nodded, determined to follow his advice.

"Thank you," she whispered, squeezing his hand back.

"Anytime," he replied with a small smile. "You're good, they're the evil ones."

Her lip trembled as he added, almost whispering, "Your mom was the strongest woman I ever knew. Don't tell Nina. But you... you might be even stronger."

The dam broke. She sobbed, the weight of his words pulling everything out of her. Max stood without hesitation, pulling her into his arms. His hug was strong, unrelenting, the way a father would hold his child. And as the tears soaked into his shirt, she knew he was the only father she had left.

Moving with a detached calm, she retrieved the USB drive from her computer and slipped it into a hidden compartment in her apartment, burying it like a secret she wasn't ready to confront. Back in her room, she took her medication and, with trembling fingers, called Dr. Clover for an emergency appointment. The numbness began to creep back in, but this time, she was determined to push through it. Silas pulled her into his arms and held her until sleep pressed upon her.

Twenty-Two

LuLu sat across from Dr. Clover, her voice trembling as she recounted everything that had happened. The words spilled out, each one heavier than the last, and Dr. Clover listened intently, her usually composed demeanor cracking as her eyes widened in shock. At times, her mouth parted in disbelief, the weight of LuLu's story rendering her momentarily speechless.

Dr. Clover's eyes widened, and she leaned back in her chair, letting out a breath she hadn't realized she'd been holding. "Holy shit," she muttered under her breath, momentarily abandoning her professional composure. "I'm sorry for the language, but... that's a lot. Too much."

She shifted forward, her tone hardening, eyes locking onto LuLu's with a sudden intensity. "You need to take this to the police. All of it. You can't keep carrying this alone— it's too dangerous, LuLu." Her voice, though still gentle, carried an unmistakable urgency, as if every second mattered.

LuLu nodded, though a pang of unease twisted in her

gut as she realized she hadn't heard from Rebecca about setting up a time to meet with the authorities. "I will," she replied, trying to sound resolute. "I'll meet with them next week."

Dr. Clover gave a small, approving nod, her professional mask slipping back into place. She adjusted LuLu's prescription, renewing one of the medications with a quick scribble on her pad, before handing it over.

As LuLu left the office, a tight knot of anxiety settled in her chest. The walk back to the bar felt unusually long, every sound and shadow amplifying the unease that prickled along her spine. Dr. Clover had assured her that it was normal to feel on edge after everything, but the sensation that someone was watching her clung to her like a second skin. She forced herself to keep moving, trying to dismiss the thought as paranoia.

"It's probably just the police," she muttered under her breath, trying to rationalize the gnawing feeling. But when she reached the parking lot, her heart skipped a beat. The silver police car that usually sat there, a silent sentinel, was gone.

The absence sent a chill down her spine, her footsteps faltering as she glanced around, half-expecting someone to step out of the shadows. The familiar comfort of the bar was just ahead, but even as she quickened her pace, the unsettling feeling lingered, refusing to be shrugged off.

The black car in the parking lot caught LuLu's eye, a familiar presence that tugged at her memory. She approached it, her knuckles tapping lightly on the window. The glass slid down, revealing Heath's concerned face.

"You know Silas went home," she remarked, her voice edged with fatigue.

"I'm here for you," Heath replied, his tone gentle but firm. "Silas thought it would be a good idea. Are you okay? He's really worried, and... he was super upset when he left the other day. Don't tell him I told you that."

"I won't," LuLu promised, but the truth spilled out before she could stop it. "And no. Everything is not okay."

As soon as the words left her mouth, the tears began to flow. Without a second thought, Heath opened the car door and pulled her into a bear hug, enveloping her in his massive arms. For a moment, she felt small, like a child seeking comfort in the embrace of someone much larger. She took a deep breath, the steady rise and fall of his chest grounding her.

When she finally stepped back, Heath released her gently, a hint of apology in his eyes. "I'm sorry. You looked like you needed it."

"Thank you," she murmured, wiping her eyes. "But go home. I am fine."

With that, she turned and walked away, feeling the weight of his concern following her, but grateful for the brief moment of solace he had offered. She could hear him get back into the car and turn it on. She did not need babysat.

LuLu pushed open the door to the bar and made her way up the stairs to her apartment. As she reached the top, Doodle was already there, his eyes darting past her in search of someone else. When he realized it was only her, he let out a huff, his disappointment clear. LuLu narrowed her eyes at him, a hint of exasperation in her voice.

"I'm not liking this new attitude," she muttered, watching as Doodle turned his back on her and slipped outside through the small hole in the door.

Her phone buzzed, pulling her attention away from the dog. It was Silas, checking in. She quickly typed a reassuring reply and sent it off, her fingers lingering over the screen. Several unread messages from Sasha stared back at her, but she couldn't bring herself to open them. It wasn't anger that held her back—just a deep, gnawing sadness, a sense of betrayal that she couldn't quite process.

LuLu wasn't that girl anymore. She refused to be that girl anymore. With a steadying breath, she opened Sasha's messages, not bothering to read the flood of texts that filled the screen. Instead, she typed out a single, concise message, rereading it to ensure it conveyed exactly what she wanted.

LuLu: We unlocked the USB drive. I know.

As she hit send, a sudden realization struck her like a jolt of electricity. She bolted downstairs to the bar, where the evidence and research she'd been poring over was still scattered across the table. Her hands shook as she rifled through Ryan's financial records and then Sasha's. There was no overlap, no common transactions—nothing that hinted at blackmail for money. LuLu sank back into the chair, her mind racing. What was she missing? The pieces were all there, but the puzzle refused to come together.

Her phone buzzed again, dragging her out of her thoughts. She glanced at the screen.

Sasha: Please. I can explain everything. Please.

The message hung in the air, heavy with desperation. LuLu's mind churned as she stared at the text, knowing that whatever explanation Sasha had, it wouldn't be enough to erase the sense of betrayal. And yet, the pieces were still scattered, the full picture just out of reach.

LuLu sent a quick text to Silas, and when his reply came, she could sense his relief in the brief but warm response.

The idea of getting a new lawyer crossed her mind, something she mentioned casually in her next message. Silas agreed, though his words were careful, urging her not to rush into anything too quickly. The concern in his tone was clear, even through the small screen, as if he was trying to protect her from making any hasty decisions she might regret.

LuLu reached for the bar's account books, flipping through the pages with a growing sense of anticipation. As she tallied up the numbers, a flicker of surprise crossed her face. The bar's profits were better than she had expected, even outpacing the days when her parents ran it. Matty's efforts were clearly paying off—the new business he brought in, along with the steady flow of college students, was making a real difference. Buoyed by the positive outcome, she took the "Help Wanted" sign from behind the counter and placed it in the front window, feeling a small spark of optimism. Afterward, she methodically went through the inventory, making sure everything was in order for Wednesday's reopening, her movements precise and purposeful as she prepared for the days ahead.

LuLu's mind wrestled with the contradiction of her life —how everything could feel so catastrophically wrong while still managing to appear, on the surface, so unexpectedly good. Glancing at the clock, she sighed and decided it was time to turn in, knowing she needed to follow the routine Dr. Clover had recommended. She changed into her tank top and sleep shorts, and climbed into bed, letting Doodle's warm, familiar presence by her side lull her into sleep.

But the peace was short-lived. Just as she slipped into a rare, deep slumber, Doodle's sudden, frantic barking yanked her back to the surface. Disoriented, LuLu blinked into the darkness, her heart already pounding in response to Doodle's escalating barks, which morphed into a low, menacing growl. He was focused intently on the door, every muscle in his small body tense.

LuLu's breath hitched as she slipped out of bed, the heaviness of her steps betraying the dread creeping through her veins. The dim glow from the hallway barely reached her, stretching shadows across the room that seemed to crawl toward her like creeping fingers. When she noticed the kitchen door slightly ajar—a door she was certain she had closed—her stomach clenched in fear. A chill skittered down her spine, a wordless warning that something was very wrong.

Doodle's growl deepened, vibrating with a ferocity she'd never heard before, his eyes locked on the door leading to the bar, as if he could see something lurking in the darkness that she couldn't. The air around her thickened, pressing down on her, making it hard to breathe as she approached the door. Her hand trembled as she gripped the cold metal handle, her heart thudding so loudly she feared whoever—or whatever—was out there could hear it.

Slowly, she pushed the door open, the creak of the hinges loud and grating in the suffocating silence. She peered into the black void of the bar, the darkness so absolute it seemed to swallow the faint light from the hallway behind her. Doodle's growl echoed, making the stillness all the more unnerving.

"Hello?" Her voice barely escaped her throat, a fragile, trembling sound that was instantly devoured by the darkness. Her eyes darted around the floor, searching for the papers she had left there—the research she'd been working on. But instead of the neat stacks she remembered, she found the documents scattered, torn, whole sections ripped away, leaving eerie gaps that filled her with a cold sense of dread.

Her breath quickened, panic rising as she tried to comprehend the chaotic scene before her. The temperature seemed to drop, the cold seeping into her bones as the darkness pressed closer, more oppressive. Doodle's barking became more frantic, a desperate cry of terror, his small body trembling with fear until she heard a thud and a whimper.

LuLu spun around, her pulse roaring in her ears, only to be met with a blinding pain that exploded at the back of her head. The world tilted violently, stars bursting in her vision as she stumbled. Her knees buckled, the strength draining from her body as the darkness seemed to reach out and pull her under. She crumpled to the cold, unforgiving floor, the last of her consciousness slipping away as Doodle's barks grew faint, swallowed by the encroaching blackness that consumed her whole.

Twenty-Three

LuLu slowly resurfaced from the darkness, her senses returning in fragments. A relentless, pounding ache throbbed in her skull, each pulse sending waves of nausea through her. Her surroundings were a distorted blur, as if she were peering through frosted glass, with a foggy haze clouding her vision. She tried to move, but her body wouldn't obey, her limbs bound tightly to something cold and unyielding. Panic began to rise as she realized she was completely immobilized.

Distant, muffled sounds gradually broke through the thick silence, like echoes from the depths of a cavern. At first, they were just noises—indistinct clatters and shuffling, punctuated by the low hum of voices that seemed to grow nearer with every passing second. As her mind fought to focus, the sounds sharpened into distinct actions: cabinets being opened, their contents rustling, and then closed with dull thuds.

A voice, sharp and tinged with anger, cut through the fog. "You told me you weren't going to hurt her." The tone was familiar, tugging at the edges of her memory, but her mind was too cloudy to place it.

Another voice responded, this one gruff and defensive. "Next time you want to steal evidence, you handle it yourself."

The tension between them was palpable, the air crackling with barely restrained hostility. LuLu's heart pounded harder as the exchange continued, her dread intensifying with each word.

"You are such a dick. I fucking hate you," the first voice spat out, now unmistakably female, laced with venom.

"Back at you," the male voice shot back, his tone icy and dismissive.

The familiarity of the voices gnawed at her, the realization that she knew these people deepening her fear. She strained to remember, to make sense of the situation, but the pounding in her head drowned out her thoughts, leaving her adrift in a sea of confusion and pain.

Desperate to see, LuLu forced her eyes open, but even the dimness of the room was an assault on her senses, the darkness somehow too bright for her disoriented vision. Her breath hitched as she registered her surroundings, the faint outlines of familiar objects in her bar twisted by the unfamiliar terror of the situation.

She glanced down, and a wave of panic surged through her—her hands and feet were lashed securely to a bar table chair, the rough rope biting into her skin. The voices around her, though clearer now, still felt distant, like they were filtered through layers of cotton, their words echoing in her mind without meaning.

As she struggled to focus, a sickening sensation crawled over her. She felt something wet and warm trailing down her neck, a sticky substance that dripped slowly onto her leg. Her eyes followed the path of the blood, realizing with a jolt of horror that it was her own, oozing from a wound she could only assume was where they had struck her. The reality of her situation sank in, the voices continuing their ominous chatter as LuLu's mind raced, trapped in the growing fog of pain and fear.

"Where the fuck is it?" The man's voice was sharp, laced with frustration. "It has to be here."

"We have to hurry before she wakes up," the female voice replied, urgency dripping from her words. "Let's check the apartment again."

A cold realization washed over LuLu—they still thought she was unconscious. She listened intently as the two sets of footsteps retreated up the stairs. Her pulse quickened; this was her chance.

She knew this bar like the back of her hand. Every creaky floorboard, every piece of furniture was a relic from her father's time, kept out of sentimentality until they were on the brink of collapse. Lucky for her, she was tied to one of those fragile chairs.

With steely resolve, LuLu started to rock back and forth, her every motion laced with urgency. The creaking of the chair grew louder, each tilt more precarious than the last, as if the fragile balance between hope and despair hung in the air. Sweat trickled down her brow, her movements growing faster, more frantic. The old chair groaned under the strain, its legs skittering against the floor.

Finally, with a resounding crack, the chair collapsed, sending her crashing to the ground. Pain shot through her, but there was no time to react, no time to acknowledge the sting. She froze, straining to hear the inevitable.

Then it came—the rapid thud of footsteps descending the stairs, a sound that tightened her chest with fear. She forced herself to move, adrenaline propelling her as she scrambled for cover, knowing she had only seconds before they would burst into the room.

LuLu scrambled under a nearby table, the long, tattered tablecloth concealing her just as the door burst open. She held her breath, heart pounding in her ears, as the intruders approached the fallen chair, their voices rising in heated argument.

This was her moment. With every muscle in her body on high alert, LuLu emerged from her hiding spot and bolted for the stairs like a hunted animal. Her heart thundered in her chest as she reached the first step, but before she could take another breath, she heard one of them shout, "There she is!"

Her whole body froze as she whipped around, locking eyes with the two figures standing before her – Liam and Sasha. The realization of their betrayal hit her like a physical blow, sending her reeling. But there was no time to process it, no time for hurt or anger. Survival instincts kicked in and she turned and sprinted up the stairs, the sound of Doodle's frantic cries echoing behind her.

As she reached the top, panic coursing through her veins, LuLu frantically tried to grab her phone to call for help. But in her haste, she dropped it and remembered her necklace – pressing the gem for emergency assistance. Just as her finger hovered over the call button, an unseen force slammed into her from behind, knocking her to the ground.

Liam towered over her, his face twisted in fury as he grabbed her roughly and threw her onto the couch like a discarded toy. Pain exploded in her head as it hit the armrest, leaving spots dancing in front of her eyes. She knew without a doubt that she had a concussion.

Without wasting a second, Liam tossed rope to Sasha who stood nearby with a tense expression. But instead of restraining LuLu right away, Sasha hesitated and looked at Liam with pleading eyes. "Please... I don't want to hurt you," she trembled.

For a brief moment, LuLu felt relief flood through her – thinking that maybe Sasha would help her escape. But before she could react, Liam stormed over and grabbed Sasha's gun from her. Without hesitation or hesitation or remorse, he pointed it directly at LuLu, the cold metal promising nothing but violence and pain.

Sasha moved quickly, her movements fluid and precise as she bound LuLu's wrists in front of her with the rope. LuLu struggled against her restraints, but it was useless – she was trapped and at their mercy. Her mind raced, trying to make sense of it all. Sasha – her best friend, the person she trusted more than anyone, stood next to the man she hated above all else. It was a nightmare come to life.

As Sasha tied the last knot, LuLu's voice shook with disbelief and hurt. "Why?" The single word was like a stab in her chest, each syllable bringing fresh pain to her throbbing head.

Liam sneered, pointing the gun at Sasha with a dismissive wave. "I didn't kill him."

In a flash of movement, Sasha snatched the gun from his hand, her grip firm and unwavering. "Give me that," she demanded.

And then it clicked for LuLu – the weapon in Sasha's hands was her own gun, the one she had been searching for since she woke up on this hellish rollercoaster. But before she could process the shock and betrayal of it all, Sasha admitted, "I took it the night of the engagement party. I was never planning on using it. You have to believe me."

Staring up at her former friend with tears in her eyes, LuLu could only feel numbness and confusion. The person she loved and trusted most in the world had turned against her, holding her own gun as if it were nothing more than an afterthought. It was a nightmare she couldn't escape from, leaving her lost and broken in a web of betrayal and deceit. And in that moment, as everything came crashing down around her, LuLu couldn't help but regret sending Heath away.

Sasha's body convulsed with sobs as she choked out her confession, tears streaming down her face like a raging river. "I couldn't take it anymore," she gasped, her voice hoarse and raw. "You saw the video...if that got out, I'd be ruined. I can't have my sex life plastered all over the internet, and then there was you..." She trailed off, unable to continue as her emotions overwhelmed her.

Liam's eyes burned with anger and disgust as he listened to Sasha's words. His irritation was palpable as he let out a heavy sigh. "It was just one time," Sasha pleaded, desperation lacing her voice. "We were both drunk and it was during that phase when you had broken up with him. I know I cheated on Ryan, but if you found out..."

LuLu's voice cracked as she interrupted Sasha, her pain evident in every word. "I would have forgiven you," she whispered, her tone barely above a pained whimper. "You didn't have to kill him."

Liam snorted, a cruel smirk playing on his lips. "Don't flatter yourself," he spat, his sneer twisting into a sick smile. "He was blackmailing her too, just not for money."

Sasha's gaze dropped to the floor, shame washing over her as she revealed the truth behind the murder. Her voice trembled as she spoke, barely audible above a whisper. "We had scheduled hook-ups," she admitted, her cheeks burning with humiliation. "He was making me sleep with him or he'd release the tape. I didn't understand why...especially since he had a beautiful girlfriend." Her breath hitched as she struggled to continue, her voice shaking with emotion. "It was about control...he wanted to stop me from being happy with Rebecca...to keep me from being faithful to anyone after him."

Her voice faltered as she paused, wiping away tears with the back of her hand. Her once flushed face now pale and ghostly, haunted by the weight of her confession. "After what I saw at the engagement party..." she whispered, unable to finish her sentence.

Liam's laughter cut through the heavy silence like a sharp knife, his amusement bordering on sadism. He leaned back in his chair, a cruel smirk etched on his lips. "And how did that work out for you?" he taunted, his words dripping with malice.

Sasha's eyes blazed with a mixture of shame and rage as she continued her story. "He laughed at me...told me... he told me... to get on his dick or he would make me," she spat out, her voice filled with venom. "I couldn't do it...so I pulled out the gun." She closed her eyes, reliving the moment in her mind. "I pressed it against his temple and he just laughed even harder. Said I'd never have the guts to pull the trigger...started unbuttoning his pants. And that's when I shot him." Her words were laced with bitterness and regret.

With a fierce grip on his phone, she spoke through trembling lips. "That idiot never changed his passwords...so I deleted everything I could, just to be safe," she explained, her eyes hardening with determination. "But he had a backup plan."

Liam's gaze shifted to LuLu, now filled with malice. "That's where you come in," he sneered, his voice dripping with venom. "I can't let what's on that drive get out. And you, of all people, know why. So tell me—where is it?"

Her mind raced for a solution, but fear paralyzed her body. The playful façade Liam once wore was now replaced with pure menace, and Sasha's grip on the gun tightened as tension filled the room. Panic clouded LuLu's thoughts as she struggled to find a way out.

Without warning, Liam's hand struck her cheek with brutal force, sending her head snapping to the side and filling her mouth with blood. As she gasped for air, Sasha's protests grew louder but Liam crouched beside her and whispered threats in her ear. She fought back the urge to scream, forced to lie through gritted teeth in an attempt to buy time.

But Liam wasn't fooled. Another vicious slap brought her back to reality, his dark tone now laced with fresh threats. Sasha pleaded with him, desperation etched on her face.

"We don't have time for this!" Liam growled, glancing at Sasha whose patience was clearly wearing thin. "Just kill her and let's get out of here!"

Sasha hesitated, her breath hot against LuLu's skin as regret and anger battled in her eyes. In a split second decision fueled by desperation and adrenaline, LuLu lunged forward and struck Sasha's forehead with a sickening crack. Sasha stumbled backwards, dropping the gun onto the floor.

But LuLu's actions had also caused the chair beneath her to break, and she scrambled towards the weapon.

A chaotic struggle ensued as all three of them fought for control. LuLu's muscles burned with exhaustion, but she refused to give in, crawling towards the gun with every ounce of strength she had left. Sirens blared in the distance, or was it just her heart pounding in her ears?

The door burst open as Silas and Chase entered the room, their eyes scanning the chaos. Chase grabbed Sasha who broke down sobbing, while LuLu focused on reaching the gun inches away from her grasp.

In a final clash, Silas and Liam fought for control of the gun, both determined to have it. But LuLu's fingers grazed the cold metal, slick with sweat as Liam's grip tightened around it. The struggle reached a fever pitch, movements and voices merging into a dizzying blur.

And then came the deafening sound of a gunshot.

A searing pain ripped through LuLu's body, stealing her breath. Her hold loosened on the gun and her vision blurred, everything fading to black.

Twenty-Four

The dream unfolded like a scene from a play, familiar yet twisted in that eerie, dreamlike way. The table and chairs were set under the usual harsh spotlight, but the grotesque figure that haunted her nightmares was gone. Instead, LuLu sat at the table like she always did, but across from her now was Sasha. Her eyes were glassy and swollen, like she'd been crying for hours. Her curly hair was pulled messily away from her face, and she wore those same oversized plastic glasses from when they were kids—ones LuLu hadn't seen in years.

They stared at each other for what felt like forever. Neither of them moved, the weight of unspoken words heavy in the thick, oppressive silence.

A faint, rhythmic beep broke through the stillness—a sound so subtle, LuLu barely noticed at first. But it was there, persistent. Beep... beep.

"What the hell does this mean?" LuLu's frustration cracked through the silence, her voice shaking with anger. The beeping echoed behind her words, growing louder.

Sasha's figure, strangely real for a dream, cocked her head, her voice hollow and distant. "What do you mean?"

LuLu's patience snapped. "What the fuck is all of this? Some sort of fucked up test? I am tired of these games." Her hands slammed onto the table, shaking with rage. The beeping, still soft but growing more insistent, beep... beep.

The sound became sharper, cutting through her rising anger, pulling her attention away. It was like a distant alarm, reminding her that something—somewhere—was real and waiting to drag her out of this nightmare.

Sasha's words floated through the dim, surreal air like smoke, curling around LuLu's mind. "You're playing with yourself then, friend." The word friend stung. It made LuLu's skin crawl, a deep ache swelling in her chest. She leaned back in her chair, arms crossing defensively, trying to shield herself from the impact of that one word.

"Don't be like that. One mistake, and years of friendship are gone?"

LuLu's response was venomous, her voice a sharp, cutting edge. "One mistake?" she sneered, her mouth twisting bitterly.

Sasha leaned forward, her eyes locked onto LuLu's, unblinking. "How did I treat Greg when you two got engaged?"

"You hated him. You refused to be in my wedding party —hell, you didn't even want to come to the wedding." LuLu's voice cracked, anger barely masking the hurt she was feeling. Sasha nodded as if it all made sense. "I always thought it was because of Annie," LuLu added, her voice softer now.

Sasha shook her head slowly. "Not everything is about

Annie. I think you forget—when was the last time we talked about me?"

LuLu's eyes narrowed, uncertain where this was going. Sasha's voice pressed on. "And you—so obsessed with the case. You made sure I met with Rebecca, didn't you? Just in case something went wrong." She paused, letting the words sink in. "Would anyone but a friend do that?"

LuLu swallowed hard, her body tense, leaning forward in her chair. "Yes. You wanted to know what was going on. You used Rebecca, too."

LuLu pushed herself up from the chair, but Sasha's voice cut through the motion like a blade, halting her in her tracks. "You don't believe that. I only reached out to Liam when I had no other choice, Lu. You know I was desperate. Think about what he was doing to me."

Suddenly, a screen flickered to life behind Sasha, projecting images of her forced encounters with Ryan. The images were brutal, raw, and LuLu's stomach turned. She couldn't look at it. She shook her head, trying to block it out, but the images were burned into her mind.

"After everything I went through," Sasha's voice broke through the noise. "You're going to hate me."

"I don't hate you," LuLu whispered, the pain threading through her words. "I could never hate you... but I'm hurt. You hurt me."

"You need to say it." Sasha's voice was firm now, unwavering.

LuLu's breath caught in her throat. "What?" she managed to ask, though she already knew.

"You know, LuLu," Sasha said, her eyes piercing through the dream's haze, "I am you."

LuLu's heart clenched as the weight of those words

pressed down on her, suffocating. She knew what she had to say, what she had been holding back for so long.

"You broke my heart, Sasha. I loved you more than anyone... and you broke my heart."

The familiar beeping sound echoed again, three soft beeps in the distance. Beep. Beep. Beep. Voices hovered at the edge of her awareness, but they were too faint to make out. The dream began to blur, everything shifting out of focus.

Warmth enveloped her, gentle but firm. Arms circled her from behind, and she twisted her head, her breath catching. There, her mother stood, her eyes soft, glowing with the kind of love that made LuLu's heart ache. Behind her, her father appeared, a steady presence.

Her mother's voice, tender and sure, whispered, "We love you." The words hung in the air, weightless yet full. "You're our strong girl."

LuLu's body jolted as she was pulled to her feet, a force beyond her control propelling her towards her mother's outstretched arms. The bubble of safety that surrounded them was suffocatingly warm, almost too much to bear, but she clung on tightly, afraid to let go.

Her father joined in the embrace, his powerful arms encasing them both like a shield against the harsh world outside. LuLu squeezed tighter, desperate to hold onto this moment forever.

Tears streamed down her face, but they were not tears of sadness. She never wanted to leave this perfect sanctuary. It couldn't end here.

"Is it my time?" Her voice trembled as she spoke, uncertain and frail. "I don't know if I'm ready."

Her father shook his head reassuringly, but it was her mother's gentle voice that broke through the haze.

"Not yet, my dear," her mother whispered, her voice like a soothing breeze. "You still have so much to do. Your life is waiting for you, filled with joy. Live it for us, and be happy."

The words reverberated through LuLu's heart, pushing her back towards the world she wasn't sure she was ready to face alone.

"Now wake up." Sasha's voice grew fainter, fading into the background. "I need you. I need you more than ever before."

"I don't want to face reality." LuLu's voice cracked with emotion, trembling under the weight of everything waiting for her outside these walls. "I want to stay with my parents. I miss you both. I miss what Sasha and I had. I can't keep going without you."

"But you must," Sasha replied firmly, turning away and disappearing into the shadows.

As LuLu fought against the blinding light filtering into her vision through thin slits of eyelids, a loud beeping sound filled her ears, growing more insistent by the second. Beep. Beep. Beep.

She clenched her fists, determination coursing through her body. "I have to wake up," she whispered to herself, her voice steady now. "I am not finished yet."

With great effort, LuLu forced her eyes open wider, taking in the sterile scent of antiseptic and floral air freshener that permeated the room. This was no ordinary hospital room. The sleek furniture and plush bed spoke of a luxurious place, worlds apart from the standard hospital setting. Her gaze settled on the small cot in the corner, its makeshift appearance indicating someone had been sleeping there for days, maybe even weeks.

Despite the throbbing pain throughout her body and the pounding ache in her head, LuLu's resolve strengthened. She was determined to face whatever lay ahead outside these walls, no matter how difficult it may be. She was alive and she was not done fighting yet.

Gingerly, she shifted, her muscles protesting the movement as though they were waking up after a long, deep slumber. Her fingers hovered over the call button for the nurse, but before she could press it, the door creaked open.

Silas walked in, his face buried in his phone, one hand cradling a cup of coffee that had clearly gone cold. He looked... ragged. His usually sharp, composed appearance was a distant memory, replaced by the shadow of a man who hadn't slept, showered, or eaten in days. Dark circles carved deep hollows under his eyes, his hair disheveled, and his clothes wrinkled and unkempt.

She wanted to speak, to call his name, but her throat burned, dry and raw, the words stuck somewhere deep inside her. Instead, she shifted slightly, the faint rustling of the bedsheets catching his attention.

Silas froze mid-step, his gaze snapping up from his phone. For a second, he just stood there, his eyes widening in disbelief, as if he couldn't quite process what he was seeing. Then, in a blur of motion, the coffee cup and phone clattered to the floor, forgotten. He rushed to her side, his hands trembling as they found hers.

He pressed her hand to his lips, his grip tight as if afraid she might vanish. Tears brimmed in his eyes, raw emotion flooding his face as he let out a choked sob. Without another word, he bolted from the room, calling for a doctor, his voice breaking as he disappeared down the hall.

The door swung open, and the doctor entered, clipboard in hand, his face composed but kind. Silas stood by LuLu's side, his eyes never leaving her, as the doctor approached the bed and began his examination. His hands moved gently, assessing her as he spoke.

"You've been through quite a lot," the doctor said softly, glancing up at her. "You suffered a severe concussion and a gunshot wound to your shoulder. The brain swelling was significant, but it's come down now, and you're healing well."

LuLu blinked, the words settling slowly into her foggy mind. She reached up instinctively, her fingers brushing against the bandages wrapped tightly around her head. Her left arm, however, refused to cooperate. A sharp jolt of panic flickered across her face as she tried, and failed, to move it.

"You've been in a coma for a month," the doctor continued, his tone reassuring. "But the fact that you're awake now is a very good sign. With time, you should make a full recovery."

Her breath hitched. A month? Her gaze darted to Silas, wide with worry, her unspoken question hanging in the air.

Before she could voice it, Silas leaned forward, knowing exactly what was racing through her mind. His hand found hers, squeezing gently, offering comfort through his own tear-streaked face. "Doodle's fine. He's been at my apartment, living the good life. Honestly, I'm not sure you'll ever be able to get him back home. He's got quite the routine going now. Matty has been running the bar with Heath. He is quite an impressive bartender." Silas said, managing a watery chuckle through his tears.

Relief washed over her, and she tried to smile, though the weight of everything that had happened still pressed down on her.

The doctor wrapped up his examination, explaining that she'd need to stay in the hospital for a few more weeks to recover fully. Eventually, when she was well enough, Silas took her home—not to her apartment, but to his. He doted on her, helping her through the long days of healing. Weeks passed, and slowly but surely, LuLu regained her strength, her body remembering how to move without pain. When she was finally strong enough to care for herself again, it was as if a new chapter of her life had begun.

Twenty-Five

One Year Later

Silas leaned down, his lips brushing tenderly against the scar on LuLu's shoulder, the faint mark of the bullet wound that had once threatened her life. She stirred, rolling over with a smile as Doodle snoozed contentedly between her legs. Silas was dressed in her favorite suit—the very same one he'd worn the night she first laid eyes on him.

"It's Wednesday, babe. You're going to be late. Rebecca's probably on her way," he murmured, his voice soft but teasing.

LuLu groaned, burying her face in the pillow. The bed was impossibly comfortable, and the warmth of Silas beside her made it all the harder to leave. A year had passed since the chaos that almost tore her apart, and two months after her recovery, they had moved in together. The bar was thriving under Matty's management, and Heath had even moved into her old apartment with Matty. Life had found its rhythm, with weekly dinners with them and the small, sweet routines she and Silas had built.

She stretched lazily before slipping out of bed, running her fingers through her hair as she got ready. "Dinner at Nina's tonight?" she asked, glancing at him as he wrapped up a few work emails.

"You know it," Silas smiled, pulling her into a quick kiss before heading out the door.

"I hope it is ok, but my parents are joining us." He said in passing.

"Yes, of course." She responded. "Is there a reason why everyone is getting together?"

He shrugged, but his mischievous grin made her wonder. If she was right, he was about to give her everything she ever dreamed about. She felt like the curse was finally broken.

LuLu made her way downstairs just as Rebecca's car pulled into the driveway. They exchanged warm greetings, their conversation flowing naturally into wedding plans as they drove toward the prison. The sun cast long shadows as they parked, and after signing in, they waited in the visiting room.

When Sasha finally appeared, dressed in her usual brown jumpsuit, her face lit up at the sight of them. Despite the cold regulations that barred them from hugging or touching, their smiles and shared laughter bridged the gap, and the three women sank into conversation as if no time had passed.

LuLu leaned in, her lips twitching with satisfaction as her voice took on a sharp edge. "Liam finally got arrested."

LuLu's laughter pierced the air, sharp and bitter as she relived the chaotic moment in her mind. Each word dripped with anger and betrayal, laced with a hint of desperation. "When I got shot, all hell broke loose," she seethed, her voice like shards of broken glass.

The memory of that day still burned within her, stoking the flames of resentment. Her eyes glinted with a fiery hatred as she spoke. Sasha looked down at that comment. It was not a memory that Sasha wanted to recall.. Rebecca raised a perfectly arched eyebrow and mimicked air quotes with a sarcastic tone, adding fuel to the fire.

"An anonymous tip led the police right to his hiding spot," she said, exchanging a knowing look with LuLu. "Yeah, 'anonymous'," LuLu went on. "And isn't it funny how every finger on his hand was broken along with both of his arms? No one knows how that happened." A wicked smirk stretched across LuLu's face, mirroring Sasha's dangerous grin.

"Such a shame," Sasha purred, satisfaction evident in her low voice. It was clear that these three women were not to be trifled with as their tension filled the room like electricity.

"He was practically begging for them to arrest him." LuLu said with a laugh.

Their laughter rang through the sterile visiting room—laughter that held more than humor. It was laced with understanding, shared history, and the knowledge of hard-earned justice. They allowed the conversation to drift into lighter territory, wedding plans and future dreams filling the space between them. Sasha and Rebecca's wedding loomed on the horizon, a beacon of hope amid the wreckage of their past.

But as the guards signaled their time was up, Sasha's

demeanor shifted. "Lu, wait," her voice cracked with emotion. LuLu froze, turning to face her, their eyes locking.

Sasha trembled as she spoke, her voice cracking with emotion. A single tear escaped from the corner of her eye, cutting through the stoic expression she tried to maintain. LuLu felt her heart twist in response to Sasha's vulnerability, and she reached out to gently wipe away the tear. "I do love you," Sasha whispered. "Thank you for forgiving me."

The weight of their history hung heavy in the air between them, but despite it all, LuLu's smile remained soft and genuine. "Remember, mistakes are just that - mistakes. You don't have to carry them forever," she said, her words a comforting anchor in their unbreakable bond. "You already had my forgiveness, and you will always have my love."

As she and Rebecca walked out of the prison, the world outside felt different—brighter, lighter. The sunlight kissed LuLu's face, warming her skin as she stood still, soaking it in. No more hiding, no more running. This was her life now, a life she had fought for and one she intended to fully embrace.

Rebecca's voice cut through her reverie as she started the car. "You ready?"

LuLu's heart felt fuller than it had in a long time, a small, quiet strength building within her. She glanced out the window, eyes tracing the horizon, then turned back to Rebecca, nodding with a certainty that ran deep. "Yes," she said, her voice steady. "Take me home."

As Lulu settled into the passenger seat, the weight of Sasha's words lingered in her heart—a reminder that forgiveness, true forgiveness, was a gift they had both given and received. She took one last look back at the prison, the walls that had once confined not only Sasha but parts of herself as well. Today, she was finally free of them.

As they pulled away, Rebecca turned on the radio, filling the car with a soft melody. Lulu glanced over, a small smile tugging at her lips. "So, wedding planning...are we talking pastel or bold colors?" she teased, nudging Rebecca.

Rebecca laughed, the sound light and contagious. "Bold, of course! This is us we're talking about."

They spent the drive home like that, weaving dreams of weddings and futures, each detail symbolizing the life Lulu had fought so hard to reclaim.

When they reached Lulu and Silas's place, the sun was beginning to set, casting a warm glow over the house. Silas was waiting on the porch, hands tucked casually in his pockets, his smile as radiant as the first time she'd seen him. She stepped out of the car, her heart swelling with the kind of peace she'd only ever dreamed of.

As she walked toward him, Lulu paused, glancing back one more time at the life she was leaving behind. The memories, the scars, and the battles—all of it had brought her here, to this moment. She felt an overwhelming gratitude, not just for the people who stood by her but for herself, for surviving and finding her way home.

Silas opened his arms, and as Lulu stepped into them, she realized she was exactly where she belonged.

"Welcome home," he whispered into her hair, pulling her close. She hugged him back, feeling a box shape in his pants. She smiled and pulled him into a kiss.

He leaned in close, his breath warm against her ear. "Let's go and meet everyone. I have a surprise for you," he whispered, his tone playful.

She raised an eyebrow, patting the pocket she suspected

held the secret. "You know I hate surprises," she teased, her grin spreading wide.

He chuckled, giving her a knowing look. "Not much of a secret then, is it?" he replied, a smirk lighting up his face.

Her laughter burst out, clear and unguarded. She was glowing, the weight she'd carried so long lifting. This was happiness—true, simple, and finally hers. She pulled him close, planting a soft kiss on his lips before stepping back to take in the people around her, faces filled with love and warmth.

She inhaled deeply, letting the moment sink in. For the first time in as long as she could remember, Lulu felt it—she was home.

Acknowledgments

This book is dedicated to my best friend, Kayla Hostetler. Your unwavering support and meticulous editing brought my words to life. I am endlessly grateful for the years of friendship, encouragement, and belief in me.

To Heather Hamilton, thank you for lending your keen editorial eye and being a source of strength during this journey. Your help and encouragement made this process so much easier.

To my husband, Walt Grata, your love and support have been my anchor. Thank you for standing by me and believing in my dreams.

Lastly, to my Grandma and Pop King, though you are no longer here to celebrate this moment, your love and faith in me have carried me through. You were my biggest fans, and this accomplishment is a testament to the inspiration you gave me.